David Wingrove is the celebrated author of the Chung Kuo series, co-author of *Trillion Year Spree* with Brian Aldiss, and the *Myst* novels with Rand Miller. He lives with his family in North London.

Praise for *The Empire of Time*

'Brilliant . . . I was gripped . . . most ingenious'
Brian Aldiss

'Wingrove is a master storyteller and *The Empire of Time* is a gripping epic that slingshots the reader across human history alongside characters enthralled by their own passions'
Michael Cobley

'It's immense fun for anyone who likes their SF writ really large'
SFX

'[an] impeccable sense of setting . . . *The Empire of Time* could be the beginning of something brilliant: Blackout meets Bond in a relentless race war Wingrove depicts with deftness and deference'
Tor.com

THE
OCEAN
OF TIME

ROADS TO MOSCOW
BOOK 2

DAVID
WINGROVE

DEL REY

1 3 5 7 9 10 8 6 4 2

Del Rey, an imprint of Ebury Publishing
20 Vauxhall Bridge Road,
London SW1V 2SA

Del Rey is part of the Penguin Random House group of companies whose addresses
can be found at global.penguinrandomhouse.com

First published in the UK in 2015 by Del Rey
This edition published in 2016

www.eburypublishing.co.uk

A CIP catalogue record for this book
is available from the British Library

ISBN 9780091956189

Printed and bound in Great Britain by Clays Ltd, St Ives PLC

Penguin Random House is committed to a sustainable future for our business,
our readers and our planet. This book is made from Forest Stewardship
Council® certified paper.

Contents

To Robert Carter, Brother-in-Arms

CHARACTER LIST

Alexandrovich, Alexander — Carpenter's Assistant at Cherdiechnost, in 13th century Russia.

Arkadevich, Yakov — Master of the Carpentry shop at Cherdiechnost, in 13th century Russia.

Arminius — also known as Hermann, Chieftain of the German Cherusci tribe and victor over the Roman legions in the Battle of the Teutoburg Forest (17BC to AD21).

Baeck, Leo — son of Minister in German government in 2343.

Bakatin, Fyodor Mikhailovic — river haulier in 13th century Russia. Has three sons.

Behr, Otto — our narrator, a German '*Reisende*' or time traveller.

Belikof — *posadnik* at Tver, in 13th century Russia.

Ben — jazz fan at the *Unbeachtet* jazz club, in California, June 1952.

Birgitta — Mikahil Razumovsky's second wife.

Bismarck, Otto von — German statesman who unified Germany (1815-1898).

Blagovesh — The Bandit King; leader of the marsh bandits in 13th century Russia.

Bobrov — Russian time agent and killer of at least a dozen German agents.

Burckel, Albrecht — German time agent and 'sleeper' in 2747 AD.

Chkalov, Joseph Maksymovich — otherwise known as Yastryeb, 'the Hawk' and Grand Master of Time for the Russians.

Dankevich, Fedor Ivanovich — Russian time agent. Otto has shot him at least twice, the last time fatally.

Dick, Kleo — First wife of Philip K. Dick.

Dick, Philip K. — Science Fiction writer in Fifties California.

Dmitri — innkeeper in 13th century Russia.

Efimenko, Anna — old widow from Cherdiechnost, in 13th century Russia.

Eisenstein, Sergei Mikhailovich — Soviet film-maker of the mid-20th century (1898-1948).

Ernst — see Kollwitz.

Fedorchuk — 'Head Man' of Belyj in 13th century Russia.

Franke, Roland — student at the Akademie in Neu Berlin, in 2343.

Frederick I, 'Rothbart' or 'Barbarossa, King of Germany and Holy Roman Emperor (1122-1190).

Frederick The Great — Prussian King Frederick II, known more commonly as 'Old Fritz', Germany's great hero.

Freisler, Jurgen — German '*Reisende*' or time agent. Hecht's special henchman – his *Jagdhund*, or 'bloodhound', responsible for doing all the dirty work.

Gehlen, Hans — aka, 'The *Genewart*'. Architect of Four-Oh, scientific genius and inventor of time travel. Has existed for 200 years as a gaseous presence in the midst of Four-Oh's artificial intelligence.

Greg — friend of Philip K. Dick in 1952.

Grigor — chief hand to Shaposhnikov.

Grikov — Head Man of Velikie Luki, in 13th century Russia.

Gromov — Official in Rzhev, in 13th century Russia.

Gruber — one of the eight *Reisende* carrying Seydlitz's DNA. 'Turned' by the Russians.

Gunsche — student at the Akademie in 2343.

Haller — student at Four-Oh.

Haushofer, Klaus — liaison officer at the Akademie in Neu Berlin in 2343.

Hecht — 'The Pike'; Meister of the Germans at Four-Oh.

Hecht, Albrecht — Hecht's older brother and keeper of the archives at the Haven, way back in time.

Heinrich — 'Henny', Burckel's friend, and a revolutionary, *Undrehungar*.

Horst — researcher at Four-Oh.

Hudner, Irmin — 'Grand Master' of Four-Oh in its early years.

Iaroslavich, Alexander — see Nevsky.

Ignatev, Tikhon — 'Young Tikhon'; field worker and runner at Cherdiechnost, 13th century.

Ilyushkin — *boyar* in Rzhev in 13th century Russia.

Inge — one of the women at the platform in Four-Oh.

Iranov — 'Priest' at Cherdiechnost in 13th century Russia.

Jablokov, Master — runs a workshop in Novgorod's central market, 13th century.

Jamil — nurse/nanny to Katerina and Otto's daughters (in 13th century Russia). Also twin to a time travel agent centuries up the line.

Katerina — Otto's beloved. See also Razumovsky.

Kaunitz, Stefan — young student at the Akademie in Neu Berlin, in 2343.

Kempner — 'Master'; one of Four-Oh's Elders.

Kerenchev — Kolya's false name in 1952 California.

Kessemeier — '*Reisende*' or time agent, at Four-Oh.

Kilik — innkeeper at Rzhev, in 13th century Russia.

Kirchoff — Master in charge of mental health at Four-Oh.

Kleist — Blacksmith at Cherdiechnost in 13th century Russia.

Koeler, Edmund — '*Reisende*' or time agent in Baturin in early 18th century.

Kollwitz, Ernst — '*Reisende*' or time agent. Otto's best friend and travelling companion; damaged in the Past.

Kramer — '*Reisende*' or time agent.

Kravchuk, Oleg Alekseevitch — agent of the Mongols in 13th century Russia, and, in some time-lines, married to Katerina.

Krylenko — boatman in 13th century Russia.

Kuhn, Matteus — (aka Matt Caldecott). Sleeper agent for the Germans in California in 1952.

Lishka — a haulier in 13th century Russia.

Luwer, Hans — artefacts expert, based in Four-Oh. Uses his other selves to multi-task.

McLean, Jackie — American jazz musician/alto saxophonist.

Maria — German woman in charge of the platform at Four-Oh; replacement to Zarah.

Natya — Katerina's maid, in 13th century Novgorod.

Neipperg — German time agent at Baturin in 18th century.

Nemtsov, Alexander Davydovitch — Russian time agent, operating in the Mechanist Age (23rd to 25th centuries).

Nevsky, Alexander Iaroslavich — Russian Orthodox Prince of Novgorod in the 13th century. Victor of the 'Battle on the Ice' (or Lake Peipus) in April 1242, a battle which ended the expansive Northern Crusades.

Odin — Chief God of the Germanic mythology; 'father' of his people.

Old Mesyats — boatman in 13th century Russia.

Old Schnorr — 'Master' at Four-Oh in charge of project to trawl Time for faces; Elder.

Otto — see Behr.

Pavlenko, Igor — steward at Cherdiechnost, in 13th century Russia.

Peter — Katerina's first betrothed, who died, in 13th century Russia.

Peter the Great — six foot six Tsar of Russia, from 1672 to 1725. Architect of modern Russia.

Podnayin — 'Master' and *boyar* at Rzhev in 13th century Russia.

Puskarev — black ex-slave; field worker at Cherdiechnost in 13th century.

Rapushka — innkeeper in 13th century Russia.

Razumovsky, Katerina — eternal love of Otto Behr. Daughter of Mikhail Razumovsky in Novgorod in the 13th century.

Razumovsky, Mikhail — rich *boyar* (or merchant) living in Novgorod, Northern Russia, in the 13th century. Father of Katerina.

Reichenau, Michael — *Doppelgehirn*, also Supervisor of Werkstatt 9. Somehow involved in time travel. Product of a genetics experiment, he has two skulls 'hot-wired' together.

Rieber, Lothar — aka Aaron; '*Reisende*' or time agent in Baturin in 18th century.

Ripke — records clerk in Four-Oh.

Rollins, Sonny — American jazz musician/tenor saxophonist.

Rudy — jazz fan at the *Unbeachtet* jazz club, California, 1952.

Sanger, Gerhardt — student at the Akademie, 2343.

Saratov, Sergei Ilya — harbourmaster at Tver in 13th century Russia.

Schelepin — boatman in 13th century Russia.

Schikaneder, Jakub — 'Sleeper' time agent in 19th century Prague; painter and exile.

Schmidt, Andreas — alias for Russian time agent Dankevich.

Schultz, Auguste — Chief Operative of the Investigative Institute in 2343.

Semevskii — field worker at Cherdiechnost, in 13th century.

Seydlitz, Max — '*Reisende*' or time agent, in charge of Project Barbarossa.

Shafarevich — German time agent; henchman to Yastryeb, 'The Hawk', Grand Master of the Russians.

Shaposhnikov — captain of a trading boat in 13th century Russia.

Smith, The — a smith, also possibly a time agent; from Belyj, in 13th century Russia.

Stahlecker, Dr Walther — commander of *Einsatzgrupen A* in the 1940s.

Stein — German time agent in 18th century Baturin.

Svetov, Arkadi — Russia's chief agent in the 24th century.

Sviatislav — Grand Prince of Vladimir in 13th century Russia.

Talyzin — *posadnik* of Rzhev in 13th century Russia.

Terekhov — the miller at Cherdiechnost, in 13th century Russia.

Urd — Goddess of Norse mythology.

Urte — one of the women at the platform in Four-Oh. Also an expert physicist, technician and mathematician.

Werner — brother of the Northern Crusades in 13th century Prussia.

Woolf, Paul — student at the Akademie, Neu Berlin, 2343; son of Chief Geneticist Woolf of the Institute in Vienna.

Yakovlev, Alexander — *boyar* in the Tver *veche* (or council) in 13th century Russia.

Yastryeb — see Chkalov, Grand Master of Time for the Russians.

Zarah — most senior of the women who run Four-Oh's operating system, the platform. Sweet on Otto.

Zhukof, Georgy — marshal of the Soviet/Red Army (1896-1974).

Part Seven

Upriver

'Thus his path had been a circle, or an ellipse or spiral or whatever, but certainly not straight; straight lines evidently belonged only to geometry, not to nature and life.'

– Hermann Hesse, *The Glass Bead Game*

154

It is August 1239 in Novgorod, northern Russia. The weather is hot and dry, the sky the deepest cerulean blue. Close by, the window – a Western touch – is open wide, giving a view across the central garden.

This is *my* house, the land purchased with *my* silver, made from *my* DNA, the house itself built only this spring to my own design. A Russian-style house, of course, but with Western touches, such as the sanitation.

Ernst stands beside me at the huge pine table, poring over the hand-drawn map. It looks crude – as crude as anything in this god-fearing, god-forsaken century – but the details are accurate. It only mimics crudity.

Ernst is frowning, as he always does when he's concentrating, then he looks up and, meeting my eyes, smiles.

'It looks fun. I only wish I was coming with you.'

'You can if you want,' I say, but he knows I don't mean it.

'No, no . . . I've plenty to do here. Besides, when winter comes . . .'

He doesn't say it, but I know what he means. When winter comes, it would be best to be inside a town, not out in the wilds of Russia.

'You'll need to keep good time,' Ernst says, tracing the course of my prospective journey with his finger. 'If you delay . . .'

Again, it doesn't need to be said. There are few roads in the Russia of this age and none at all between Novgorod and Moscow. Russia's rivers are its main means of transportation, and when winter comes . . .

The rivers freeze. Those roads are closed.

Besides, Ernst has been ahead of me already, checking out the route beforehand and making deals. Arranging things.

There are four points marked along the way in bright red ink. Those are my supply dumps, already set up and in place. Again, this is Ernst's doing. At each dump are duplicates of everything I need: food, equipment and weaponry.

And a focus. To jump to if in need. Or to send a message up the line to Four-Oh. We've worked it all out, you see. Each dump is marked by a tracking signal, which only I, in this non-technological age, will be able to locate. To make the hazardous journey safer, less subject to accident.

And there's a good reason for that this time. Because I'm not going alone.

Ernst looks past me, and, in his quaint Germanic manner, comes to attention and bows his head. I turn and smile.

'Katerina . . . you didn't have to get up.'

She grins. Her long, dark hair is tousled and she's still in her sleeping gown. But that doesn't worry her this once. It's Ernst. She squeals and hurries over to him, hugging him to her, like a long-lost brother.

'Otto, why didn't you tell me Ernst was in town!'

For a moment, in her happiness at seeing Ernst, she doesn't notice the map spread out on the table. But then she does and looks at me sternly.

'Otto . . .?'

'What?' I say nonchalantly. She turns and looks at the map, struggling to take in its details, but knowing what it means. Then, looking up at me again, she scowls, a hurt expression in her eyes.

'Otto . . . are you going away again? Is that why Ernst is here?'

'Yes,' I say, and see the disappointment in her eyes. But I'm teasing now, and I really shouldn't. She goes to speak again and

I raise a hand. 'And before you ask, no. Ernst *isn't* going with me. Ernst is staying here in Novgorod for the winter.'

'You're going *alone*?'

And now I smile. 'No, my darling little one. You're coming with me.'

155

The apprentices have wandered from their benches to come and stare over each other's shoulders at the drawings that their master, the chief carpenter, has unrolled and fastened to his worktop.

The old man is frowning heavily and pulling at his beard, in a state of what, for him, is almost agitation.

'I've never seen the like,' he says. 'Never in all my life.'

It's true. The design comes from the future. It's one of Hans Luwer's, a beauty if you ask me, but the master can't see that. All his life he's been used to making sleds a certain way – the way his father made them and his father before that – and this is too new, too revolutionary for him.

He sighs deeply, then straightens up and looks at me across the bench.

'No, Meister Behr. I am afraid I cannot make this. This . . . blueprint, as you call it . . . it makes no sense.'

It makes perfect sense, of course, but that's not what he means. He is frightened of it. Frightened of the departures in its design. It is, after all, radically different from any design he's seen or is ever likely to see. But next to him, his senior apprentice is staring and staring at the diagram, his eyes filled with pure wonder at what he's seeing. He wants to make this new thing. In fact, he absolutely burns to turn my drawing into something real, something he can touch with the palm of his hand.

'But Master . . .' he begins, daring to interrupt the old man in his excitement. 'This is—'

'Be quiet, Alexander Alexandrovich. I cannot make this thing. It would not be *safe*.'

'But Master . . .'

This time the old man turns and even raises a hand. Alexander Alexandrovich desists. But his eyes still burn.

I take the old man aside.

'Here,' I say, handing him a small bag filled with silver coins – dirhams, freshly copied, using my own DNA, in Four-Oh not six hours past subjectively. It's the only way we can transfer such copies, from place to place and age to age. Only our DNA can survive the jump. 'Let your boy take this on. If it doesn't work . . .' I shrug. 'I'll pay you anyway, understand? Another twenty dirhams.'

The master's eyes have lit at the sight of all that silver and the promise of yet more. I have paid him lavishly – ten times the worth of the sled, as much and more as a prince might pay – and so he bows low before me.

'Whatever you wish, Meister.'

'Good. Then I want the job done for St Vladimir's day.'

His head jerks up. 'St Vladimir's day? But that's—'

'Ten days away, I know. Is that a problem?'

Before he can answer, Alexander Alexandrovich steps in. 'It will be done, Meister. I guarantee it.'

'Good. And there'll be a bonus if you do a fine job.'

But now I've overstepped the mark. Both the master and his senior apprentice straighten, almost bristling at this insult to their pride.

'Meister Behr,' the old man says sternly. 'Understand one thing. When Yakov Arkadevich takes on a job, it is done not just well, but perfectly. We are the best, you understand. The finest in all Russia.'

156

Walking back to Katerina's father's house, I find myself smiling broadly. I know the sled will be built to my design. I knew it long before I knocked on Master Arkadevich's door. After all, with the slight improvements Alexander Alexandrovich makes to it, it forms the basis of those sleds we copied and which wait, even now, at the supply dumps along the way – the same basic design that will be used throughout Russia for the next seven hundred years.

Razumovsky greets me off-handedly. Something is bugging him and he's in a bad mood, even for him. I tell him of my plan to travel east and he asks me why I should want to do that. Isn't everything I need right here in Novgorod? I tell him no; I'm taking a very special cargo of goods inland with me and this single trip could make my fortune, and that with the proceeds I plan to buy an estate and a thousand serfs. That impresses him, but when I tell him that I'm taking his daughter with me, he objects strongly.

'That's no place to take a woman, Otto! There are thieves and bandits and ruffians of every kind out there!'

'I know,' I answer, 'but there are thieves of a different kind right here in Novgorod and I am as loath to leave Katerina here as she is to let me go alone. Besides, I *am* her husband!'

That, irrefutable as it is, settles matters. But Razumovsky still doesn't like it. He comes up with a dozen reasons why his daughter should stay. And most of them have merit, only . . .

I can't bear to be parted from her. And this journey gives me a valid excuse to be with her every day for the next six months. *And every night . . .*

Razumovsky is saved from coming up with further reasons by the arrival of Ernst.

Ernst, I know, has been back to Four-Oh to get the latest news, but he tells Razumovsky that he's just come over from the Peterhof, the German Quarter of the town, where he's struck a deal for fifty furs. Ernst wants to celebrate, and this surprises me somewhat, but I can't ask why. Not with Razumovsky there. It's not the 'deal' Ernst wants to celebrate, that I know, but there is a definite spring to his step as he calls out to Razumovsky's servants to bring us wine.

Razumovsky needs no encouraging. When the servants bring three flasks of wine, he sends them away for a dozen more. So it is that, as evening falls, the three of us sit drunkenly at the bench, laughing and slapping each other's backs.

Razumovsky's ability to consume endless amounts of liquor without needing to excuse himself is legendary. Even so, he eventually needs to use the midden, and when he does, I lean across and ask Ernst what's going on.

'They've killed Shafarevich!' he says, his eyes gleaming. 'Freisler shot him between the eyes. Then they snipped off time behind him, neat as a sewn wound!'

I laugh, astonished. Shafarevich is the Russians' equivalent of Freisler, in charge of all the dirty jobs, the nasty sort that even us hardened agents want to wash our hands of, and he's been a thorn in our side for as long as I've been an agent – yes, and for long before that. No wonder Ernst wants to celebrate.

When Razumovsky returns, I call for more wine, then climb on to the table and raise a toast to my father-in-law – a toast that has the sentimental Razumovsky in tears.

'You're a good son to me, Otto,' he says, hugging my legs, not letting me get down from the table. 'A man could not ask for a better son.'

Only I'm glad I'm not Razumovsky's son, for if I was, how then could I have married Katerina?

Ernst wakes before me and he's making breakfast when I stagger out into the kitchen. There's no sign of Katerina, and when I ask one of the servants, he says that she's gone to the market to buy food for our trip. My head is thick and painful, my wits dulled by our prodigious bout of drinking, but just the memory of Ernst's news makes me grin.

'So the bastard's dead,' I say, and laugh.

'Time-dead,' Ernst says, and that special phrase sobers me, because it's what we all fear. All of us who travel back and forth in time. Because death's not final for us. Not until there's no way anyone can change it. Not until Time itself is snipped off and sealed and made inaccessible to change.

Time-dead.

Ernst serves me breakfast: a thick slice of ham with eggs. It's delicious, but my stomach is feeling none too good after its evening exertions and I push the platter away unfinished.

'Did you put in the designs?' Ernst asks, taking my plate and beginning to pick at what's left.

'Yes.'

'I bet Master Arkadevich was horrified.'

I laugh. 'He was. But his senior apprentice . . .'

We meet eyes.

'Strange, isn't it?' Ernst says. And I know what he means. Alexander Alexandrovich is a very clever young man, quick and flexible of mind. In our own time he would have made a fine technician or engineer; yet here he is in this age of darkness and superstition, wasted, one might say, on making things from wood.

Some of my younger students make the mistake of thinking themselves more intelligent than the men and women of the past. They think that the context in which they live reflects the degree of their intelligence. It is not so. And how could it be? Could mankind really have evolved so far in so very short a time? No. It's an impossibility. What might seem like ignorance is merely lack of insight. Or of potential.

I decide on the spot to go and see our young friend and try to speak to him alone, away from his master. And so, having washed and shaved, I set off for Master Arkadevich's.

It is midday when I get there and, picking my way through the jumble of wood and half-finished carts and sleds that clutter the front of the building, I ask where Alexander Alexandrovich might be found.

'He's asleep, Meister,' one of the apprentices answers me, grinning broadly.

'He was up all night,' another adds, 'working on the new design.'

'Has he been sleeping long?' I ask, and there is laughter.

'He fell asleep over his bench. He did not *want* to sleep.'

I grin. Clearly I have found the right man for this job. 'Then let him sleep. I will come back in an hour or two. I'll wake him then. Only there are a few things I wish to discuss.'

'But the master—'

I give the apprentice a handful of small bronze coins and wink. 'There is no need to trouble the master, eh, my boy?'

The 'boy' – forty if he's a day – grins toothlessly. 'No need at all, Meister Behr.'

158

With time on my hands, I go down to the market to see whether I can spy my Katerina among the stalls. At first there's no sign of her and I begin to think that she has gone already, but then I see her, her back to me as she examines a bright blue cloak, her servant Natya beside her, discussing the quality of the garment.

I smile, the day lit up by her presence.

I walk across and stop on the other side of the stall, watching her until she looks up and notices me there. She looks down, smiling shyly, playing a game we often play, as if she doesn't know me yet, but quite likes me. As if she is a young maiden again, waiting to be swept away by her future husband. Natya, slower on the uptake, looks from her mistress to me, then back again, then does a comic little double-take, surprised that it's me who's standing there, and not some boyar's son. Dull-natured as she is, Natya cannot understand the powerful chemistry that is between Katerina and I. She thinks her mistress could have done better, and that she is wasted on some 'old man' like me, tall as I am, rich as I am.

But Natya and her like can go to hell. When Katerina looks at me I feel seventeen again, fresh from the Garden, the whole of life laid out before me, like it was all new and promising. *Unsullied*.

There's part of me, of course, that knows it isn't so: that Time is Time and sullied. That life, far from being romantic, is a vale of tears. And that a man's destiny – whatever it may prove to be – is never what he expects.

Yet when I look into her eyes and see her smiling back, I can easily believe that nothing in the universe is more powerful than this.

Not even Time can destroy this bond.

Katerina walks slowly round the stall, leaving Natya to bring the basket.

'Otto, so you're up?'

'So it seems.'

Her right hand lifts from her side, crosses the space between us and gently touches my chest. Like a blessing. I look down at it, then place my own over it. Her eyes are watching me now with such an intensity, such a seriousness, that I wonder how the noise and bustle of the marketplace can continue – how it is that everyone there in that crowded space is not watching us?

'I missed you this morning.'

'Did you?' she asks. And again, the intensity within those words is almost too much for them to carry. She would die for me, and I for her.

'Your father—'

'Got you drunk last night?' The smile returns. 'You *need* help, then?'

I smile at her teasing. 'We were celebrating.'

'Celebrating?'

'Us going away.'

'Ah . . .' And she looks more thoughtful. 'You told him, then?'

I nod.

'And he agreed?'

'He didn't like it, but he has given us his blessing. I told him that the journey would make us rich. That I would buy an estate when we returned with a thousand serfs.'

She frowns at that. 'You want that, Otto?'

'It would make things easier. Our own place.'

'But we have that.'

'Here in town, yes. I meant a place away from here. In the countryside. With just you and I . . . and our children.'

Her eyes widen. For a long moment she says nothing, her eyes searching mine, and then she lifts herself up on to her toes and kisses me softly, gently on the lips.

'Ah, my sweet *batiushka*,' she says, and I feel a small tremor pass down my spine at the words, for it is a kind of private code between us. *Little father*. It is what she always calls me when she wants me to make love to her.

'Natya,' she says, raising her voice, but never moving, never looking away from me. 'Take the basket to my father's house and wait there for instructions.'

'Mistress?'

'Go!'

And Natya scuttles off, frowning unhappily at having her shopping expedition curtailed. But I don't spare her a thought. Walking back, my arm about Katerina's waist, the enticing warmth of her against my side, I am aware of nothing but her.

We go to bed and stay there until the evening comes. Leaving her there, sleeping on her back, I slip on my robe and go out to use the midden and as I'm there, smiling to myself, remembering the afternoon's sweet lovemaking, there's a hammering on the door, and old memories make me frown, recalling how cruelly my happiness has been shattered in the past. But not this time. This time it is Razumovsky, come calling on me, returning Natya and the basket, though that's not the only reason for his visit. The council of city elders – the *veche* – wish to see me, and so I wash and dress and, leaving a note for Katerina, venture out into the warm evening darkness, Razumovsky at my side.

He seems excited, yet he will not tell me why. 'You'll find out,' is all he says, his dark eyes shining, a broad grin splitting his thick beard. It's a beautiful evening, a full moon laying a coat of silver over the town as we climb the hill toward the assembly building.

I look back at the river, then beyond it to the forest, recalling what Katerina said as we lay there after our first bout of lovemaking.

'Are you afraid?' I had asked.

'Of the journey? Yes. But I want to go. Nothing matters, as long as I'm with you, Otto. If I were here . . . it would be awful. Every moment I'd be wondering where you were, worrying that something might have happened.'

'Nothing will happen.'

13

'Yet if it did . . .'

In my mind I see her there, naked beside me, and see again how she turns her face away briefly, a look of pain in her lovely eyes. When she looks at me again, her voice is the merest whisper. 'If you died, I would die too. I couldn't live without you, Otto. The times you are not here . . .'

She doesn't have to finish her sentence. I feel that too. To be apart from her is hell. And when did I ever feel that for anyone?

Razumovsky nudges me, and it's only then that I realise I have stopped and am staring back towards the house, as if to see her through the solid layers of wood and stone between her and me.

'Otto? Are you all right?'

'I'm fine,' I say, and wonder what he'd make of it if I told him the full content of my thoughts, and how each waking, breathing moment of my life is dominated by my love for her.

He would think such love excessive and unmanly. '*A man must be the master of his emotions, Otto, not a slave to them.*' Yet how can I feel other than I feel? For Katerina is the other half of me, the part that makes me whole. Without her . . .

Jump back in time, Otto Behr, and you will see an unhappy, unfulfilled fellow, not knowing what he lacked, not even guessing.

'I was thinking,' I say to Razumovsky as we begin to walk again.

'*Thinking*? About what?'

'That maybe I should ask one of the members of the *veche* to look into the matter of the estate.'

Razumovsky glances at me frowningly. 'But I thought—'

'No disrespect, Father,' I say hurriedly, 'but I am thinking in terms of the benefits to our family. Were I to leave the matter in your hands, I am certain you would find me the very best of estates and at a bargain price. But my thinking is as follows. If we ask one of the *veche* to undertake this matter for us, it will create an obligation.'

Razumovsky stops dead, then turns to me. 'An *obligation*? But surely that's a bad thing?'

'Not at all. What is trade if not a web of mutual obligations? And what binds men together better than trade? No . . . if we ask one of the *veche* to do this for us, it could well be the beginning of greater alliances between our family and the boyars. And in time, well, I do not wish to presume, but to have a grandchild of yours on the *veche*, that would be something, would it not?'

It would indeed. Razumovsky, now that his imagination has been stirred, fairly glows at the thought of it. He reaches across and grasps both my shoulders in his massive hands. 'Otto, you are a genius.'

'And a German,' I say. 'And so a stranger here in Novgorod, however long I live here. Yet my sons, and daughters, will be Russians. And it is their future that I must attend to.'

Razumovsky positively beams. He draws me close and hugs me in a bear-like hug. 'Why, yes,' he says. 'And they will be fine boys, I know it!'

Another time I might have agreed with confidence, having gone forward to see how the future transpired. But this once . . .

This once I am loath to glimpse what yet will be. This once I want to *live* it. To watch it unfurl, hour by hour, minute by minute, whatever fate has in store.

Like ordinary people with their ordinary families.

As Razumovsky releases me, I realise another thing. That I like him. That it pleases me to have this large and colourful man for my father-in-law, and that my toast last night was honesty, not policy. That what I love in Katerina I also glimpse in him.

We come to the assembly house to find the *veche* already gathered, the boyars seated about a massive wooden table in a raftered hall that swelters in the evening's heat. The place is lit by torches, which hang in small braziers on the walls. In their light these

15

bearded figures seem like something from a dream. They are all here, the *posadnik* at the head of the table, Novgorod's military commander – the *tysiatskii* – standing just behind.

If Razumovsky had not been so excited, I might be fearful, for there is a distinctly sombre feel to this gathering, yet the *posadnik* greets me cheerfully enough.

'Meister Behr, welcome to our *veche*. If you would take a seat . . .'

I sit in the only vacant chair, Razumovsky standing behind me. Looking about me, I see how every eye is on me. These are rich, powerful men – boyars all. Nor is their power illusory. In the past century they have won the right to nominate their own candidate for prince, expelling – even killing – those they felt were unsuitable to rule. They sit there in their furs in the heat, their full beards specially combed for the occasion.

Gathered together thus they look very strange, very primitive, and I feel like smiling, only a smile would be inappropriate, *disrespectful*.

'Gentlemen,' I say, 'thank you for inviting me. But tell me . . . what do you want?'

At another time and in another place this might seem too forward, too pushy, but these are practical men, used to great suffering and hardships. Novgorod has suffered many famines. In 1128 the town was ravaged by starvation when an early frost destroyed the winter corn and its people were forced to eat birch-bark and wood pulp mixed with husks and straw to survive; only a few years ago, in 1230, more than three thousand died, the people feeding on moss and snails and even eating the dead bodies of the fallen.

For all its apparent wealth, this land is still a wilderness, and Novgorod is still vulnerable and can be brought low by disease and bad harvests. Thus its boyars like directness. They are blunt to the point of rudeness, and I have learned to be like them.

The *posadnik* grins and looks about him before addressing me again. 'I understand you are about to leave on a journey, Meister Behr. To Moscow. A trip that, it's rumoured, will make your fortune.'

Behind me Razumovsky shuffles a little, uncomfortable. If there are rumours flying about, it's clear who started them.

'That is so.'

'Good. Then we have a proposition to make you, Meister Behr. As a body, we would like a share in your mission, and thus – naturally – in the profits to be made.'

'And in return?'

The *tysiatskii* answers this time. 'In return you have the favour of the *veche*. And whatever internal passes you require.'

The *posadnik* turns slightly in his seat and looks back and up at his fellow, and nods, his long beard bobbing in the light from the torches.

I smile. 'I have no problem with that. What share does the *veche* wish?'

The *posadnik* hesitates a moment, a hardness in his eyes, then says calmly. 'A half.'

'A third,' I say, my voice brooking no argument, and strangely enough the *posadnik* does not argue. Instead he laughs, his laughter joined a moment later by that of others, until the whole table is laughing, and I with them. The deal is done. They have just gained themselves a third of my profits for almost no material effort.

It's a bribe, of course, but that is how things work here, and at least I do not now have to go with cap in hand to the *tysiatskii* and beg for a passport to travel overland to Moscow.

We drink huge goblets of wine to seal the deal, and afterwards I take one of the boyars aside and – as I rehearsed with Razumovsky earlier – ask him if he would be my agent in the purchase of an estate, somewhere to the south of the town. The man says he is honoured, and we embrace like old friends, then drink yet another goblet of wine.

Later, walking home unsteadily, Razumovsky puts his arm about my shoulders and, drawing me closer, breathes wine into my face.

'I wasn't sure about you, Otto. But now . . . You are a fine chap. A most excellent son. To think that I might have had that nauseous little toad for a son in law!'

Kravchuk, he means. But I don't want to think about Kravchuk right now.

'Father?'

Razumovsky pushes himself back away from me a little and straightens up, trying hard to appear dignified. 'Yes, Otto?'

'I'll look after her. I promise on my life. I'll make sure she gets back safely.'

159

Young Alexander Alexandrovich whips off the rough glue-stained sheet and beams at me with pride.

'There! What do you think?'

I am standing in the workshop, Ernst at my side, an excited crowd of apprentices hemming us in, old Yakov Arkadevich, the master, looking on, concerned.

I step forward, then go down on to my haunches, examining it carefully, then reach out to touch and feel the solid reality of the sled. It has been polished and varnished, and it looks a beauty. Straightening up, I walk round it, stopping every now and then to scrutinise something or another. But this is all for show. I know already what a fine job Alexander Alexandrovich has made of it.

As I look up and meet the chief apprentice's gaze, I am aware that everyone is staring at me, holding their breath, waiting for my verdict, old Yakov especially so. Giving the slightest nod I reach into my pocket and draw out the bag of silver coins and, almost casually, throw it to Master Arkadevich. His toothless grin brings laughter from all sides. The laughter of relief.

Looking to the younger man, I smile. 'This is an excellent job, Alexander Alexandrovich. Better than I'd dared hope for. I particularly like your own improvements.'

If the young man smiled any more, his face would split. As it is, he hurriedly bows his head, his neck and face flushed a brilliant scarlet.

'Thank you, Meister—'

'Indeed,' I carry on, 'I am so pleased that I have decided to double your bonus and –' I look to the old man '– with Master Arkadevich's permission, naturally, I would like to treat you all at the local tavern.'

There are cheers, and no protests from the old man, who, hugging his bag of dirhams, is only too willing to break off and celebrate. After all, it is not every day that one brings a new thing into the world, and this sled – this wonder made of wood and glue and varnish – is perhaps the most important innovation Russia will see for many a year.

Two hours later, and well the worse for wear, I find myself sitting across from the young apprentice, who, his tongue loosened by wine, has been spelling out to me his scheme to open his own workshop once the term of his apprenticeship has been served. Old Master Yakov is asleep at the head of the big trestle table, head slumped against the table top and snoring loudly. He is not alone. Those that are not sleeping are drunk. There will be no more work today. But these are Russians and this is how life is for them. If there is a reason to celebrate they will grab it with both hands – yes, and drink it dry.

I look around me, then look back at young Alexander, realising that for the last five minutes I haven't heard a word. Yet on whim I reach across and, with a tender smile, say, 'Alexander, you can come work for me when your apprenticeship is served. I will build you a workshop.'

The expression on his face is priceless. He is at the same time dumbfounded and overjoyed.

'What?' he says. 'What did you say?'

'I said I will build you a workshop. When I am home from Moscow. But you must do right by Master Arkadevich. He has been good to you, and you must not be ungrateful.'

'No, no, but . . .' Suddenly he reaches out and, grasping my left hand, kisses the ring on my finger – my wedding ring – and swears he will not let me down. The young man is crying now, tears of happiness that, I confess, move me deeply, such that when Ernst returns from the midden, he finds the pair of us sitting there, face to face across the table, tears streaming down our cheeks.

'Otto?'

I look to Ernst and laugh. 'Oh, it's okay, Ernst. We're fine. We really are fine.'

160

Yet I wake in the night, wondering what's happening to me. Am I becoming like them? Is living here among them changing me?

I sit up in the darkness, then reach across and undo one of the shutters, letting in the moonlight. In its pale glow, I turn and look at Katerina, lying there asleep beside me, and realise that I have never been so happy in my life. All my life I have travelled in time and space, doing my duty by the *volk* and never once wishing to settle. But now . . .

Katerina stirs, then wakes. 'Otto?' she asks sleepily. 'What is it?'

'Nothing,' I say.

She gives a small, sleepy laugh. 'You were very drunk again.'

'I know.' But now I am feeling very sober. 'Everything's ready,' I say. 'We're going to leave the day after tomorrow.'

She is suddenly wide awake. Sitting up, she stares into my face. 'But I thought . . .'

She thought she'd have another week, that's what she thought.

I reach out and take her hand. 'There's no reason to delay. The sled is ready and all the goods are packed. We've provisions and the weather's good.' I hesitate, then say, 'I thought we'd spend tomorrow saying our farewells, then set off at dawn the next day.'

I can see that she is suddenly fearful. For a time she's quiet; then, sighing, she nods. 'All right, but Otto . . .'

'Yes?'

'Promise me you'll do something for me on the journey. Promise me you'll teach me German.'

161

It is July the fifteenth, St Vladimir's day, named after Prince Vladimir Sviatislav, son of the first Grand Prince of the Rus'; the same who took an army to Constantinople and came back with the Byzantine Emperor Basil's sister Anna as his bride; he who, returning home to Kiev, tore down the graven images of the six gods – of Stribog, the god of the sky, Dazhd'bog, the god of light, Mokosh, goddess of nature, Hors, the sun god, Simargl, god of fertility, and Perun, the old Norse god of thunder and war – and set a great cross in their place, leading the people of Kiev – all fifty thousand of them – down into the waters of the River Dnieper, there to be baptised in the faith of Christ.

Long ago that was, yet I remember it well, for I was there,

standing waist-deep in the river beside the Grand Prince as, one by one, he submerged his people, drawing the sign of the cross upon each brow and washing away their sins as that long hot summer afternoon wore on.

On another summer's day two hundred and fifty years later, I lie back, my darling Katerina beside me as our boat slowly crosses Lake Ilmen, the shorelines to either side of us lost in distance, the oars of the boatmen pulling strongly against the northward current.

Behind us, the sled is packed upon a cart, secured with chains and padlocked, the only key secreted on my person. Though its loss would not be a total disaster, it would make things hard for us, and so I take cautious measures.

As well I might, for we venture now into lawless regions.

There is a secret compartment beneath the floor of the cart, accessible from beneath, wherein I've stored certain items of importance. As for the cart itself, a thick tarpaulin – not of this age – covers the load, strapped tightly so that no thieving fingers can get in.

Katerina is wearing a large straw hat and a summer dress, like a peasant girl, and from time to time I catch one or another of the men staring at her. But I make no issue of it. These are good men; as good as one might find in a wilderness town like Novgorod, and the *tysiatskii*'s pass carries weight with them. They might dream of having her, but they know better than to act on the desire. Besides, there is the prospect of a handsome bonus if I return safely, so they row hard and keep their thoughts to themselves, even if their eyes sometimes stray.

For the past half hour I have been writing in my journal, but now Katerina interrupts me, asking me to run through things just one more time, so that she has it clear in her mind.

I take out the hand-drawn map, then turn, pointing north

across the great lake towards the distant mountains. 'Look,' I say. 'See the clouds gathering already. In eight, maybe nine weeks the rainy season will begin. We must be in Gzhatsk before then.'

I draw a line on the map with my right forefinger, tracing it from where the River Lovat begins, on the south shore of Lake Ilmen, down through Velikie Luki to the tiny village of Zajkava.

I say village, but it is little more than a trading post. A wooden jetty and a cluster of small wooden buildings built for the river trade. There we leave our friends, the boatmen, and travel south-west overland some twenty miles to Velizh, another trading post, but this time on the River Mezha.

Katerina listens attentively. She is keen to be no burden but to be an equal partner on this venture. If I am hurt, she tells me, then she will get me home.

I like that, even if it's unnecessary. Because if I am badly hurt, then someone from Four-Oh will come and get me, and Time will be changed so that no hurt has been done. Nor will any burden be placed on Katerina's memory, for with that change her recollection of everything will also be erased.

But she doesn't know that. As far as she's concerned, I'm Otto, a German trader from her own century, and that is *all* I am.

I put the map away, then lie back, stretching out, totally relaxed for the first time in weeks, and after a while she lies down next to me, her head resting on my chest, her eyes closed, dozing in the warm sunlight. It's a pleasant way to spend time: the sound of the oars, the rush of the water going by the hull of the twelve-man *ushkui*, the call of birds high in the clear blue sky above us. After a while, the boatmen begin to sing and I hear – and feel – Katerina humming the tune to herself.

And so we sail on, as the afternoon becomes evening. The sun slowly sinks beneath the trees far to our right as we sit there, watching the land draw closer.

It's a beautiful evening, the thin wisps of cloud on the horizon painted crimson by the setting sun, and as we row into the river's mouth, I have a sense of the enormity of Time, of the weight of the long centuries surrounding us, and I want to say something to her, only I can't. She must never know.

The land here is unspoiled, the virgin forest stretching away unchecked to either side, and as the last trace of sunlight disappears, so the night rushes in, the sky dark suddenly, the stars burning above us.

Katerina snuggles close as I put my arm around her and begin to tell her about the stars – the truth this time, not some romantic myth – and after a while she stares at me, astonished, then laughs.

'You're making it up, Otto! Teasing me!'

'No,' I say, then let her have it her own way. Maybe she is not ready for that yet. Maybe . . .

Her kiss surprises me. Reminds me where I am and when. *Home*, I think. For wherever she is, is home.

162

Shaposhnikov, the captain, moors the boat at a turn in the river and, leaving us on-board, takes his men ashore. From where we lie in the darkness we can see their campfire burning brightly, throwing up cinders into the night, and hear, in the stillness, the deep, low murmur of their voices. For a while I hesitate, wondering if any of them have perhaps crept back, to hide in the dark nearby and watch us, but it's no good, the warmth of her naked body beside me on the fur-lined pallet makes me forget myself and, after a long and pleasant while, I come to myself again as if from the depths of dream, the stillness of the night much more intense than before.

I frown, then realise that the boatmen have fallen silent, listening to us. *Imagining* us. Beneath me, Katerina stirs and softly laughs.

'Do you think they heard us, Otto?' she whispers.

Her pupils reflect the stars. So beautiful, her eyes. Like mirrors into the cosmos itself. I smile and touch my lips to hers. My flesh is still within her, is still hard despite all her best attempts to blunt its ardour.

'Maybe,' I whisper back, moving slowly against her, making her catch her breath. 'But you know what?'

'What?'

'I don't care.'

She is moving now, pushing herself up against me to meet each slow, deliberate thrust. She giggles. 'You were very noisy, Otto.'

'Noisy? *Me*? What about *you*?'

She answers with a kiss and, in a while, the voices round the fire take up again, even as my love and I begin again, the warm Russian darkness surrounding us, without and within, timeless and eternal.

163

We make good time. At midday on the tenth day we come to Velikie Luki, the small town nestling into the trees on a bend in the river. There was a Rus' fort here a century ago, but it fell into ruin, its log walls rotting away. Then, thirty years back, Mstislav Mstislavich, Prince then of Novgorod, strengthened its defences against the Lithuanian threat, making it his principal garrison in the south. Since then, however, it has fallen into disrepair once more. It's a ramshackle place, and every last one of its inhabitants, young and old, come out to stare at us as we tie up at the jetty.

Katerina, particularly, gets their attention. She has changed her style from peasant girl to boatman, borrowing the clothes of one of the men and even taking a turn at the oar for a while. The crew are in love with her, with that fierce protective love elder brothers have for younger sisters. A mere ten days in and I do believe they would die for her, were they asked to. As it is, they eye the natives of this town suspiciously – the young men especially so – with warning glances as if to ward off any possibility of trouble.

We go ashore, meeting Grikov, the town's head man, in his 'house' – a glorified hut with two rooms rather than one – and I do a little trading, and drink a little of his awful wine and, because these seem good people, trustworthy people, I offer to pay for a feast, and the whole town – all three hundred – are soon to be found carousing deep in drink, their faces greasy with fat. Roast bear, someone tells me, as well as wolf, alongside the more recognisable lamb and dog.

As evening falls, the party continues, and one of the locals brings out a fiddle and starts up a tune, and soon there's a crowd of villagers dancing in the firelight beside the dark-flowing river, and after a while Katerina joins in, lifting her hands above her head as she dances, in the Russian fashion, and twirling about, clapping with the rhythm, and there is laughter and singing and later – much later – we return to the boat as the last of the villagers straggle home.

And it's as she snuggles against me on the furs that she tells me how happy she is and how glad she is she has come with me, and how very, very much she loves me. But when I turn to answer her, she is already asleep, her beautiful face against my shoulder, her soft breath on my neck.

I am tired, but sleep does not come easily. And there's a reason for it. For you see, I remember the last time I came to Velikie Luki, in 1942. It was a very different place then, much bigger and uglier, though no less ramshackle. The river still flowed through it, but it was a dirty, grimy place and there was a sheen of oil on the water, and the scum of detergent from the massive industrial complex three miles north of the town.

I was there with Dr Walther Stahlecker and sixty of his men from *Einsatzgrupen A*, posing as a war correspondent for the *Volkischer Beobachter*. Not that any words I could write about what Stahlecker was doing in the *Reichskommisariat Ostland*, as it was then known, would ever be published, but because the man was keen to show me – in a boastful kind of way – what he was up to there. Stahlecker smiled a lot, as if he really enjoyed his work, but those days I spent in Lithuania and the Smolensk region had the feel of a nightmare. Stahlecker had almost a thousand men under his command, trained SS killers who had no interest in fighting a war but in mopping up behind the lines after the regular soldiers, the *Wehrmacht*, had fought their way through. They were after Jews and Romanies and known communists, and in Velikie Luki they found almost four hundred.

The memory of what happened – of what I was witness to that day just south of the town – returns to haunt me now, troubling me much more than usual. There was nothing I could do, of course, nothing but watch and keep my silence. These things have happened throughout history, and there is little we can do to change that, but sometimes, just sometimes, it worries me. Sometimes Albrecht Burckel's words, spoken to me in another time, another place, come back to haunt me:

'*We act like policemen, Otto. Time cops, when we really ought to be acting like revolutionaries.* Undrehungar. *We could change things.* Really *change things. Not piss about meddling in historical events – what good does that do ultimately? The Russians only change it back! No. We need to get to grips with the underlying phenomena, with the* infrastructure *of history, not the surface froth.*'

Perhaps he's right. Perhaps we really ought to do things

differently. Yet I'm not convinced. Not yet, anyway. Besides, there's time enough to worry about such things. Time enough and more. Closing my eyes, I let the night swallow me up, my love pressed close, her soft breath in my ear.

Tomorrow, I tell myself. I shall address such thoughts tomorrow.

164

Only tomorrow is a bright, clear, sunny day, and the shadows of the night are little more than phantoms. The whole town comes out to see us off and, as we row away, the ragged children run alongside the boat, waving and calling, until Velikie Luki has been swallowed by the distance and there is nothing but trees to either side of us.

It is three days' journey to Zajkava, then at least three, maybe four, across land from Zajkava to Velizh, where we are to pick up our boat on the Mezha, but we are making good time and the weather is perfect. Katerina sits on the prow of the boat, her bare feet dangling over the edge, her toes trailing in the clear, cool water. She is wearing the straw sun hat, but her face and neck have got a real colour these past few days, and I have never seen her quite so happy, so free of cares.

At noon we moor beneath the shade of some overhanging trees to give the crew a break, and while they prepare a meal, the captain, Shaposhnikov, takes me aside.

Shaposhnikov is a short, stocky fellow with a silky black beard and heavy, almost bushy eyebrows. He is in his thirties but has kept himself trim and runs a good boat. Yet while he's deferential to me, he's also troubled by my behaviour. All morning he has been silent, but now, out of earshot of the others, he speaks out.

'Forgive me, Meister,' he says, 'but it isn't right.'

'*Right?*' And I think immediately he's talking about Katerina. I bristle and make to argue, but he quickly speaks again, lifting his broad, strong hand expressively to silence me.

'Hear me out, Meister Otto. Please.'

I nod at him to continue, but I am tense now, strangely angry. How *dare* he criticise her?

'You are a generous man, Meister, there's no doubting that. Only, the feast last night. It wasn't right. To waste so much on such . . . *riff-raff*.'

I almost laugh. So that's it. I make to answer, but once more he hurriedly interrupts me.

'It is your money, of course. Yours to do as you will, only . . .'

Only he would rather I spent it on him and his crew than on strangers. But Shaposhnikov is not going to say that in so many words.

'They seemed like good people,' I say. 'Yet you call them riff-raff.'

Shaposhnikov does not flinch or look away. He prides himself on his honesty, and so he answers me bluntly now. 'You have not had to deal with them these past years. When things were bad . . .' His eyes narrow, as if he is remembering how it was, and then he nods. 'I would not have stopped there, except that it was your wish.'

'And yet they treated us well.'

Shaposhnikov laughs at that, as if I am naïve. 'They understand one thing, these river people. That a rich man might be robbed. There is no kindness in them. Which is why I've asked my men to take care until we are far from that place. I would not put it past old Grikov to send his men after us, to track us and, when the chance came, rob us.'

I reach out and hold his upper arm in a friendly grip. 'Dear Shaposhnikov, I thank you for your concern. but do not fear. I have travelled in wilder places than this and survived. But I hear what you are saying and will take greater care in future.'

My little speech does not, of course, address his main point – that he would rather have me spend whatever money I wish to throw about on him rather than strangers – but he will not find me ungenerous.

Returning to the boat, I find Katerina fishing, with a pole and a line. One of the younger crew members is nearby, offering her advice, but, seeing me, he quickly lowers his head and moves away.

'What's this?' I ask gently, settling alongside her, and staring down into the bright, fast-flowing water. 'Learning to fish?'

She looks sideways at me and smiles. 'I thought it might be a useful skill to learn.'

'It is.'

I say no more, but watch her for a while, enjoying the look of concentration in her face.

'Otto?'

'Yes?'

'When are we going to begin?'

'Begin?'

'You promised me, remember?'

'Ah . . .' I smile. 'Right now if you like.'

She grins. 'Okay.'

'What you're holding, that is *die Stange.*'

'Dee-stan-ger?'

'That's right. *Die Stange.* The rod.'

'And the fish?'

'Is *der fische.*'

'Der fish-er.'

I laugh, then, moved by her beauty, reach across to lay my fingers gently on her neck. '*Siehe, wir lieben nicht, wie die Blumen, aus einem einzigen Jahr; uns steigt, wo wir lieben, unvordenklicher Saft in die Arme.*'

The German words are not the Old High German from the early years of the twenty-first century. There are those who consider my native tongue ugly and cumbersome, yet in the hands of a poet it can sing.

Katerina gives a little shiver and then looks to me, seeing the seriousness in my eyes. I have never spoken in my own tongue to her before this moment, yet while the words mean nothing to her, she seems to sense their meaning.

'What was that, Otto?'

'A poem,' I say, then, realising she has no clue as to what a poem is, I add. 'A song without a tune.'

'What does it mean?'

I consider, then, putting on my best oratory manner, translate for her: '"Look, we don't love like flowers, with only a single season behind us; immemorial sap mounts in our arms when we love."'

She stares at me, astonished. 'Otto, that's beautiful. Did *you* write it?'

I could lie and say yes. I could claim it for my own and she would never know. Only I would never lie to her.

'No. It was written by a countryman of mine. A young man called Rilke. Rainer Maria Rilke.'

'Maria? But that's a woman's name.'

I smile. 'Yes. But not always.'

She looks away, then, frowning, lets the pole drop into the water.

'Katerina?'

As it floats away, she watches it a moment, then turns back, meeting my eyes.

'Speak to me once more, Otto, in your own tongue. Tell me you love me. Tell me you'll never go away.'

165

As evening falls, Shaposhnikov lights torches all about the gunwhales of the boat, and as the darkness intensifies, so the world takes on a different, almost magical look. With Katerina resting at my side, I watch the mist-wreathed river flow past, soothed by the song of the boatmen as they pull on the oars. The water is wide here, the current sluggish. At the prow, Grigor, Shaposhnikov's chief hand, leans out, staring into the darkness up ahead, trying to locate a place to moor for the night.

The forest is dense on either side, pressed close against the water's edge. As we follow a left turn in the river, however, it begins to thin out, and as the light from the burning torches illuminates the far bank, a gasp comes from the men.

Katerina is dozing, but the sudden interruption to the regular stroke of the oars, the lurch to one side as the boatmen stand and stare, wakes her.

'Otto . . .?'

I swallow, taking in the sight.

There, on the far bank where the trees have been cleared, is a makeshift gibbet. The long, straight trunk of a tree has been trimmed of its branches, lifted up between two trees and wedged between them to form a beam. From that beam hang six shadowy figures, their heads lolling to one side, the necks snapped, their arms dangling lifeless at their sides.

As the boat drifts closer, I hear Katerina catch her breath. Of the six, two are boys, one barely out of infancy.

'Robbers,' Shaposhnikov says, reading the sign that has been painted crudely on a plank propped up against the left-hand tree.

As the torches throw more light upon them, so the horror increases. Their faces are black, the eye sockets empty, and their flesh . . .

They have been partly eaten by animals. One can see the bones poking from among the weatherworn rags of their clothes.

Katerina turns from the sight, burrowing into my side. 'God protect us . . .'

I look past her as we drift slowly past the gruesome sight, watching it unflinchingly, reminding myself that this is how it is back in this age: lawless and brutal. Only rich men rely upon the courts in Rus'. Out here, in this wilderness, *this* is justice.

That night we sleep onshore, among the others, Katerina held close in my arms. The sight has disturbed her, robbed her of her gay spirits, and though she sleeps, her sleep is troubled and more than once she calls out, as if seeing the dangling men once more. And not just the men.

'*Boys, Otto. They were only boys.*'

I sigh, then try to sleep, but sleep will not come, and as the morning light seeps back into the world, I wonder what other sights we shall see on our travels, and what Katerina will make of them.

She has seen a great deal, in her own way. Novgorod, while paradise compared to most of Rus', is still a frontier town, and twice in her short life she has suffered hardship. Out here, in the wilds, however, things are very different. Out here there is nothing between you and your fellow man. Nothing but your own wit and strength. Was I right to place her in such danger?

Then again, could I have left her? Would I even have made such a journey without her?

With her pressed close and warm I know the answer: I would risk everything just to be with her. I would defy a thousand cut-throats and river pirates if only she were there beside me.

Besides, I have something no river pirate has. A Kolbe model 9.3. The best needle-gun ever made. If the worst comes to the worst I'll shoot my way out of trouble.

Katerina wakes and looks up into my face, then gets up on to her elbow, yawning, a puzzled look in her eyes. 'Otto? What is it? Why are you smiling like that?'

'It's nothing,' I say, smoothing her brow with my fingertips. 'Nothing.'

Sometimes – just sometimes – there's a dark humour in anachronism.

166

Zajkava is a shit-hole: a collection of ragged huts and a rotted wooden jetty. Nor are the old man and his boy – my guides across country to Velizh – anywhere to be seen.

'We're a day early,' Shaposhnikov says, as if to excuse him. 'He'll be here. He always is.'

But I'm not happy. He should have been here *now*. I've paid him to be.

My bad mood is reflected by the weather. It's been overcast all day, but now – for the first time on our journey – it begins to rain; not heavy rain, nor cold, yet it seems ominous somehow.

The boatmen unload the cart, and while I check that the sled is okay, Katerina explores the village, trailed by Mikhail, one of Shaposhnikov's younger hands, to ensure she comes to no harm.

It doesn't take her long. As I say, there's little here. But there's the problem of where to stay overnight. None of the huts look suitable and Shaposhnikov wants to get back, otherwise we'd stay on-board the boat. From the look of the sky, however, it's set to rain all evening.

In the end I persuade Shaposhnikov to stay on. He counts the silver coins I've tipped into his hand, then grunts his satisfaction.

'All right,' he says, 'but we leave at first light.'

By nightfall there's still no sign of our guide, so Shaposhnikov has two of his men guard the cart, while Katerina and I settle on-board, beneath an improvised awning. The boatmen don't worry whether it's raining or not. It's a warm night and they simply strip off their tops and sit there in their rough hessian trousers, drinking and talking late into the night, their laughter reassuring us.

We are up before the dawn, and once Shaposhnikov has fed his crew we make our farewells, the men queuing in a line to kiss and hug their darling Katerina goodbye. It's all very amiable, and my hand is grasped time after time, my back slapped, and we are wished 'good fortune and a safe journey' a dozen times before finally they climb into the boat and depart.

It will be an easier journey home for them, going with the current, and Shaposhnikov takes with him a letter I've penned to Ernst. But it will be a week or more before Ernst gets to see what I've written, and our concern now is that the old man has let us down. Katerina and I wait by the river, the cart with our sled on resting nearby, never out of our sight.

The villagers keep out of our way, yet we are watched every moment with a hostility that only living in a place like this could breed.

I am beginning to despair of our guide ever turning up when, just after noon, he walks out of the forest, his boy – a mute who can be no more than six or seven – a little way behind, leading a small, very stubborn-looking donkey.

'Ah,' he says, wiping his mouth with his hand and then pulling at his long grey beard. 'There you are.'

He looks like a vagrant and I sense at once that there's no point being angry with him. We have lunch of sorts – a meagre meal bought off the locals, mainly consisting of over-cooked vegetables – and then set off, Katerina and I, like our guides, barefoot, the donkey drawing the cart reluctantly, it seems, and only after the boy has beaten it with a stick into moving.

Russia, I think.

The old man wants to talk, of course, but his words are those of an untutored imbecile, and after a while I find myself wishing he'd be silent. It's now that Katerina proves her worth, for, sensing my irritation, she takes on herself the task of talking to him, treating him deferentially, almost as if he were her father, and after a while the two of them are laughing and joking.

There is a path of sorts through the trees, though it would be easy to stray from it, and the old man and his boy take it without the need for thought. In places we have to clear the way to get the cart through, but otherwise our afternoon is uneventful. We walk for three, maybe four hours, then, as the sun begins to sink, the old man looks to me and raises his eyebrows expressively.

'You want to stop?' he asks, as if I were the one who was asking.

'*Here?*' I ask, looking about me.

'Here's as good as anywhere. It's all much the same.' And he gives a roar of laughter, as if it's the funniest thing anyone has ever said.

I shrug, then look to Katerina, who nods.

'Okay,' I say. 'But let's clear a space. We can put the cart at the centre and make up pallet beds.'

The crude beds are packed in the sled, atop the tarpaulin, along with our food, axes and furs.

The old man, of course, makes no attempt to help, but watches us with an air of amusement as Katerina and I – and the boy – chop down several of the nearby trees to clear a space a dozen paces in circumference.

At the centre of it, just a little way from the cart, I clear away the leaf mould underfoot and, using an entrencher, dig a small hole and begin to lay a fire. As I do so, the old man comes closer and, leaning over the hole, studies it intently, as if it is the most interesting thing he's ever seen. After a moment the boy too joins him there, staring down.

'Strange,' the old guide says, shaking his head and drawing his fingers repeatedly through his grizzled, unkempt beard. 'But then, I guess you *are* a *Nemets*.'

Katerina looks to me, to see if I'm offended, but I just shrug. Pulling out my tinderbox I strike the flint and get the fire lit. As I make to put the box away, the old man puts out his hand. I give him the tinderbox and again he studies it, as if he's never seen the like. Which is so. It is, once more, anachronistic, out of its proper time and place, though not overly so.

'That too is *Nemets*,' I say, taking it back.

While Katerina tends the fire, I go off into the surrounding woodland, returning in a while with two small hares. I throw them down, then proceed to skin them. The old man is impressed, then grateful when I share the meat with him. I even go to give the boy some, only our guide doesn't allow it.

'You will spoil him,' he says, wolfing down the boy's share. 'And then how will I get him to work?'

But later, while the old man talks to me, I notice Katerina slip the boy a piece of the dark, cooked meat, and see the youngster turn his back as he secretly eats it.

I don't like the old man – not one bit – but I only have to put up with him for the best part of four days, and so I bite my tongue and let the old rogue say what he wishes.

I ask him about the robbers that we saw and he laughs. 'There are ten for every one the authorities catch. It's a wilderness out here. Even the wolves are afraid.' And he roars with laughter again.

The old man sets the boy to watch the first part of the night, but when I wake to take my turn in the early hours, I find the fire out, the boy asleep and snoring, flat on his back beside his master. But the cart is fine and no harm's done, and I sit there beside the rekindled embers, awaiting the dawn, listening to the noises of the wild animals in the surrounding forest, remembering other times and other places not so dissimilar from this..

The next few days fall into a routine. We walk, and all the while the old man talks and we listen, for even Katerina has run out of things to remark upon. From time to time we have to change course, to bring the cart around some natural obstacle that has appeared since our guide last took this path – fallen trees, a landslip or the like – but eventually, on the afternoon of the fourth day, we emerge from the trees and find, there across a broad, fast-running river, the trading post of Velizh.

Katerina, especially, is glad to see it, for in the last few days she has been badly bitten by insects. We have only one problem now: how to cross the river.

I mention this to our guide and, in answer, he puts two fingers to his teeth and lets out a piercing whistle. Heads appear from the makeshift houses on the far bank and a moment later there are shouts. Men and women run to and fro on the far bank and then a long, flat-bottomed boat is launched. One man jumps in, then holds the boat still against the bank as a second hurriedly joins him. Swiftly and with great skill they bring the craft across, their short, blunt paddles digging deep into the rushing flow, the boat tacking back and forth against the fast-flowing current.

'Meister Otto, I take it,' one of them calls up to me, grinning at me with a mouth full of rotten teeth. 'We were told to expect you.'

'Is Krylenko here?'

'He's moored about a mile upstream, with his sons. They have an encampment there.'

'Ah. And the cart?'

He looks past me and gives a little shrug. 'It'll be okay there until Krylenko comes. I'll get one of the youngsters to look after it. But Meister, *please* . . .'

He puts a hand out, welcoming me on-board. I help Katerina get in, then wait patiently as the old man and the boy clamber aboard before I finally join her in the stern.

'You've had a safe journey, I hope,' the boatman asks, turning his head to grin at me again, even as he pushes away from the bank and, digging his short paddle steeply into the water, begins to turn the boat's prow against the current.

'Yes, thanks to our guide here.'

'Old Mesyats knows every tree in the forest. Yes, but he loves to talk, eh? He could talk my mother-in-law to death and that's the truth!'

It is, and I laugh for the first time in days, and old Mesyats, seeing the funny side of it, laughs too, and so we arrive in Velizh in the best of moods, even as the sun finally breaches the cloud cover and lights up the afternoon, blazing on the river's surface.

Russia . . . how beautiful it sometimes is.

167

Krylenko, when he finally arrives, proves as dour and unhelpful as he could possibly be. He refuses to take me upriver, and will only take me to Surazh, to the south-west, which is in completely the wrong direction. I object strongly, and remind him of the advance Ernst paid him, and of his handshake on the deal, but Krylenko is unmoved. He looks at me from under his heavily hooded eyes and shrugs.

'My wife is with child,' he says. 'If I leave her for so long . . .' And he shrugs again, as if I'm to take it or leave it.

I begin to wonder if this is yet another attempt to squeeze more money from me, the foreigner, the *Nemets*. Nor, I know, is it any good me flashing the *tysiatskii's* pass at him. We are two full weeks from Novgorod and these people are not afraid to snub their noses at the good commander, no, nor kill his tax collectors if they become too persistent. In the end, I bite the bullet and offer to pay the man an extra six dirhams, but even this seems to have no effect.

'I'll take you to Surazh,' he says. 'You'll get another boat from there. Someone mad enough to go into the marshes.'

I fall quiet, understanding. Krylenko is afraid. Where the River Mezha turns south towards Zarkovsji, it runs through extensive marshlands, home to river pirates and bandits.

I say nothing more. Surazh it is, then, and a week lost at the very least.

His sons, when they arrive, are carbon copies of their father and every bit as surly, and in transporting the cart and its load across the water, I have to tell them more than once to stop poking at the parcels stacked on-board the sled. For the first time on this journey I feel I am among dishonest men, and come to a decision.

At Surazh I shall have them. All five of them, if needs be. But I don't tell Katerina what I'm thinking. I tell her calmly that there's been a change of plan and when she queries it, I tell her it's for the best. And maybe it is, for to travel into bandit territory with such men might prove disastrous.

Even so, I am angry at the delay. Surazh is a good day and a half's journey downstream, and Krylenko will not leave until tomorrow. And if I cannot find a boat to hire at Surazh . . .

I feel like forcing him to stick to his agreement – to *make* him take me – only the practicalities of that are insurmountable; at best it's an eight-day journey to Belyj on the River Obsca, our final destination, and I can't imagine how I'd make him take me, short of holding a gun to his head and then keeping awake for eight whole nights.

No. It has to be Surazh. But he'll not get away with this.

That night I sleep on the cart, Katerina on a pallet underneath. And it's a good job I do, for in the early hours someone sneaks up and, not noticing me there, tries to take something from the sled. I am awake and on them in an instant, beating them off with my stave. They run away, whimpering, into the trees. In the dark I'm not sure who it was, but one thing's for sure: they'll have the bruises to show.

Krylenko is twice as surly when he finally arrives, an hour after noon, and I note that only three of his sons are with him. The fourth is conspicuously absent.

They lift the cart on to their boat – a flat-bottomed *strug* – then, letting us settle in the stern, push off into the current.

There's little talk. Krylenko is content to mutter instructions now and then to one or another of his sons. Taking his lead, they try their best to pretend we're not there, and even when Katerina needs to stop to answer nature's call, Krylenko makes as if he hasn't heard my request to pull the boat over to the bank. It's only when I make my way forward and, grabbing his arm, turn him round and speak roughly into his face that he acknowledges me.

He makes some comment under his breath and his sons laugh. But it doesn't matter. I'll have the bastard, see if I don't.

While Katerina is among the trees, I stand there in the boat, looking from one of them to another, defying them to look her way. She's not long, and when she climbs aboard again, Krylenko makes another of his under-his-breath comments, making his sons roar with laughter.

I hear part of it this time; something about 'the *Nemets'* slut'.

This time it's just too much.

'Krylenko, why are you such a pig?'

He half turns and looks at me lazily. 'I merely speak the truth,' he says. 'My wife, she's a bitch, and my daughters and my daughters-in-law cows, all of them!'

His sons laugh and nod their heads.

Krylenko is smiling now, an ugly, sneering smile. 'Women are good for three things only. Fucking, cooking and beating.'

'You think I should beat my wife, then, Krylenko?'

He nods slowly. 'You should beat her while you fuck her.'

His sons are giggling now, tears streaming from their eyes. I look from one to the other and wonder what I'd do if things got out of hand. The Kolbe is in my pack, easy to reach, and I could shoot them dead before they knew what was happening. Only then I'd have to explain to Katerina what the Kolbe was, and why it wasn't magic.

We're barely halfway there when Krylenko calls it a day and moors the boat. It's clearly a spot he knows well and that's used by the river-men, for the edge of the forest here has been cleared and there's evidence of many fires. The boat secured, we make camp.

Krylenko tries every means to coax us ashore, and I know then for a certainty that he was hoping that we'd leave the cart unguarded on-board, and that had we camped onshore, he and his sons would have been away just as soon as they heard us snoring.

As it is, I have a restless night, waking several times and starting up. On one occasion I notice Krylenko, seated by the fire, whittling a piece of wood and staring sullenly across at me, as if planning the best way of outwitting me.

With the morning my spirits rise. It's a bright, warm day and we will we be rid of the odious Krylenko by that afternoon.

There's a brooding silence as we set off on the last stage of our journey down to Surazh, and I begin to wonder if they haven't concocted some scheme after all.

I'd not put it past them to try to murder us and dump the bodies, then share out our goods, but as the hours pass and they make no move, so I relax. Besides, if Krylenko wanted to murder us and steal our goods, why not do it on the journey north, where the river traffic is less, rather than on this busier, southern stretch of the Mezha?

Cowardice, that's why. Simple cowardice.

Surazh heaves into view just after noon, with the sun beating down from directly overhead. It's the hottest day yet, and it appears that the rain that has swept across the land further north has left Surazh unscathed, for the earth between the ramshackle wooden houses is bare and dry with not a blade of grass to be seen. Even the trees – birch and cedar for the main part – seem to wilt in the excessive heat.

Surazh is a proper town, not just a trading post, and as we drift in towards the main jetty, I note a dozen or more vessels tied up against the shore. Beyond the makeshift harbour, formed by a wide sweep of the river, lies the town itself, a sprawl of two or three hundred houses, set within a wooden palisade, and – that rarity out here in the wilds – a stone-built church, complete with a bright blue cupola. Seeing it, Katerina looks to me. It is two weeks now since her last confession.

'Okay. But don't be long. If I can find someone who'll take us, it would be good to set out at once.'

She understands and, even as we tie up, jumps onshore and, without so much as a glance back, hurries across to the shadowed doorway of the church, a crowd of curious locals watching her go.

Which leaves me with Krylenko and his sons.

Krylenko is sitting there, in the very centre of the boat, on a long worn, wooden bench, staring up at me with a kind of mocking smile.

'Well,' he says, lifting his head sneeringly. 'We've brought you here.'

'So you have.'

There's a moment's silence. His sons look to one another, as if not quite sure what's going to happen next. Krylenko wants paying, of course. The bastard actually wants paying for putting me to such inconvenience – yes, and on top of what Ernst's already given him – but he's going to have to ask.

'Well?' he says, a slight impatience in his voice. 'You pay us and we'll unload the cart. Otherwise . . .'

Otherwise what? You'll steal my cart? Take all my goods?

I meet his eyes. 'Unload it and I'll pay you.'

He laughs and looks away, then spits into the river to his right. 'You pay me. *Then* we unload.'

I'm conscious of exactly where each of his sons is standing. In the last few hours I've watched them, noting how each one moves, attempting to gauge which of them I'd need to deal with first, for there's always a best way of handling these situations, and these fellows always look to one of their number for their lead.

Thus I'm acutely conscious of how Krylenko's eldest straightens and turns slightly to face me. Beneath me the boat gently sways. That's another factor, and it's the one that finally decides me.

'Okay,' I say, 'here's the deal. Half now, half when the cart's onshore.'

Krylenko grins. 'Done.'

I dig three coins out of my leather purse, and hand them across, then, as the eldest holds the boat still, climb up on to the jetty.

If he wanted, Krylenko could cast off and sail away with my cart and all my goods, only perhaps there are too many witnesses and even he knows he needs a reason – a refusal to pay, maybe – before he could get away with that and not be called a thief. Besides, he's got what he wanted, an extra six dirhams, and for what?

For being an arsehole and breaking his word.

I watch them untie the wheels of the cart, then lift it carefully onshore. Krylenko, meanwhile, has not moved. He still sits there, picking at his teeth and watching me.

It's his eldest now who puts his hand out, asking for the remainder of the money.

I smile and shake my head. 'Go fuck yourself.'

It's like he doesn't hear me properly. Either that or he can't believe I've just said that. 'What?' he says. Then, a moment later, *'What?'*

'I said—'

But I don't have to repeat it. Finally, it's sunk in, and as it does, he growls and takes a swing at me.

I parry it easily, then watch his face crumple with pain as I knee him in the balls. He goes down on to his knees with a grunt.

The other two are slow to follow up, and the youngest is on his back before he knows what happened, gasping for breath where I've punched him in the throat. The last of them yelps and makes to leap on to the boat, only I kick his legs out from under him and he falls between the boat and the jetty with a startled cry and a loud splash.

Krylenko is on his feet now, his eyes wide and frightened. He thinks I'm coming after him, and, taking a step backward, he tumbles awkwardly over the bench seat. But I'm not going to sully my hands. Reaching down, I slip the knife from my belt and cut the mooring ropes, then heave the boat out with my foot.

Slowly it drifts away, Krylenko's second son, coughing and spluttering from his unexpected dip, trying to clamber on-board.

The eldest son is behind me, wheezing, trying to get up off his knees and take another swing, but I'm not about to let him. Besides, I remember what his father said about Katerina, and how he laughed.

I grab the collar of his smock and jerk him to his feet, then whirl him about and, with the help of the toe of my boot, launch him into the river after the boat.

The youngest doesn't wait for me to act. Still holding his throat, he throws himself into the water, surfacing a moment later with a spluttering gasp.

It's over, and barely a minute has passed. As I turn my back on them, I find a crowd of locals gathered at the top of the jetty, staring at me with a mixture of amusement and awe. It makes me realise that Krylenko must have a reputation for his double-dealing, for there's nothing but admiration for what I've done, and when Katerina emerges from the church, she finds me at the centre of a crowd of townsfolk who want nothing so much as to pat my back and shake my hand and offer to buy me drinks at the dock-side inn.

'Otto? What's going on? Where's Krylenko?'

'Gone,' I say, recalling how he and his sons glared at me and shook their fists even as they rowed away.

'You paid them?'

'I paid them.'

'Good. And the boat?'

I'm about to answer that I haven't yet hired a boat, when a stranger – a huge, dark-haired man with a long jet-black beard who's been standing off a little way, watching me – speaks up.

'If it's the hire of a boat you want, then a boat you have.'

He steps forward and, leaning down to my level, offers me a hand easily twice the size of my own. A veritable blacksmith's hand. 'Bakatin,' he says. 'Fyodor Mikhailovich Bakatin, and it's an honour to meet you, Master . . .'

'Behr,' I say and take his hand. '*Meister* Otto Behr.'

168

Fyodor Bakatin proves to be not just a large man, but a man of large appetites. As we sit at a trestle table in the inn, I marvel at the amount of food he manages to eat, and begin to wonder if there is a boat big enough to carry the provisions it would require to feed such a man for the eight days we'll be travelling.

The cart is outside, within sight, but to ensure its safety Bakatin has had his sons guard it, in his words, 'against the thieving fingers of the locals'.

Bakatin has three sons, though I'd not have guessed they were his, had he not told me so. The eldest is long and lanky with a squint and a wispy beard, the middle son short and heavy, bordering on fat, with long, flaxen-blond hair and pale blue eyes. The youngest, however, is the oddest, with his light, athletic build, his bright red hair and green, cat-like eyes. A smooth-faced, handsome boy. Far too handsome to have come from Bakatin's loins, or so it seems.

While we wait for more wine to be brought, I ask him how it is they don't resemble each other. Bakatin laughs. 'That comes, I guess, from them having different mothers.' He grins. 'I have three wives.'

Katerina giggles and I nudge her.

'Oh, it annoys the priest, but what of that? I'm a good husband and a good father, and besides, the church does well out of me. Some around here are mealy-mouthed. They give lip-service to the faith, but I –' he taps his chest expressively '– I, Bakatin, give *money*. I understand the *value* of religion.'

'And our journey, Fyodor,' I say, trying to bring him back to what we were discussing earlier. 'Are you not afraid of the marshes?'

'*Afraid*?' Bakatin throws out his great chest proudly. 'Show me the man of whom Fyodor Mikhailovich Bakatin is afraid and I will show you Satan himself!'

At which he roars with laughter, then finishes his wine and bellows at the serving girl to move her pretty little arse and get some more wine over to our table at once.

Beside me, Katerina giggles, enjoying Bakatin's company, loving

his larger-than-life outrageousness, his *Russianness*. She's capti-
vated, and when I say he has a deal, and that I'm happy to sail
with him, she squeezes my right hand under the table and turns
her head to grin at me.

'You'll not regret it,' Bakatin says, nodding to himself. 'Though
I say it myself, there's no one knows this stretch of river better
than Bakatin. Ask anyone, they'll tell you. As for Krylenko . . .'
Bakatin leans to one side and spits, showily, as if on Krylenko's
grave. 'Krylenko,' he continues, 'is a liar and a bully and a coward
and a sneak-thief and you, Otto, are my friend until the Day of
Judgement itself for what you did today. Glorious, it was. Simply
glorious!'

At that moment the girl arrives with two fresh jugs of wine,
and Bakatin seizes one and pours the rich red liquid into our
goblets, the wine splashing everywhere. Then, slamming the jug
down and lifting his goblet, he stands and makes a toast.

'To adventure! And to my dear new friends, Otto and Katerina!'

169

I would have happily left that night, travelling in the dark, only
a sore head prevented it. Katerina alone of our little party was
sober when we called it a night, and it is late morning before we
finally set off, the cart nestled in the hold of Bakatin's surprisingly
large boat. It's an *ushkui*, not unlike the one we travelled down
from Lake Ilmen on, though smaller. Even so, it's big enough to
make me concerned whether Bakatin and his sons can row such
a vessel, loaded as it is not only with us and our cart, but with all
manner of goods Bakatin is transporting for other clients.

But Bakatin and his sons prove to be as strong as oxen when
it comes to rowing, and whenever the wind blows in our favour

– which it does often on that first day – he puts up a great sheet of a sail and, leaving it to the youngest, ships oars and rests, taking the chance to engage Katerina and me in conversation.

It is on one of those occasions that he raises the matter of Krylenko and what I intend to do about him.

'I intend to do nothing. Why, do you think I should?'

Bakatin nods. 'At the very least the man should be taught a lesson. But that's not my point. He'll be waiting for us, somewhere up ahead. You can be sure of it. He and his sons.'

'So we take care.'

'I think we should do more than that. I think we should ambush the rogue.'

'But if he's waiting for us, hiding somewhere in the trees, watching us sail past . . .'

'You have spare clothes, Otto? You and Katerina?'

I nod.

'Good. Then listen. I have a plan . . .'

170

But the ambush doesn't happen – not that evening – and while Bakatin and his sons make camp and keep guard, Katerina and I take the opportunity to bathe.

It's a long journey, and even when lazing about on the boat you can still begin to smell after a day or two. Which is why we try to wash every day and bathe every third day at the least. Katerina, new to such hygiene measures, has taken to the ritual in a big way and is as excited as a child. She likes her washing me, and I . . .

Well, how can I lie? I love the sight of her pale, beautifully formed limbs glistening wetly, the delight of her wonderfully curved body crouched above the river's edge. How could I not be aroused by such a sight? And so we make each thing we do a sensual game, and if it usually ends with her in my arms, beneath me, where's the harm in that? Only this time we are on our guard. Krylenko's still a threat, and there's nothing he'd like more, I'm certain, than to come upon us naked, in the act of lovemaking, so this once we simply wash, though, as ever towards the end of the ritual, Katerina squats before me, watching as I shave, endlessly fascinated by it.

'You should grow a beard,' she says, and when I laugh, she adds, 'It would make you look more Russian.'

I smile and, tilting the small circular mirror, study my chin for tufts of hair, the razor-sharp blade in my left hand.

'I am a *Nemets*. A German. This is how we look. Besides, I thought you liked the smoothness.'

'I do, only . . .'

'Only what?'

But she doesn't say, merely reaches out and gently touches my face where I've missed a bit.

'*There* . . .'

I lower the mirror and look directly at her. For a moment I almost – almost – tell her about Peter – Peter the Great, that is – and his amazing gesture on his return from the 'Great Embassy', his grand tour of the West. It's pertinent – a story about beards – but it won't happen for another four hundred and fifty years.

'I'll grow one,' I say. 'One of these days.'

I can't tell her why I don't. That I couldn't jump back, sporting a beard. Because that *would* make Hecht suspicious.

'Otto?'

'Yes?'

'Why didn't you get married, back in Germany?'

It's quiet in those moments before it begins. Very quiet. The river, which, just north of Surazh, had been narrow and fast-flowing, is broader here and muddied, like a sheet of molten lead. In the heat of the early afternoon the boat moves sluggishly, the big, off-white sheet of the sail hauled down, the four oarsmen – Bakatin and his sons – heaving us at great effort through the water.

There's the faintest of breezes up on deck, but it's against us, blowing from the north-east, and where Katerina and I sit in the bottom of the boat, our knees drawn up beneath us, the supporting struts of the body of the cart only inches above our heads, it's still and stiflingly hot, like an oven.

Bakatin and his sons are quiet, too. Oddly so, for they seem a merry bunch and prone to sing at the drop of a hat, but they're like silent automata just now. Hung-over, maybe. For a brief moment there is nothing but the rustling of the trees on the banks to either side, the rhythmic pull of the oars through the water, which rushes and gurgles past us. The day is hot and still. And then it happens.

There's a massive, splintering crash up ahead, followed almost instantly by a series of huge splashes – three or four at least – that send a great wave of water back at us. At once Bakatin's up and yelling to his sons, getting them to dig in the oars and backstroke, only as slow as we're moving, we're still moving too fast, the boat has too much momentum, and it crashes into the tangled barrier of fallen trees that now completely blocks the river.

The shock throws Bakatin off his feet. He gets up, cursing, his face filled with a dark anger.

Telling Katerina to stay where she is, I duck out from under the cart and quickly look about me. There are more than a dozen figures among the trees to our left, and a similar number to the right. Krylenko has got reinforcements.

Things are going badly wrong. This isn't the kind of ambush Bakatin was expecting, nor have we prepared for it. They've boats ready to launch on both banks, and as Krylenko's boat pushes off from our left, I make a quick decision. Not the Kolbe, but something almost as good under the circumstances. The *staritskii*.

I'm breaking rules, I know, but sometimes it's a question of expedience. Fists and feet won't do right now, not with the numbers they're throwing against us.

I crawl back under the cart, slip the catch to the secret compartment, and reach inside. It takes me a moment to undo the strap and open the bundle, but then it tumbles out into my hand, long and smooth with its fine, needle-like nose and its thick handgrip. It doesn't look very elegant, but it's highly effective.

'Stay where you are,' I say to Katerina, kissing her forehead. 'And don't – for *any* reason – come out!'

I turn back just in time. Krylenko's boat is almost on us. They're manoeuvring to place themselves directly alongside. One of his sons reaches out to grab hold of our gunwhales and secure the boat against his own, but even as he does, I aim the *staritskii* and blow his arm off from the elbow down.

The noise out on the water is deafening and everyone turns to stare at me – Bakatin and his sons, as well as Krylenko and his men. They look to the thing in my hand, then to the screaming man's missing arm, the severed elbow of which is spurting blood, and they don't make the connection. They think I must have thrown something – an axe, maybe, or a very sharp knife – only there's a strong burning smell in the air. I change the setting on the *staritskii* and aim again.

Krylenko's furious. He's almost spitting as he points to me and yells at his men to get me. He's screaming that he wants me dead, but midway through his rant he falls back, dead, a neat, coin-sized hole burned straight through his forehead and out through the back of his skull.

If it's a fight to the death, I don't believe in fighting fair, not even with decent men, let alone some bad fucker like Krylenko.

But I've barely time to think. Even as Krylenko falls, the prow of the second boat ploughs into ours, knocking us all off our feet again. There are shouts and screams and then one of them jumps across, a boat-hook in one hand. I aim up at him from where I'm sprawled on my back and burn a long, steaming gash from his groin to his neck. He falls back, clutching at himself and screaming, his clothes on fire, his eyes wildly staring, unable to believe what's happened to him.

And he's not alone. They are beginning to panic now. Several of them leap from the boats into the water, making swiftly for the shore.

I get up on to my knees, knowing that I'm likely to have a better centre of gravity thus than standing and, seeing Krylenko's eldest, let him have it full power.

There's the smell of roasting flesh and he topples, dead, into the water, his burning entrails sending up bubbles of steam from below the surface.

That ends the fight. With Krylenko and his eldest dead, the others flee as if from Satan himself. And to make sure that they don't come back, I fire the *staritskii* one last time, turning one of the trees on the shore just beyond them into a flaming pyre. They run, screeching, into the forest.

In the silence that follows, I look about me and see them all watching me, astonished and fearful, as if I've changed my shape. Bakatin, brave as he is, looks almost comically upset.

'Sweet Mary, Mother of our Lord,' he says, in a tiny, cracking voice. 'What *is* that?'

'It's a gun,' I say. 'A weapon. Like a bow. Only instead of shooting arrows, it shoots fire.'

'A *weapon*?' Bakatin asks, disbelief heavy in his voice. He frowns deeply, trying to take it all in, but I have turned away, looking to Katerina. She is cowering beneath the cart, staring up at me, completely shocked, unable to believe what she has witnessed. Her eyes flick toward the *staritskii* then back to meet mine.

'It's okay,' I say quietly. 'It isn't magic.'

But she's looking at me like she doesn't believe that. After all, she's seen the vivid flashes of light, the way it ate away at the men's flesh like some awful, burning acid, and how it cut a neat hole through Krylenko's head. No normal tool – no weapon *she's* ever heard of – could do such a thing. No, this is big magic and I some kind of sorcerer.

'*Katerina* . . .'

But it's no good. I've frightened her badly, and when I crouch down and make to gently touch her, she cries out and moves her whole self back, as far away as she can in that cramped space.

I am tempted to jump back and change it all. I could make Bakatin stop the boat a mile downstream and sneak up on Krylenko and his men.

Only I can't. If I did, Hecht would want to know why. And then he'd find out about Katerina.

How do I know that? How can I be sure? I don't, and I can't, and yet I'm absolutely certain of it. If I go back, he'll start asking questions, whereas as it is . . .

As it is, he thinks I'm with Ernst, travelling overland to Moscow to meet up with Prince Alexander – Nevsky – who is spending the winter months there. Hecht wants me to establish myself at Nevsky's side and win his trust, so that I might subsequently undermine him. All this before the great battle on the frozen lake. Before the single event that will change this whole section of history.

Katerina isn't in this scheme, not in any shape or form. Hecht doesn't know about Katerina, and if he did he'd want to know who she was, and whether I'd checked her out properly. And knowing Hecht, he'd sniff me out, discover my true reasons.

And if it came to a choice, I know for a certainty that Hecht would view her life as a trifle, as merely a single piece in the greater game, to be surrendered – *sacrificed* – if necessary.

And if he found out that she was *my* woman . . .

I daren't think of it. And so I can't jump back. Not unless her life's in danger. Not unless there's really no alternative.

I look down at the *staritskii* and sigh. It's not one of ours, of course. I took it from a Russian agent – from Pelshe, the little snake – shortly before he coughed his last bloodied breath. But it's a handy weapon and I've used it often since.

I turn and look to Bakatin.

'Fyodor,' I say, my voice ringing with command. 'Let's get the boat ashore and see what damage has been done. It would be good to be away from here before nightfall.'

172

For the next few hours we barely talk. We shipped a lot of water in the collision and there's considerable damage to the cargo. We sort out what can be saved and, after making repairs, set up camp among the trees. We're all tired and miserable, and I can see that all they want to do is get some sleep, but I decide to confront the issue head-on, there and then. I call Bakatin and his sons to me and, standing there, explain what's happening.

By now it's getting dark, and in the light of the fire I can see how uneasy they are. Their eyes watch me warily, their body language defensive.

Katerina won't come off the boat. She hasn't moved from beneath the cart since I tried to touch her, and though it worries me, I know I'm going to have to take my time and win her trust back slowly. But first, Bakatin and his sons.

'All right,' I say, deciding that a kind of brutal frankness will serve me best. 'You want to know what happened back there. It must have looked to you like magic, only sometimes magic isn't what it seems . . .'

I take a silver coin from my pocket and, closing my hand and quickly opening it again, make it 'disappear'. The three sons give a little gasp. Bakatin himself stares, interested suddenly.

For the next ten minutes I show them tricks with cards and coins – things I learned as a child from old Molders, back in the Garden. Then, to take the mystery away, I show them how each trick was done, and see how they relax.

'So it was all a trick?' Bakatin says.

'In a way.'

He stares at me thoughtfully, scratching at his great black beard, while his sons look to him, and when finally he shakes his head and grins, so they too grin.

'Okay. So you're not a sorcerer, *Nemets*. But will you show me the weapon? Let me study it myself?'

'Of course. But you must be very careful, and do exactly as I say.'

'It won't destroy me, then, like it did Krylenko and his eldest?'

I smile. 'Not unless you point it at yourself.'

'Like a wand,' Bakatin says, narrowing his eyes.

I go to the boat and, trying not to notice Katerina crouched beneath the cart, her dark eyes staring up at me fearfully, I unwrap the *staritskii* again and carry it across.

'Here. It's safe right now.'

Bakatin stares at it long and hard, turning it in his hands, then looks back at me. 'Safe?'

I hesitate, choosing my words. 'It's . . . *asleep*, if you like. When it is, it's perfectly harmless. But when it's awake . . .'

I take it back from him, then turn and, squeezing it gently – activating it – I aim it across the river and let off a bolt.

In the twilight the flash of searing laser-light is much brighter than it was earlier, leaving an after-image on the retina, but it's the explosion that awes them. The tree is practically up-rooted, splintering into matchwood which, in the great ball of heat from the explosion, ignites in a shower of flaming leaves and branches, which fall hissing and sizzling into the water. It's spectacular, and when I turn to look at them, I see how each of their faces is filled with awe.

'You want a go?' I ask Bakatin.

He swallows, then nods.

'Here,' I say, placing it in his hand carefully. 'Let me show you. You lift it thus, and aim it, and then you squeeze. So . . .'

I let my hand fall away as he lifts the *staritskii* and, squeezing, lets off another bolt.

It seems to leap from his hand to the tree, which jumps into the air in a great ball of flame.

This time, the three sons cry out gleefully and whoop, jumping up and down excitedly like children.

Bakatin turns, looking at me, grinning broadly.

'Fyodor,' I say abruptly, seeing where he's pointing the *staritskii*. 'Keep it pointed away from us. Look . . . let me take it from you.'

Bakatin does as he's told, jerking the weapon round to face the far shore again.

'How does it do that?'

I pluck the weapon from his trembling hand, then answer him. 'It's like I said. It gathers in the air and binds it together, then sends it out as a stream of fire.'

'Ah . . .' But I see that for all my attempts to disabuse him of the notion, it's still magic to Bakatin. Powerful magic. He tries to look at me, but his eyes are drawn back across the river to the flaming stumps and the dark patch of smouldering undergrowth that are all that remain of the two trees.

'Ah . . .'

173

That night, for the first time since the start of our journey, I sleep 'alone', in the bottom of the boat, alongside Bakatin and his sons.

We wake early and make breakfast in the half light before dawn. I'm about to go and check on Katerina when I see her, leaning out over the side of the boat, retching into the water.

I sigh and look away, upset by the sight. Have I scared her that much? Is she *that* afraid of me?

I must do something. Only for once I don't know what. As she retches again, I slip away, returning to where Bakatin and his sons are packing up. Bakatin looks to me, a knowing look in his eyes, then throws me my pack. He seems to want to say something, then decides against it.

We set off before the sun has risen, the river wreathed in mist as the day begins. I take a turn at one of the oars, and am still there, toiling away, as we approach the trading post at Velizh.

Bakatin calls on us quietly to ship our oars, and we do so, drifting slowly past the jetty and the clutch of ragged huts.

Velizh is abandoned, not a sign of anyone, and further upstream, Krylenko's compound – a small palisaded fort, built on a turn in the river – is likewise bereft of life.

Word of our coming – perhaps of the great sorcery I worked – has clearly gone ahead.

'They are afraid of you,' Bakatin says. 'You can imagine what was said.'

The trouble is I can, and hope that the ripples won't spread too far, the rumours get too much out of hand. It was a mistake, I know, to use the weapon, but it was my only option. Now I must hope that word of it dies down – that nothing gets into the history books, even as a footnote – in case the Russians get to hear of it and send an agent back to check things out.

We burn the compound to the ground, then row on until, just after noon, the wind picks up, blowing from directly behind us, allowing Bakatin to ship oars once more and raise the sail.

Katerina is asleep, turned on her side in a foetal position beneath the cart. For a time I crouch there, staring at her, moved by her beauty. Then, from habit, I take my journal from my pack and begin a new entry.

I'm partway through when I hear Katerina waking. I turn in time to see her turn about and stretch. Her eyes open and for the briefest instant she looks directly at me, a faint smile coming to her lips. Then memory kicks in, and she turns her face away, her whole body stiffening, withdrawing into her shell.

I close the journal and put it away, then look to her again.

'I'm still *me*, Katerina,' I say quietly. 'I haven't changed.'

She's listening, I know, but she makes no answer.

'They would have killed us. And it would have been much worse for you. I couldn't stand that. The thought of that bastard Krylenko touching you.'

There's the faintest movement, but still she's silent.

'I know how it must have seemed, but I'm still the same. I'm still your Otto. Your *batiushka*.'

I leave it there and return to the prow, where Bakatin is whittling a piece of wood and humming to himself.

I smile, recognising what he's making. It is a copy of the *staritskii*. I take it from him and examine it, then hand it back.

'It's good. Almost a perfect copy.'

He grins at me, then, lifting the 'wand', points it at one of the trees on the left-hand bank and makes the distinctive whooshing noise of the laser, followed by the sound of an explosion. It's so realistic, it makes me laugh, and after a moment or two, all of us are laughing. All, that is, except Katerina, but when I glance around I see that she has come out from beneath the cart and is standing there, brushing out her hair.

Noting where I am staring, Bakatin turns and looks.

'She'll come round, Otto,' he says softly, keeping his voice low so as not to carry to where she's standing. 'See if she doesn't.'

Then, because it got a laugh before, he points the wand again and makes the noises, and we all laugh.

'My God,' Bakatin says, suddenly remembering. 'The look on Krylenko's face!'

And he laughs, as if it's the funniest thing in the world. 'The look on his fucking face!'

174

I sleep, and in the early hours of night wake from a dream in which Krylenko is stalking me, following the boat, half-hidden among the trees on the shore. I know it's Krylenko because he has that darkly rounded hole in the middle of his forehead, while behind him his sons – two of them dead, two alive – follow him silently, waiting for his command.

I sit up, my heart racing, and look across at the night-shadowed shore. We are tied up in the middle of the river, a rope securing us to a massive rock, which forms an island in the stream. Bakatin's sons are asleep, snoring like bears, but Bakatin himself is awake. In the light of the three-quarters moon I can see him, sitting in the prow, staring out into the depths of the forest.

I make my way forward and sit beside him. Turning his head, he looks at me, his dark eyes thoughtful. 'Couldn't you sleep?'

'I was dreaming. Of Krylenko.'

'Ah.' He nods. 'So it is. I always dream of the men I kill. For a day or two, anyway. And then they fade. Very few of them return.'

It's true. And I've killed my share over the centuries. I feel like telling him that, only I've broken enough rules as it is, and he'd not believe me anyway.

'When will we get to the marshes?'

'Tomorrow, maybe the day after. It depends.'

'On what?'

'On who we meet, and whether this weather holds.'

I nod. Though the moon shines brightly down, much of the sky is obscured by ragged, fast-moving cloud. It's much colder than it was, and there's the feel of rain in the air.

Bakatin yawns and stretches. 'We'll need to stop at Belyj, though. Stock up on provisions. We lost most of ours when we hit the barrier. And I warn you, it may cost you, my friend.'

'If we must, we must.'

He looks at me again, giving me a long, thoughtful stare. 'You are a strange fellow, Otto Behr. A very strange fellow. That thing you do with the box.'

'The box?'

'The box with leaves. The one you make marks in.'

I almost laugh. He means my journal. 'It is a book, Fyodor. Like the priests use.'

'Like the church scrolls, you mean?'

'That's right. Only whereas they write in Latin, I write in my own private code.'

'Code?'

'Never mind. It's merely another language. Like German, you know, *Nemets*.'

'Ah . . .'

But the more I say, the stranger he finds me. For once, however, I'm not overly concerned. We're far enough from civilisation to be safe from prying Russian eyes. Future ones, that is.

Even so, I probably need to take a bit more care.

'You'll need to take care.'

I look up sharply. The coincidence of thought and words is strange, and it almost makes me wonder. Only it's just that: coincidence.

'Why's that?'

'If you think Krylenko was sly . . .' Bakatin takes a long breath, then leans forward to scratch his knee. 'They'll try and cheat you, and, if they can, they'll steal your goods, even slit your throat if they must.' Bakatin shrugs. 'But so it is. There are five scoundrels to every one good man on the river.'

'And what made *you* good, Fyodor Mikhailovich Bakatin?'

'My mother's love and fear of the Devil.' And, having said it, he roars with laughter, such that his sons are woken from their sleep and come and join us in the prow, yawning and rubbing their eyes.

'Tomorrow,' Bakatin says and nods vigorously, as if agreeing with himself. 'Oh, you'll see some rogues tomorrow, Otto, make no mistake!'

175

The marshes prove as bleak as I imagined. Mostly the river keeps its banks as it cuts its way through that watery waste, but here and there it spreads itself, for long miles merging with the marshlands to form a kind of dreary shoreless lake, great beds of reed accentuating the shallowness of the water.

What makes it worse is the greyness of the sky, the thick cloud that drifts in from the north, and in the early afternoon it begins to rain: a thin, cold drizzle that depresses my spirits even further.

Bakatin is especially quiet today, speaking only to instruct his sons as to which channel to take, his knowledge of these waters keeping us from running aground on one of the many mud banks which make this part of the river almost impassable.

When the rain eases a little, I go forward and sit beside him. I'm quiet at first, then:

'I thought this was bandit country.'

'It is.'

'Then where are they?'

Bakatin glances at me, then stands up and, in what for him seems a display of bad temper, barks at his youngest, telling him to pay attention and watch what he's doing with the steering pole. But this has nothing to do with the youngster. Bakatin, I can see now, is tense.

'What is it?' I ask quietly.

He looks to me, then comes and sits again, leaning closer, as if to prevent the others from hearing. 'Something's up.'

'What do you mean?'

'We should have seen one of them by now. One of their boats. It's how they operate. They come and take their cut for passing through their lands. That is, if you're a regular on these waters. As for strangers . . .' He lifts his hand and draws an imaginary knife across his throat.

'So what do you think is happening?'

'I don't know.'

I study Bakatin for a time, until his discomfort at my gaze makes me look away. But I know now. It's the not knowing that disturbs him – Bakatin doesn't mind danger – it's uncertainty that he's afraid of.

'D'you think they're afraid of us, Fyodor?'

'Afraid?' He spits theatrically over the side. 'Blagovesh is afraid of no man, nor any devil, come to that!'

'Blagovesh?'

'The bandit king. Or so he calls himself. He's the leader of the marsh bandits. They say he has over five hundred men in his service. And no one – *no one* – passes through his land without paying him tribute.'

'What's he like, this Blagovesh? Is he a big man?'

'Big? No. But *big* . . . you could say so. Fearless.'

'Like you, then, Fyodor Mikhailovich.'

There's the suggestion of a smile on Bakatin's lips, but then he shakes his head and looks down. 'No one is like Blagovesh. No one.'

'Ah . . .'

We fall silent and remain that way for a long while, as the boat drifts slowly through that wasted, watery land. Then, just when it seems we might pass through this colourless, windswept landscape without event, Bakatin's eldest sends up a cry.

'Boats! Up ahead! Lots of boats!'

Bakatin heaves himself to his feet alongside me and we both stare across the faintly misted surface of the water, looking east towards where, in a patch of ominous darkness, a dozen or more boats seem to be gathered.

I look to Bakatin. 'What are we going to do? Turn around? Try another way?'

'There is no other way. There's only one channel through this part of the marshes. There's a village just south of here – Zharkovskij – but it's no use looking to that direction. No, Otto. It looks like Blagovesh has sent us a welcoming committee, and we've little option but to be welcomed.'

I hesitate a moment, then turn, meaning to get the gun from the cart, but Bakatin grabs my arm.

'No, Otto. You wouldn't stand a chance. Oh, you might kill a good few of them, but Blagovesh has archers. Cossacks, so it's said, from the far south. They would be sure to target you.'

'So we do nothing.'

Bakatin nods. 'It seems the best course, wouldn't you say?'

I wouldn't, and I'm beginning to wonder at his confidence, his self-assurance, for ever since we've spied the bandit fleet, he seems to have perked up, all of his previous tenseness vanished. I'm almost waiting for him to laugh or hum some sprightly little tune.

'What if they decide to kill us anyway?'

But Bakatin says nothing, just stares straight ahead as the boats come closer. And as they do so, I see that our first estimate didn't do Blagovesh's fleet justice, and that there must be at least thirty, maybe even forty craft in all, hugging the banks on either side of the river up ahead.

'You think he wants to impress us, Fyodor?'

Bakatin smiles. 'I'd say he *has* impressed us, no?'

Each boat is crammed with bandits, and as we come closer, we're surprised by the silence, the stillness of that large host. As we slowly drift between the first of the boats, there's not a single jeering call, not a whistle or a wolf's-bay to taunt us, just a cold, hostile silence and the glare of several hundred watching eyes.

I turn, looking to my right, seeing how this ragged band – some missing eyes, other hands or whole arms – simply stare at us with a kind of mocking contempt. I've never seen an uglier, more ragged group of men, yet there's a curious dignity in them at this moment.

'*Look!*' Bakatin says in a low whisper, nudging me.

There, to the left, where the river makes a slight turn north-wards, is a big galley, much larger than all the other boats, and on its prow, on a wooden platform, stands Blagovesh himself, no more and no less ragged than his men, a red cloth tied about his forehead. For a moment he stares at us coldly as we approach.

Then, with a show of mighty arrogance, he spits into the water and turns his back on us, then stands there, his arms folded across his chest, ignoring us.

It is a signal, and a moment later, with a great shuffling noise, all of his men do likewise, turning their backs and standing there in that self-same pose as we drift slowly by.

'Urd protect us,' I mutter beneath my breath. And I realise that all this while my hand has been hovering above my chest, ready, at the least sign of them attacking, to jump.

Bakatin wets his lips, then lets out a long, shuddering breath. 'Some man, eh, Otto? Some man.'

And for once I agree, and, as we slowly draw away, I turn and look back, watching the bandit king until he's out of sight. Watching, yes, and wondering what such a man might have been in another time and under different circumstances.

176

Belyj proves to be a sprawl of hovels, set inside a partial wooden palisade. Bare-arsed Russian children are everywhere, their unwashed faces staring curious-sullen back at us as we moor the boat.

Worse, there are slaves here, the first we've seen on our journey. We glimpse them in the pens beside the river: two young women, four young men and two children, a boy and a girl. Chud, by the look of them, chained at the ankle to prevent them from escaping.

The locals know who we are. I can feel it. It's not far upriver from where the fight happened, and rumour has swept before us. The adults stand in the shadowed doorways and look on, their eyes suspicious; hostile, but strangely not afraid.

Of all the places I have seen, this is the worst, and it makes me wonder how anyone could live in such a godforsaken place.

I leave Bakatin to make our introductions while I look about the place, never straying too far from the boat, but keeping a wary eye, just in case. Bakatin's sons are aboard, but that's no guarantee that my goods – or my wife – will be safe here.

This place *feels* wrong. And it isn't just the slaves. No. Slaves are a fact of life in this age – just another commodity, second only to furs in the volume of trade between the Rus' and their Muslim neighbours to the south and east. Slave girls for the high officials' beds, young men – Christian as well as pagan – for the galleys.

Walking between two of the unkempt, stinking huts I come upon something I'd not expected. A makeshift smithy. Though the smith himself is absent, there are signs that he has been working here recently. His kiln is lit and hot, the great leather bellows on the floor nearby, while a piece of unfinished work lies on top of the great metal block of an anvil.

I'm about to turn away and go and find Bakatin again when the smith returns.

He's not a big man but he's strong and wiry. His beard is neatly trimmed, his clothes – his leather apron – in reasonably good condition. Seeing me, he narrows his eyes and slows his pace, then ducks inside his workshop.

I'm wondering what he's doing here, out in the wilds. He must be the only blacksmith for a hundred miles. You would expect him to be in Surazh or one of the bigger towns, not here in this pisshole.

'Yes?' he asks me, looking up at me sideways.

'Will you make me something?'

He looks down at the unfinished object on the anvil, then back at me. 'That depends.'

'Depends?'

'On what it is, and what you're willing to pay. I'm not cheap.'

'But you're good?'

He laughs at that, as if it doesn't need an answer. But looking past him at the objects hung up on hooks behind him on the back wall, I see that he *is* good. For this age.

'I want you to make me a brooch. A leaf-shaped brooch, from copper.'

Not looking at me, he takes a hammer from the basket by his side, then reaches out to grasp a pair of long-handled pliers.

'I haven't any copper.'

'That's all right. I have some.'

At that he looks up, interested. Then, conscious that he's given himself away, he smiles. Picking up the rough-cast piece of metal with the pliers, he walks over to the kiln and holds it in the heat.

'Maybe we could come to some kind of deal,' he says, as if it's neither here nor there to him.

'Maybe.'

I watch him, see how skilfully he handles the metal. Skills like that can't be duplicated easily, and my suspicion melts away. He's just a smith. Anyway, if he *was* an agent – a Russian agent – I'd be dead by now.

We're both silent for a time as he beats out the piece, turning it and shaping it, sparks flying from his hammer, and then he looks up at me again. 'When would you want it by?'

'This evening?'

He considers that, then nods. 'I can do that. You tell me what kind of leaf you want, and you pay me – up front and in copper, eh?'

'Half up front, half when it's done.'

He considers again. 'It depends.'

'On how much copper?'

He nods, and as he does, I note how dark his eyes are. Dark like Katerina's eyes, only whereas hers reveal her soul, his eyes hide his. It's like there's nothing there behind them. It ought, perhaps, to worry me, only it doesn't.

'I'll bring the copper. But first I must eat and speak to your head man.'

He laughs at that. 'Good luck. On both counts.'

177

I find Bakatin by the boat, his huge figure looming over some wizened little man, the two of them head to head, arguing furiously, bargaining, it seems. Seeing me, Bakatin backs away a little and nods to me, acknowledging my return, but I can see that he's angry with the man for some reason.

The wizened little creature turns out to be the head man, Fedorchuk, and everything about him is as unpleasant as can be, from his heavily pocked and distinctly elf-like face with its exaggeratedly insincere smile, to his way of pawing your shoulder as he talks to you. It's like being in the company of some particularly unappetising insect, an insect that's taken human form. From time to time the smile slips slightly and the man's naked avarice shines through.

We're food for the spider here, it seems. Wrapped flies to be drained of whatever goodness is in us.

But it doesn't matter. Not this once. Fedorchuk can be as odious as he wants, demand what he wishes, it doesn't matter. There's a supply dump just outside Rzhev, and I can replenish my stores from that, if necessary. All we need is the means of getting there. Enough to get us by. And the brooch, of course. For Katerina.

Time and again Bakatin tries to butt in and prevent me from agreeing with the little shit, but I don't let him. It's daylight robbery, and all three of us know it, but I act as though I'm delighted with the bargain I've made. And in a way I am, because we *are* getting what we need. What with the river bandits and their curious gesture of defiance and respect, I had begun to think that maybe the villagers would have fled before our approach.

Back on the boat, Bakatin berates me for being such a fool. 'You should have let me deal with that little arsehole.'

'Maybe, but don't you think it curious?'

Bakatin's voice rises. '*Curious*? Being robbed?'

'No. That they're not afraid. None of them. Blagovesh I can understand, but not these villagers. You'd think they'd be terrified. After all, we used powerful magic back there on the river.'

That stops Bakatin in his tracks. For a while he's silent, trying to work it out. Then he shrugs. 'Maybe they haven't heard.'

I laugh dismissively. 'No, Fyodor. It isn't possible. Besides, two of them are right here, in the village.'

His surprise is almost comic. '*Here*? In Belyj?'

'Yes. I'm sure of it.'

And I am. One of them was in Krylenko's boat when I shot the bastard. The other was in the right-hand boat, one of the oarsmen. But here they are, in Belyj, as calm and unaffected as if they'd witnessed nothing back there on the river.

Which is strange. Taking one of the packages of copper from the cart, I return to the smithy.

The smith looks up as I appear in his doorway. The 'unfinished' item is now an elaborate-looking ladle – a real luxury item, by the look of it – and I wonder who it's for. Blagovesh, perhaps?

I stand over him, waiting for him to finish before I speak. 'Do you know who I am?'

The smith sets his tools down and wipes his hands on a piece of sacking. 'I know you, yes. You're the sorcerer.'

'I'm . . .' I shake my head, more confused than ever. Yet when I look at him again, I see the ironic smile.

'You don't believe that, then?'

'That you're a sorcerer?' He looks me up and down, then shakes his head. 'Not impressive enough. You'd be more arrogant, more . . .'

'*Strange*?'

He doesn't answer that. Instead he asks a few questions of his own. 'What did you use? Fire arrows? A crossbow?'

It's my turn to be surprised. The man's a rationalist! Smith that he is – powerful mythical figure that he is in his own right – he clearly does not believe in myths and legends and the hobgoblins of rumour. I laugh.

'What's your name?'

'My name?' He turns aside. 'My name's *my* business and mine alone. Now . . . have you the copper?'

'Yes, and you can have it all. Only . . . answer me a question.'

He turns back. The darkness in his eyes is still and empty, like a night without stars.

'Okay. Ask me.'

'The two who were with Krylenko when he attacked us. What did they say?'

The smith smiles drily. 'That you used great magic to uproot trees. And that you sucked the brains out of Krylenko's head through a tiny hole, just like a child would suck the inside from an egg.' He takes a long, sighing breath, as if such talk tires him. 'I told them at the inn that it was nonsense. Oh, I'm sure *some-thing* must have happened, but there were such rumours. Such outlandish rumours! And look at you! Can you suck my brain out of a tiny hole, *Nemets*? Can you uproot this smithy with your magic wand and send it tumbling through the air in a great ball of flame?'

'No.'

'Good. Then I was right.'

And he turns away, all matter-of-fact, a one-off in this age of mumbo-jumbo and superstitious clap-trap.

If he *is* from these times.

Only I've little doubt that he is, for why would the Russians place a man here in this shit-heap of a place? Simply to wait for me and make me a leaf-shaped brooch? That makes no sense. Besides, the Russians don't have skills like this man displays; they haven't the time to waste on developing them.

No. The smith is just an oddball. As out of place in time as he is in space. A rationalist – a seeker of simple explanations – in an age that sees a dark, distorting mystery behind events.

I smile, then hold out the cloth-wrapped package that contains the copper.

He turns, stares at me a moment, then comes across and takes it from me and unwraps it. Placing it down carefully, he removes one of the tiny ingots and weighs it in his hand. He sniffs at it and licks it, and then he nods.

'This is good.' And for the first time he looks at me, and smiles. 'So, what kind of leaf do you want?'

178

Our business in Belyj is done. The food is loaded on the boat, bought at an exorbitant price – famine rates, so Bakatin says – and we have removed ourselves to the opposite bank, mooring just upriver from the village for the evening. As the sunlight fades and the moon begins its slow climb up the sky, I send Bakatin and his sons ashore and, hoping that my timing's right, begin to try to win her back.

The brooch is in my shirt pocket. It's a real beauty, a genuine work of art, the metalwork so light, so delicate, it looks as if a real leaf has been transmuted into metal.

Katerina is sitting just beyond the cart, on the long bench seat in the stern, so still and silent that in the half-light she seems to be part of the boat. Moving carefully, the boat swaying gently beneath me, I make my way back, then sit across from her.

'Katerina . . .'

She is looking away, as if into the depths of memory, but at my words she turns and looks at me.

'What?'

It is the first word she has spoken to me since the fight.

'I wanted to say sorry. And I want you to forgive me for frightening you. For making you afraid of me.'

She's silent a moment, then, 'You scared me. I thought I knew you, only . . .' I wait, and in a while she continues. 'Only I didn't. I don't really know you at all, do I, Otto?'

There's something in the way she says it; something in the way she looks at me in that moment, that makes me realise she wants the truth. The whole truth, no matter how strange or disturbing it might be. But can I tell her that?

I look down, almost afraid to meet her eyes and lie to her. 'Katerina, I—'

'You're a stranger, Otto. You walked out of the night and stole my heart. And now . . . now I can't trust you any more.'

The thought of it shocks me. But why should I be so surprised? That glimpse she had of the weapon's power was a glimpse of a different me, of a more powerful, more *secretive* person than the one she thought she knew.

She speaks again, her eyes searching mine. 'I want no barriers between us, Otto . . .'

'I can't promise you that.'

'Why?'

'Because . . .'

'Have you another wife . . . back in Germany? Is *that* it?'

'Katerina . . . no . . .'

But she has touched upon a raw nerve. Not *wife*, but *wives*. A hundred wives and more.

Mein Volk. Mein Schwestern.

'It's because you, well, you just wouldn't believe it.'

'Try me.'

I laugh, then look away, pained. 'You'll think me mad. And then I'll lose you. Lose you for good.'

She reaches across the space between us and gently turns my face towards her. 'No, Otto. Not if it's the truth. However strange it is, however . . . *odd*. I want us to be as we were – as I thought we were. No secrets. No hidden rooms in our heads.'

I stare at her, surprised by her maturity. By how quick and intelligent she is. By her inner strength. Or is it, rather, the idealism of youth? The untarnished hope that lies within a young heart? Whatever it is, it moves me – moves me more than anything she's ever said or done – because it's what I too want, deep down. A life without barriers. A life shared – in every single aspect – with the one person in all of time and space who completes you.

Urd protect me, but that's it. *Completion*, that's what I crave, more than anything in the whole vast universe: utter, unconditional completion.

I stare at her, seeing the beauty within her and without. 'Okay. But you have to take what I say on my word. I can't prove it. Not now, anyway. Later, possibly, but right now you have to believe me. You have to take me on trust.'

Her eyes look back at me clearly. 'If it's the truth, I'll know.'

I nod, suddenly, almost absurdly convinced of it. Right now I could tell her anything – anything at all – providing it were true, and she would know.

'I'm not from here,' I say. 'Oh, I'm German, German through and through, only . . . I'm not from this time.'

'Not . . .?' She struggles to take that in, then gives her head a little shake as if to clear it. 'What do you mean?'

'I mean that I come from the future. From the days to come. I can go there and come back.'

She laughs, and then her face clouds over once again. 'I don't understand. You can't just—'

'Oh, but I can. And I have. Hundreds of times. I've travelled back and forth across the centuries.'

'Then tell me somewhere you've been. Something that you've seen.'

I think a moment, cursing the fact that this is such a benighted age. If Katerina knows any history at all, it is of Novgorod, or at best, of Kievan Rus'. But then I think of something.

'I have seen Christ.'

'*Christ*?' She is visibly shocked. 'You have *seen* our Lord?'

I nod. 'I was with him in the garden of Gethsemane, with Jesus and his disciples, in that last, awful moment before the Romans came and took him. I saw Judas come slowly up the path in the twilight and greet him with a kiss. His hand cupped Jesus's cheek so . . . I . . .'

I falter, because she is looking at me now as if I am the world's greatest liar. But it is true. I have seen so many things. I was there, for instance, when Barbarossa, in June 1190, in the very moment of his triumph over the infidels, fell from his shying horse into the River Salef in Armenia and drowned, the weight of his armour carrying him down into that fast-flowing current. And I was there, on-board the *Standard* in 1703, when Peter, later called 'the Great', looked about him at the wild, flat empty marshlands of the Neva delta and decided he would build a city there.

I take her hands, willing her to believe me.

'Oh, Katerina, I have seen so many things. Things both wonderful and terrifying. I have seen great kings deposed and imbeciles set up in their place. I have seen vast cities rise from the smouldering ruins of the old, and I have seen the sky turned black with bombers.'

'Boh-mahs?'

'Ships, only with wings, sailing in the sky, throwing down great pots of fire – bombs – on to the people below.'

She looks away, troubled. 'All this is true, Otto? You see things that are yet to happen? You have . . . *visions?*'

'Yes. Only these aren't visions. I've actually been to those places and witnessed those things with my own eyes.'

'But . . . why exactly are you *here*, Otto Behr? What are you doing here?'

Being with you. Only I know that won't be enough. I can see that she'll need to know it all. And so I begin, explaining it, piece by piece, trying to make sense of it all to her. Four-Oh and Gehlen and the great dark castle of Asgard. And the War, and Time and . . .

Dawn comes and we are still sitting there, only I'm quiet now, letting her digest what I have told her.

'Well?' Bakatin asks me, as I come ashore. 'Is it all mended?'

I shrug. 'I'm not sure. But at least we've talked. At least . . .'

'At least?'

At least she knows now. Only I could change it in a moment, jump back and last night would not have happened. Only now that it has, I want it to remain. I realise now just how heavy a burden it has been, keeping it from her. And though I'm still afraid of how she'll take it, I feel a real relief.

I look to Bakatin. 'At least it's done.'

For no particular reason, I feel in my pocket and my fingers close over the delicate shape of the brooch. I take it out and stare at it a moment, surprised that I'd forgotten, then turn, meaning to go back and give it to her, there and then. But I stop. Now is not the moment. Just now it's best to leave her, to let her brood on what I've said.

It's a fine, clear morning, the kind that lifts your spirits, only I'm not sure what to think. Katerina is retching again. And who can blame her? What I've told her is enough to make any sane person anxious. All the same, I go back to her and, waiting for her to finish, ask her if she's all right.

She splashes water over her face, then turns and looks at me, and smiles. 'I'm fine. *Really*. It's okay. Besides . . . it's not me . . . it's the baby.'

179

'Otto?'

'Yes, my love?'

'Can we start again?'

'Again?'

We are midstream, half a day north of Belyj, the sun shining down, the forest a solid barrier of green to either side. Light glints off the surface of the river as Bakatin and his sons pull hard on the oars, drawing us swiftly through the water.

'You were going to teach me German. Remember?'

I reach out and trace the line of her jaw. 'I remember.'

'Only it would be useful.'

'Useful?'

'If we need to speak of . . . *things*.'

'Ah . . .'

I understand. Though they seem as if they aren't listening, Bakatin and his sons hear every word we say. In a few days' time, we'll be saying farewell to Bakatin and his sons, and they'll be heading back downriver to Surazh.

'Okay,' I say. 'Then let's begin right now.'

She sits up a little straighter, her face all attentive, like a pupil at her desk, which makes me laugh. But as I hand her the brooch, I see her face change, an expression of pure wonder and delight entering her eyes.

'*Das Blatt*,' I say. '*Das Esche Blatt*.'

180

That next evening we arrive at Antipino. It's another Belyj, only worse, and I'd prefer not to stop, only Bakatin has business there.

We go ashore, Katerina holding my hand, curious to see the village, even though it's clearly a stinking hole of a place. Chicken bones and other discarded things litter the ground between the ill-built, shabby huts, and – worse than anything in Belyj – there are dogs, half-feral beasts with dark oily coats that sniff at us and growl and show their sharp yellow teeth threateningly.

There are more slaves here, too. Six scrawny-looking young men in ragged clothes sitting with their backs against the wall of a hut, chained to each other at the ankle, one of their 'owners' – a Swede without any doubt by the axe and sword he carries – standing close by, keeping an eye. They look underfed, and from the bruises on their arms and legs it would seem that their masters have been none too kind.

Feeling despondent, we cut the tour short and search out Bakatin. He's drinking beer and laughing with a merchant friend in the riverside 'inn', a crowd of locals pressed into that hot and fetid room. The smell is awful and I wonder how they can stand it. I say hello and am about to make my way back to the boat when I see them standing in the shadows of the far corner.

The two men we saw in Belyj. The ones who were with Krylenko.

Noticing my eyes on them, one of them speaks quickly to the other's ear, and immediately they begin to push through. But they have to get past me, and I move slightly so that they can't do that without either pushing me aside, or asking me to move.

Katerina glances at me, then looks again, noting how I'm watching the two men.

'Excuse me, cousin,' the first one says, trying not to make eye contact.

I put my hand flat on his chest, stopping him. Immediately, every eye in the room is on me.

'How is Krylenko?'

The man swallows nervously and glances at me. He's trembling now. His answer's almost a whisper. 'Krylenko's dead.'

'And you?'

'Sorry?'

'You? Are *you* dead?'

He's shaking now, afraid I'll strike him down. 'I . . . I . . . No . . . No, I'm alive.'

'Good. Then stay that way, eh?' And I remove my hand from his chest and stand aside, and the two of them stumble past me and then run out of the door, as if all the devils in hell were chasing them. You might think there'd be laughter at the sight, but the room is deathly silent. Even Bakatin is quiet, watching me from where he sits, tankard in hand, waiting to see what I'll do next. But I do nothing, merely look to him and smile.

'I'm sorry, Fyodor. Don't mind me, I'm just saying hello to old friends.'

Bakatin's face is serious a moment longer, and then he smiles, the smile broadening until he gives a great roar of laughter and the tension in the room breaks and suddenly everyone is laughing – with relief, it seems. But I know something now. They all know who I am – or who they believe I am. A sorcerer. A powerful

79

magician. And behind every smile, every laughing face, I see an element of naked fear.

I have made a mistake. I know it now. There is not a single village or settlement on this river that hasn't heard of me and what I did back there. Only it's to be hoped it won't follow me across land to Rzhev. Because if it does . . .

I turn and leave, taking Katerina with me. She's silent, too, thoughtful, and back at the boat she asks me quietly what I mean to do about the men.

'Nothing,' I say. 'I can't blame them for what Krylenko did.'

It's true. But it's not the only reason why I won't go after them. I could track them and find them, and even kill them if I wanted, only it would mean leaving Katerina here while I did. Besides, I don't think they're a danger. They're much more afraid of me than I am of them. Even so, I'm slightly worried. Why were they here? On Blagovesh's orders? Or maybe they're cousins of Krylenko and this is a kind of vendetta? Only, if so, why not sneak up on us and kill us while we sleep? Why slink about from village to village, following us?

Because they think you are a sorcerer, Otto. They probably think you never sleep.

It's dark when Bakatin returns, not drunk exactly, but unsteady. His business has gone well, and he wants to talk, and maybe to drink some more, only I've another idea.

'I want to go, Fyodor. I want to leave here now.'

'To go? But it's late, Otto. And, my friend, my purchase won't be ready till the morning . . .'

'Forget that. Tell him you'll come back for his goods later. I'll pay you both for the inconvenience. But let's get out of here, now.'

'But Otto—'

'Fyodor. Do as I say. We're in danger here. Trust me. I know what I'm talking about. If we stay here, they'll attack us.'

Bakatin looks at me as if I'm mad, but he shrugs and, hauling himself up off the bench seat, gives orders to his sons.

The moon is high and it's late when finally we moor on an island three hours upstream from Antipino. It's far enough not to be followed by foot, but there's always the possibility that they'll follow us by boat, and so while Bakatin and his sons get some sleep in the bottom of the boat, I sit at the stern, keeping watch.

I've told Katerina to rest, but she wants to sit with me. She's said nothing thus far, but now that Bakatin and his sons are asleep and snoring, she asks me why we didn't stay in the village.

'Just a feeling,' I say. 'An instinct I had. Those two . . . they've been trailing us for a reason.'

'You don't think they simply had business in Antipino?'

'Yes, and their business was us.'

'But surely . . .?'

I turn and look at her. 'I made a mistake back there, Katerina. I revealed what I was. Not just to you, but to everyone. And even if they mistake what it is, they know I'm something different, something special. And that's dangerous. Very dangerous indeed.'

'Then maybe you should have dealt with it back there. Maybe you should have followed them and—'

'Killed them?' I shake my head and look away. 'No. I can't kill people just because I suspect them.'

'But they'd have killed us.'

'Maybe. And maybe not.'

She's silent for a time, then, putting her arm about my back, she leans close and whispers to my ear. 'Otto?'

'Yes, my love?'

'Forget watching for a while. Take me ashore and make love to me.'

81

It's two days' journey to Tatarinka, our last stop on the river, and from the start the weather is awful. We wake to an overcast sky, a solid layer of thick, grey cloud blocking off the sun, and then it begins to rain.

For the rest of the morning it doesn't stop, and Katerina and I sit huddled together beneath the makeshift awning as Bakatin and his sons pull against the current.

The heavy rain has swollen the river, which here cuts through a rougher, less even terrain. We have left the flatlands now and the land to either side rises steeply, fold upon fold towards the distant, rain-obscured hills

After a while Katerina complains of the cold, and I go to the cart and carefully unpack one of the furs I've brought for colder weather, securing the load again before returning to her and wrapping it about her shoulders.

There is the slightest plumpness to her now – barely anything, yet last night I took care to be gentler than usual with her and she, noticing it, laughed softly and asked me if I didn't think her made of sterner stuff than that. And maybe she is, yet the thought of her carrying our child fills me with such tenderness for her, such an aching softness, while at the same time . . .

At the same time, I would kill anyone who harmed her.

As we sit there, listening to the rain fall and the birds call forlornly in the trees, to the slush of the oars and the rush of the water past our hull, I am conscious of just how vulnerable she makes me feel. Which, perhaps, should worry me. I am, after all, a time agent, my life a complex, dangerous one. Yet without this . . .

She sleeps a while, and when she wakes the rain is still falling, and very little in the landscape seems to have changed. Sometimes the sheer size of this land encroaches on the mind. Great armies have floundered in its vastness. It has been a month and more since we set out from Novgorod and still we seem a long, long way from our goal.

But I am happy today, despite the rain, despite the thought of all the bad weather to come – for the rainy season is now upon us, and after the rains comes the snow. Happy because, for the first time in some while, I feel at peace. It will be hard, juggling my life to fit everything in, but when was life easy for anyone? Hecht's the only problem, but even there I can work my way around him, find ways and means to come back here as often as I can. To be with her. And with our children.

It's that last thought that melts me. That makes me smile despite all obstacles to my happiness. And there's even part of me that wants to jump ahead and see it, now – right now – as if to guarantee its future reality. But I can't do that. In fact, I won't let myself do that. This has to be as it is – *lived through*, day by day. To anticipate would kill it – would make it . . .

I'll be candid here. The truth is, I want this because it's something I can't have back in Four-Oh: a woman who is mine and mine alone; a family; and all of the uncertainties, the *risks*, that go with that.

Oh, there are risks enough in my life, but not of this kind. Nor, for all my dedication to the *volk*, to the cause for which we fight, have I ever felt so attached, so . . . *connected* to anyone or anything. And maybe that's a flaw in how things are set up in Four-Oh. Maybe, by breaking down those bonds of family – of *Mutter*, *Vater* and *der Kinder* – we have broken some essential link, and substituted one vulnerability for another. Maybe we need the strength of family – true family – to get us through the days, and kinship – mere kinship as we have it in Four-Oh – is not enough.

Maybe. I don't know. But my head is filled with such thoughts, and when I smooth my hand over the slight roundness of her stomach, well, it is like I have been transformed, my life made real, no longer such a game as it was.

And that's what worries me most. For I can see now that it *is* a game – however much we risk in playing it. *It is a game.* And Hecht . . . Hecht is not our father, Hecht is merely our master. Through us he plays the game. And surely that's a flaw, too? For humans were not meant to be pawns in a game.

Don't get me wrong. I don't mean to throw it all up. I know where my duty lies. Only I see things a little more clearly today. I see the comparative importance of things and I am left wondering if there isn't a better way than the way we do it in Four-Oh, and that maybe – if there were changes – it might not work far better than it does.

There are dark clouds just ahead – storm clouds blowing in from the north – and Bakatin, seeing them, decides to take a break and we moor over on the north bank, pulling the boat up on to the shore as far as we can. And just in time, for though it has been raining all day, the rain descends upon us in a torrent, and we huddle beneath the trees, our cloaks over our heads, listening to the crashing of the thunder, the sudden darkness of the afternoon lit up now and then by terrifying flashes of lightning.

Katerina crouches at my side. She loves storms and is not afraid of them, but Bakatin's youngest seems anxious and after a while I call him over and let him shiver alongside me, my arm about his shoulders, as if a sorcerer's protection might make him safe.

The rain falls endlessly, swelling the river yet further, and slowly soaking us, until it seems better to throw off our covers and just let it fall. We'll get no wetter.

As the thunder passes into the distance, and with it the electric storm, so Bakatin walks over to the boat and, taking out a cooking pot, begins to bale. His sons join him, lending a hand, and shortly afterwards, despite the continued downpour, we push off on to the water again.

For a time the rain intensifies, and we are forced to bale yet again. But then it slackens and, after a few minutes, ceases altogether. There's a break in the clouds and, for a time, a glimpse of blue sky and sunlight.

Bakatin laughs, then breaks into song. An old river song, about the river-man's daughter. A rather crude song, as it turns out, which his sons sing along with lustily, even as they increase their pace. For a time you would think they were racing someone, but then, as Bakatin ends the song, they stop, letting the boat drift on in the sudden silence, their oars lifted, water dripping from them as the boat slows against the current.

Bakatin turns and grins at Katerina. 'You like our little song, eh?'

If I was expecting her to blush, I'd be disappointed. She laughs and, improvising, makes up a verse of her own, much to Bakatin's delight. He roars, and slaps his hand against his thigh, then sings her verse again, his sons joining in at the last.

At another time I might feel uncomfortable, but we have come to know each other extremely well, Bakatin and I, and if Katerina isn't offended, why should I be?

I look to her and grin, then lean across and kiss her.

The hardest part of our journey lies ahead: across land to Rzhev, and thence down the Volga to Gzhatsk. At least, that's the plan. For in Russia, everything is dependent on the weather. The rains swell the rivers and make them difficult to cross, even to navigate upon. Yet by river and across river we must travel. Traversing the great stretch of forest that lies between Rzhev and Moscow is not an option in this weather – we would make three or four miles a day at best. But the snows will change that. Come the snows we shall unpack the sled and then hopefully the miles will fall away behind us.

Tatarinka proves a surprise. It's an orderly, pleasant little town, with a well-kept palisade and a sense of bustling life about it, rain or shine. It's also the end of our journey with Bakatin and his sons, and though he is not setting off back down the river for another day or two, I feel saddened that we must make this parting. But first he helps us find a room and a place to store our cart until we can hire a guide to take us north-east to Rzhev.

The inn is a surprise too, not merely for its size, but for the fact that it's one of the few two-storey structures I've seen in this age. There are Novgorod's churches, of course, and the hall that the *veche* use, but almost everything out here in the wilds is single storey – log cabins, essentially, with either a single room, or two at most. The inn – while built of logs – has eight rooms and a barn attached. It's run by a jovial, red-faced fellow named Rapushka, who leads Katerina and I through a crowded room where drinks are being served and out the back, where we find a sturdy ladder going up to the second storey.

'There,' he says, 'on the left.'

I climb up first, and step inside, lighting my flint and looking about me at the room.

The floor is packed with earth, on which are laid rush mats. As the light falls on them, insects scuttle away into corners, or burrow down again between the logs, but it looks clean enough and dry, and there's a large pallet bed in the corner, stuffed with straw.

I hold the flint up as Katerina steps into the room.

'At least the roof doesn't leak.'

She looks to the bed, then giggles. 'We'll have to be quiet,' she says, her voice almost a whisper. 'Half the village is down there, listening.'

But the look of her in that wavering light is too much for me. 'Let them listen,' I say. 'Let the whole world listen . . .'

And, pushing her down on to the bed, I extinguish the flint and begin to make love to her, there in the insect darkness, with half of Tatarinka listening below.

182

'Otto . . . there's someone I'd like you to meet.'

I turn and look up from where I'm sitting at the table, my drink before me. Bakatin, it seems, has brought a friend to introduce to me. I nod and bid them sit across from me.

'This is Lishka. He's a haulier.'

Lishka nods his agreement, then grins at me, showing a set of blackened teeth.

He's a good ten years or more older than Bakatin – with a wispy grey beard – but of a similar build. Only whereas Bakatin seems as if he's built of granite, Lishka looks as though he's made entirely of lard. He looks in ill health and, to be frank, I find myself wondering if he'll even make it to Rzhev.

'Fyodor?'

'Oh, Lishka is a good man. A very good man. You can trust Lishka. And he knows all the best routes. He's travelled everywhere. Down to Smolensk and across even to Orel and Tula.'

Again Lishka nods and shows his blackened teeth. I turn and hold my hand up, signalling to Rapushka to bring us more beers. Katerina, I note, is looking dubiously at Lishka, as if she's thinking precisely what I'm thinking.

'Fyodor, I—'

'Lishka is my cousin. And he's cheap. There's not a man to be had so good at twice the price Lishka charges. And he's reliable.

He won't run off in the night and leave you prey to bandits. Lishka's a fighter. A stayer.'

I almost laugh. Lishka looks like he'd run a mile at the first sign of trouble. But I don't say that. Instead, I decide to question Lishka myself.

'Tell me, Lishka . . . do you know what they say of me?'

Lishka grins and looks to Bakatin. But Bakatin nudges him. 'Answer him, Lishka. Show the man you have a tongue.'

I'm beginning to think that maybe Lishka is a bit of a simpleton, but when he finally speaks, there's no sign that he's a simple man.

'They say you are a sorcerer, Meister, but my cousin Fyodor says that's nonsense and lies. He says you are merely a trader and a *Nemets* . . . oh, and a good fighter, too.'

'He says that, does he?'

'Yes, and if Fyodor recommends you, then Lishka will be honoured to guide you to Rzhev. Yes, and keep you from the wolves.'

'There will be wolves, will there?'

'Undoubtedly, this time of year. But Lishka knows how to deal with wolves. Lishka has great experience with wolves.'

I look to Bakatin and raise an eyebrow, but he merely shrugs. 'Lishka is a good man, Otto. I wouldn't put you in the hands of any other, believe me.'

That makes me think. Lishka may look soft, but if he's done what Bakatin claims, he can't be *that* soft. Wolf packs are one of the hazards of trade in this age, and if Lishka has survived to the age he's reached, then he must have been good at dealing with them.

Our drinks arrive and for a while we busy ourselves making toasts and emptying tankards. Then, wiping my mouth, I look to Bakatin again. 'I'll think about it overnight.'

'Good!' Bakatin says, and grins, as if I've said yes. 'You'll not regret it, Otto.'

'I said—'

'Oh, I know what you said, Otto. But once you've had the chance to think about it, you'll know that Bakatin was right. That he wouldn't place you in the care of any but the best man for the job, cousin or no cousin. Why, I would take you there myself, if I only knew the way, and if I didn't have four wives waiting for me downriver.'

'*Four* wives, Fyodor? I thought it was three.'

Bakatin looks at me, surprised. 'Oh, didn't I say? That's what my business was in Antipino. I've bought myself a new wife, a young one, fresh from the south. She'll be waiting for me when I get back.'

I laugh, astonished, then look to Katerina, who merely raises her eyes, as if she's heard it all before.

Bakatin's right. His recommendation carries weight with me. Lishka may look soft, he may look a simpleton, but I can't believe Bakatin would palm me off with someone who couldn't do the job. So the next morning I decide to hire him.

Only when I ask Lishka when we're setting out, he shakes his head.

'Not yet,' he says. 'Not until the rains die down. The paths will be unpassable. The cart would just sink into the mud! And where would we be then? Look at the river, how high it is. The land between here and Rzhev will be nothing but a marsh!'

'So how long will we have to wait?'

Lishka shrugs. 'Two weeks? Maybe three?'

It's a delay I hadn't counted for, and for a moment I consider hiring myself another guide, one who'll take us now, only Lishka is probably right. If, as Bakatin says, he knows these lands, I should trust in his experience and believe him when he says that the terrain is impassable in this weather. In the day and a half we've been in Tatarinka, it has barely stopped raining for an hour, and the river is close to bursting its banks.

There's every reason to hold on and await the snows. However . . .

'Is there no other way to get to Rzhev?'

Lishka gives me a blackened grin. 'There *is*, only . . .'

'Only?'

'Only it would mean travelling at least three times the distance, south and then east and then along the shore of the lake, and then north, following the Volga into Rzhev.'

'Then let's do that.'

Lishka laughs. 'You *want* to?'

'Why not? I can't stay here.'

'Can't stay . . . *here*?' Lishka looks puzzled by that. 'But in eight, maybe nine weeks from now the snows will come, and then . . .' He skims his hand along an imaginary road of ice and makes a faint whooshing sound. 'Here you are cosy and warm. You have good food and fine beer. You and your woman.'

That's true. Only I don't want to sit on my hands, waiting for the weather to change. I want to get to Rzhev. Once we're there we can await the snows. Not here. Not in Tatarinka.

Even so, I decide to delay the decision until Bakatin leaves, and that night, as I'm lying there beside Katerina, I ask her what she wants to do.

'I want what you want, Otto. Don't you understand that?'

'Yes, but . . .'

I fall silent for a time, thinking about it. I am not used to doing nothing, that's the problem, because if the idea is to spend time with Katerina, then I can do it here as well as anywhere.

And so I make my decision, to stay and await the snows, only that very night I'm woken by voices, outside, just below where we're sleeping. Careful not to wake Katerina, I creep to the door and, looking through a gap between the logs, I see two men a little way off, beside the barn. I watch them for a moment, then realise what they're doing. They're trying to break inside, to steal the cart!

I feel my way back across the pitch-black room and, slipping on my trousers, take my dagger from the pack. Then I go back and, trying to make as little sound as possible, push the door open enough for me to slip through. Ignoring the ladder, I drop and roll and come up facing them.

One of them turns and, seeing me, gives a little cry.

'Mother of God!'

The other turns, panicked, and draws a knife, only it's clear he doesn't want to use it. They're both visibly shaking with fear. I raise my hand and point at them, and they whimper and then, their nerve breaking, turn and run into the night.

But it doesn't matter. I got a good look at them in the moonlight and it was definitely the same two who were at Belyj and Antipino. Krylenko's friends. But why are they here? Why are they still following us?

One thing I do know. We're leaving here, first thing, whether Lishka thinks it a good idea or not. Here we're sitting targets, easy to find. Much too easy.

I turn as Katerina pushes open the door and looks out.

'What's happening?' she asks, even as the innkeeper, Rapushka, emerges from within, his smock tucked into his breeches, a stave in his hands.

'It was nothing. Just some wild dogs.'

Rapushka looks at me suspiciously, then shrugs and goes back inside. But Katerina is less easily fobbed off. She knows it wasn't dogs.

'Was it them?' she asks, as soon as I'm back inside the room.

'Yes. It looked like they were after the cart.'

She's silent a moment, then. 'We'd better go. If we wait here—'

'I know. We're going. First thing tomorrow.'

'Good. But Otto . . .'

'Yes?'

'I think you need to give me a knife.'

183

I don't like the idea of arming Katerina, and yet it makes good sense – like teaching her German, and confiding in her about Four-Oh.

Over breakfast, I tell Bakatin and Lishka about last night's visitors, and that I want to leave Tatarinka that morning.

Lishka's still against the idea, and offers to sleep in with the cart, but I won't be put off. Besides, this once Bakatin agrees with me. Today's the day he's going home, and he says he'd feel better about it if he knew I was on the move.

I'm surprised. I thought he'd agree with Lishka. These Russians seem to make any excuse to sit on their arses and do nothing, blaming the weather for their idleness. But that's unfair to Bakatin. Though he likes to drink and enjoy himself like the next man, he works hard, and his agreement with me impresses Lishka, who says he'll be ready to leave by midday, once he's sorted out a few things.

The rain has held off all night and most of the morning, but as Katerina and I step out of the inn it begins again, laced with a thin sleet that gusts into our faces.

Lishka appears an hour later, leading a tired-looking horse. I help him bring the cart out from the barn, then stand back as he yokes up. While he's doing this, Bakatin and his sons arrive to see us off.

I embrace the big man warmly. He has been a good friend to us, and I tell him that he is welcome to visit us in Novgorod at any time – and to bring his wives. He laughs at that and scratches his big black beard, then grins. 'Perhaps . . . if I'm ever that far north.'

I stand back and let him hug Katerina, who kisses his bearded cheek, then goes over and gives each of his boys a kiss and a hug. They seem embarrassed, after all, they are but peasants – sons of a river haulier – whereas she is the lady wife of a *Nemets* trader, and they seem conscious of that difference in status. But Katerina has no airs. She is a young Russian girl, that's all, and she tells them she will miss them, and they wish her a safe journey to Rzhev and on to Moscow.

And so we set off, walking beside Lishka and the cart, our heads covered, our faces lowered, as we walk into the gusting rain on a grey afternoon in Tatarinka.

Three hours in, we stop and shelter in a cave, the rain outside incessant, falling in a grey unending curtain from the sky. We are soaked to the skin, and while Lishka clears a patch of ground and starts a fire, I unpack fresh clothes for Katerina. Dressed, she settles on her haunches, then looks to our guide.

'Have you family, Lishka?'

Lishka looks up from where he's crouched down, feeding kindling to the growing flames, a surprised, almost guilty look on his face.

'Pardon, mistress?'

'A wife? Children?'

'No, mistress. I was never lucky with women.'

'Never . . .' Katerina turns and looks at me, then turns back. 'And your parents?'

'Dead. Long dead. The fever took them.' He sniffs, then stares away into the past, his face bright in the glow of the fire. 'I was only a boy. This high.' And he raises his hand to a point two feet above the floor.

Katerina steps closer, then kneels, facing him across the fire. 'What did you do?'

Lishka shrugs. 'What *could* I do? I found a master. I worked. I earned my crust. And in time I became my own master. But I could never stay too long in any one place. That's why I became a haulier. To escape all that.' He looks up at Katerina again and smiles. 'Something to eat, mistress?'

Lishka brings bacon and cabbage and bread and a skillet pan, and in a little while we eat while outside the rain falls endlessly.

We stay there in the warm and dry for the rest of the afternoon and as night falls and as the rain hasn't stopped, we decide to stay there until the morning.

Katerina and I make our bed from furs and cloaks on one side of the cart, Lishka and the horse on the other. Sleep comes easy, but halfway through the night I'm woken.

I'm only half awake at first, still following the thread of a dream, and then I realise that there's movement in the cave. In the glow from the fire's embers, I can see faint shadows moving on the far side of the cart. At first I think it's Lishka, got up to piss, only I realise it can't be, because I can hear Lishka snoring. I turn and look beside me. Katerina is still there, on her back, asleep.

The horse snorts restlessly. A moment later a twig snaps.

That's it. The sound that woke me.

I reach under the cloak for my knife, then slowly, careful not to make a noise, I slip from beneath the covers and lift myself up into a position where I can peek over the cart without being seen.

For a long time I stay there, motionless, watching and listening for something from the back of the cave. But there's nothing. Either I imagined it, or it was something very small – a nocturnal beast of some kind. Relaxing, I go round the cart and look about me. No. There's nothing. Only Lishka and the horse.

Relieved, I go over to the entrance and stand there, peering out into the moonlit night.

The rain has stopped and in the silvered light the surrounding forest seems newly fashioned, like on the very first day of creation. The overhanging branches sparkle with raindrops, while the moon seems to wink back at me from a hundred tiny pools among the trees. Overhead the stars blaze down from a black velvet sky. It's beautiful, and for that one brief moment its beauty pierces me, touching my soul, the way Katerina does whenever she looks at me. And I realise that I have fallen in love with this land, so different from my own.

I'm about to go back to bed when I see him suddenly, standing among the trees about fifty yards away, to my left. He's looking straight at me: a tall man with almost silver hair. A man my own height and build. His presence there, so still and silent, chills me. For the briefest moment he watches me, then, with a casualness that speaks volumes, he turns and walks away.

I strain to follow him with my eyes, but in a moment I have lost him among the tangle of tree trunks; either that, or the ground there slopes down out of sight. Whichever, he has gone, as effectively as if he'd disappeared. Which makes me wonder.

I go back to the cart and, reaching underneath, get out the Kolbe, then sit on a rock in the entrance, keeping guard. It's here that Katerina finds me, just before the dawn.

'Otto? What is it?'

'We had a visitor. In the night.'

'Those men again.'

'No. A different one. One we've not seen before. I think he may have been in the cave at some point.'

She turns and looks behind her, fearful suddenly. Our plan to leave Tatarinka doesn't seem so clever now.

'We should move on,' she says. 'Quickly. Try and lose them.'

'You think that likely? It won't be hard for them to track us with the cart. We can't move fast, and the deep ruts it leaves could be followed by a blind man. No. We'll just have to watch our backs and hope.'

'Backs?' Lishka says, coming out from behind the cart. 'What's this about watching our backs?'

'We had a visitor,' Katerina explains. 'Otto saw him.'

Lishka narrows his eyes. 'You want to go back?'

'No,' I answer, slipping the Kolbe away, out of sight. 'But we take greater care from now on, and we take turns to watch at night.'

'Do you know these people?' Lishka asks.

'Not the one I saw. I've never seen him before. But he was some way distant and, despite the moon, it wasn't easy to pick out what he looked like. His face was in shadow. But I know it wasn't one of the other two who were skulking about in Tatarinka.'

'What was he like?'

'Tall. My height and build. Silver-haired. He seemed . . . calm. Not afraid of me at all.'

Lishka shrugs. 'I've not heard of such a one. Not in these parts, anyway.'

And then – from nowhere – it strikes me. *Shit! He didn't have a beard. The bastard didn't have a beard!*

184

I say nothing to Lishka, but at the first chance I get, I take Katerina aside and discuss the matter of the missing beard with her. All the Russians of this age have beards, so the figure I saw, I'm certain, was a time agent. But ours or theirs?

Whichever, it means that I've caused ripples, and that could prove a problem. I was hoping to make this journey anonymously – at least, as anonymously as I could while being tracked every second from Four-Oh.

I am extra alert the next few days, as we journey through that rough, heavily wooded terrain, but there's no further sign of our pursuers. Lishka knows his stuff, and eventually brings us out into a valley that runs from west to east. I can see from the deeply scored ravine that there was once a proper river here, back in the Ice Age, but now it's little more than a stream. We walk alongside, the cart swaying and dipping with the path, the old horse happier now that we're out in the sunlight.

It's late morning when we stop to eat. It hasn't rained for a full day now, nor have we had any further sign of our pursuers. But that's not to say that they aren't there, biding their time – waiting until the 'sorcerer' drops his guard.

Katerina's morning sickness has grown worse these last few days, her nausea lasting well into the afternoon. If I could jump back to Four-Oh I could get her something for it, but as it is she has to do what women have done through the ages: grit her teeth and persevere. But I feel for her. She seems so miserable sometimes.

'How far is it to the shore of the lake?' I ask Lishka as I help him to make a fire.

'Three days. I thought we might stop at Sychevka first.'

'*Sychevka*?' The place isn't marked on the map Ernst had drawn up for me.

'It's at the southern foot of the lake. We can rest there overnight. Get feed for the horse.'

I sit back on my heels and think about that, then shake my head. 'No.'

'No?' Lishka's surprised.

'We avoid it. Press on.'

'But we need food.'

'I'll hunt for food. The horse can graze.'

'I don't understand. If you're afraid of an attack . . .'

It's true. They are as likely to attack us in the wilds – more likely, probably – than in a village. But my instinct is to avoid all centres of habitation. I don't know why, but I feel safer out here, paradoxical as that seems. Maybe it's the thought of being caught inside a building. Of being trapped. Out here we can always run.

Lishka stares into the fire a moment and then shrugs. 'If that's what you want.'

'It's what I want.'

As it is, we have to pass right by Sychevka. The valley opens out into the lake and Sychevka sits in the gap.

No one's about. The huts look deserted. And while the rain might explain that, I don't like the feel of the place, and so we keep to the left, following the rocks closely, until Sychevka is behind us.

I'm beginning to relax a little when, rounding a rocky promontory, we come in sight of a boat, out on the lake. There are two men in it, fishing, and for a time they don't notice us. Then one of them spies us and, nudging the other, points in our direction. Almost at once, they've pulled in their nets and are rowing hard, back towards the village.

It doesn't look good, and I ask Lishka if there is some way we can get away from the shore, but he doesn't think so. It's only because it's so stony here that we can pull the cart. If we go further inland we'll hit mud again and the cart will get bogged down.

Nor can we hurry much. The old horse is doing its very best, drawing a load which at times seems beyond it, especially on slopes, where Lishka and I have to give it a hand.

But now I sense danger and, making Lishka stop, I scramble under the cart and get out both the weapons. They ought to be enough, but if not, Katerina has her knife and Lishka his stave.

I look to Lishka a moment, wondering if he was in on this. Whether he told them, maybe, that he would bring us out to Sychevka. It would make sense of why they've not attacked us before now. Only I've come to trust old Lishka, and I don't believe for a moment that he'd make that kind of deal.

I look to Katerina. 'We may have to fight.'

She nods nervously, then, bravely, gives me a smile.

'It'll be okay,' I say. 'We'll get through. Trust me.'

But the words have no sooner left my mouth than I feel a thud to the back of my head and the world goes black.

I come to an instant later, my ears ringing, nausea overwhelming me. I'm slumped against the cart, steadying myself with one hand, Beside me, on the ground, is the piece of rock that hit me. My head hurts like blazes. There's a hot, throbbing pain at the back of my skull and a wetness. My vision swims.

There's a sudden awful braying and yelping, as of wild animals, and then the first of them are upon us.

I look up, alarmed, as one of them tries to skewer Katerina with what looks like a butcher's knife. But she's too fast for him and jerks aside. Lishka, meanwhile, has met the charge of another of them full on, thrusting his stave into the man's face, then bringing it down hard into the fallen man's stomach.

I haul myself up, even as Katerina ducks under her attacker's swipe and plunges her knife deep into his guts. The fierceness in her face astonishes me. But I've no time to watch her. Two of them now target me, one with a long curved knife, the other with a woodman's axe. I've lost the guns and have only my hands now to defend me, but it's enough. I straight punch the swordsman even as he seeks to cleave me from head to toe, breaking his nose, then turn and kick away the right leg of the axeman.

And almost faint from the sudden pain in my head.

I stagger back, knowing that others are coming, that we're

outnumbered heavily and that my best chance – the guns – has gone. As the axeman scrambles up and grips his weapon anew, I place my hand against my chest, preparing to jump. Only even as I do, I am knocked sideways, out of the way, as Lishka charges through and, with a vicious swing, takes the axeman's remaining teeth out.

Lishka is laughing now, enjoying himself. As another of them rushes him, he trips them and, with a deft turn I'd not have believed him capable of, smacks him across the back of the head as he sprawls.

Katerina is also thriving in the fight. She's cut another of them badly, and as a third attacker seeks to grab her hair and pull her down, she swings round under his arm and stabs him in the thorax. He gives a gurgling scream and falls away.

But now things turn. As I get up yet again, I sense someone behind me and, turning, find myself facing one of the two who'd followed me to Tatarinka. Before I've time to lift my arm, he swings his club, and only poor judgement on his part makes him miss my head. Yet he tumbles into me and brings me down again. Getting up, I see that Lishka has been hit. He's holding his bloodied head and staggering. Looking just beyond him I see the culprit – a young boy, barely a man – bending to find another rock for his slingshot. As my own attacker tries to get up and grab me, I thrust an elbow viciously into his face, then – ignoring the aching pulse in my head, the great sheets of blood-hot pain that wash through my whole body – I get to my feet again and, half-jogging, head towards the sling-thrower.

He looks up as I overshadow him, just in time to get my boot full in his face. But as I turn, swaying now, almost spent, I hear Katerina cry out, and feel my heart ripped from me. She's down, and even as I watch, some bastard sticks her a second time with a knife.

I bellow and, finding reserves from somewhere, run at her attacker, stooping briefly to pick up an axe. As the man turns, surprised, I bring it down savagely and he falls back, an astonished look on his face, a line of blood running from where the blade of the axe is embedded in his forehead. Dead.

That seems to do it. The rest of them – three or four at most – flee from us, even though it's clear we're on our last legs and easy pickings. But I'm barely conscious of that. Stooping down, I try and lift Katerina, groaning at the sight of her injuries. The whole right side of her upper body is covered in blood, and her face is ash pale, her eyes closed, the eyelids fluttering.

'No! Urd help me, no!'

I turn my head, looking about me, then half-carry, half-drag her over to the cart, where, cutting through the securing straps, I search through the load until I find the medical kit I've packed at the very bottom. Then, on my hands and knees beside her, I cut into her bodice, tearing at it with quick, almost desperate movements. As it comes away, I wince. There are two stab wounds, and though neither are in critical areas – through the heart or lungs – they're both deep and she has clearly lost a lot of blood.

'Katerina, can you hear me?'

She gives a little moan, and then her eyes flicker open.

'I need to do something to you. But don't be afraid. It'll help you.'

'O-oh . . .?'

She tries to speak, but then her left hand comes up and grabs at me. Pain makes a rictus of her face. The sight of it hurts me more than my own suffering.

I realise I need to work fast. Searching among the medical pack, I find the injector and quickly load a capsule. Then, praying that her thirteenth-century body won't react badly to it, I inject her with a shot of heal-fast.

Her eyes look at me beseechingly, as if I've just done something bad to her, but that look quickly fades and she slumps in my arms as the powerful drugs take effect.

I shouldn't be doing this. It's totally against the rules. And I know there's a chance that she may even die as a reaction to the drugs. Only . . .

Only it's my only chance of saving her. Without jumping back, that is. Without having to explain to Hecht just why I've got into this mess.

Quickly I dress her wounds, using special combat strips from a thousand years hence, and then I slump back, exhausted.

Resting my head gently against the cart, I realise that I've overdone it and that I need to sleep; my body is about to slip into unconsciousness. Yet even as my eyes begin to close I sense a shadow standing over me, and I wonder if it was all in vain.

185

It's evening when I wake, and I'm surprised to find myself lying on a bed of furs beneath a bivouac, Katerina beside me. For a moment I think I must have dreamed it all, but then, as I try to lift my head, the pain reminds me it was real.

There's the crackle of a fire nearby and the smell of something cooking, and when I manage – slowly – to turn my head and look, I see that it's Lishka, sitting on a rock beside it, chewing on a piece of meat.

He looks across at me and grins his black-toothed grin. 'Hungry, Otto?'

I swallow painfully. My throat is dry, my lips cracked. I really ought to see to my own injuries before I do anything else, but I'm curious. 'What happened?'

'Most of them ran off. The rest . . .' Lishka draws an imaginary knife across his throat and grins. 'I made sure they wouldn't be a problem.'

Lishka's face, I note, is a mass of bruises, but he seems happy enough.

I stare at him a moment, feeling a new respect for him, remembering the sight of him swinging his stave. Bakatin was right: Lishka *does* love a fight.

I get up on to one elbow, then carefully turn my head, looking down at Katerina. She's pale still and her breathing is slightly erratic, but the bleeding has stopped and her brow when I feel it is cool, with no sign of a fever. The drugs are working. I take her wrist and feel her pulse – it's good, strong and regular – and let out a long sigh of relief.

I get up slowly, then look about me.

'You want the box?' Lishka asks, and points to just under the cart where I see the medical kit.

'Thanks, I . . .'

I look across at Lishka. He's watching me very matter-of-factly as he chews on the haunch of meat. Finishing a mouthful, he wipes the back of his hand across his mouth, then says, 'I kept one of them alive for a time. Asked him a few questions.'

'Yes?'

'Things I thought you might want to know.'

I nod, but I'm genuinely surprised. 'Go on.'

'It's like I thought,' Lishka says. 'They weren't from around here. They were from the south. Polovtsy.'

'So why were they this far north?'

'They were promised a lot of gold.'

'By whom?'

'The one I asked didn't know.'

'And where is he now? Did he run off?'

Lishka throws the bone into the fire, then breaks off another piece from the carcass on the ground beside him. 'Like I said.' And he makes the throat-slitting gesture again, only this time he gives a little laugh, like it was fun to do.

'And the bodies?'

Lishka makes a gesture with his thumb, back into the trees.

I swallow, then kneel down by the kit and begin to rummage through. It's only then that I remember. I turn and look at Lishka again.

'Lishka?'

'Yes, Meister?'

'Where are the guns?'

Lishka stares back at me, then stands and, dropping the piece of meat, puts his hands to his waist and, like a gunslinger, pulls the two guns from his belt.

'Here. I was keeping them for you.'

I hobble across and take them, nodding my thanks. But Lishka hasn't finished.

'Bakatin told me about them,' he says, sitting again and picking up the meat. 'He says he fired one of them.'

'He did. It blew a tree into matchwood.'

'Matchwood?'

Again, I realise that it's not a concept they have in this time. Matches come later.

'Into splinters,' I say.

'Bakatin claimed there was a great ball of fire.'

'There was.'

'Then 'tis a pity you dropped the fuckers before our friends attacked today.'

And he laughs, and after a moment – as much from relief as anything else – I begin to laugh with him.

A while later, after I've bandaged my head and taken a shot or two of various drugs, I sit with Lishka and share his meal, and we talk, and I begin to see this world through Lishka's eyes.

The world of this age is vast. It has no edges to it. You can travel for long months and still not come to the end, even of Russia. Within it there is only chaos or, should I say, only the small, scant order that a single man can impose. There may be laws, but few men understand them, and in any case, justice is a thousand miles away out here in the wilds. Out here there are no hard-and-fast rules, only the law of survival. That's why Lishka is such a good fighter. He has had to be. He could not have lived this long without being good with his fists. But that's only a small part of it. I listen to all he's done and seen, and though I have travelled the length and breadth of Time, I'd find it hard to claim that I have seen more than him of Man and his ways. Lishka expects both the worst and the best of every man he meets, and he is never disappointed.

'Take you,' he says. 'You are the oddest of mixtures, if you'll forgive me for saying so. Such gentleness and such savagery, and all in the same frame. Why, when you buried the hatchet in that fellow's head, there was such a look on your face, you'd have thought the man had raped your mother!'

I give a short laugh. 'Well, it's like he *did*! He hurt my Katerina!'

'You see!' Lishka says, as if he's made his point. 'Another man would have saved his own skin and married again. After all, as the proverb goes, wives are like the fish in the river. But you, you risked all for her!'

I make to speak, then fall silent, thinking about what he's said. Because it's true. I could have jumped straight out of there at the first sign of trouble – yes, and almost did. Only now that I think of it, Lishka shoving me aside notwithstanding, I don't think I could have. Not if it meant leaving her there. Not if it meant, even if only briefly, she might die.

Because . . .

And now I face it. Now I stare directly at it and begin to understand.

Because I couldn't be sure that I could save her any other way. Because if I went back, and Hecht said no . . .

I look down, and then I look back at him and nod. 'I had to,' I say, my voice quiet. 'I didn't have a choice.'

'I know,' Lishka says. 'I've seen it all along.'

186

We make up a narrow sled from interwoven branches and harness it to my shoulders so that I can pull Katerina along behind me. She seems much better now. Her breathing has regularised and her colour is almost back to normal, but the drugs have heavily sedated her and made her sleep.

I am a big man and pride myself on my ability to endure, but what with my own injuries, I find it hard to drag her weight, and though I'm willing enough, I find, after two hours toiling through the rain, that I have to stop.

Lishka eyes me strangely, confused. He is convinced – like Bakatin – that I am a sorcerer, and thus possessed of great powers. Yet my weakness in this instance disturbs him. He has seen me take potions from my magic box and heal both my own and Katerina's wounds, yet he sees me struggling with the makeshift sled and cannot understand why I won't conjure up some spell to ease my burden. Indeed, I could. There are drugs in the pack that would boost my strength and allow me to do entirely without sleep for several days. Only such drugs take their toll. I am only human after all, and I cannot risk collapsing two days hence.

So we stop again and camp beneath a ledge of rock as the rain falls steadily. It's there that she wakes, and just the sight of her, looking up at me through the dark circles of her eyes, makes me feel that everything I've been through has been worthwhile.

She tries to speak, but I place my finger gently to her lips.

'It's okay. You're better now. You just have to rest. Lishka and I are taking care of you.'

She gives the faintest smile, then closes her eyes again, the smallest flicker of remembered pain crossing her face. The wounds have healed nicely, but she'll carry the scars all her life. Reminders of this adventure. Of what she went through just to be with me.

That makes me think. Makes me wonder yet again whether I was right to bring her. She almost died back there. Should have, maybe, from the wounds she got, the loss of blood. And there's a paradox. For just as my presence here out of time has endangered her, so what I've brought with me – the drugs, the combat bandages – has saved her life.

And there's one other thing – about the attack itself. They were upon us too quickly for it to have been the villagers – the fishermen – who set them on our trail. They had to have been waiting up ahead, ready to ambush us. Nor, when I think of it, could they have known about the guns. If they had, they would never – surely? – have attacked. That fits with them being Polovtsy – Cossacks – from the south. But who sent them? And how did they know where we were heading?

I am beginning to think that maybe the Russians know about me. Know where I'm heading and why. Only if that is so, why not just send in their own agents? Why go through this complicated charade, if all they want to do is kill me?

I chew that over for a time, and it's only Lishka, reminding me that it will be dark in a few hours and we must decide whether to press on or camp here for the night, who breaks my reverie and forces me to act.

It's time to take a few risks. To press on while we can. And so I take a handful of the small yellow tablets from the pack and swallow them down. Then, getting Lishka to harness me up once more, I look to him and smile.

'Okay. Let's get moving. I want to be a long, long way from here by morning.'

187

I wake to find Katerina sitting just across from me, watching me. She smiles. It's night, the sky intensely black, dark, but her long dark hair shimmers with warm tints of gold in the light from Lishka's campfire.

She reaches out and strokes my brow. 'I wondered when you'd wake.'

'Have I slept long?'

'Not long. But you needed the rest. Your head . . .'

For a moment that seems strange, her worrying about me, but then I smile and, reaching out, lace my fingers into hers.

'It's okay,' I say. 'It's healing well.'

Her eyes look past me, and I realise it is Lishka, returning from finding provisions.

'He's awake then, is he?' he asks gruffly, coming into view, then crouching to throw more logs on the fire. 'I was beginning to think he was going to sleep for a month!'

I lift myself slowly, a faint wooziness making my vision swim. It's the drugs.

'Where are we?'

'On the way to Rzhev,' Lishka says. 'Don't you remember?'

I do, only—

'I don't believe what you did, Otto,' Katerina says quietly, squeezing my hand gently. 'Carrying me on your back like that for three days . . .'

I lean across and kiss her. She presses back urgently, pushing her tongue between my lips, and as we break from it, I understand everything.

I would have walked over burning coals for her. Through hell itself.

'Lishka?'

'Yes, Meister?'

'Would you leave us for a while?'

188

Rzhev sits on the top of the hill like some ancient stone-age encampment, its huge earth ramparts giving it a look of great antiquity, yet the town is barely a century old and its importance as a trading centre is dubious, despite its position on the Volga.

It has taken us two weeks to get here, and it was a good thing Katerina could walk the last ten days, or we would still be back there in the forest.

Lishka stops me while we are yet within the trees and looks at me earnestly.

'Don't say *anything*,' he says. 'Leave everything to me. I know these people. They can be scoundrels. Worse than bandits.' I clearly look confused, because he carries on to explain. 'The Grand Prince's officials. They are like a plague on all civilised men. But these are worse than most. These are Prince Alexander Iaroslavich's men, and the prince serves the Great Khan.'

I am surprised Lishka knows this. But then, why not? If anyone knows what's going on in this part of Russia, Lishka does.

'Ah, yes,' he says, noting my surprise. 'The Horde's influence stretches to Rzhev all right. And it will not be long before you in Novgorod feel it too. The Horde is hungry beyond the greed of many thousand men.'

'Hungry?' Katerina asks.

'For tribute.' Lishka indicates the cart. 'It might be worth your while to hide most of that load. Bury it somewhere nearby and come back for it later, when you've found a boatman you can trust. I'll help you there. I know these men.'

I smile. 'Thank you, Lishka, but I'd rather keep my cart intact. Besides, I have the *tysiatskii*'s pass. They wouldn't dare risk offending him by robbing me.'

'No?' But Lishka doesn't push the matter. He merely stares at me a moment then, shaking his head, turns away. 'Whatever . . . let me do the talking, Meister Otto. If one must deal with wolves, best leave it to one who knows their habits, eh?'

A steep path leads up the side of the hill to the main gate which is to the west of the town. Guards delay us while someone hurries off to fetch the steward. As we stand there, Lishka up front, Katerina, cloaked, her face concealed, a small crowd of inquisitive locals forms behind me.

Again, it's my beard – or lack of one – that provides the talking point. Men and women stare openly at me and point, and some even laugh, as if I'm deformed. But they know what I am from a single glance at my clothes. A trader. A *Nemets*. And thus a rarity this far inland.

We wait almost twenty minutes before the runner returns, breathless. He says nothing, merely waits to one side, and after a moment we see a small procession coming our way between the shabby wooden houses, five or six armed men – militia, by their look – surrounding one particularly corpulent fellow, dressed in furs despite the warmth of the day. As he comes nearer he slows, taking on an air of importance, until, as he steps before us, you would have thought it was the Grand Prince of Kiev himself who was facing us. But he's clearly a small man pretending to be big. He has a bony, hairless head, a cast in his left eye and heavily pocked skin, and I'd say at a glance that he's been soured by his ugliness, made hard and cruel and self-important.

The pomposity in his voice confirms it for me. 'Who is it who seeks to enter the prince's town?'

Lishka is watching me with hooded eyes. I look to him and nod, and he turns, facing the official.

'My master is Otto Behr, trader, of Novgorod, converted to the Faith and travelling under the protection of the *veche* of that town, and of its *tysiatskii*.'

The official doesn't even blink. Lishka's words clearly don't impress him. He studies Lishka a moment, like he's looking at a turd some dog has left in his path, and then, with an exaggerated movement, turns his attention to me.

'You have a *pass*?' he asks, and manages to make it sound both insult and mockery. The crowd laugh, enjoying my discomfort, every eye looking for my response. But I say nothing, merely take my leather purse from my belt and, unstrapping it, remove the folded pass and hand it across.

The official holds the corner of the document, like it's diseased, and stares at it a moment, then throws it back, so that it lands in the mud by my feet.

There's more laughter. The official is now looking at me coldly. 'Your pass is not valid in Rzhev. You will need to buy a new pass.'

'But that pass . . .' Lishka begins, only to receive a blow to the head with a cudgel from one of the official's men, who has quietly positioned himself behind him. As Lishka sprawls forward, I glare at the thug and vow to hurt the man plenty when I've the chance. Lishka clearly feels the same, for, getting up, he scowls a warning at the rogue.

Lishka goes to speak, but I raise a hand and, in a fluent Russian that clearly surprises most of them there, ask the man, 'How much is such a pass?'

He almost smiles. It's robbery, and he knows it. My pass is good throughout Kievan Rus'. But I am in Rzhev now, not Novgorod, and if I want to hire a boat here I'll have to go along with this.

'Thirty ounces of silver.'

There's a gasp from the crowd. The sum is outrageous. Lishka takes a step forward, as if he's about to strike the man, but I intervene. 'Lishka! Leave it!'

Lishka whirls round to face me, real anger in his face now. 'But this is robbery! Thirty ounces! Has this Judas no shame!'

I see the flare of anger in the official's eyes at that and quickly move to make things good. 'Lishka! Behind the cart! *Now!*'

Like a dog that's been chastised by its master, Lishka turns and does as he's been told. But he's not happy. His eyes are smouldering with fury.

I face the official again and smile. 'Forgive my servant. He does not always know when to speak. But *thirty* ounces? It seems . . .'

The official makes a face, as if he's considering matters. Then, with a little shrug, he nods and a kind of smile appears on his lips, if not in his eyes. His eyes are still cold and calculating. They look past me at the loaded cart, as if to assess just how much he can take me for. Finally he folds his arms and nods.

'Let it never be said that the Steward of Rzhev is an ungenerous man. Our laws state that a man must have an authorised pass before he can trade in the marketplace at Rzhev. Such laws cannot be bent or broken. Yet I can see a way, perhaps, where local law can be satisfied.'

I smile at him. 'Go on.'

'There is a meeting tonight. Of the *veche*. If they could be persuaded somehow to . . . *endorse* your existing pass, then maybe we could reduce the required fee. Then everyone would be happy, no?'

Lishka makes to speak, but I silence him. 'Lishka!'

I smile my apologies to the official, then nod. 'We are to attend this meeting, I take it?'

'Indeed, but until the matter is decided, it might be best to place your cart under our protection. For the benefit of all.' And again he smiles, his eyes – cast and all – like ice.

Lishka, I know, is about to burst a blood vessel, but I merely smile and bow to the man. 'That would be most kind. We can keep our packs, I take it?'

I can see that he'd rather we didn't, but my very politeness – which seems to be playing directly into his hands – makes him concede. 'Of course. Until tonight, then.'

And with that he turns and, moving through his little entourage, walks away.

I watch him go, then take our packs from inside the cart. And not a moment too soon, as his men come over to the cart and, without asking my leave, begin to trundle it away.

'Take good care!' I call to them. 'If anything's missing you will have your master to answer to!'

There's muted laughter at that from the men, and at any other time I'd be worried, only it doesn't matter. There's a supply dump only a few miles from here and I can replace the whole lot if I need to. No, what matters is to get that pass and hire a boat, because I need to be in Tver' before the snows fall.

Lishka, however, is incandescent with anger. 'How could you let him do that, Otto? Thirty pieces of silver! Mother of God! The man's a thief!'

'Maybe. But let's deal with that later. Right now let's find us an inn and some food.'

Lishka narrows his eyes, my very calmness alerting him to the fact that *something* must be going on in my head. He lowers his voice, so that the mob won't hear.

'You have a plan, Meister?'

I smile and nod. 'Oh, I have a plan, Lishka. I *always* have a plan.'

189

Only I don't. Not this time. Not unless you consider giving in and abandoning the cart a plan. Which I guess you could, seeing as I have duplicates not far away. Only how do I explain all that to Lishka?

As sorcery, of course.

Lishka finds us an inn, run by what he calls 'the only honest man in all of Rzhev'.

The man's half-oriental – a silk-trader, I learn, in his youth – and he goes by the name of Dmitri. It's not his birth name, which he'll tell to no one, but in this part of Russia it's fit in or move on, and so he has adopted a Russian name and Russian ways, and thus is tolerated, if not much liked, by his neighbours.

The food is none too bad, either, and his ale is good, even if our accommodation proves spartan. But then, this is thirteenth-century Russia and to hope for anything better would be pointless.

Besides, as long as Katerina is beside me, it doesn't matter.

The official clearly has been having our movements watched, for his messenger finds us without trouble, and I am told to present myself at sundown at the great lodge, which is in the centre of the town. Lishka, I'm told, is not required to attend.

Lishka, fuelled now by several pots of ale, is almost bear-like in his anger. He growls and prowls about the room, and curses the local boyars, calling them thieves and villains. He would rather burn their great lodge to the ground than have me step inside and trust to their untender mercies. But it's my choice. Besides, I want to see the kind of men that Prince Alexander has appointed here, for it'll give me some clue as to how to behave when we're in Moscow.

You see, a ruler can be judged by the men he gives power to, and by what he permits, and if I'm to judge Nevsky and find a way into his confidence, then maybe I'll find a few clues here.

As the sun begins to set, Katerina joins me once again in the main tap room of the inn. She has combed her hair and changed her dress and looks quite stunning. The deep blue of the cloth sets off her figure wonderfully. She's showing now, but not enough to suggest more than a matronly plumpness. But her face glows with good health, such that one would not suspect how ill she really was, after the ambush.

Taking my arm, she walks beside me up the hill toward the lodge. And as we walk along, so people come outdoors to watch us, their curiosity naked. Bare-arsed children tail us the full length of our walk, crying out and running about us, tugging at our cloaks now and then, while their parents look on, envy in the women's faces at Katerina's looks and dress, hostility in the faces of the men.

Rzhev, I think. *The devil's made this place his home, for sure.*

Guards bar our way at the main gate to the lodge and make us wait as night falls. We stand there, kicking our heels until, finally, we are admitted.

The official meets us just inside the compound that surrounds the lodge. It's a tiny fort, I realise. A safe haven for the elite within the greater fortress. And that too speaks volumes, for these people know that their power depends on force, not popularity. As for our official, he greets us coolly, offering no greeting at all to

Katerina, only a disdainful glance, before leading us through into the main banqueting hall.

It's a poor show compared to Novgorod, but then, Rzhev has neither the wealth nor history of that greater northern town. Twenty men sit around a massive table, wearing their furs like badges of office – proof of their wealth, though a glance about the table reveals more than one fur that's seen better days.

I bow my head, then wait, looking to the one among them who I can tell, from instinct, is their leader. And so it proves. He's a small fellow, grey-bearded and almost delicate in his features, yet there is something in his eyes that gives him away; that marks him out as the one who has real power in this town. Even so, if you shaved away his beard, there would be nothing of him.

He stands, and as he does, so silence falls.

'*Nemets*,' he says, quietly but authoritatively, 'I understand you require us to endorse your pass, to make it valid for Rzhev.'

'That is so, Master.'

He likes that. Likes the reverence I'm paying him.

'But I also understand that you find the fee . . . a little *high*, is that so?'

I hesitate. 'Forgive me, Master. Were I my own man, I would not hesitate to pay what is due. Unfortunately, that's not the case. Half of my load belongs to the *veche* of Novgorod, and I must account to them for all payments.' I smile, and look about the table. 'Were I able to say to them that the *veche* of Rzhev was generous enough to reduce that fee then – who knows? – maybe other traders would make their way here from Novgorod.'

Surprisingly it's not something any of them have considered, and for a while there's a real buzz of conversation about the table. They clearly like the idea. Only they also like the idea of fleecing me. After all, what's in the hand is real, while what's *promised* . . .

The old man raises a hand, and they fall silent again. He looks at me and nods. 'You speak well . . . for a *Nemets*. And I understand that you've converted to the Faith.'

'I have, Master.'

'And yet . . . your beard. Or lack of one.'

'It is the style of my people.'

'Hmmm . . .' He sits, considering a moment, then looks about him, as if seeking their approval before he speaks again. 'Very good,' he says suddenly. 'We will halve the fee for the pass. Fifteen ounces of silver.'

'And the pass, Master?'

'Will be ready in a week or so. In the meantime, I hope you will enjoy our hospitality. Come, take a seat at table, Meister Behr. Let's drink a toast and seal the deal. To good friendship. And to trade!'

190

And Katerina all this while? Much as it wounds my soul, she is ignored by them. It was a mistake to bring her, and not one of them goes so far as to even offer her a chair, let alone something to eat or drink, and when finally we leave, she has been standing there for three full hours.

Back in our room, I hold her close and whisper my apologies. 'It's okay, my love. It wasn't your fault. You weren't to know.'

'No, but I should have guessed. It is the same in Novgorod, after all. The men eat and drink, while the women . . . the women stay behind the screen and wait.'

'Otto, it's okay, really it is.'

But I know it isn't. It was the last thing she needed in her condition. And thinking that, I grow really angry with them. It makes me feel like riding roughshod over them all. Like taking my guns and . . .

A week! We must stay in this hellhole a full week at least before we get the pass!

That is the worst of it.

I get Dmitri to bring her food, and while she's tucking into a bowl of soup and a loaf of fresh-baked bread, I find Lishka and tell him what happened.

Lishka's anger at their treatment of Katerina mirrors mine, but he has some good news. It seems he's found someone willing to take us up the Volga to Tver'. Someone reliable. We are to meet the following day, down at the harbour. Until then, there's nothing to be done.

I return to the inn to find Katerina talking with Dmitri. I sit down, barely listening to them, brooding upon the situation. I'm tempted to hire the boatman, arrange to meet him somewhere upstream, then go and get the duplicate cart. Lishka, I'm certain, would go along with that. But the boatman? How reliable is reliable? Because I can't afford to lose a second cart.

I decide to sleep on it. After all, I've yet to meet our friendly boatman. Once I have I'll make up my mind.

'Dmitri?' I ask, interrupting them. 'Has it always been like this in Rzhev?'

'Always?' Dmitri considers, then shakes his head. 'No. But for a long time now. Some blame the young prince Alexander, but his father, Prince Iaroslav, is the real villain. And now that the Horde has come . . .' Dmitri lowers his voice, as if even saying this might cause him great trouble. 'Their *baskaki* was here in the spring. He and several dozen of his men. Big, fierce men. Horsemen from the far side of the world. They are to return and settle here, it seems. To farm the land and take their *tamga*.'

'*Tamga*?' Katerina asks.

Dmitri turns to her. 'It is a tax. A tithe on everything we own, everything we make or sell. And the *baskaki* collects it for the Great Khan. Or rather, the *veche* does. For they're afraid of the *baskaki* and his men. They have heard how Kiev was burned to the ground, and not a house, not a single person saved.'

'It is true,' I say.

'Yes,' Dmitri says, leaning closer, his voice going down to what is almost a whisper. 'And that is why they seek to rob you, *Nemets*. Because the *tamga* is so great. They are greedy, yes, but they are also afraid.'

All the more reason for us to leave this place as soon as possible.

I sit back, lift my goblet and down the last of my ale, then stand, smiling down at Dmitri. The drink has made me tired, the talk depressed. 'You are a good host, Dmitri,' I say, and he gives me a little nod of acknowledgement.

We are about to retire to our room, when Dmitri's boy comes in.

'What is it?' Dmitri asks kindly, one arm reaching out to embrace the lad.

The boy glances at me fearfully. 'Masters Kilik and Podnayin are here. They say they wish to speak to the *Nemets*.'

'At *this* hour?' Dmitri gets up unsteadily.

'It's okay,' I say. 'I'll see them.'

Not that I have a choice.

The boy goes out, returning a moment later with two of the company I met earlier. They look to each other, and then the taller of them speaks. 'Forgive us, *Nemets*, for the lateness of the hour, but we have been thinking of our meeting earlier. We felt you were a trifle, how should we put it . . . disappointed?'

I shrug, waiting for the man – Podnayin? – to elaborate.

The other – Kilik, I'm sure of it – now interrupts. 'Only we felt we might be able to . . . help you. Smooth your way, if you like. Help hurry things along.'

I nod. 'Go on.'

Podnayin glances at Katerina. 'Also, we felt that maybe you found our hospitality somewhat lacking. Making your wife stand throughout. Talyzin sometimes forgets such small delicacies.'

Talyzin was the greybeard. The *posadnik* of Rzhev.

'I'm grateful for your kind thoughts, but—'

'No, hear me out. We wish to make amends for that oversight. To properly welcome you to Rzhev. If you – you and your wife, that is – would be our guests at my house tomorrow evening . . .'

I am surprised. More than surprised. But why? There must be good men, men with a conscience, even in such a place as this.

I smile and bow my head. 'Thank you. That would be a great pleasure.'

Podnayin gives a nervous little smile. 'I'm glad you think so.' He looks to his friend, then bows his head to me. 'I will send my man to fetch you. At sunset, yes?'

'Yes, and thank you. I shall look forward to our meeting.'

When they are gone, Dmitri whistles through his teeth softly. 'Well, well,' he says. 'Wonders never cease. I'd have put those two down for rogues. But there you are.'

I shrug. 'Maybe they see a possible advantage in being kind?'

'Maybe.' But Dmitri falls silent.

Alone with Katerina, I find myself thinking through the alternatives. If those two *can* smooth my path, then maybe there'll be no need to cut loose. They seemed contrite enough. But Dmitri's comments nag at me, and I begin to wonder whether this is not simply another ruse to make me part with my silver.

If so, then I'll confront that at the time.

Katerina turns into me, snuggling against me in the darkness. 'Otto?'

'Yes, my love?'

'Are you plotting something?'

I laugh quietly. 'Why are you so sure I am?'

'Because . . .'

I'm quiet for a while, then, quietly, whispering in the dark, I begin to share my thoughts.

191

The boatman is a small man named Schelepin. Lishka and I examine his boat, then take him to the harbourside inn and buy him beer while a deal is agreed. I like him, and when Lishka suggests we go and check up on the cart, I ask Schelepin to accompany us, which he does with great delight. Though he expresses no opinion on the matter, I sense that he finds officials as much of a pain as we do.

The cart, Lishka's discovered, is in the compound by the lodge. We go there and ask to look at it, but no one is willing to allow us in, and we are told that the official we first met – Gromov, we learn – has gone to Zubtsov that very morning and will not return for three days at the very least, and until he does . . .

Lishka wants to argue, but I draw him away. He doesn't know it, but it doesn't matter. Not now that I have Schelepin. Besides, I say, placating him, I'll raise the matter when I see the two boyars, later that evening.

I go back to the inn and, collecting Katerina, decide to make a tour of the town, ignoring the ragged mob who come out to stand and stare wherever we walk. I'm particularly interested to see where the town's merchants live, and we find them at the top of the hill, in a separate little enclave, tucked inside the outer palisade, beyond which is a stretch of cleared ground about a quarter of a mile wide before the forest begins again. They're good, well-built cabins, but not to be compared to those of Novgorod. These aside, there's really not much to see. Rzhev is a town of two, three thousand people, and an hour sees us back at the harbourside, where Lishka is still ensconced with Schelepin. I introduce him to Katerina, and he's at once in love with her – as a father with his daughter – and I decide there and then that if it doesn't pan out with the two merchants, then we'll abandon Rzhev, pick up the second cart and meet up somewhere on the river. Lishka will know a place, I'm sure.

The thought of it raises my spirits, even though the rain – which has held off these past three days – now returns with a vengeance, washing down the sloping streets of Rzhev in torrents, turning every path into a quagmire.

It is the ninth day of September, and the rainy season is now truly upon us. If we're lucky we will have five, maybe six weeks of this, but when the snows come . . .

I need to be in Tver' before then, ready for the snows; ready to make that last long push down to Moscow in the sled.

As evening falls, Katerina brushes out her hair, then looks to me. In the candlelight she looks magnificent. Like Russia itself, her beauty is ageless, timeless, and as her eyes smile back at me, I find myself wishing that I could take her back with me to Four-Oh, to be beside me every waking moment, to travel the width and breadth of time with me. Such marvels I would show her. Such astonishing things. But it is not to be. This here is all. And it would be enough, only I fear for her in this age of pestilence and banditry. I fear for her, and the child she carries in her belly.

Dmitri knocks at the door and tells us a man has come to lead the way, and so we set off through the back streets of Rzhev, lifting our booted feet high out of the squelching, oozing mud, Katerina picking up her skirts to stop them being spoiled.

Podnayin's house is much like Katerina's father's, only smaller and somewhat shabbier. Podnayin welcomes me and, once a serf has cleaned our boots, leads me inside, into a room that's set for a small feast. Kilik is there, and a man named Ilyushkin, but no women, and that surprises me, for I had assumed they would bring their wives to dinner, if only to provide company for Katerina. Yet they seem gracious enough, and when we have made a toast to friendship, servants bring food – fish and chicken and what tastes like venison, but turns out to be bear.

For a time the talk is light. They ask me about my travels, and my suspicion is confirmed: no one here in Rzhev has heard of my fight with Krylenko on the river. No one here thinks me a sorcerer, no one apart from Lishka, that is. But instinct warns me against becoming too close with any of these men. Ilyushkin, particularly, seems a shifty sort, and I catch him ogling Katerina more than once. Not that it's so surprising. I've not met a single woman on our travels to compare with her, and tonight she looks particularly splendid.

It's not that I feel uneasy with Ilyushkin, it's just that I find him unpleasant: a grasping man with indifferent manners. But then, that too is of this age. They belch and fart and throw their chewed bones down like animals. And Katerina – my darling Katerina – accepts that this is how most men must act.

It's about an hour into our meal that, noticing a slight sourness to the red wine we are drinking, I lean closer to Podnayin and tactfully mention it. At once he insists on tasting mine and, theatrically spitting it out, bids a serf bring a new bottle – 'the best wine' he says, and nods decisively.

Turning to me, he smiles and says, 'I bought some from a Turkish merchant a year ago now. I've been saving it for a special occasion such as this. If you would have the first cup, Otto?'

The others are watching me, smiling. Since I arrived I've been expecting them to come to the point and make their offer, only they seem in no hurry to do so. But then that too is very Russian, and no doubt they hope a drink or two and their good company will help them make a better deal in the end.

The serf brings the wine, corked in a flagon, and Podnayin pulls the cork and flamboyantly pours me a fresh goblet of it. It's good – surprisingly so for this age – and I take a long mouthful. Only . . .

I grip the table. It's like a wave has just washed over me. Or like a time-change, only . . .

My vision swims. The wine. The bloody wine.

I get up and stagger to the doorway, conscious of every eye on me. Katerina stands, concerned for me. 'Otto?'

'I'm fine,' I say, my voice seeming to echo in my own head. 'I've just got to pee.'

And make myself throw up. At once.

I stagger out into the warm darkness, then fall to my knees beside the midden. They've drugged me; I know it now. Forcing my fingers down my throat, I make myself vomit, but whatever this is, it's strong, and my head sways and pulses. It's in my blood, I can feel it. Not poison, no. Something subtler. And then, from behind me, I hear a crash and shouts and a single sharp shriek. I can hardly stand, let alone walk, but somehow I drag myself back there, each step a gargantuan effort, until I'm stood there, swaying in the doorway, looking on.

Katerina is on the far side of the room, her back to the wall, the three men surrounding her. One – Ilyushkin, is it? – is clutching his bloodied face while the other two snarl angrily and call her all manner of foul names.

I find it hard to focus, to see exactly what she's holding in her hand, but as Podnayin makes to grab her, I see something come up fast, a flash of silver, and he falls back, shrieking with pain.

And now it's like some stop-start film, as Katerina seems to lurch across the room and, grabbing my arm, turns me and drags me, step by limping step, from there.

That journey, back through the dark and rain-washed streets of Rzhev, is a nightmare. Katerina half leads, half carries me along, and more than once I stumble and we fall, sprawling and slipping in that awful slime, until – somehow – we are back at Dmitri's, Lishka – dragged from his carousing – staring down at me where I'm slumped against the wall, anger and fear in his eyes.

'We must go from here,' he says. 'Now!'

'Yes,' I slur. 'Go.'

Or that's what I try to say, only my tongue is too thick in my mouth and all that comes out is a kind of slurred moan, and anyway, Katerina won't go. She won't leave me. Not in this state.

And there's the small matter of her honour. It is no small thing in Russian law to insult a woman in the way they've insulted her and, though my head is in turmoil, I am very conscious of how angry she is. I have never seen her like this, seething, like a pot of water coming to the boil. I hate to think what she did to Podnayin and his friend.

Dmitri brings me a kind of gruel, and after a few spoonfuls I begin to retch again. But it's no good. Whatever drug they've given me is having a totally debilitating effect. It's not just that I can't think straight, I can't do anything. My legs feel like they belong to a mannequin, and even my hands, though I can clench and unclench them, seem to be a long, long way away from me, at the far end of a dark and telescoping tunnel of vision.

There is an answer, of course. I could jump. Back to Four-Oh. Back to safety and antidotes. Only what antidote will allow me to come back and rescue Katerina?

Besides, the room is full. Curious locals peer at me, pushing past each other to stand and stare at the drunken *Nemets*.

It gets worse. There's a fresh commotion at the door to the inn, and then soldiers – dressed raggedly, but armed, their short swords drawn – push their way into the room and their leader, a cold-eyed man with bright red hair, has them seize Katerina. Lishka makes to fight them, but they knock him down and, seizing him too, bind him tightly with ropes.

Katerina has gone very still. Though they hold her arms, she looks about her with contempt, her natural pride – her strength – triumphing over this setback.

'It's okay, Otto,' she says. 'I'll be all right. Just come for me.'

She knows I will. As soon as I get better; as soon as I can stand and walk and move my eyes without my head spinning. But in the meantime my heart breaks, seeing her led away. Seeing those savages tug the rope and almost pull her off her feet.

Rzhev. If I had my way I'd raze this fucking place to the ground.

192

I wake, and for a moment think I'm in my room in Four-Oh. There's such a silence, such a stillness. And then I hear a dog bark, and I sense the dampness of the floor beneath me and groan, remembering.

'Otto? Are you awake?'

I sit up slowly, resting my back against the cool, log wall, and try to peer through the gloom.

'Lishka?'

There's a vague, looming shape just in front of me, and then I feel a hand grip my shoulder.

'How are you?'

I stretch my neck and try to flex my toes. Everything seems normal. Working, anyway. 'I . . . think I'm all right.'

'The bastards want to see you. They've summoned a special meeting of the *veche*. It seems Ilyushkin has lost an eye. As for Podnayin—'

Lishka's sudden silence frightens me. 'What about Podnayin?'

Lishka sighs. 'He's dead. Katerina stabbed him through the heart.' He swallows. 'She says they tried to rape her. That as soon as you left the room they made their move. The little one, Kilik, grabbed her arms and pulled them behind her while the other two . . .'

'No!'

I don't want to know. I don't want those pictures in my head. But now I'm glad. Glad that Podnayin is dead, and that Ilyushkin has lost an eye. Only that means that Katerina is now in serious trouble.

I close my eyes, trying to think – trying to see a solution that doesn't involve telling Hecht everything.

'Well?' Lishka says. 'Are you ready?'

'Ready?'

'To face the *veche*. They want to see you now.'

'Ah . . .'

Lishka crouches. I feel his breath on my cheek as he whispers to me. 'Otto? Why don't you use your guns?'

193

To get through this – to do the very best I can for her – I must be hard of heart and pretend she matters less to me than she really does, for these men feed upon weakness, and if they were to know how much I love her, they would use that as a weapon against me.

I wait outside the gate to the compound as they search my pack.

'What's this?' one of them asks, pulling out the *staritskii*.

'It is a pepperpot,' I say. 'From far Cathay.'

The guard makes a face, then shoves the gun back down into the pack before handing it back to me. 'Go through,' he says gruffly. 'Master Talyzin awaits you.'

'Master Talyzin? But I thought—'

But the guard says nothing more, just gestures for me to cross the space between the gate and the council lodge.

Talyzin is alone inside. He sits at the far end of that huge table, drumming his fingers on the surface as I approach. His face is hard, unkind. He never much liked me, and it seems he likes me even less now that Podnayin is dead. His small, bird-like eyes spit malice at me as I stop and bow my head.

'We have a problem,' he says.

I say nothing. I want him to spell it out. But I'm also disappointed. I was expecting them all to be here, along with Katerina. Now I have no plan, if you could ever call shooting my way out of Rzhev a plan.

He speaks quietly, but his dislike of me colours every word. 'Were it a simple case of wounding we might come to an arrangement. But a man is dead. The law demands punishment.'

'They drugged me. Tried to rape my wife.'

'So you say.'

'You think she would attack them without provocation?'

'One would think it most unlikely. Only she did.'

'You take Ilyushkin's word?'

'Over hers? Yes. You, I understand, were drunk.'

'*Drugged.*'

'So you say.'

He interlaces his fingers, tries to stare me out. Only I'm angry now. Angry that liars and rapists should be believed before Katerina.

'So when is the *veche* to meet?' I ask.

'The *veche* has met. We have already decided.'

'You can't. You haven't heard what happened.'

'We've heard enough.'

'I wish to make a counter-claim. For *mestnichestvo*.'

The old man's eyes narrow angrily. *Mestnichestvo* is an insult to honour, yet unlike its commoner form – *beschest'e* – it refers only to society's elite. By claiming it, I am elevating Katerina beyond the status they have thus far given her as my wife.

'Ridiculous!' Talyzin says.

'Her father is an important man. A boyar and a member of the *veche* in Novgorod. When word gets to him of what has happened here . . .' I calm myself and say the words quietly but with great authority. 'I am certain he'll appeal to Prince Alexander himself.'

Talyzin answers me angrily, almost coming up out of his seat. 'It has been decided—'

'Then I appeal against that decision.'

Talyzin bangs the table with his fist. 'You wish to join her?'

I almost smile at that. 'Where is she?'

'In a safe place.'

'She is unharmed?'

'Meister Behr. I do not have to answer your questions.'

But I've had enough of talking. It's time to act. Pulling my pack from my back, I dump it on the table and reach in.

The *staritskii* feels good in my hand, and as I walk round the table towards Talyzin, I am aware of the trouble I am storing up for myself by doing this. *If* word gets out. *If* Talyzin or any of the others survive this.

I hold the gun out, aimed at his head, as if threatening him with a piece of branch.

'Take me to her.'

Talyzin laughs, then goes to get up and call for help.

'Sit down!' I say, quiet but threatening, and to make my point, I aim the weapon at the desk beside his hand and burn a neat round hole through the wood.

Talyzin's eyes bulge. The smell of burnt wood is overpowering.

'Okay,' I say, reaching out and grasping his to pull him up. 'The next one goes straight through your head unless you take me to her.'

194

I give Lishka the Kolbe and tell him not to squeeze the trigger unless he really wants to kill someone, then, thanking Dmitri, slip out into the darkness.

No one knows anything, yet. But it won't be long before they find them, and then . . .

Katerina follows me, stooping low as we run across the space between the back of Dmitri's inn and the palisade wall. She's discarded her skirt and is dressed in men's clothes. Lishka is last to come, wheezing a little, but happy now that we're going.

Ilyushkin is dead. Kilik I couldn't find, else he too would be dead, but the rest – including Talyzin – are bound and gagged. I would have killed Talyzin, too, only his villainy was of a lesser order. Besides, the thought of travelling on to Moscow with the death of Rzhev's *posadnik* attributable to me made little sense. We are in enough trouble as it is.

Lishka wants to go back to get the cart, but I persuade him against the idea. But even though we've freed Katerina and got some vengeance on the bastards, he's still unhappy that they've robbed us.

Note that *us*. For Lishka has definitely become family. He would die to defend our honour or stop us being cheated. Like a brother he is. That is, if all brothers were half-crazed maniacs.

Right now, however, getting away is the priority. We need an hour, maybe more, to make good our escape.

We follow the palisade until we're in the shadows, twenty feet from the gate. There's only a single guard on duty, and he's crouched beside a small fire, making soup. Seeing that, Lishka grins and moves past me silently, keen to despatch the man.

As he draws out the Kolbe from his belt, I find myself wanting to shout out to him, to tell him not to use the weapon, when I note that he's reversed it, to use as a club. The savagery of the blow makes me wince, but Katerina, beside me, is expressionless. After what she's been through, she wouldn't care if all the soldiery in Rzhev were burned alive.

We drag the body behind a hut, then slip outside, following the north course of the palisade, keeping close to it to avoid being seen. But as we're passing the northern compound, there's a whinnying sound and Lishka turns to me. 'It's little Nepka,' he whispers. 'We have to get her.'

Nepka is his horse. I'm about to say no, that we have to move on and how, anyway, are we to lift the horse over the fence, when he begins to climb the stout wooden barrier.

'*Lishka!*'

But it's no good. He's gone, and I hear him drop the other side and run off. A moment later he is back, the unmistakable sound of a horse's hooves accompanying his voice.

'Otto, help me breach this thing.'

I curse him, then, trying to get my fingers between two of the poles, try to heave it towards me. Only it's tightly wedged, and won't budge even a fraction. It would take us hours to loosen enough of these massive poles to make a gap.

Yes, but there is the staritskii.

It's mad, but it might just work. The forest, after all, is only two hundred yards away, to our north, and by the time they work out just what's happened and who's responsible, we'll be deep inside the trees.

'Lishka!' I hiss urgently. 'Stand well back!' And I draw the gun.

I count to ten, then aim at the bottom of one of the poles and squeeze the trigger. The result is a great flare of incandescence in the darkness and a thunderclap of sound. Lishka, vividly revealed through the sudden gap, is grinning in the brilliant light, one hand holding tight to Nepka's reins as she bucks, her eyes terrified.

I fire again, and then a third time, shattering the palisade, then turn to Katerina. She's looking on, no emotion in her face, but when I tell her to run towards the trees, she runs.

Behind the burning palisade, in the town itself, there are now shouts and screams and a fearful moaning. People are running about and staring at the gap in the palisade and at the burning timbers and are wondering what in God's name has happened. But we are busy running, Katerina, Lishka and I, and Nepka, who cannot get away from there fast enough.

It's two hours before we finally stop and make camp. I think we're lost, but Lishka says he'll know where we are when the morning comes, and anyway it doesn't matter because we'll hit the river at some point. And he's so pleased to have his horse, that I don't moan at him or tell him what a stupid thing he did back there.

And besides, we'll need a horse. To pull the cart.

While Lishka builds a fire, I take the tracker from my pack and activate it. For a moment I stare at it in disbelief, and then I turn to Katerina and laugh. 'It's here. We've walked straight to it.'

Lishka looks up, inquisitive. 'What's here?'

'Come. Come and see.'

I follow the tracker's signal until we're directly above it. We've walked barely thirty paces from where we stopped. When I turn to look, I can see our camp directly behind us, Nepka tethered to a tree.

Bending down, I begin to clear away the branch and leaf cover, until I've revealed what looks like a massive wooden door in the ground. Lishka stares at it amazed, then crosses himself.

Katerina, too, is puzzled.

I look to Lishka. 'Give me a hand.'

The cover is heavy, but between us we lift it and throw it back, to reveal the pit, and in the pit . . .

'God help us!' Lishka exclaims. 'What sorcery is this?'

In the pit is the copy cart, fully loaded, the sled tied on the back.

I grin, then reach down and press the switch to activate the platform. At once there's the noise of hydraulics and the cart begins to rise up towards the surface.

Lishka gives a little cry.

'It's okay, Lishka. This is friendly magic.' And I look to Katerina and see the hint of a smile on her lips – the first since we left Rzhev – and thank Urd that she's come to no great harm.

Lishka examines the cart in amazement, then turns to me again. 'But how . . .?'

Then he shrugs and, accepting it all in an instant, begins to laugh until his laughter fills the space between the trees.

'Oo-oh,' he says finally, wiping the tears from his eyes. 'I would love to see their faces when they find it missing. I would dearly love to see their faces . . .'

'I like it,' Katerina says, stroking the week's growth on my chin. 'It makes you look distinguished. And *very* Russian.'

I grin. 'That's the idea.'

But Lishka merely shrugs. We have been travelling ten days and seem to have made little progress. Tver' is still some distance and the weather is getting worse by the day. Autumn has come with a vengeance and already half the trees are bare, such that we trudge through great drifts of golden-brown leaves, and when it rains they seem to coat themselves to everything, adhering with a layer of mud for good measure on whatever surface is free.

Lishka, however, is happy with our progress. He's used to travelling at this snail's pace and chides me when I grow impatient. We will get there when we get there is his attitude.

Katerina, by now, is speaking German fluently. That is, what German she knows. Daily her small stock of phrases grows, and even Lishka now and then chimes in with something – proof that, for all he pretends not to, he is listening to every word we say.

'*Danke*,' he says, in answer to almost everything. '*Danke*.'

Not that it matters. I would trust Lishka with my life. Yes, even with Katerina, come to that. The only difficulty is the nights, for Katerina and I are noisy lovers, and poor Lishka has his own demons to contend with. But somehow we get through. Somehow it works.

We are making our way down a long slope, a low range of hills to our left, a river to the right. And as we go, so we sing, a little song I've taught them both, one I first learned in the Garden, long years ago – a fragment of Hölderlin's nature poem, 'Autumn', written some five hundred and thirty years in the future:

Das Glänzen der Natur ist höheres Erscheinen,
Wo sich der Tag mit vielen Freuden endet,
Es ist das Jahr, das sich mit Pracht vollendet,
Wo Fruchte sich mit frohem Glanz vereinen . . .

Lishka stops suddenly, the song faltering on his lips, and we fall silent too, listening, trying to make out what he's heard. And then we hear it too.

The sound of an axe, somewhere ahead of us, in the forest.

Lishka looks to me and after a moment I nod. It's been some while since we slept under a roof.

The village is typical of its kind, nestled in a large clearing amid the trees. The villagers move on every few years, using a method of farming known as slash and burn. They choose an area of the forest and cut deep into the bark of the trees and leave them to die, then – when they're dry – they burn them. The ash adds the necessary nutrients for two or three years' harvesting – and then they move on again, preparing a new site even as they farm out the old.

Their huts are in the centre of that huge, cleared space – crude, single-room affairs on low stilts to keep them off the damp ground – the nearby storage pits lined with birch and pine bark. As for the ground itself, they tend it with crude rakes they call *sokha*, and sickles and scythes, letting their animals – pigs, sheep, goats and poultry – graze and scavenge. They are a clan, a *miry*, sharing common pasture land and meadows, using traditional skills to get the best out of the short growing seasons and the grey, infertile soil. A way of life that has lasted a thousand years and more.

Lishka goes in first, arms raised, hands empty, hailing them heartily, a big smile on his face. They're suspicious of us, naturally, but once they see Katerina, they greet us cheerily, and children are sent out to the fields and work suspended for the day, the villagers milling about us and touching our clothes, anxious for any news from the outside world.

Lishka is happy to oblige, and, sat there by the cooking fire, a crude wooden cup of beer in one hand, he holds forth about the villainy of the world, and especially of townsfolk who, as these villagers know, are godless folk.

Not that we are among Christians here. No, these people are pagans to the core. They might wear the cross about their necks – for who knows when the Grand Prince's men might visit, demanding tribute – but they also wear other charms about their necks and wrists and ankles, tokens of the old gods.

That night we feast on a great hog specially slaughtered for the occasion. They bring out a massive cauldron, the village treasure, the outside black and greasy from long decades of use. As it all cooks, the villagers produce drums and pipes and one-stringed lutes and set up a fast, insistent rhythm, the tune hauntingly Russian. The villagers, young and old, dance and clap and whirl about and, after a while, Katerina and I join in, our bare feet pounding the earth about the roaring fire, reminding me of the evening at Velikie Luki at the beginning of our journey. But what I most remember of this evening is the faces of the villagers – such open, honest faces, all of their hopes and fears expressed in the folds and lines, in the sparkle of their innocent eyes.

Innocent, but not unknowing, for as the evening draws on and much wine and beer is drunk, so all inhibitions are discarded and, throwing off their clothes, the villagers rut indiscriminately, beyond God's judgement, beyond caring who might watch.

Katerina, tucked in to the hollow of my arm, looks on wide-eyed, and afterwards she asks if I wanted to join in with them, and I tell her no, that she is enough for me, that she is both *all* women and the only woman in my life, now and for ever. Not that there's any harm in what they're doing. Only, I am changed from what I was. *She* has changed me.

Morning comes grey and hazy, the mist like smoke blowing in through the silver boles of the birch trees. I stand there in that silence, the huts behind me, the forest in front, and think of all the places I have been, all of the things I've done and seen.

A bird calls and I turn, listening, feeling the faintest ripple down my spine. It's a haunting, timeless sound, the very voice of the forest, and as the sun slowly climbs the sky, burning off the mist, so the village slowly wakes, the villagers sore of head yet smiling, men and women grinning and nodding at me as they emerge, blinking, into the sunlight.

Good people. *Russians.* And it makes me ask myself: how can these people be my enemy? And yet they are. All my life they've been. To the death.

Only . . .

Only this morning I can't see it like that. This morning I am filled with the beauty of this place. Filled with a sense that, for all that I am German, I am in love with this land of theirs.

Katerina comes up behind me and puts her arms about me, and for a moment I close my eyes and surrender to the simple feel of her, there at my back, her hands on my chest. And, gently taking those hands, I turn and take her into my arms and kiss her.

'We must go.'

Her dark eyes meet mine. 'Must we?'

I nod. Oh, it's tempting to stay a day or two among these folk, but we really need to get to Tver'. For, unlike Lishka, I *know* when the first snows will fall.

When, after an hour, there's no sign of our friend, I go inside the hut and try to shake him awake, and when that doesn't work, fetch water in a bucket and throw it over him. He sits up, spluttering, ready to fight, then blearily sees it's me and laughs. 'Oh, it's you, Otto. Why didn't you wake me?'

I go back outside, to where Katerina and I have fed Nepka and checked the cart. Not that we really needed to, for the headman ensured that no one touched a thing of ours. I smile thinking of that, for the honesty of these villagers impresses me. We have encountered so many bad, deceitful people on our travels, that to be among trustworthy men and women is refreshing. And it makes me think that here, out in the wilds – out in the forest – is the real Russia, hidden away, like a secret kept from the world.

Finally, Lishka emerges and, watched by the whole village, strolls out and pisses against a tree, looking round at them and grinning while they laugh and clap their hands in delight. And I realise that we have brought a sense of holiday into their dour, hard lives, and that they will talk of us and our visit for months to come.

To live like this, to be so confined in time and space: again, I find it hard to fathom, hard to understand how curious, intelligent beings could survive this without going stark, raving mad. But so it is.

Children follow us deep into the forest, then trail off, hallo-ing to us as they depart.

And then we are alone again, the three of us and Nepka and the cart, making our way through the endless trees, trying to find a path, back-tracking when our way is blocked, and always – always – heading north.

196

The next four days are uneventful, one might almost say dull, except that being with Katerina is never dull. Nor Lishka, come to that. Lishka has a store of old tales, and needs little encouragement to tell them. Only sometimes the details seem, well, a touch *exaggerated*.

'With your own hands?' I ask, for a second time, and Lishka glances at me angrily, as if challenging his word were a request for a fight.

'Didn't I just say so?'

'Yes, but you said he was a big man. A mountain of a man.'

'So he was. But I was younger then. Quicker on my feet. And I had a few tricks.'

'Ah . . .' But I leave it there. Besides, it may be true. I've seen Lishka fight, and even at his age he's quite adept, not to say brutal, in his methods.

I'm about to ask him something else when we come out from under the branches and see, just ahead of us down a moss-covered slope, not a stream but a proper river, a broad, slow-flowing mass of grey-green water, almost up to the level of the grassy bank.

I look to Lishka. 'The Volga?'

He shakes his head. 'No, the Volga's that direction . . .' And he half turns and points back the way we've come. 'This is the T'ma. It flows into the Volga just west of Tver'.'

'Then we can follow it?'

Lishka nods, but he seems disturbed by something.

'Lishka?'

He looks to me and laughs. 'You know what? I was lost and didn't know it. I thought, well, I thought we were further south than this.'

'But we're okay now? We can follow the river to Tver'?'

'We can do that. Or we can get a boat. At Vysokoe. That is, if word hasn't gone ahead of what we did at Rzhev.'

But we don't reach Vysokoe by nightfall, and we're forced to make camp beneath the trees again, on a hill overlooking the river.

Lishka has been unusually quiet all afternoon, as if deep in thought, but now, after a supper of baked pigeon and mushrooms, he finally says what's been on his mind all day.

'Otto, we should build a raft.'

'A raft? But I thought . . .'

He looks down.

'What is it?'

'I think,' he says, not looking at me, 'that we may have gone past Vysokoe.'

'You mean it's back there somewhere? That we're upriver from it?'

He shrugs, which I take for a yes.

I consider the idea, then nod. 'Okay.'

Lishka too gives a single nod, but he's still not looking at me. 'Lishka?'

He glances up at me, then looks down again, agitated now. 'It's just . . .' He lets out a great sigh, then, placing his hands firmly on his knees, meets my eyes. 'I just thought, with your powers, that you might—'

'*Magic* us there? To Tver'?' And I laugh, and keep on laughing until the tears are streaming down. 'Oh, Lishka, if only you knew . . .'

'Then tell me,' he says, and there's a serious light in his eyes. 'Tell me exactly *who* you are, Otto Behr. For you're not from here, that I know.'

Katerina looks to me, then back at Lishka.

Lishka's face in the firelight is suddenly different. And for a moment – just for the briefest moment – I am tempted to let him into my secret. Only it's already enough that Katerina knows, and that kind of knowledge – that there's a world *outside* his mundane world, *framing it*, if you like – would not help Lishka. It would not help him to know that all journeys are not as straightforward as the one we are taking together and that to get to a place one need not toil for weeks through the primeval forest. What use would it be for him to know of alternate timelines and future wars, of no-space and ten-dimensional physics? Only, I need to tell him *something*.

And so I tell him a half-truth. I tell him that I am a servant of the World Tree, and then I tell him about Asgard and the gods, and of the great war in Heaven, and at the end of it Lishka, who has not stopped staring at me all the while, wide-eyed, simply nods, as if he finally understands.

'And these gods,' he asks. 'Are you one of them, Otto?'

Katerina, too, is watching me intently as I answer.

'No . . . I'm a mere mortal. Kill me and I die.'

Again, it's not entirely true, but it's not a lie. Not a total lie, anyway.

We rise early the next morning and begin to make our raft. And as we work, so Lishka asks me question after question – about the gods, and Asgard, and how I see the world. And I try to answer him as honestly and completely as I can, only now – in the daylight – I'm beginning to think that maybe it wasn't such a good idea. Not if Lishka is going to incorporate my stories into his own treasure-trove of tales. Then again, maybe that's how these myths start – as tales told by time travellers to their time-constrained companions. Maybe that's how everything works, every single innovation in the world. Maybe it's all one great complex time paradox. Only that, I guess, would be taking it too far.

It takes us the best part of the morning to make the raft, but by midday we've floated and tested it and, satisfied, have carefully loaded the cart, poor Nepka tethered securely to the raft. Water laps over the edges of the raft as we pole our way slowly down the river, keeping close to the left-hand bank, but we're perfectly seaworthy, and it's a good job, too, for about three or four miles downstream, the land closes in on either side, great slabs of rock forming a kind of canyon, while the river narrows and speeds up. For a while we cling on, struggling to keep the raft afloat as we rush down a series of small white-water falls, praying we don't hit one of the massive rocks that are jutting from midstream, or lose Nepka or the cart as we judder and tumble our way down through the churning waters. For a time it's touch and go; the waters buffet us cruelly, trying to tear at our hand-holds and smash the raft. There's a great thud as we collide with something and the raft lurches to one side, the cart jolting round and then holding . . .

And then, suddenly, it's behind us. The landscape opens up ahead, the river spreading itself like a fist slowly opening, the current slowing, until we've almost drifted to a halt. But neither Lishka nor I make any attempt to push on apace. For a while we simply sit there, slumped with relief. And then Lishka laughs and lifts a hand to the sky. '*Danke*,' he says. '*Danke*.'

And I look at him and grin.

197

It's two more days before we arrive at Tver', the old town sitting on a hill overlooking a turn in the river. It's much bigger than Rzhev, and far more important politically. Eight years from now, Sviatislav, Grand Prince of Vladimir, will place his nephew in the town as prince, but already it is an important military base. Major campaigns have been launched from here, and for the next two hundred years, its princes will vie with the princes of Muscovy – often in warfare – for control over northern Russia.

Indeed, had history turned out otherwise it would be better known than its eastern neighbour Moscow, only the tide of history passed Tver' by. Moscow – a mere trading post when Tver' was a town of three thousand citizens – has already become the greater power. Nor has it anything to do with geographical location. It has to do with men and their ambitions.

Let me explain.

In the official record, the first mention of Moscow is in 1147, some sixty-two years before there's any mention of Tver'. Only Tver' is a whole lot older than Moscow. Or was. You see, this is one of the big changes. As in BIG. Because Moscow *wasn't* the capital of Russia when this whole shooting show began. Moscow was only a provincial, backwater town, famous for nothing.

But Moscow was where the Russians built their command bunker, more than half a mile underground. Moscow was where the last remaining Russians were when it all went badly wrong. When the bombs fell. And Moscow was where they were when they first heard of Gehlen's wonderful machine. A machine that could travel through time.

Which is why they've defended it all these years, through Time and Space, and in doing so they have changed history, turned it into the history we know, with the Muscovite princes slowly taking over from their Kievan counterparts until, by the sixteenth century, they were unassailable. *Tsars.*

But it didn't begin that way. First time round it was Kiev that was the capital, and Tver' the second-largest northern town. After Novgorod, of course.

If you look at the old road maps from the twentieth and twenty-first centuries, Moscow looks like a giant spider, crouched at the centre of a web of great roads, every one of them leading in to the centre. Podol'sk, Odintsovo, Krasnogorsk, Himki, Mytisci, Noginsk, Balashiha, Elektrostal, Ljubertsy and Lytarino: these are the towns that circle Moscow like electrons at the heart of an atom, while a whole series of huge roads, thousands of kilometres long, spread out from the centre of that web like the spider's silken strands, across to Kazan in the east, to Volgograd and Donets'k in the far south, and to Minsk and Riga in the west.

So it is with BIG changes. They impose a whole new pattern on the map. They refocus everything and make it seem so normal, so *natural*, that it's hard to believe it could have happened any other way. And yet it did.

And there's a lesson there. That there's nothing natural when it comes to the works of men.

Lishka, of course, knows nothing of this. He knows only what he's seen and experienced. The idea of reality being anything other than it is would never occur to him, nor to anyone in this age, for their belief in a rigidly preordained order to things, their fatalism, as I'd term it, is ingrained. They have no idea how *elastic* reality is, just how many ways it can be changed, and to what startling effects.

We secure our raft on the beach to the north of the harbour, then sit and wait, and sure enough, within minutes, a small group of 'officials' make their way down the steps and come across to us. Yet if I'm expecting a reprise of what happened at Rzhev, I'm wrong, for when their harbourmaster sees the *tysiatskii*'s pass, he is immediately as helpful and courteous as he can be, treating all three of us like honoured guests. He arranges for our cart to be brought ashore and safely stored, while we are led off to meet the *posadnik* himself.

I like this harbourmaster immensely. He's a young and clearly vigorous man and you can see he will go far. That is, if he makes no enemies, and keeps in with the right friends. For even good men can go wrong in these times. Yes, and not just in these times. It is the way of the world that, without patronage or luck, a good man often finds himself the victim of others, less able yet less scrupulous.

While we're waiting for the *posadnik*, I ask him his name and he tells me that it's Saratov – Sergei Ilya Saratov. Of course, he's smitten with Katerina, and though he tries hard not to stare, the slight colour in his cheeks betrays him. Seeing my amused smile, he gives an embarrassed nod and then leaves us, but he's back in an instant, the *posadnik* in tow.

In appearance, the *posadnik* could quite easily be the twin of the scoundrel, Talyzin, whom we encountered in Rzhev, only they're as different in their natures as chalk and cheese. Old he might be, and long of beard, but he's a gay, humorous fellow and, after a cup or two of wine, we feel like long-lost relatives.

Which is a great relief. For here we must stay now, until the snows come.

The *posadnik*'s name is Belikof, and it seems he travelled much in his youth, though never as far as Novgorod. In fact, he's such a nice old fellow that I begin to wonder how he ever came to power or managed to keep it once he'd gained it, but then his sons appear – six strapping lads, each one of them a good two or three times his size – and I begin to understand.

Two hours pass and then the harbourmaster, Saratov – though he begs us to call him Sergei – reappears to inform us that our rooms are ready. Belikof comes over to me and hugs me like I'm another of his sons – which I well could be, for they're each as tall as me – and asks us to return later on; that there's to be a feast of welcoming, to celebrate the beginning of a new friendship with our 'cousins from Novgorod'.

Walking back through the narrow, log-lined alleyways of Tver', I ask Sergei if Belikof has been *posadnik* long, and he glances at me then shakes his head. 'Only this last year. Before then . . .'

I seek to draw him about the circumstances, but all he will say is 'Not here. Not now.' As if someone might overhear him in the street. Which intrigues me, because I had begun to think that Tver' was a happy place. Only there seem to be undercurrents.

Our lodgings are simple but clean. The dirt floor of the room has been swept and new rush mats thrown over it. What's more, there are linen blankets filled with duck down – an unexpected luxury – which Sergei tells me are an 'eastern touch'.

Katerina is delighted, though Lishka – dour Lishka, who would rather spend a week on the forest floor than ten minutes in the comfort of a proper bed – moans that he'll never get a proper night's sleep.

Leaving Katerina to sort herself out, Lishka and I go with Sergei to inspect the cart.

As at Rzhev, they've placed it in the town compound, but here, I note, the guards are simply guards – not the surly, overbearing thugs of Rzhev. Belikof runs a tidy ship, so to speak, and I comment on the fact, only to have Sergei glance warningly at me again.

Alone inside the rough shed where the cart is, I stand close to Sergei and, in a quiet voice, ask him what's going on.

He whispers back. 'Belikof is on top, for now. He won the last vote in the *veche*. Only—'

But he doesn't finish. At that moment the captain of the guards arrives and, without any niceties, asks Sergei what the fuck he's doing there without his permission.

I've seen this kind of horn-locking often, and know well enough to keep out of it. The two young men clearly dislike each other intensely; maybe there's a woman behind it. Even so, the sheer rudeness, the unnecessary nastiness of the captain surprises me.

We leave, Sergei fuming but apologetic, to us, anyway. Back at our lodgings he makes to go, but I reach out and hold his arm.

'Sergei, what's happening here?'

He turns and meets my eyes, and I realise, for the first time, that they're a deep blue, not brown or green like most of the people here. 'Not now, Otto. They're watching us.'

'They?'

He nods, but when I press him he won't say any more, only that his duties call him. And for the first time on this journey I ache to jump right out of there and then jump back, at night maybe, and have a poke about for myself to find out what's going on. But I can't, and it feels like I've got one hand – maybe even both – tied behind my back.

When he's gone, I turn to Lishka and Katerina and, speaking quietly, tell them to be careful, and not to say too much about our business, not until we've a much clearer idea what the situation is. Then, leaving them a moment, I step outside and look around, and sure enough, there's a pair of men standing idly across the alleyway, watching our inn, though when I stare at them, they look away and begin to talk, as if it's mere chance that they're there.

But that tells me something. Tver' is not the happy town it first appeared to be. There are stresses here, rivalries. And it doesn't take much to guess that the greatest source of rivalry would be over who should be *posadnik*.

It also makes sense of the welcome we received, for what better opportunity could there be than for the *posadnik* to be able to claim the friendship – yes, and a 'trading agreement' – with Novgorod? If he's desperate for support – for votes in the *veche*, which, I guess, is the bottom line – then we're a god-given, golden opportunity, for there's nothing the boyars value more than the chance to make money.

Only I sense that that isn't all. That there's something else.

One of Belikof's sons comes for us just before nightfall. He's not alone, either. As we step outside, I note that he has a dozen or so peasants, armed with staves, with him. That, too, sends alarm bells ringing.

Even so, the evening is a pleasant one, and the earlier tensions don't show themselves. In fact, the atmosphere is so carefree that

I begin to wonder if I've misread what was going on, only that doesn't account for Sergei's behaviour, and, because he wasn't at the celebratory feast, there's no way I can speak to him again.

Which makes me determined to do just that.

Back at our lodgings, I wait for Katerina and Lishka to fall asleep, then slip out quietly and make my way down to the harbour.

I'm good at this, at *skulking*, only the moon is bright, almost full, and for once I'm aware of just how crucial it is not to be seen. I've no real plan, of course, other than to try to locate Sergei. I'm not even sure that he lives close by; only he *is* a young man and, it seems, unattached, and as he wasn't at the feast, I'd guess that he isn't a wealthy man, so he won't own one of the big houses up at the crest of the hill. Only how do you find where a man lives in a strange town in the early hours of the morning?

Luck is the answer. For he's there, sitting out on the wooden jetty, his legs dangling over the side, looking out across the slow-moving river.

I walk out on to the jetty and stop. Sergei half turns and looks up at me, then smiles, almost as if he's been expecting me.

'Otto,' he says quietly. 'Would you like to go upriver?'

198

As we drift in to the right-hand bank, Sergei ships the oars and jumps ashore, using the boat's momentum to haul it up the tiny beach. The Volga is almost a quarter of a mile wide at this point, cutting through the landscape like a dark, star-filled wound, but in seconds there's no sign of it as I follow Sergei, who has plunged into the trees and up a slowly rising path.

Moonlight filters down through the tall birches, giving everything a stark black-and-white appearance. Emerging from the dense foliage at the top, we step out on to a massive ledge of rock that gleams like a thick, smooth piece of bone beneath the blue-black, star-spattered sky.

And there, on the far side of the ledge, is a hut.

Sergei turns to me and smiles. 'Sanctuary,' he says. And the way he says it seems strange, momentous somehow, and my inner antennae twitch.

Only I don't know why.

And there, inside, the door pulled tightly shut behind me, I stare, astonished, as, switching on the electric lights, Sergei stoops down and, opening the refrigerator door, offers me a beer.

There's a big, black, fluid-looking plasbox in the corner and a floatcouch in front of it, while on the wall . . .

I look to Sergei. He's grinning now.

'Relax,' he says. 'We're safe here. There are tripwires on the path. Invisible. Laser-operated. If anyone tries to come up here they'll be fried.'

My stomach is a tight ball of fear. 'Who *are* you?'

Sergei holds out the beer to me. A Schmackhaft, I note, from the Weissenfels brewery. A twenty-fifth-century beer, and my favourite.

'An agent,' he says. 'Like you.'

'Yes, but for *who*?'

'Don't worry. I'm on your side. I was put here. To help you.'

My head swims. Hecht doesn't know. He *couldn't* know. Could he?

I take a step back mentally and try to sort through the jumble of facts that are in my head, for that's how we do it, we agents. We're supposed to be flexible, to be capable of making instant judgements from limited information.

The best of us, that is. The rest panic.

Oh, I don't panic. Only this once I'm at a loss.

Instinct, then. I like him. He *says* he's on my side. And he *must* be an agent, else why the fridge, the plasbox, the floatcouch?

'Why don't I know you? I know *all* our agents.'

'Because I'm from the future.'

The words chill me. So this is the second time round. All of this. Every moment with Katerina. Or is that so? Maybe it only became so the moment I met him.

'What's your *real* name?'

Sergei laughs. 'That's unimportant. What you need now is what I know. Without it . . .'

'Without it *what?*'

'Without it you die. You and Katerina.'

I take the beer from him and pull the tab, then take a swig. It tastes wonderful. *Wonderful.*

'Okay,' I say. 'Then brief me.'

And so we begin. The strangest evening of a strange life.

Back in Tver', I embrace Sergei, then, conscious that dawn is only moments away, hurry back to the inn.

Katerina wakes as I enter and, sensing the night's coldness on me, asks me sleepily where I've been.

'Upriver,' I say, and feel the sheer weight of the words I've uttered. 'I've been upriver.'

199

Knowing what's to come sometimes makes it harder.

Sometimes.

Because nothing is foreordained. Nothing is certain.

Sergei is confident, but I've a doubt or two. I'm not so sure that the Russians will let us get away with this.

For Sergei it's second time round. For the Russians it could be third or fourth or fifth, for that's the nature of things.

At best I know now for certain that my actions on the river – the anachronism of me drawing the needle-gun and firing it – has set off all kinds of reverberations in time.

At worst, I am outside it all. Impotent to change a single thing.

There's to be a meeting of the *veche* at noon, at which the boyars are to decide the very future of Russia.

Of Russia, yes, not just of Tver'. For, contrary to our earlier analysis, it begins here, *right here*. Not in Moscow, nor Berlin; not with Peter, nor with Frederick – nor Hitler, come to that – but with Belikof.

Poor bloody Belikof.

Because he's going to die tonight. He and his sons.

My head swims, thinking about what Sergei told me.

It's simple and yet complex. Vast forces are at work here – the Horde, the Kievan princes – yet everything depends upon this single town, this single time, for in one timeline, the refusal of the Tver' *veche* to cooperate with the Horde will set off a chain of events that will stretch the Mongols' fragile supply lines and snap them. An unexpected weakness in their organisational structure – allied to other factors – will result in a sudden internecine struggle and the abandonment of the West. Specifically, of Kievan Rus'.

A single vote will end the Mongol incursion. Will collapse it like a pack of flimsy cards and free Russia from Mongol control for the next two hundred and forty years.

If today's events run true.

Which is why I'm scared, Because, in my experience, nothing *ever* goes to form.

'Otto?'

'Yes, my love?'

'Why are you so tense?'

'Am I?'

She looks down, smiling.

'I'm sorry,' I say, 'only . . .'

'Only what?'

Lishka is sleeping. Or seems to be. Dare I risk it?

'Only . . . last night I went upriver.'

'Upriver?'

'With Saratov. He's an agent.'

She stares at me. 'What?'

'Sergei. He's a time agent. One of ours.'

'Then . . . Hecht knows.'

'I don't know. He's from the far future.'

'How far?'

I shrug. The truth is, I didn't ask. And that's not like me. I guess it was the sheer unexpectedness of it that threw me.

'He says Hecht died before he was born.'

She nods, but I can see how hard it is for her to take this in. Her imagination doesn't work like ours. We've logic circuits in our brains that allow us to think in Time. But she . . .

'Belikof is going to die,' I say. 'And we can't stop it. He and his sons. But it's for the good.'

She frowns. 'Belikof is a good man, Otto. How *can* it be for the good?'

'It can. Trust me.'

'Sergei told you this?'

'Yes.'

'And you trust him?'

'Yes. Don't you?'

'I'm not sure.'

That pulls me up sharp. In all those hours I was with him, I didn't think to question him. Not at gut-instinct level, anyway.

But I trust Katerina's instincts better than my own, maybe *because* she's outside the loop.

'So what should I do?'

'I think you should see Hecht,' she says. 'I think you should tell him about me.'

200

Only I don't. Not yet.

Just as Sergei said it would, the summons comes late morning, and at noon I find myself entering the great house at the very top of the town, where, behind closed doors, the *veche* are in session.

Sergei's briefing was very detailed, yet looking about me I see no sign of him and wonder for the first time just how he came to know so much about events. Even so, it follows what he said almost to the letter.

The boyars want to know how things are in Novgorod, and what their boyars are offering in trade.

I look to Belikof before answering, and note how he's looking down and smiling, clearly the instigator of the enquiry.

I am prepared, of course, and, turning, snap my fingers. At once Lishka steps forward and throws samples of our goods – furs, jewellery, and cleverly painted wooden icons – down on to the surface of the council table. All around the table the boyars stand, craning to see, and the items are passed around and examined, even sniffed, before things settle.

'I was heading for Moscow,' I say, 'but if we can strike a deal with Tver', well, all the better!'

'And your prices?' Belikof asks, his shrewd eyes fixing on me.

I give them the figures Ernst and I worked out, and from the surprised whispers around the table, I know they're interested.

Belikof grins. 'I ought to haggle. To tell you that you're robbing us. Only, both you and I know how things stand. Your prices are most reasonable, *Nemets*. I only wonder how you manage to keep them so low.'

It's time to drop my bombshell.

'Because I can afford to. Because . . . Novgorod has decided not to pay the *tamga*.'

There's a collective intake of breath. Belikof stares at me aghast. 'They've *what*?'

'I'm surprised you hadn't heard. The *veche* voted to throw out the Khan's *baskaki* and they did so. He was bound hand and foot, then carried to a boat, and shipped back to his masters.'

There's a great tumult around the table at this news. As it dies down, Belikof leans towards me. His eyes are burning now.

'No word of this has come to us. And Prince Alexander, does he know?'

'Not yet. At least, not as far as I know.'

Belikof looks about him. As he does, so a number of boyars rise and go to him, leaning in to exchange quiet, hurried words, while elsewhere about the table a dozen or more conversations go on.

It's all a lie, of course. But if what Sergei said was true, it could – and should – prove the trigger to events. For these boyars hate the thought of giving a single piece of their hard-earned silver to the *baskaki*. For them the *tamgar* is one imposition too many and the majority of them can't understand why the princes haven't joined together to rid Kievan Rus' of the hated Mongols.

So news of this kind from Novgorod is incendiary.

'Remember,' one says loudly, over the hubbub, 'they burned Kiev. Left not a single building standing.'

'True,' another counters, 'but Kiev is far to the south and much closer to the steppes. They would not *dare* bring their army this far north. Not with winter coming. Besides, without our tribute, how do they clothe and feed their men?'

It's not true. The Mongols *would* dare. In fact, they do most of their fighting in the winter months when frozen rivers make it easy for their horses to cross the terrain.

But there's a lot of sympathy for that view. Heads nod and beards wag. I have only now to push it one stage further. Yet even as I make to speak again – just as Sergei said he would – Belikof's chief rival in the *veche*, Alexander Yakovlev, makes a great show of getting to his feet.

The whole room falls silent.

I nod to him, giving way before him.

'Meister Behr,' he begins, smiling at me, his voice heavy with a fake reasonableness, 'is it true that you killed two men in Rzhev?'

I stare at him, astonished. This isn't in the script. This isn't what Sergei said would happen. I think on my feet and answer with a confidence I don't feel.

'*Killed*? What nonsense is this? You think I would dare show my face in Tver' if it were so?'

Yakovlev stares at me coldly. 'A certain kind of man would.'

The words are a challenge. They impugn me. Now I must fight him or admit to being a criminal.

Sergei has let me down badly. What's more, I'm totally unarmed. If they wanted, they could seize me and chain me and there would be little I could do about it, not against this number of them.

Only Belikof isn't having any of it. He stands, glaring across at Yakovlev. 'Have you any evidence to support your accusation?'

Yakovlev nods. 'Word came from Rzhev four days back. Of this *Nemets* and his woman. It seems, between them, they killed two of Rzhev's leading citizens – Ilyushkin and Podnayin. What's more, they committed violence against the person of the *posadnik* himself, Talyzin.'

Belikof slumps down in his chair, the wind taken from his sails. He looks to me. 'Meister Behr, what have you to say?'

I decide that honesty would serve me best.

'Okay. I killed them. But there was good reason. They invited me to Podnayin's house, along with my wife, Katerina, and there they drugged me and tried to rape her – the daughter of a senior boyar in Novgorod. Talyzin had Katerina arrested and refused to hear my side of things. He sentenced my wife in my absence.'

'So you claim that your actions were rightful vengeance.'

'I do. And if there is a fine to be paid, I'll gladly pay it. Only Rzhev is a corrupt place and the prince's justice did not prevail. I denied the charge because I did not want us to fall into their hands again. Why, they even charged me for a new pass, even though I held the *tysiatskii*'s visa, paid for in good silver.'

There's a long pause while a murmur of discussion passes back and forth about the table. Then Belikof stands.

'Forgive me, Meister Behr, but I am left with no option. You must submit yourself to trial. You and your wife. But be assured. You will be heard. And here, not in Rzhev, if that allays your fears. But we must send to Rzhev for witnesses, and that might take some time.'

I bow my head submissively. 'I understand, and thank the *veche* for the chance to clear my name.'

But when I look up again I see how Yakovlev is glaring at me, furious, and know it is far from over.

We are escorted back to our inn and a guard is posted. And there we wait, until gone dark. It's only then that Sergei appears, looking a little sheepish.

I stand, confronting him. 'What went wrong?'

'Things are different,' he says. 'That business with Yakovlev and the news from Rzhev. That didn't happen last time.'

'It's the Russians,' I say. 'The Russians have changed it.'

But Sergei laughs at that. 'The Russians? We *are* the Russians.'

I sit there for a long time after he's gone, shocked, not understanding. Is Sergei a member of a rebel faction, split off from Yastryeb? Or . . .?

Or what? Because I can't explain it. Can't understand why a bunch of Russians are helping me, unless they're renegades.

All I know for sure is that something's happened up the line. Some twist that has thrown itself back in time. As it must, eventually, because here in this strange dimension nothing ever stays the same for long.

I tell Katerina, but she's as much at a loss as me.

'What will happen?' she asks.

'They'll keep us here,' I say, 'under guard until they can bring witnesses from Rzhev. Then we'll appear before them and state our case.'

'And then?'

I look away. I don't know, and I hate not knowing. I hate not being in control, especially when it places Katerina's life at risk.

As this does. For short of jumping out of here, there's really fuck all I can do about the situation. My guns are in the cart, which is in their compound. To get to it I would have to fight my way halfway across town.

Which might even work, only more than likely it wouldn't.

I slump down, placing my head in my hands, trying to think, to come up with an answer.

'I think you should see Hecht.'

Katerina's words echo in my head. It's crazy, sure, but so is this whole situation, and it's getting worse by the day.

Only . . . before I can do anything, I hear, distant yet unmistakable, shouts and cries, and then the screams. Awful screams. And then, equally distinctive, the strong, pungent scent of woodsmoke.

Going to the window, I see, at the top of the town, a flickering glow in the sky, growing brighter by the moment. Great clouds of smoke are billowing up into the moonlit sky, and I know, without being told, what it is.

So Sergei was right.

News comes an hour later. Belikof is dead, and all his sons and their wives and children. The whole clan gone. We overhear the guards talking and learn that many of them were cut down in the streets, naked, running from the flames, by Yakovlev's men, and I wonder if they'll come for us next. It seems the logical thing to do. Only no one comes, and soon the town falls quiet again, with only the awful burning smell in the air to remind us of what's happened.

It puzzles me why they didn't come and finish the job, but it's not until the morning that we find out why. Yakovlev was drunk, celebrating his success. And we were overlooked. But now, as dawn breaks, he sends for us, and Katerina, Lishka and I are taken to him, hands bound behind our backs, up the hill and into the hall where, only yesterday, we were honoured guests.

Yakovlev, seated in Belikof's chair, looks to have the mother of all hangovers. Even so, he's in control, and makes us stand there waiting, while he gives orders to this minion and that. Finally he looks up at me and, coldly, his eyes like ice, asks me what I think he ought to do with me.

'Try me,' I answer. 'Just as Belikof was going to. Let the *veche* decide.'

For a moment I think he's going to say no. But then he gives the smallest nod, and I note, as he stands and walks away, that he's smiling.

And why not? For he thinks he controls the *veche* now. And why take the further risk of being blamed for our deaths when the *veche* could legitimise them?

We are taken back, the guard doubled. No doubt they've heard what we did at Rzhev, so no chances are being taken. Only Sergei is allowed to visit us, and I wonder at that, at why Yakovlev would allow it.

Sergei has news. The witnesses from Rzhev are already here. They arrived last night, even as Belikof's house was going up in flames.

'And what of that?' I ask. 'Are the other boyars just going to let him get away with it?'

Sergei laughs. 'They've been expecting it. Ever since Belikof insulted Yakovlev openly in council. It seems he called Yakovlev "the Great Khan's dog . . . nestling at his feet."'

'Even so . . .'

'They are proud men.'

'And violent, too.'

'Of course.' Sergei grins, but then the grin fades and he lowers his voice. 'But listen. I have a plan . . .'

202

Plans. What are plans except vague hopes? Walls of sand built against the incoming tide of chance?

Even so, Sergei's is a beauty, even if he is a Russian.

I ask him about that, but he evades my questions, telling me that there will be time to explain everything once we are safe.

When Sergei's gone, I discuss the matter with Katerina, and we decide to trust Sergei, only I'm not as sure as she is. I have begun to wonder if this isn't an elaborate trap, a ploy to get me cornered in a cul-de-sac of time, and then snip me off – *time-dead* – and no way back.

So, when we are brought before the *veche* once again, I am not surprised to find Sergei among a small group of men I've not seen until that moment. Russians, by their beards and manner. But are they agents, too?

It turns out that they aren't. In fact, they're citizens of Rzhev, brought here by Sergei in anticipation of such a trial as this. Men who will speak up for us.

Which means he's gone back in time and made an alteration. There's no other explanation, because two days ago he didn't know that Yakovlev would bring his witnesses.

The trial begins with Yakovlev making an empty speech about justice. He invokes the *Russkaia Pravda* – 'Iaroslav's code', the written law of the land – and calls upon the *veche* to administer it 'without prejudice or fear'. But everyone knows what a lie that is, and that certain members of the *veche* will not oppose him if he finds us guilty. That doesn't mean that we've lost before we've begun, nor – even if we lose – that our lives will be forfeit. Article one of the code stipulates the financial penalties for homicide, and Yakovlev has little option but to abide by those. Only I have a feeling that Yakovlev doesn't plan to keep us alive that long. He's hoping we'll try and make our escape, as we did from Rzhev, and then . . .

Well, you see it, as clearly as I. As long as we behave ourselves and go along with the mockery of this trial, we'll survive. There's only one difficulty: Katerina.

Katerina wants to fight their accusations. She wants no blemish against our names, which, of course, there will be if we let this go. She claims – and rightly – that those men deserved to die for their villainy and for their attempt to dishonour her. Such men, she says, deserve nothing better than a knife in the heart, and the world's a cleaner place without them. And I don't disagree. Only there's no possibility – not with Belikof dead – of us getting such a decision.

So my problem is keeping her quiet. Stopping her from venting her anger against the *veche*.

Lishka has been silent these past few days, like he's afraid to say what's clearly bottled up inside him. But I'm not fooled by his silence. Like Katerina, he is furious that we are standing trial, while the real villains are sitting there, waiting to pass judgement.

But there's still Sergei's plan, and if it works . . .

We stand before them for the best part of three hours, listening to our accusers speak. And Katerina – pregnant and weary from it – bears it all without a murmur. But when it's over her pallor makes me ask the captain of the guards whether she might not be seated for the afternoon session. He goes away and returns to say that Yakovlev has refused our request.

That infuriates me so much that before the 'great man' can open the second session of the hearing, I interrupt him and angrily ask for his explanation.

'My explanation?'

'For making the daughter of a boyar stand. Would you dishonour your own daughters so? *Any* of you?'

And I turn in a half circle, making my appeal to them all, hoping that they'll be shamed into overruling Yakovlev. Some look down, some look to Yakovlev, but I have misjudged the mood of the assembly. After Yakovlev's strike on Belikof it appears that none of them wish to take him on. He's master here now. I look back at him and see how much colder he's become. He wants to crush me. To humiliate and destroy me. But we'll see about that.

I stare him out. 'The prince will hear of this. Make no mistake.'

Yakovlev laughs at that. 'You think Prince Alexander has time to speak to mere *traders*?'

But I'm not to be belittled that easily. 'I'm sorry. I forgot, Master Yakovlev. You have a money tree, rooted in the shit of your midden. You have no need to be besmirched by *mere trade*.'

At another time I think that might have brought a laugh. Looking about me, I see how several of the *veche* have their heads down, so as not to reveal their smiles. But Yakovlev is almost apoplectic. Spittle sprays from his lips as he stands and yells back at me. 'You will not show me such contempt! It is *you* who are on trial, not me!'

'No? You think yourself *above* Iaroslav's code?'

It's not a wise thing to say with your hands bound behind your back, but I can't help myself.

He comes round the table and, standing before me, makes to slap my face, only Lishka intercedes, ducking in and head-butting the man full in the face, the crack of Yakovlev's nose audible in the sudden silence.

And then there's uproar.

203

I come to, my vision blurred, such a pain in my head that I wonder if my skull is still in one piece. It's dark but for a thin sliver of moonlight that slips in through the narrow crack between the door and the frame.

I sit up slowly, groaning, the blood pounding in my head, the pain almost blacking me out again. For a moment I just sit there, my hands tenderly exploring my skull, feeling the bumps, the clotted blood. Someone gave me a good beating, it seems, but I'm still alive, and I find that fact amazing after what Lishka did.

'Lishka?'

My voice is cracked and frail in that dark silence.

'Katerina?'

But there's no answer. It seems I am alone.

I rest for a time, then, moving warily, begin to explore that tiny space.

Nothing. No sign of either of them.

I move back, a few inches at a time, until I'm propped up against the log wall of the hut.

And go very still, listening.

The river. I can hear the river flowing past outside. Only somehow it's different.

For a while I sleep. When I come to again the door is open, the cool night air flooding into the room. For a moment I see only the pale night sky, but then a figure steps into the doorway.

'Otto? Are you okay?'

It's Sergei, and for the briefest moment I feel like crying with relief, only where is Katerina? And, for that matter, where is Lishka? But I can't speak. I can only sit there, staring back at him.

'It's okay,' he says, crouching before me, his eyes taking in the injuries to my head. 'You're safe now.' Gingerly he touches my scalp. I flinch and he takes his hand away. 'You'll be okay. We'll patch you up. Make you good as new.'

'Katerina?' I ask.

'I don't know,' he says. 'Yaklovlev took her. But where she is . . .'

I close my eyes briefly, a separate, different pain flooding through me.

'And Lishka?'

'Lishka's dead.'

The news shocks me. I know it shouldn't, but it does. Somehow I'd begun to think of Lishka as immortal, but he head-butted the wrong man in Yakovlev. Some men, it seems, are unforgiving.

I put my left hand to my face to wipe away the tears, then look back at Sergei.

'I've a medpac,' he says quietly. 'You're not allergic to any of the standard drugs, are you?'

I shake my head. What they use we use, and vice versa. It's one of those things that happens when you fight someone for any length of time. Your technologies converge. You learn from each other and adapt. *Enhanced evolution*, Hecht calls it.

Sergei goes outside and comes back moments later with a box not so different from my own. He takes several vials from it and fits them into an injector, then, tearing my shirt from my arm, injects me with a couple of standard cure-fast mixtures, as well as an anti-shock booster.

It's only minutes before I feel the pain begin to subside and a kind of woozy pleasant feeling take its place. Pleasant, I say, only it's hardly nice to feel my anxiety for Katerina dissolve along with the chemicals in my blood. She deserves better than that.

I find words. 'Was she . . . unharmed?'

'Katerina?'

'Yes.'

'I think so. It all got rather manic. Getting you out was my priority. Yakovlev would have killed you.'

I should have jumped. I should have got out of here the first moment I could.

And then what?

'We have to find her.' But the drugs rob the words of the urgency they ought to have. I feel warm and drowsy. And safe . . .

I sleep. Sergei shakes me awake some hours later. It's light, the call of birds, the nearby rush of the water downriver filling the silence.

'How do you feel?' he asks, smiling at me.

'Okay,' I say, sitting up, feeling renewed, the pain gone from my head, the drowsiness washed out of me. And then I remember.

'Where would he have taken her?'

'Dolrugy, maybe.'

'Dolrugy?'

'It's a village, north-west of Tver'. It's Yakovlev's estate.'

'Ah . . . so she'll be there?'

Sergei shrugs. He doesn't know. Which means all of this is new. A departure from what happened before.

'What happened to your plan?' I ask.

'We can still use it, if needs be.'

Only the whole situation has changed. Lishka is dead and Katerina taken. And I don't know what I'll do if Yakovlev has harmed her.

No . . . I daren't even think of it. Of what he might have done in the night. To gain vengeance. To humiliate me.

Only I know now – without a doubt – that I will kill him. He's had his chance and failed. Now it's my turn.

I get to my feet. My head's fine, my legs sound. If anything, I feel energised. Only I know that that's only the drugs, and that, in reality, I'm still weak and overdoing it could prove harmful.

I need a day, at least, to recover. Only I haven't got a day. I need to rescue Katerina now.

I have one advantage: Yakovlev won't be expecting me to come calling, not after the beating I received.

'Are you on your own?' I ask Sergei. 'Or are there other agents?'

'It's just me,' he says, and laughs. But I can see that something's worrying him.

'What is it?'

'Nothing,' he answers, avoiding my eyes. 'Are you up to travelling?'

'I think so.'

'Then let's go at once. Unless—'

'No. No, let's go. Let's give Master Yakovlev a visit.'

204

We cross the river then go north, skirting Tver', travelling quickly but carefully, conscious that there's a hue and cry out for us. It takes four hours, but finally we're there, among the trees, looking across at Yakovlev's *dacha*, crude as it is. There's lots of movement, people hurrying to and fro, but no sign of Yakovlev himself, nor of Katerina. But I know she's there. Word from Sergei's contacts in Tver' have confirmed it for us.

Just be alive, I say silently, sending up a prayer to Urd herself. *Don't be dead. Please don't be dead.*

Beside me, Sergei stiffens, then makes a small sound in his throat. As I look at him, he points, and I see it, wondering why I didn't notice it before.

Lishka, hanging by a rope from a tree, his neck snapped, his body swaying gently, senselessly, in the mild afternoon breeze.

I groan and sink to my knees. The bastard. If I had reason to kill him before, I have added reason now.

'Here,' Sergei says, and hands me a gun – a *spica*.

I stare at it, amazed. But why? He's a time traveller. He can get such things, even if I can't. Even so, it's unexpected.

'Go on,' he says. 'Walk in there. Shoot him between the eyes.'

I stare at him, wondering again if this isn't, perhaps, a trap. But this is Sergei, and if he'd wanted me dead . . .

I check the charge then, tucking it into my belt, leave the cover of the trees and walk towards the house.

The guard at the door falls dead, a neat hole burned through his breastplate and clear through his heart. As he slumps, I step over him and kick the flimsy door open. It splinters and falls away with a crash.

Yakovlev looks up. Two of his henchmen look to him, then hasten to draw their swords. I blast one of them, then aim the *spica* at the other. He freezes.

'Where is she?'

Astonishingly, Yakovlev smiles. 'Hurt me,' he says, 'and you'll never know.'

I raise the gun and fire – one through the head, one through the heart – then turn to his sidekick, who's trembling now.

'*Well*? Or shall I burn your bollocks off?'

He jerks, then points back past me. 'There,' he says. 'In the storage pit . . .'

205

My heart breaks at the sight of her. She is lying amid a pile of freshly slaughtered carcasses, her mouth gagged, her wrists and ankles bound tight. Insects crawl over her face, trying to escape the sudden sunlight as I crouch at the edge, looking down.

I jump down and, drawing my knife, cut her free, then hold her to me, feeling her press her face into my chest and sob. There are bruises on her face and arms, and on her breasts, visible through her ripped garment, where Yakovlev has violated her.

I want to go back and kill him again. Kill him in a thousand, painful ways for what he's done.

I move back from her slightly. 'Is the baby . . .?'

She can't look at me. But I gently lift her chin and make her. 'Katerina, I love you. Through time and space I love you. What he did . . . that was *him*, not us. You've no reason to feel ashamed.'

But she's distraught. 'It was horrible. I fought him.'

'I know.' And I hold her to me again. 'I know . . .'

'Otto . . . we'd better get going.'

I turn and look up at Sergei, a dark shape framed by sunlight. 'We'll need a ladder,' I say, 'or a rope.'

Sergei turns and barks an order. Moments later, two serfs lower down a crude wooden ladder. I secure it and push Katerina up ahead of me, then follow, surprised, as I emerge from the hole, to find a crowd of serfs gathered about us, but they seem more curious than anything.

Then, suddenly, a group of men – better dressed than the serfs, and armed with swords and axes – appear between two of the huts on the far side of the clearing and make towards us purposefully. At their head is a tall, balding man, presumably Yakovlev's steward.

I draw my gun and face them. Beside me, Sergei does the same.

'We'd better give them a little demonstration,' he says, and aims. A searing beam of light leaps from the *spica* and one of the huts behind them goes up in a ball of flame.

The shock on their faces is almost comical. They crouch near the ground, their hands over their heads. Behind us, the serfs do the same, as if they've just witnessed great sorcery.

'I didn't think they could do that,' I say, and Sergei looks to me and grins.

'No. But mine's not standard issue.'

'Ah . . .'

Sergei turns back to face the steward and his men and takes a step towards them, brandishing the gun. 'Fuck off! Go on! Back where you came from!' And, resetting the charge, he blows a great hole in the ground between us and them. It's like a land mine going off, great clods of earth flung up into the blue, late-afternoon sky.

They run, howling, back into the trees.

I nod to Sergei, then look back at Katerina. She is standing a little straighter than before, some of her pride restored to her, but there's great hurt in her face and in her eyes. She needs comforting. But first there's something else I have to do.

'Lishka,' I say. 'Let's cut him down and bury him.'

I offer up a prayer to Odin, then wiping the dirt from my hands, stand and look to Sergei. 'What now?'

'We go back to town,' he says. 'Get the cart and go on. To Moscow. That was your plan, wasn't it?'

I nod. Only it feels strange. Sergei seems to know too much. 'We need to talk,' I say.

He nods. 'I know. But not now.'

We hasten on, and for a while it's fine, only Katerina begins to get cramps, in her chest and stomach. We stop and let her rest and they subside. Sergei wants to press on while it's still light, but I'm far from happy. Katerina says nothing, but I know she's worried about the baby.

'Do you think you can go on if we walk slowly?' I ask her.

'I'll try.'

And it's that perseverance that I love about her. Only I'm worried now, and even as we limp our way through the forest back towards Tver', I wonder if this really is the best thing to do. Whether I oughtn't to jump back and throw myself upon Hecht's mercy and beg him to save Katerina and my child.

Only I'm not going to. Not until I have to. Until there's no other option.

Slowly the sun sinks and the darkness of the forest deepens about us. But the dark, when it comes, isn't complete: there's a half moon shining down from our right as we approach the town from the north.

The palisade is brightly lit, torches set up every twenty paces or so, and even as we look on, from our place among the trees, a hundred metres distant, we hear a sudden commotion and see, from the great wooden gate to our left, a host of people stream out, torches held high.

As in a nightmare the crowd turns, heading directly for us.

'Your gun, Otto.'

I look to Sergei, then shake my head. 'I can't kill them all.'

'Why not? They'll kill us if they take us.'

'Yes, but . . .'

I didn't make this journey to become the slayer of whole towns.

I am about to argue, to take Katerina and head back into the trees, when she gives a great groan of pain. I look to her and see she has one hand pressed to her groin. As she lifts her hand, she gives a little whimper of fear, and in the moonlight I see that her hand is wet. Wet with blood.

Sergei looks to me. The gun in his hand is trembling, I note. 'What is it?' he asks, seeing the strange look in my eyes.

'It's Katerina,' I say. 'She's having a miscarriage.'

He stares at me a moment longer, then, like a phantom, places his hand against his chest and vanishes.

207

We are in the inn at Tatarinka, when Bakatin approaches.

'Otto . . . there's someone I'd like you to meet.'

I turn and look up from where I'm sitting at the table, my drink before me. Bakatin, it seems, has brought a friend along. I nod and bid them be seated.

'This is Saratov, Otto. Sergei Saratov. He's a haulier.'

Saratov nods, then smiles at me. He has good teeth. Strong, white teeth, unusual in this age, and he's young, younger than Bakatin by a good ten years. There's a natural vigour about him, too, and an intelligence in his eyes that's unmistakable. But can he be trusted?

'Fyodor?'

'Oh, Saratov is a good man. A very good man. You can trust

Saratov. He knows this part of the country like the back of his hand. He's travelled everywhere.'

I look back at Saratov. He nods, but I have my doubts. He looks far too young to have travelled everywhere.

'Where do you want to go?' Saratov asks.

'Rzhev.'

The young man shakes his head. 'If I were you I'd not go to Rzhev. Nor on to Tver', come to that. They're both bad towns right now. A man could find himself in great trouble in those places. Especially a *Nemets* with such a beautiful Russian wife.'

I stare at him, surprised. 'You know this for a certainty?'

'The *veche* in Rzhev are as corrupt as the lowest insects. They have tribute to pay to their Mongol warlords and do not care how that sum is met, provided it's not from their own pockets.'

'But I have the *tysiaritskii*'s pass—'

'Worthless,' he says. 'They would make you buy a new one.'

'And Tver'?' Bakatin asks, pre-empting me. This is news to him, too, apparently.

'Tver' is a dangerous place right now. There is a faction that wants power, and if they get it . . . well, Rzhev would be like paradise compared to Tver'.'

Our drinks arrive, and Saratov takes one of the battered mugs and lifts it, offering up a toast to my health. 'If I were you, Otto, I would head directly for Gzhatsk, on the Moskva River. That is, if you wish to arrive safely at your final destination.'

'And you know where that is?' I ask, curious now, because this is something I haven't even told Bakatin.

Saratov smiles, showing those perfect teeth once more. 'Your road, if I guess right, Meister Behr, is to Moscow.'

'And you can take me there?'

Saratov nods. 'I and I alone. But let's drink now and shake hands on the deal.'

I look to Bakatin. 'I'll think about it overnight.'

'But Otto . . .'

'Overnight,' I say, with a firmness that surprises him. But I have already decided. We'll go with Saratov.

208

The snow falls softly from the pale October sky, drifting across the Moskva River like a fine gauze of lace, before settling in the branches of the trees on the far bank.

The river moves slowly now, sluggishly, ice forming in its glaucous depths. Winter – the hard Russian winter – is almost upon us.

Behind us lies the town, shrouded in ice.

Beside me, Katerina blows warm breath into her hands, then turns to me and smiles. 'It won't be long.'

I smile back at her. 'No. Not long now.'

Gzhatsk is a hundred miles west of Moscow, and as soon as the river freezes over we shall be gone from here, heading east on the sled on the final stretch of our long road to Moscow.

Sergei has gone to make sure that everything's prepared: the horse fed and groomed, our provisions stored inside the sled, all passes stamped and verified.

Three weeks we've been here now, waiting for the weather to turn, enduring the silent stares and the scornful, vindictive looks of the locals. Putting up with their petty insolence and their rudeness.

If *this* is a good town, Urd knows what the others are like.

'You should have grown a beard,' Katerina said, laughing it off. 'They might have liked you with a beard.'

Only these people – provincials to the core – like nothing better than a foreigner to pour their scorn upon. It's as if they can't exist without a target for the venom that's inside them. Small, they are, with a smallness that is almost evil.

Sergei, though, has been a diamond. Without him we would have suffered far greater indignities than we have. Though our passage has been far from smooth, we have at least arrived at this point, untouched, unscathed, able to move on. It might, as he has said a dozen times and more, been worse.

Tomorrow, I think, smiling inwardly. *Tomorrow we'll be gone.*

I take Katerina's arm and lead her slowly along the riverbank toward the jetty.

'I had that dream again last night,' I say.

'The one about Rzhev?'

I nod. 'It seemed so real. I keep seeing you, the shard of glass in your hand as you struck out at him.'

'The thin man?'

I nod.

She's silent for a time. The grass beneath our booted feet is limed with ice and brittle. There's a fine powder of snow on everything and, stopping, I reach up and gently brush the whiteness from her lustrous dark hair.

She smiles at me, all of her in her eyes. 'Do you think he's still in Moscow?'

'Nevsky? Yes. I'm certain of it.'

Prince Alexander has not yet become 'Nevsky' – the battle has yet to be fought – but it is what we call him between ourselves.

'What if he won't see us?'

'He'll see us, don't worry. If he thinks he can by any means gain influence in Novgorod, he'll grab the chance. We'll be like long-lost cousins, you'll see!'

We walk on, out on to the jetty. It is newly built that summer and the logs are strong and firmly joined. Careful not to slip, we walk out to the very edge and stand there, above the turgid flow of the Moskva, looking across towards the darkness of the forest on the far shore. The snow has grown heavier these past few minutes and the sky is now a solid sheet of falling white. As it settles on the water's surface, it melts slowly, as if some critical mass is being reached.

I take both of Katerina's hands in my own. 'You should have worn gloves,' I say, but she shakes her head and laughs.

'It's not cold enough. Besides, I like the feel of it on my skin.' And she tilts her head back so that the snowflakes collect on her cheeks, her brow, and on her lashes, and for a moment I am spellbound by the beauty of it.

And then I turn, to hear Sergei calling out and waving what looks like a package in the air.

As he comes closer, so he seems to materialise from the mist of whiteness, taking on more solid form. He joins us on the jetty, standing there above the leaden flow.

'It's from Ernst.'

'*Ernst?*' This is a surprise. 'When did it come?'

'Today. A trader brought it.'

The timing is too good to be coincidence. Ernst must know that we're here right now, and that we're leaving in the morning. This has to be a message of some kind.

I take it and heft it in my hand. It's light. Most of its weight is taken up by the ancient wrappings. The rest . . .

'Let's get back,' I say. 'Let's see what Ernst has to say.'

Leaving Katerina and Sergei in the other room, I unwrap one end of it and, tilting it up, let the slender playcard fall into my right hand.

There's a tiny three-by-three screen at the top of the card and, beneath it, a kind of stipple in the surface. I put my thumb to that and feel it prick me. Blood oozes on to the card and a moment later the screen lights up, activated by my DNA.

Ernst's smiling face stares up at me. 'Otto . . . so you made it. This time . . .'

This time . . .

'. . . I had to get you now. It'll be harder once you're in Moscow to get a message through to you. It's like we thought. The Russians have infiltrated Prince Alexander's *druzhina* – his personal body-guard. Memorise the following faces and names. These are the ones we know about, as of now.'

Now being when? I think, knowing the complexity of Time, then clear my head, letting the whole of my concentration focus on the faces that appear one by one on the tiny screen.

'Zasyekin . . . Rakitin . . . Pavlusha . . . Tyutchev . . . Kalinych . . .'

'They're all new agents,' Ernst says, confirming what I'd suspected. 'Or at least, new to us. Some of them, we estimate, have been in place for fifteen to twenty years. Alexander considers them his brothers. But they'd slit his throat in an instant if he stepped out of line.'

'We don't know what their plan is. Whether it's to keep present history on track, or whether there's a better plan, but . . .'

Ernst pauses and seems to look around, as if someone has entered the room where he's recording this.

'Oh . . . oh yes . . .' he says, then turns back and faces me again. 'I almost forgot. On no account go to Krasnogorsk. You oughtn't to stray that far north, but if you do, avoid it like the plague.'

I want to ask why. I want to question him more about what's going on and why he's sent the message, only that's it. The card fades to black.

'Well?' Katerina asks as I step into the room. 'What did he say?'

'All's well,' I say. 'Your father had a chest infection, but he's better now. And they've found us an estate, north of the town. Ernst is seeing to the details.'

Katerina goes to open her mouth, then closes it again. She knows I'm lying, but she doesn't know why, nor is she about to ask me in front of Sergei. Because Sergei doesn't know who I am.

'Oh,' I say, looking to Saratov. 'He said something about a place called Krasnogorsk. We're to avoid it, it seems. He said the place is bad news.'

'*Krasnogorsk*?' Sergei looks surprised. 'But there's nothing there. It's just a staging post. Two huts and a jetty. And not much of a jetty at that. *Avoid* it? Why, you'd be lucky to *find* it.'

I shrug. It's probably of no significance anyway.

'So is everything else sorted out?' I ask. 'The sled? The passes? Our horse?'

'All done.' He looks down a moment, then looks back at me. 'I'm sorry we have to part here, Otto. I'd come too, only . . .'

Only there's no room in the sled.

Katerina looks to me, as if to prompt me, but I'm already ahead of her. I turn and go over to my pack, then return with a bulky package wrapped in cloth.

'Here,' I say. 'For all you've done for us.'

He unwraps it and shakes it out, his face filling with awe. It's a fur. And not just any fur. This is a black bear fur, glinting red and brown and gold in the candlelight. Saratov stares at it then looks to me, overwhelmed.

'But this . . .' He makes to hand it back. 'It's too much. I—'

A tear rolls down his cheek. Katerina reaches out and holds his arm.

'You must have it, Sergei,' she says. 'We would not have got here without you.' She smiles. 'Go on. Put it on. Let's see what you look like in it.'

He hesitates, then does as she says. It looks good. Makes him look stronger, more substantial.

I grin at him. 'It was made for you.'

Sergei can't help but grin back. He gives a huge sigh of content-ment, then reaches out and hugs me, the scent of the fur strong as he grips me like a brother.

'You are a good man, Otto,' he says quietly to my ear. 'Such a good man.'

209

There is nothing – nothing in all space and time – to compare with a sled journey across the Russian snows. To feel that breath-taking rush, the exhilaration and the danger. To hear that endless tinkling of the bells. It is as Pushkin says, 'so fast and free'. And to share it with the woman that you love, to be pressed close in the darkness of that tiny, jolting carriage. Nothing compares.

We are heading upriver, across the moonlit ice. Ahead the Moskva broadens to a narrow lake, and beyond that – some fifteen or twenty miles distant – is our destination, Mozhaisk. That's where we'll stop, more than a third of our journey complete.

I hold the reins tightly in my gloved hands. Ahead of us the horse snorts and spurs itself on. It's a dark, fine beast that cost us dear but is probably worth twice what we paid for it. The snow is still falling, flakes gusting through the narrow slit at eye level.

But we don't mind. It's warm inside and cosy, and the feel of her hip against mine, her arm beneath my arm, is all I need. I am happy beyond all measure.

I can smell her in that darkness, and now and then our faces meet to kiss. Oh, such kisses. And still the onward rush, that breathless, unrelenting hurtle through the moonlit dark.

But not unthinking. Indeed, I've done little else but think about things since Ernst's unexpected message. Especially his '*This time . . .*' I've not told Katerina about that, but now, as we move out on to the lake, I do.

'So what does it mean?' she asks, having to raise her voice a little against the noise of the sled. I stare out ahead as I answer her, pulling gently on the reins to keep the horse running close to the northern shore, away from the centre where the ice might still be thin.

'It means something went wrong last time. Ernst must have jumped back and changed things.'

I glance at her, and see she doesn't quite understand. But then, nor do I. If Ernst jumped back, it meant he would have had to go through the platform at Four-Oh, and if so he'd have had to speak to Hecht. So what excuse did he make? Or does Hecht now know about Katerina and me?

He can't. Because if he did . . .

'Imagine you were embroidering something,' I say, 'and you make a mistake. Imagine that all you had to do was go back to the point on the cloth at which you made the mistake and – like that! – the mistake was gone, the thread unstitched, and you were back where you were before you made it.'

'That whole particular thread removed?'

'Precisely.'

'And Ernst did that?'

'He must have done. There's no other explanation.'

At least none I can think of. For I certainly didn't make a jump. I'd have remembered if I did. As it is . . .

The dreams . . .

I frown, then tug the reins again, bringing the horse's head back to the left.

It isn't possible, of course. It's not how it works. But my dreams have seemed curiously real lately, more like something remembered than ordinary dreams. Their very vividness has marked them out as different. Not that dreams can't be vivid. It's the repeated detail of them; the quality of . . . oh, I don't know . . . of *having happened*.

Or not now. That timeline having been erased.

Which means, of course, that I oughtn't to remember any of it. Not even as dreams. So they have to be just dreams.

So why do they disturb me so? Why do I continue to suffer them, each and every night?

The night rushes past us, our sled hissing across the snow, the thud of our steed's hooves against the thick-packed ice mingled with the tinkling of bells. But we are not the only things abroad this night. There is the cry of wolves in the distance. Not one, but many. And not so far away, at that. But they'll not harm us, not at the speed we're travelling.

I am silent for a while, then jerk awake, having dozed momentarily, realising that Katerina is asleep beside me, lolling against me, her head on my shoulder. I blink my eyes and try to see through the narrow slit just where we are, and whether there's any sign of the lake narrowing up ahead, but I can't properly see.

I pull on the reins, slowing the horse, bringing him to a slow trot.

I turn, nudging her gently with my shoulder. 'Katerina . . .'

She lifts her head slowly, sleepily, and smiles at me. 'Are we there?'

'No. But I need to check precisely where we are.'

I don't think we've drifted, but then, I don't know how long I dozed for. We seem to be out on the lake still, so it can't have been long, and if the horse ran in a straight line then we should be okay. But it's best to be sure. Best not to be lost in this wilderness of a land.

I slow the horse further, then apply the brake, grinding the sled to a halt. Beside me, Katerina raises her hood, then looks to me and nods. Unfastening the catch, I throw the hinged lid back and stand, the sudden, bitter cold swirling about me.

It's such a still, crisp night, and now that the snow has almost stopped, everything glistens in the moon's pale light. I look about me, puzzled, for the land seems distant to either side. We've drifted, that's for sure, and are out now near the very middle of the lake. I lean over the side, and sure enough, the ice is darker, thinner than I'd hoped to see. Even as I lean back I hear it creak and groan, as if our weight's too much for it to bear.

We need to move, and quickly. But which way?

I tighten the reins, then make the horse walk on, slowly at first, listening to the sound of the ice beneath us. Is it my imagination or is that cracking I hear?

Indecision could be fatal now, and, tugging on the left rein, I make the horse veer to the left, heading across the ice towards the northern shore. If I'm wrong we're dead. Slowly I make the horse go faster, standing up all the while, my knees pressed against the front bar of the sled, my arms aching from the tension of holding the reins, my eyes seeking out any sign of open water up ahead.

A minute passes, then another. Beneath us the ice seems once again thick and hard. I let go a breath and laugh with relief, then look down at Katerina. 'Urd's sake, that was stupid of me!'

She looks away.

'Darling?'

'I feel sick. I—'

I slow the horse, then pull the handbrake on. The sled once again grinds to a halt. Stepping out, I turn and offer her my hand. She takes it and clambers out. And only just in time.

I walk across and pet the horse, stroking its flank and the long side of its neck and face, giving it a handful of chestnuts from my pocket.

'Otto?'

I turn and look at her. For once she looks drained and bedraggled. Still beautiful, of course, but not her best. 'Yes?'

'I've finished.'

'So I heard.'

She almost smiles. I walk across and, taking her hand, help her back in. I'm about to join her, to seal us back in and drive on, when I notice something.

We're being watched.

Far off – maybe half a mile away – there is another sled on the ice. It's not moving and I'm not entirely sure how many of them there are, only when I take a step towards them they vanish as if they were an apparition. But I know they weren't. They were there.

I don't tell Katerina. I don't want to scare her. Not while she's feeling so fragile. But as we make our way onwards, I begin to register a strong sense of wrongness about the whole thing.

Just *why* am I being watched? What exactly is going on here?

But of one thing I'm convinced. Hecht knows. Hecht damned well knows.

210

My first sight of Moscow is through the early morning mist. We have stopped high up on a ridge overlooking the town, at a place known to the locals as the Sparrow Hills. Beneath us the ground slopes away slowly towards the Moskva River, through snow-covered water meadows and small copses towards the cluster of wooden buildings – no more than a hundred in all – that perch atop the low hill to the north, where the frozen river bends in a great, white inverted 'U', pointing south.

It looks what it is – a trading post: a tiny island in this great northern wilderness. Nothing in its humble aspect suggests its future. Nor should it. The real centres of power are far from here, in Kiev to the south, and in Novgorod. Moscow is a backwater, important only because Prince Alexander chooses to make it so. He has friends here and enjoys the hunting. And there's another reason. It's easy to meet with the Horde's representatives here in Moscow. His friends, the Muscovites, are discreet. No word gets out of what's discussed here. And that's important right now, for Alexander doesn't wish his people to know just how in thrall he is to the Great Khan. If they knew, they would probably overthrow him. As it is, he can play the hero – the saviour of the Rus' – and no one knows any better. Not outside of this backwater, anyway.

And that's why I'm here: to meet with Alexander and become his friend, because when the time comes to spring the trap . . .

Katerina climbs from the sled and comes across to me. Her voice, when she speaks, is filled with surprise. 'Is that it?'

I turn and smile. 'Yes. Not what you thought, eh?'

There is a crude wooden palisade about the town, and a small stone tower – the Kremlin! Beyond that, it's little different from Tatarinka, or any of the other places we have stayed along the way. It's hard to imagine how huge it will become, unless, like me, you've seen it in its later glory.

The sky is clear, the day bright, and so we decide to walk behind the sledge, letting the horse plod slowly, and in less than an hour we arrive at the gate and wait to be admitted.

They are surprised to see us, a beardless German trader and a beautiful Russian girl, but the town's officials are courtesy itself and lead us along the main logged path, past staring locals, to the great hall – the only two-storey building in the town – where, unexpectedly, we are brought directly and immediately into the presence of the prince himself.

They are having breakfast, I note, as we duck inside, into the fire-lit gloom. Two long, trench tables fill the upper half of the room, about which several dozen men – Nevsky's *druzhina* – are busy eating. Our entrance makes heads turn suddenly, the great buzz of conversation falters. Nevsky looks to the official, who has hurried ahead of us, listens to him a moment, then stands and smiles.

'Welcome, *Nemets*. And your good wife, welcome, too.'

It is courteous enough, and the smile seems without edge, but I have met Nevsky before – though he doesn't know it – and I know the kind of creature he is. Nineteen years old, he is a strong and handsome man – more so than I – and his good looks and long blond hair have turned the head of many a young girl, yet I am surprised when I turn and see how Katerina has looked down, a faint blush at her neck.

I say nothing, concentrating on making a good first impression, but that glimpsed moment disturbs me, because Katerina is my rock. My foundation.

Room is made for us at the table, between – as fate would have it – two of the Russian agents, Tyutchev and Rakitin. Of the others there's no sign, but I'm certain they're not far away.

Breakfast finished, we are found quarters near the prince's – a simple *izba* but clean enough – and are invited to a feast that evening in our honour. The letter I am carrying from Novgorod's *veche* will be handed over then, but before that there is this other matter to be sorted out.

Alone with Katerina, I turn to her and gently ask her what she thought of him.

'*Of whom?*' she asks, speaking in German, even though I have not.

'Of the prince,' I say, persisting with the Russian, refusing to be drawn into a game about this.

'*I thought he was very gallant*,' she answers, and for once her German is so fluent, that single word – *ritterlich* – so unexpected, that I simply stare at her.

'*Ritterlich?*' I ask finally. The precise meaning is 'knightly', 'chivalrous'. And outwardly it fits. Only I know what true knights are like. I have been among them, and lived among them, and Nevsky isn't one of them. Nevsky is a snake pretending to be a knight. He has the look of it and the mannerisms, but otherwise . . .

'Did you like him?' I ask, still in Russian.

Unexpectedly, she pouts and looks away, like a little girl caught out. 'Yes,' she says quietly. 'What's not to like?'

Russian. This time she's speaking Russian. The German, then, was for distance. But why?

She looks across at me. 'Why? Am I not supposed to like him? Am I only to like who you tell me to like, Otto?'

The question takes me aback. Before now I'd not have thought she'd need to ask it. But for the first time – the first time since Kravchuk, that is – I feel jealous.

I close my eyes a moment, trying to still my thoughts, my racing heart. 'Nevsky is a villain. I've told you that. What's more . . .'

'Yes, Otto. You've told me. Only—'

'Only you *liked* him.'

'Yes. I couldn't help it. He was nice to us. Kind. The feast—'

'He's a politician, Katya. He's nice to an end.'

'That's not what I've experienced.'

I meet her eyes, meaning to stare her down, to make her acknowledge that she's wrong, only what I see there shakes my certainty.

'Instinct is all I have, Otto. Until I know better.'

'Then trust me. You don't mess with the man. And you especially don't flirt with him.'

'Otto, I didn't—'

'No. But you might.'

She turns abruptly, a flash of anger in her face. But she says nothing. Just stands there, waiting. And eventually I step across and, reaching out, turn her gently to face me again.

'I'm sorry,' I say quietly. 'I'm being silly, I know. Only this is a tiny place, and Prince Alexander is a powerful man. I keep remembering that dream . . .'

She looks up into my face, her eyes imploring me. 'It was only a dream, Otto. As for the prince . . . he won't act like that. If he did, well, you said it. He's a politician. He'd not want word of what he did to get back to Novgorod.'

'And yet he still might try.'

'Then I'd rebuff him.'

I'm quiet a moment, then, 'Would you?'

'Yes. Of course I would. I might like him, but you're my man, Otto. *You*. Now and for ever. Until the stars die.'

My mouth falls open slightly. *Until the stars die.* She has never said that before, not even in the extremities of passion.

And so we kiss, and kissing leads us on. Until, with a tiny cry, I make her mine again, there on the packed earth floor. There, in Moscow, in the very heart of Russia.

211

It is mid-afternoon when we step outside once more, and something's different, though it takes me a moment to recognise what it is.

The clue is in the sound. The strong, vigorous flapping of a banner in the wind. I walk across and stare up at the tower and there, sure enough, is a long silk banner; sign that the Great Khan's representative is in residence. Katerina looks a question at me, but I shake my head. I have not explained the Mongols and their significance to Russian history to her.

I am about to find one of Nevsky's *druzhina* and ask him if we might not see the prince again before the evening's festivities when one of them, Zasyekin, I think, marches up to me and, without preamble, tells me to come at once.

We follow, back along the iced log pathway, but this time not to the hall but to a smaller building set back from it against the palisade. Nevsky is there, and two Mongols. There are also two traders, brothers by the look of them, and I'm not surprised when they are introduced to me as Arkadi and Mikhail Romanov.

But it's the chief Mongol that I'm interested in. I'm surprised to find him here without significant military backing. After all, the battle of the Sit' River – where the Mongol Horde, under Burunday, defeated the Rus' princes – was only a year and a half back, and the Mongols, for all their threat, are far from established in the north.

Their chief calls himself Kongdu and has all the air and swagger of a chieftain. Of course, he cannot speak a word of Rus', but his attendant – a small, squint-eyed fellow – more than makes up for it, his Russian heavily accented.

They're there, of course, for money. Tribute is the lifeblood of the great Mongol empire. And there's an age-old balance to be made here, between what they can bleed out of the conquered Rus' and what the Rus' claim they're able to pay. It's this debate that I come into, being drawn at once by Nevsky into discussing just how poor the harvests have been these past three years. As if my word – as a *Nemets* and a trader – will confirm it.

It isn't true, of course, but I go along with it, understanding what he's up to. And for a brief while I can almost see what Katerina means. There *is* a kind of charm about the prince. Yet the man is quite capable of the most outrageous lies. Oh, he lies for a purpose, there's no doubt of that, only it makes me question everything else about him.

Nevsky's word, I know, isn't worth shit.

The debate finishes, still unresolved, the Mongol chieftain unhappy and growling to himself – words that his interpreter is careful not to translate. But we get the gist. Either we come up with a better offer or we'll suffer the consequences.

It makes me think – if only for that moment – that maybe I'm being too harsh on Nevsky. That maybe he's only trying to do his best in a difficult situation. Only I know the truth. Prince Alexander likes power and riches, and he has an ego the size of a small moon. The situation *is* difficult, but this man milks it for all he's worth – and the history books will call him a hero and a saint, whereas he's little more than a glorified pirate, robbing his own people to pacify the enemy, while posing as the protector of his nation.

I'd kill him in an instant, only it wouldn't help us. We need him alive, just as much as the Russians need him alive.

Yes, for once it all coincides. Or almost so. There *is* a difference.

You see, we've tried killing him, and it doesn't work. The answer's subtler than that. Discredit him and the job's done for us. Not only does the Horde keep Russia from expanding for the best part of three hundred years but, without the battle on the frozen lake, the Teuton knights continue *their* expansion eastward. The result is a smaller, essentially *European* Russia. No match for a unified Germany when the great war comes. Or that's the theory, anyway. That's what our computer models predict. And that's what Ernst and I are working towards. Ostensibly. By which I mean, *if Katerina wasn't involved*.

The Russians need Nevsky because, well, because he is Nevsky. One of those figures that, in time of war, they trot out for general consumption, such iconic beings having the miraculous ability to inspire the common man.

And woman, come to that. Which brings me back to Katerina, for – though her promise not to flirt with Nevsky was strictly kept – it has not kept him from flirting with her the whole of this past hour. Even as he haggled with Kongdu, he had one eye on my woman, turning to her often and, with a silken tongue, seeking her advice and seeming to consider it.

The viper. Because I know those kind of tricks. It's flattery, just as much as to tell her that she's got beautiful eyes and hair, and lips like the sweetest, softest fruits.

Which, of course, she has.

And the awful thing is that it's worked. Katerina, I can see, is more impressed with him – with his manners, and with his 'attentiveness' to her – than she was before our little talk. She might profess to 'trust' me on Nevsky's nature, but her instincts aren't awake to what he truly is. Nor will they be, until it's proved otherwise.

But dare I risk that? What if he finds a way to separate us, to get her alone with him?

What makes it worse, of course, is that Alexander has his own woman, Alexandra, daughter of Prince Bryacheslav of Polotsk. He married her only months back, in Polotsk itself, and she is here right now, in Moscow, keeping his bed warm even as he flirts with Katerina.

Walking back, I am broodingly silent; so much so that, when we're alone again, Katerina asks me straight out what it is that's eating at me.

I turn on her. 'Why should anything be eating at me?'

She looks hurt. My tone was anything but kind. I relent.

'Look, I'm sorry but . . . that man!'

Katerina says nothing. Turning away, she goes over to our pack and, kneeling, begins to get out her things in preparation for the evening. I watch her, knowing I'm in the wrong, but unable to help it. She thinks she's right. She thinks that he's no threat. But she doesn't know. She simply doesn't know. Such men are ruthless when it comes to what they want. And if he wants my Katerina, I am sure he'll try to take her, however he can. And hide the tale of it afterwards, even if it means murder.

And that's my deepest fear. Because I didn't count on Nevsky falling for Katerina. Or not even 'falling', but desiring, which is perhaps worse. Let's put it simply. He wants to fuck her, just the way he'd like to ride a beautiful horse, or slay a difficult enemy.

Only he isn't going to. Over my dead body.

I am quiet for a little longer, then, changing the subject, ask her: 'What did you think of the other two? The traders?'

'The Romanovs?'

'Yes.'

She shrugs. 'I'd not want to marry either of them, if that answers you.'

I laugh edgily. 'You want to know something?'

She half turns, looking up at me, her blue dress bunched in one hand. 'Go on.'

'Their great-great-grandsons will be the kings and emperors of Russia. Tsars, they'll call themselves, and they'll rule a land that stretches from Poland to China.'

I know she can't envisage that – that the scale of it means nothing to her – but still there's something like surprise in her eyes.

'Them? The *Romanovs*?'

I nod. 'For three hundred years, they'll be the "fathers" of their people.'

'But they're uncouth. And this place . . .'

I can see she only half believes me.

'That's why this place is so important to us, because this is where it all begins. Besides the Romanovs, there are other families – the Zhakarins, for instance. They too will spawn emperors – the Rurikids, as they'll be known. But they, like the Romanovs, are here, right now, in this, well, in this pigsty of a place.'

Katerina stands and, shaking out the dress, holds it against herself. I know just how wonderful she looks in it and fear for her.

'Katerina, you can't wear that.'

Her eyes meet mine challengingly. 'But I am. For you, Otto. Not for him. For you.'

212

We are only an hour into the feast when I realise that our mission here has failed. I am supposed, after all, to spend the winter here, endearing myself to Nevsky, making myself indispensable to him, but already, after less than a day, I hate the man with a passion. As much as I ever hated Kravchuk.

It's not particularly the way he's so smilingly polite to me, with that 'attentiveness' of his that's a mask to his genuine indifference, it's more that he does it even as he plots to prise Katerina away from me.

Not that he wants to keep her. He just wants to have her. To try her. For novelty's sake. And if two of his men have to hold her down, well, he'll enjoy that as much as if she'd come to him willingly.

At least, that's how I picture it. And sitting there, I can't help but picture it.

The situation is made worse by the fact that the Russian agents – the five of them, all of whom are now present – have this kind of mocking smile which they award me every time I look their way, as if they know quite well who I am and are smug in that knowledge.

Which makes me feel even more that we're in danger here.

As yet, however, it's all undercurrent. Nuance. Nothing's out in the open, nor will it be. Not unless I make a fuss. Which, of course, I'm not. Providing, that is, that Nevsky behaves himself.

Katerina herself seems almost unaware of what's going on. I say that, because she smiles and laughs most naturally, like the charming creature that she is, and every male eye in that hall is drawn to her, ignoring Nevsky's wife, Alexandra, who sits there sullenly, looking down at her untouched meal.

Nevsky, particularly, watches Katerina, a half smile on his lips, and even as he gnaws at a bone, I imagine that he, in turn, is lasciviously imagining himself naked with her.

Dark my thoughts are, so dark that I want to run from there, only it's not possible. I have to endure it, as if I've found myself suddenly in hell itself.

'Meister Behr. If I could have a moment?'

I turn and look up. It is the Mongol, the interpreter. From where he sits across the table, Nevsky watches me carefully, his eyes narrowed.

'Right now?'

'My master wishes to speak with you alone.'

I look to Nevsky, suspecting him of planning this. But he's not smiling, in fact, he seems almost worried by this development.

I stand and, kissing the top of Katerina's head, bow to Nevsky and leave the table, following the interpreter.

Outside it's cold, snowflakes gusting in the sharp night wind. We cross the open space and duck inside one of the nearby *izbas*. The Mongol chieftain, Kongdu, is sitting there, on the bare earth floor, a crude map in front of him. As I enter he looks up and, without ceremony, gestures for me to sit across from him. The interpreter scuttles around and quickly sits beside his master.

'You've travelled this land,' he says, without his master speaking. 'Tell us – which is the quickest way from here to Novgorod?'

I look from one to the other and then give a little laugh. Kongdu is not in charge at all. He never has been. It is the interpreter who is the boss here. Kongdu is just a front – a kind of mask this other man wears to impress the Russians.

He sees I understand and smiles. 'I am Tengu,' he says. 'I am the *baskaki*. Kongdu here is my bodyguard.'

I give him a tiny bow, then reach out and take the map. I study it a while, then look to him. 'Why should I help you?'

'Because you are in danger here.'

'I know that. But how will me helping you change that?'

'Because Prince Alexander is afraid of us. He has seen with his own eyes what we can do.'

'He was at Sit'?'

Tengu nods.

'But I thought—'

'We spared him. And others. But they saw what we did. How ruthless we can be. How many of us there are, like the leaves on the trees.' Tengu smiles, as a tiger smiles. 'There is no arguing with the Horde. You submit or die.'

I consider it a moment. If I help him – if I show him how to get to Novgorod – does that mean he'll take the Horde there? Historically it never happened, yet I have seen with my own eyes the fate of Kiev and Vladimir, both sacked and then razed to the ground by the Horde. Not a man, woman or child was spared, and those were cities of fifty thousand souls.

Do I really want to tell this man how to get to my beloved's home?

'Do I have a choice?'

Tengu laughs. 'Every man has choices. But yours, I think, are limited. You can help us, or you can be left to your fate here.'

'Which is?'

'For you to discover.'

He studies me a moment, his dark eyes, folded into his face as they are, shining with an unexpected curiosity. 'You're not like these Russians,' he says finally. 'You can see who they are through their eyes. But you . . .'

'What about me?'

'I'd say you had seen many things that ordinary men don't see.'

I smile. 'Then you'd guess right.' I look down at the map, then hand it back to him.

'You'll find your way. With or without my help.'

Tengu shrugs. 'Ah well. I hoped . . .'

I look to Kongdu. The big man is staring straight ahead, as if he has been told to do so. Tengu reaches out and touches his arm and says something in his native tongue, which I cannot under-stand, and the warrior gets up and walks over to the door, then steps out, into the night.

Tengu looks to me. 'I would leave here, trader. Tonight. Your long journey has been wasted, I'm afraid. There is nothing here for you.'

'But—'

'Go and retrieve your wife, Otto Behr. Then run from here. Get your sled and fly into the night. Or stay and die.'

I swallow. There's something in his tone that suggests he knows what Nevsky's up to. I bow to him then stand.

He jumps to his feet, smiling once more. 'Maybe we'll meet again, Meister Behr. It would be good to talk . . . of all we've seen and all we've done, neh?'

There is something strangely familiar about the way he says it.

Yet what have we in common? Even so, I reach out and take both his hands, and he pulls me to him and hugs me, as if I am an old friend – and that, too, surprises me.

'Now go,' he says. 'While you still have the chance.'

213

Nevsky looks up as I come back into the hall. About him, his men do the same, then quickly look aside, as if they've given something away. It's that that confirms for me what Tengu said. We are in danger here.

Katerina sits amid it all, laughing and smiling, blithely unaware of the fact that she is sitting in a vipers' nest, a sword arm from death on every side.

Not that I'd let them harm her. Only how do we get out of here alive?

As I sit beside her again, she turns to me and smiles. 'Are you okay?'

'I'm fine,' I say, then place my mouth to her ear and whisper. 'We have to go. Can you feign being ill?'

She gives the slightest nod. I look to Nevsky. As I thought, he's watching me closely now, suspicion in his face. I smile at him and, reaching out, lift my cup and toast him.

'Your health, Prince Alexander!'

Nevsky ignores the gesture. Leaning towards me, he raises his voice as other voices fall silent all about us. 'What did he want, the Mongol?'

I sip from my cup, then put it down. There's silence now in the hall.

'He wanted to know how things were in Novgorod. How they were disposed to the Horde.'

Nevsky stares back at me as if he knows I'm lying. 'It's a long way to Novgorod.'

'It is, my lord.'

'And what else did he say?'

That I'm in danger here . . .

I am about to answer, to frame another lie, when Katerina clutches her belly and groans. I turn to her, as if surprised. 'What is it?'

'The child. I—'

She groans again, such a groan as would convince anyone that she's in pain. I look across and see that Nevsky's on his feet. So too are his men.

'Grab them!' he says. 'Don't let them get away!'

214

This is the place we were warned not to go. As we ride up to it along the treelined riverbank, I recognise it from Saratov's bleak description: *'It's just a staging post. Two huts and a jetty. And not much of a jetty at that . . .'*

He was right. Krasnogorsk is the deadest, most insignificant of places we have yet seen. Only Nevsky has brought us here, so there must be some significance. We stop and while his men go ahead to check things out, he turns and looks down at us from his horse.

Our wrists are bound and we are tied together, like slaves. Nevsky, of course, holds the lead rope. Two days it's taken us to get here, and I still don't understand why we've come.

'I'd have killed you,' he says, looking at me coldly, imperiously. 'Killed you and kept your woman for my slave. I would have enjoyed that.'

'Why?' I ask, my hatred of him shaping my face as well as my words. 'What have I ever done to you?'

'I was told what you planned.'

'Told? By whom?'

'By a friend.'

He stares at me a little longer, contempt in his eyes, then turns his horse and his back on me. One of his men – Pavlusha, it looks like – returns, half running. He stops by the neck of Nevsky's horse. 'They're here.'

'How many of them?'

'The old man and two others. They're armed, but—'

'We want no trouble. Tell Alexei.'

Pavlusha nods, then turns back, hastening to pass on the message. Nevsky gestures to the men about him and we move on into Krasnogorsk, such as it is.

I don't know what to expect, but it's not this. The old man stands by the larger of the huts. He's a tall, imposing-looking fellow, built like a latter-day wrestler and with long dark hair that frames the bald dome of his forehead. He wears a long black *armyak*, a peasant's cloth coat, and in his left hand is a stave, carved at one end into the shape of a wolf's head. His beard is huge and black and bushy, salted with grey, and though there's no real facial similarity he reminds me of that infamous creature of a different century, Rasputin. It's the eyes. Eyes that could be either wise and all-knowing, or simply mad.

Just beyond him are his two companions. They're both much younger – in their teens, I'd guess. One holds an axe, the other a drawn bow. They both look frightened out of their wits. And who's to blame them? Nevsky's men are bigger and better armed. What's more there's ten of them. Just beyond them is a horse, a grey, bony old creature that looks close to exhaustion. Behind it is a cart, on which two corpses are lain.

As we come close, Nevsky tugs on the rope and makes us jerk forward.

'Kolya,' he says blankly, addressing the old man. 'You have everything?'

The old man nods, his face inexpressive.

'Well?'

The old man turns towards the axeman and snaps his fingers. At once the young man puts down his axe and, going to the great leather bag that's laid across the horse's back, pulls out a cloth sack and brings it across to his master.

The old man hefts it a moment, then throws it down between himself and Nevsky.

'You can count it now, or trust me.'

Nevsky almost smiles. But he too seems nervous, and I wonder what's going on here. Are we being sold to the old man? If so, why? Why not just kill me and have done? But it's not that kind of nervousness. Nevsky seems almost in awe of the old man, like he's some kind of sorcerer.

'*You* should be paying *me*, Alexander,' he says, as one of Nevsky's men scuttles forward and picks up the heavy cloth bag.

Nevsky laughs, but again it's a nervous laugh. 'Why's that, Kolya? You wanted them alive, I wanted them dead. So we both get what we want, no?'

'But you get the silver.'

'I have tribute to pay.'

'Ah yes, the Horde.' And there is such contempt in the word that I wonder just who the old man is, and what his relationship to Nevsky is. He's certainly not intimidated by him. In fact, it's the other way round.

'Here,' Nevsky says, and, casting the rope towards the old man, he turns his horse and moves aside, leaving us facing him.

The old man's eyes fall on me and smile. 'Otto. How long I have waited for this.'

'Do I know you?'

At which the old man laughs. Laughs until the tears stream down his face. Only when he's finished it's like he's drained all of the good humour from his soul, and when he looks at me again it is with pure malice in those eyes. Malice that I can't understand or comprehend. He raises his hand and gestures for his men to bring the cart forward.

They lead the horse on, until it's almost level with us.

'Turn it,' he says quietly. 'Let the bastard see.'

As the horse turns and the litter comes into view, so I gasp in disbelief. Beside me, Katerina falls on to her knees with a little cry.

'*Mother of God!*'

But I at least know that this isn't sorcery. And though I do not know this Kolya, I'm certain now of one thing: he's a Russian agent, like the others. For the two bloodless corpses on the litter, their throats cut, their clothes crusted with blood, are mine and Katerina's. I swallow, trying to find the words to defy the old man, to show him that I'm not afraid. Only for once I am, because I can't see any way out of this, unless to jump. And that will leave Katerina here, in this festering, god-forsaken place, alone among enemies. And that I cannot do.

Dead, I think. *They finally got me.*

Yes, and the bastards brought me back to show me. To gloat over me. Only when I turn and look, it's not what I expected. The only one who's smiling is Nevsky. Rakitin, Zasyekin and the others are strangely sombre, and when I look at them, they quickly look away, as if ashamed. Only why should that be so? They've nailed me, after all. They don't even have to kill me now, because they've killed me up the line somewhere.

Katerina reaches out and grips my leg. I look down at her, pitying her, pitying us both. But for once I can do nothing – nothing whatsoever – about it. Even so, she pleads with me, breaking my heart anew.

'Do something, Otto! For God's sake *do* something!'

'Katerina, I—'

Nevsky laughs. Forgive me, but he laughs. A mocking laughter that rolls on and on.

I want to kill him. Only it's not rage I feel any longer. I sink to my knees and, facing Katerina, clasp her to me and lift her face so that she's staring into my eyes.

'This is it,' I say gently. 'Do you understand? This is the end, my love. They've won.'

Yet even as she shapes her mouth to answer me, even as her eyes meet mine, their perfect darkness filled with sorrow, so I feel the world fragment about me, my self dissolve into a thousand billion particles . . .

215

Hecht stands there, arms folded, beside the platform, facing me as I shimmer into being.

'We've got to go back there!' I cry, stepping towards him. 'Katerina, the woman I was with, we've got to save her!'

Hecht gives the slightest shake of his head. 'No. There's no time for that now.'

'No time?'

Doesn't he know? But then I realise. He doesn't. He has no idea what significance she has to me. He thinks I'm just being cranky.

'We must!' I say, shocked that he can't understand. 'We *have to*!'

But Hecht's not listening.

'Listen,' he says, speaking slowly, calmly. 'It's all falling apart. Five of our agents are dead already. So you've got to go in there, Otto, and sew it back together again.'

I stare back at him, bewildered. 'Together? What are you talking about?'

'It's Poltava,' he says. 'The Russians are about to lose Poltava.'

Part Eight
A Stitch in Time

'Studying history, my friend, is no joke and no irresponsible game. To study history one must know in advance that one is attempting something fundamentally impossible, yet necessary and highly important. To study history means submitting to chaos and nevertheless retaining faith in order and meaning. It is a very serious task, young man, and possibly a tragic one.'

– Hermann Hesse, *The Glass Bead Game*

It's hard to feel enthusiastic when you know you're dead.

Even so, I recognise the significance. *Poltava*. It's one of those historical cusps. A pressure point, if you like. And even if the word means nothing to you – in which case, you cannot possibly be a Russian – that significance can still be quickly grasped.

Poltava is the first great battle that the Russian empire wins. The grand turning of the tide. It is when the whipping boy becomes the master.

But let me take a moment to explain, if only to give this context.

Long before Hitler, long even before Napoleon, another European ruler tried to conquer Russia, to march an army across the steppes and seize Moscow. That ruler, Charles XII of Sweden – twenty-seven at the time of which we speak, that is, the summer of 1709 – was just as much a megalomaniac as his two successors. A child king and most definitely a warrior, he attempted the impossible, and failed. But not by much.

At least, that's the regular history. But things have changed. Suddenly, it seems, he's about to win, and we need to find out why.

Russia in the eighteenth century was a backward place of bearded men in long, thick furs; an insular and isolated place, as strange in its ways as Far Cathay, and, to the Western view, every bit as barbarous. The young tsar, Peter the First, changed that. He dragged his country, kicking and screaming, into the modern world, attempting to make a proper European power of it, much as Stalin, years later, tried to transform his basically agrarian state into a centre of industry.

Russia, before Peter, was landlocked. Or almost so. For six months of the year there was Archangel in the Arctic Circle. Otherwise . . .

Peter changed that. He built a fleet from scratch, and fought for footholds on both the Baltic in the north and the Black Sea to the south. And between times he modernised the Russian army, which had always – *always* – been a joke.

Oh, and he built a city, in the mouth of an icy river, in marshland, in a place so hostile that its builders often froze to death as they worked.

This is a story, then, of two compulsive young men, given by Fate to their respective countries. Implacable enemies, whose 'Great Northern War' dragged on for seventeen long years. But Poltava . . . why Poltava?

Because that is where Charles's ambitions died. That is where Peter – who had avoided open battle for two whole years – finally turned and faced his foe, and crushed him. Sent him scuttling into Turkey with a bare six hundred men – all that remained of the seventy thousand who had marched from Saxony twenty-three months earlier.

Hecht wants me to go in at once, but Freisler, who's been brought into the discussion, argues against that. He thinks I should undergo a refresher course. Maybe he's right. Only this once I don't actually care. What does it matter whether Peter loses the battle if Katerina is dead? What do I care if Russia is cut to pieces by its enemies and shared out like a giant cake?

Because if I don't start caring then I won't get back to save her. *If I can, that is. If this dreadful gut feeling I have is false.*

And so, with Hecht's concurrence, I find myself in the immersion laboratory, data flooding into every pore. Or so it seems. And maybe that's good for me, because for a while the sheer intensity of it makes me forget.

Only the moment I stop remembering, I think of her again.

Hecht is waiting for me when I come out of there.

'Are you ready, Otto?'

I hesitate, because for once I'm not sure. In fact, I'm not certain I'm ready for anything any more, only I don't say that. I just nod and let him lead me to the platform.

And so I go back. To Poltava. And to the Swedish camp, on the evening of 26 June 1709.

217

I know something's wrong the moment I step into the tent. Charles, for a start, is standing there, his back to me, looking down at the map spread out across the table. Gathered also about the table are others I recognise – Count Adam Lewenhaupt, Field Marshal Rehnskjold, the two Poles, Stanislaus and Krassow, the old Cossack 'Hetman' Konstantin Gordeenko, Mazeppa, his friend from the Zaporozhsky Cossacks and – most surprising of all – Khan Devlet Giray, the Sultan's man.

Their presence says it all. Someone has been tinkering with history big time. Making not one but four, maybe five decisive changes.

Charles turns and, seeing me, smiles. 'Otto! Where in God's sweet name did *you* come from?'

And he comes across and embraces me.

I look down, taking in the fact that his left foot is unharmed, his riding boot unviolated, then look back into his face.

'Otto?'

'It's nothing,' I say. 'Only there were rumours . . .'

'Rumours?'

'That you were hurt.'

He laughs, his heavily pocked face unsmiling. 'Haven't you heard, Otto? God looks after me. I am his favourite. He blesses me, and not merely with the strength of will and body to carry out his purpose, but with good friends and allies to help me in that task.'

I look past him at the others. 'So I see.'

At least five of them should not be here in Poltava at all: the two Poles, Mazeppa, Gordeenko, and Devlet Giray. In our time-line, all five disappointed Charles, depriving him of some 36,000 troops. As for Lewenhaupt, he was never consulted, never given his battle orders by his rival, Rehnskjold, and to see him there at the map table is as much a shock as anything.

'The supplies?' I ask.

'Are safe,' Charles says.

And that too is different. So different that that fact alone should swing the battle in Charles's favour, let alone the rest.

Peter doesn't stand a chance. The Russians, well, they might as well cut their own throats as try to contain the Swedes with such advantages as they now possess.

'Where have you been?' Charles asks, drawing me across to the map table and finding room for us between the hunched Mazeppa and his marshall, Rehnskjold.

'Kiev,' I say, and he turns to look at me questioningly.

'Kiev?' The others are watching now too. 'And what were you doing there, my old friend?'

I hesitate, and in the sudden silence, old Mazeppa speaks. 'Maybe he has a woman there.'

Charles stares at me, his steel-blue eyes intense, then shakes his head. 'Not Otto. He is like me. A warrior. Chaste. God's servant. The pleasures of the flesh hold no interest for him, isn't that so, Otto?'

'It is,' I say with conviction, and realise just what a liar I have been in my past dealings with this man. But it has been necessary, for Charles is an intolerant and unforgiving man who has chosen a hard existence. For him women are a distraction, sent by Satan himself as a test. In this, as in much else, Charles is not like other men.

'Then what was it?' Devlet Giray asks, his German – which is spoken in deference to Charles, who will speak little else – softened almost to the point of incoherence.

'Sorry?' I say, as if I haven't understood.

'If not a woman, then what?' the Turkish Khan asks, his dark, almond eyes watching me strangely.

'For information,' I say, the German word – '*Auskunfte*' – pronounced with a hardness that makes Charles's eyes come up and study my face again.

'Information?' he says softly. 'What *kind* of information?'

'About Peter.'

He waits, and, after a moment's hesitation, I go on. 'He's dying.'

Charles's face is hard. 'He'll die tomorrow anyway. That is, if he dares face me and doesn't run away again.'

There's laughter at that, but Charles himself remains grim. He continues to study me.

'Is that all?' he asks finally.

I shake my head, then, quietly: 'He means to assassinate you.'

'He tried. Nine days back. At a little place called Nizhny Mliny, north of here on the Vorskla. We caught the fellow. Racked him. Heated him up in places.'

Again there's laughter; but this time it's a cruel laughter. Mazeppa finds it particularly amusing.

'I think they'll try again. I was told—'

'Told by *whom*?'

I look about me, then look to Charles again, my eyes pleading for secrecy. But he ignores me. He wants to know.

'By whom?'

'By Patkul.'

There is a collective intake of breath. But Charles just stares at me, then shakes his head.

'Patkul's dead. Two years back and more. We broke him with a sledgehammer. Cut him apart and hung him on a wheel. I had his head set on a post beside the highway for his treachery.'

'*Johann* Patkul, yes. But he had a brother.'

Charles has a doubting expression in his eyes. He doesn't know whether to believe me or not. But I've never lied to him before. Not in any way he could have discovered, that is.

'A brother . . .' He shrugs. 'And what does this brother want?'

'To kill you. He was hoping I would help him find a way.'

'And in exchange?'

'*Auskunfte.*'

Charles smiles for the first time, then slowly reaches out and lays his right hand on my left shoulder. 'Where is he now?'

'I left him back in Kiev. But he was planning to come south. To seek you out.'

'And what name is he travelling under?'

I shrug. 'He wouldn't say. Kindler, possibly. Certainly not his own.'

'And how did *you* encounter him?'

I have rehearsed all this with Freisler, practised it a dozen times and more, just in case Charles should ask.

'A mutual friend. A Pole, working for Menshikov. One of his agents.'

Charles nods. He doesn't like it, but he understands the world in which I supposedly function. 'And what is he like, this brother?'

'Medium height and build. Dark . . .'

I deliberately keep it vague, for the truth is Patkul has no brother. Never had, and never will have, his mother having died giving birth to her only son.

Charles looks away thoughtfully. His hatred of the Livonian noble Patkul is quite legendary. He blames him – rightly – for starting the Great Northern War, and when the chance came to grab him, he did. In fact, he went as far as writing in a separate clause – Clause 11 in the treaty he imposed upon the Saxons and Poles, the Treaty of Altranstadt – insisting that peace was conditional on them handing over Patkul.

To find he has a brother is thus something of a shock, even if he only half believes it.

You might ask why I am doing this, but it's very simple. Five of our agents are dead. Dead at the hands of Russian agents, we must assume. So, if I can snare just one of those agents by this means – by accusing him of being Patkul's brother – then perhaps I can flush him out. Make him jump. And once we have one of them, we can quickly trace the rest, jumping back through time to trace them.

So this is important. This is the first step.

The conversation turns and, just as soon as seems natural, I bow to Charles and take my leave. Yet even as I turn away he reaches out and holds my arm, then tells me quietly to come to him later in his tent. After nightfall. I nod, then hurry from there, making my way through the tent city towards the town of Poltava itself, nestling to the south and west of the encampment.

Where the ground rises slightly, I turn and look back and have it confirmed for me. There are a host of Turkish troops here, and Cossacks, and – in a separate camp to the east – a contingency of Poles.

Outside the city's hastily thrown-up earthworks, guards challenge me, then, noting the decorations on my uniform, let me pass.

The town, besieged these past few weeks, is in a state of hasty preparation for tomorrow's battle. I find a quartermaster and attempt to commandeer a room, but it's a good hour or more before he finds me one. It's a poky little room on the upper floor of an inn, and I'm sharing with a cavalry captain, but the man is out, patrolling the Russian lines, finding out what Menshikov is up to.

I could save him the bother, only that's not my purpose here. Besides, I need to be alone so I can jump, because what I've seen needs to be explained. We need to send agents in to find out just what changes have been made and where.

Closing the door, I haul the bed across, blocking the entrance, then shrug the pack off my back and drop it on to the bed. Lifting my hand to my chest, I'm about to jump, when I realise something.

I don't need to go back. Not straight away. If I jump an hour from now it's all the same. And the thing is, I've had no time to myself – not a single minute – since I was brought back from Krasnogorsk.

So make some time, Otto. Now. Before you get sucked back into things.

I sit, my back to the door, my pack beside me. From the window across from me come the sounds of frantic activity outside in the muddy streets of the town: shouted orders and running, booted feet; the neighing of horses and the trundle of wagons. I look up, listening for a moment, then close my eyes and squeeze my hands tight into fists.

I can see her, lying there on the cart, her beautiful dark eyes staring sightlessly at the sky, her skin so pale it looks like ice has formed beneath the surface. And I beside her. The two of us utterly detached, so far from each other that the small distance between our hands might be a thousand billion miles for all it mattered.

A tear rolls down my cheek. The first I've cried. The first I've been allowed since I returned from there.

I wipe it away, then stand, opening my eyes, looking about me determinedly.

I will not let this defeat me. I will not. They've killed me, sure, but I don't have to stay dead. I'm a time agent – a *Reisende*. If anyone can avoid death, I can.

And then it strikes me. They brought her back. They brought her back through time. They had to, because there is no other explanation, unless her corpse was a fake. How do I know this? Because there were two of her – one dead and one alive – and they couldn't manage that unless one of them was from another timeline.

But what does that mean? Did they do to Katerina what they did to Seydlitz?

Maybe. But who's *they*? And how was the old man, Kolya, involved in all of this? Why have I never heard of him before?

Yes, and why that intense hatred of his? What have I done to him that he should hate me so?

I must get answers. Only how?

And then I laugh, because the answer's simple. Pretend he's here, in Poltava. Get Hecht and the others to look for him for me.

Oh, I don't mean to neglect my task. I'll do my best to unravel whatever's happening here. I'll find out who and why and how and change it back. Only I can't leave Katerina to that fate. *I can't.* And if a lie or two will help, I'll lie like Loki himself.

The thought disturbs me. Loki . . . Someone once quipped that Loki had to be a Russian. But he's German through and through. Or, should I say, Teuton. His inventiveness. His quick and agile mind. His ability to seem what he is not. These aren't Russian qualities. No. Russia is a landscape; Germany an idea. And Loki, I sometimes feel, embodies the *idea*. And yet . . .

I pause. For some reason the image of Reichenau with his

obscene double head comes to mind, and for no reason I shiver as if cold. But the day is warm. Even the slight breeze that moves the curtains cannot mask the fact.

Kolya, then. I'll find out who Kolya is and where he comes from and who he's working for.

And then?

But that's asking too much. One step at a time, Otto, that's the way.

218

Hecht frowns, as if my news has only clouded things further, but Freisler for once is grinning.

'It's a major push,' he says. 'It *has* to be. Why else make so many changes?'

'Yes, but why?' I ask. 'Why undermine your own side?'

I look to Hecht, but he has that distracted look he always has when he's thinking things through.

I lower my voice, then speak to Freisler again. 'Charles bought the Patkul story.'

'About his brother?'

I nod.

'Good. Then that has to be your main priority. To flush out one of them. We'll send in agents to check out the rest.' Freisler sits back a little, then shakes his head in admiration at the Russians. 'What audacity!'

Audacity? Or stupidity? Because how can it benefit them? If Peter loses, Russia will be close to collapse, the road to Moscow open to a decisive strike from the combined Swedish and Turkish armies, and there's nothing the Sultan would like better than to add the Russian steppes to his vast empire.

And how can that help their cause?

Hecht clearly feels the same. I can see it in his face. Only he says nothing, merely gestures for Freisler to go.

But this *is* intriguing. Why would the Russians want to lose such a crucial battle? I go to speak, but Hecht lifts a hand. I can see he needs to think this through.

Sensing that I'm dismissed, I stand and, following Freisler's example, leave.

Only I don't go straight back to my own rooms. Instead I go and see an old friend.

The room I step into is long and narrow, like a railway carriage, only shelves fill both walls, stacked to bursting with files and boxes and tapes, a disorderly mish-mash from across the ages.

'Otto?' old Schnorr says, looking up from his desk and peering over his massive spectacles at me, the lenses of which make his eyes seem as large as gobstoppers. 'Now here's a stranger. Must be . . . oh, a good three years since you last graced us with your company.'

There are three others in the room with old Schnorr, each at their own desk, each staring across at me through a pair of identical overlarge glasses.

'Any new faces?' I ask, and wonder how many thousands of times he's been asked that.

'One or two.'

'Anyone interesting?'

Old Schnorr smiles. 'It depends on what you mean by that. Interesting operationally or interesting genetically?'

I smile, then hand him the slip of paper on which I've written Kolya's name.

'This all you have?'

'I can describe him for you, if you like.'

Which I do. Schnorr sighs, then looks round at his fellows. 'Anyone?'

Three heads shake a no, then settle. Schnorr looks back at me. 'I'll run it through the machine. See what comes up. But without an image . . .' He hesitates, then. 'Any reason why you want to know?'

'He killed me.'

'Ah . . .' Schnorr nods and his chin lifts thoughtfully. 'Then I can see why you'd want to trace him. Even so . . .' One hand comes up and scratches at his cheek a moment, then he looks back at me. 'You got an hour?'

I smile. 'Sure. All the time in the world.'

219

Old Schnorr is an interesting fellow. Moreover, his job, which he created himself, is one of the strangest in Four-Oh.

Old Schnorr trawls Time for faces. Repeated faces. Faces so alike that they might be accidents of genetics, or – just as likely – the faces of agents operating in Time.

The idea came to him when he was looking at a reproduction of an old painting one day – Raphael's *The School Of Athens*, I believe – when he recognised one of the faces as being similar to that of a Russian agent. He told Hecht, who sent a man back, and sure enough, one of Raphael's models, back there in sixteenth-century Florence, turned out to be one of theirs: a 'sleeper' by the name of Grechko. He escaped, but not before we blew their whole operation there.

After that there was no looking back. Schnorr was allocated a budget and a team of keen young students to help him. Repeatedly going back in time, they began to build up a massive data base of names and faces, using the most up-to-date technology – that, incidentally, of the twenty-sixth century – to begin to create what we now know as 'The Record'. Old paintings, photographs, films and holo-images all went into the mix indiscriminately to be sorted and collated by a programme devised specially by Schnorr for the task.

Trawling Time. Looking for repeated features.

It's easily done. Agents go back into areas of time we know are ripe for change with discreet cameras. Posing as natives, they wander the streets, casually looking at this or at that, and all the while their cameras record everything they see. And when they return, the cameras are processed and the faces fed into the programme, and we see what we see.

I say easy, but it wasn't easy at first. Because some faces are just *so* similar, the genetics *so* close. that we can make mistakes. Faces repeat naturally – it is the way of nature – so we have to look for unnatural repetition. Faces that seem to have died out, along with that genetic line, and then suddenly are there again. Faces that leap five hundred years, that are found in tenth-century Byzantium and then, later, in Renaissance Italy.

Like Grechko's.

Since he set up 'The Record', Schnorr has traced over sixty of their agents by this means. Some we knew about already, but several – and Vosnesensky is perhaps the most famous – would have eluded us altogether without Schnorr's programme identifying him.

But Kolya . . . will they be able to find Kolya?

Schnorr sits me down in front of his machine, then leans over me and taps the screen. 'You say he's old?'

'Old for the time. Late forties, maybe. Fifties, even, but no older.'

'And burning eyes. Like Rasputin's?'

I nod.

'Okay. Then let's form a subset of possibles. Let's see if you can't see a face that's *like* his.'

And so, for the next hour, I watch face after face appear before me and try to describe in what fashion each differs from Kolya's. And as the process continues, and Schnorr fine-tunes his database, so the distinctions become finer, the faces more and more like Kolya's, until—

'That's it! It isn't *him*, but that's *almost* him. If it wasn't for the eyes . . .'

Schnorr nods. 'Good. The eyes aside, there might be a direct genetic line, and if we can trace it . . .'

'You can do that?'

'Of course. We've another six matches to this one already. Scattered, admittedly, but they're family, even if they don't know it. What we'll try to do now is fill the gaps and trace the line forwards and back. Somewhere, I'm sure, we'll find your fellow.'

'As easy as that?'

Schnorr laughs. 'Far from it. Genetic lines are real bramble trails: illegitimacy, emigration, blood feuds. There's never a direct road. But it *is* possible. Given time and a great deal of detective work.'

'If you haven't time . . .'

But old Schnorr looks down at me and beams. 'On the contrary, Otto. I'll put young Horst on the job. After all, if we can find this Kolya, then maybe we can stop you being killed.'

220

'Otto's right,' Freisler says, as he enters the room. 'They've made at least five, possibly six major changes to the pre-battle scenario.'

Hecht looks up, past me. 'On just the Swedish side or both?'

'We haven't checked yet to see what changes have been made

to the Russian side of things. I thought Otto might find that out.'

Hecht shakes his head. 'Too risky right now. They'll have Peter surrounded with their agents.'

'But he *knows* Peter. He has *access*.'

'Maybe. But Otto stays with Charles for now. Focus on what's happening around *him*. If changes *have* been made on the Russian side, then they're almost certain to have been made to further weaken their position. That is, if that's their strategy. Speaking of which . . .' Hecht looks to me. 'There's something you should know, Otto. About the situation back there. Our agents . . .'

'Five dead,' I say.

'Yes, but only two of them were from that time zone. As usual, they were being tracked, on the screens back at the platform. When they blinked out – one almost immediately after the other – we sent an agent back, to a point one minute before they vanished. He too blinked out, almost instantly.'

'And the others?'

'We sent one back an hour before, another a week. Both were intercepted by the Russians almost immediately they jumped through.'

'Do we know how?'

Freisler answers for him. 'They've saturated the area, Otto. There must be three, maybe four dozen of their agents back there.'

'But none about Charles,' Hecht throws in. 'That's why we sent you straight back there, into his tent. It was the safest place.'

Yes, I think, *but if the Russians are looking out for our agents jumping through, then surely they could have hit me once I came out of there – in the village, perhaps.*

'So we know nothing,' I say. 'Nothing except what I brought back.'

'Not so,' Freisler says. 'I went back myself. We got a map and worked out where the first two vanished, then dropped me in the day before, half a mile away, in a wooded copse, looking down across a valley at the place.'

'What did you see?'

'They were duelling,' Hecht says, a slight anger in his voice. 'Agents of mine and they were duelling among themselves! Over some gambling debt, no doubt, or a woman.'

Freisler is silent a moment, watching Hecht, then looks to me again. 'It's true. They were standing on a hilltop, out in the open, twenty paces apart. It was quite distant but you could see the two puffs of smoke. One of them fell immediately, the other . . .'

The look on Freisler's face surprises me. 'What?'

Hecht answers for him. 'A Russian sniper, that's our guess. Blew the top of his skull off. Knocked him forward, so it had to be from behind.'

'There was a thicket,' Freisler says, back in control of himself, 'just to the right of where they had set up. The assassin must have been in there, waiting to pick him off.'

'And the one who jumped in?'

'The same,' Hecht says. 'He didn't stand a chance.'

'But we can get them back, right? We can make changes and—'

'They keep anticipating us,' Hecht says. 'Out-guessing us. But it's also weight of numbers. That's why I called you back. That's why we need to capture one of their agents and find out what's going on. What Yastryeb's thinking is. Because I can't afford to send in agent after agent. We haven't got the men.'

'But Freisler showed it could be done. We just need to be careful.'

'We tried that.'

Freisler nods. 'It's like, well, like they *wanted* us to see. I felt, well, it's something I've never felt before, but I felt I was being watched. Like Yastryeb himself was somewhere in that landscape, looking across at me through high-powered lenses, a sardonic smile on his features.'

'Yes, but—'

'But what?' Hecht asks. 'Cut our losses? Let the Russians get on with it, whatever it is?' He sighs heavily. 'If it were a single agent, and if it wasn't Poltava, and if I had a single clue as to why the Russians were doing this, then yes, I'd cut our losses. Only . . .'

I count to ten, then ask, 'What happens up the line? How does it affect things historically?'

'For the Russians? The consequences are appalling. They pretty well cease to exist. And that makes no sense at all, unless—'

'Unless they want to draw us in?'

'Yes.'

'So you want me to find out what Yastryeb's thinking is?'

Hecht nods.

Only . . . would Yastryeb let his agents know what his thinking is?

Maybe not, but I understand Hecht's dilemma. If this *is* an attempt by the Russians to suck us into a massive firefight, then Hecht ought to cut his losses and keep out of it. Better to lose five agents – bad as that is – than fifty. But it's not that that's nagging at me. What intrigues me is why the Russians should want to destroy their own history – to, in effect, burn their own house down – to achieve that?

And I laugh, because the answer is right there in front of me. 'Scorched earth.'

'Sorry?' Hecht says, not following my reasoning.

But I'm gone from there. Gone to see Ernst. Because Ernst, if anyone, will know.

Ernst is halfway through a lesson, but he's delighted to see me, as are the boys – Alpers and Haller, Muller, Tomas and young Matteus.

I embrace him, then stand back a little. 'Scorched earth. What are the historical parallels?'

Ernst laughs. 'Well, it's a particularly Russian form of warfare. Almost no other nation does it, unless one counts the Portuguese in 1811, or certain Chinese warlords, who—'

'Russia, Ernst. Stick to Russia.'

'Okay.' He thinks a moment, then, as if delivering a lecture, begins. 'As far as Russia is concerned, three particular instances come to mind. The first is Poltava, 1709. Where the crisis is right now, am I right?'

I nod, and Ernst continues, the boys watching him, enthralled.

'To be more specific we're talking initially about the summer of 1707. That's when Charles XII of Sweden decided to march his army across Poland to capture Moscow. Ahead of this advance, the young Russian tsar, Peter, had vast swathes of Poland put to the torch, whole towns destroyed, so that Charles and his men were unable to replenish their supplies. And it worked. Without forage the Swedish horses suffered. They were too weak to continue. Charles's campaign faltered and finally came to a standstill at Grodno, halfway between Warsaw and Vilnius, on the Russian border. Charles dug in for the winter and awaited the fresh grass of the spring. At the same time he had Count Lewenhaupt scour Livonia for supplies – food, powder and ammunition – together with the horses and wagons to carry it all. By late spring the next year he was ready to resume his campaign. Only Peter was up to the challenge. The young tsar called a council of war and ordered the creation of a zone of total devastation one hundred and twenty miles deep, stretching north and east from the Swedish camp. Within that zone, every last scrap of food or fodder was to be burned, denying the Swedes any sustenance. And again it worked. Faced with what was in effect a region of utter desolation, Charles turned his army south, towards his Turkish and Cossack allies and away from the heart of Russia. Moscow was saved.'

'And the second instance?'

Ernst smiles. 'Napoleon. June to November 1812. His "Grand Army" of almost half a million men ran into difficulties almost immediately when they discovered that their very first "prize", the town of Vilnius, had been left in ashes by the retreating Russian forces. The bridge – their only river crossing – had been destroyed, along with the Russians' supply magazines and stores, which Napoleon had counted on for his campaign. A change in the weather, which turned the roads into quagmires, and the use by the Russian peasantry of vicious guerilla tactics, ended with a mere forty thousand ragged and almost skeletal troops staggering back into Vilnius six months later.'

A hand goes up.

'Yes, Tomas?'

'But the French *took* Moscow, Meister.'

'Yes, but they couldn't hold it. Besides, you recall what happened . . .'

There are one or two frowns, but three of the boys have their hands up, eager to answer.

'Matteus?'

'They burned it, Meister.'

Ernst beams. 'They did indeed. The Governor, Rostopchin, ordered the prison doors opened. Among those freed were over four hundred arsonists. Within hours the city was on fire, the conflagration so intense, so widespread, that three-quarters of

Moscow burned to the ground. Napoleon marched into a city that had been virtually destroyed. Not only that, but the land surrounding Moscow was systematically ravaged by local peasant bands and Cossacks, making the task of gathering enough food to feed the city an almost impossible one.'

'And the third?' I ask.

Ernst's smile is thin. 'Hitler. Barbarossa. In particular, late November 1942. Stalingrad. The German Sixth Army under General Paulus, trapped deep inside enemy territory after Zhukov's counter-attack. The Russians destroyed everything within the Germans' reach.'

'The *Kessel*.'

I'm talking now of what the Germans in Stalingrad called 'the cauldron' – the enclosed killing-ground in which they ebbed out their remaining weeks, dying by the thousand every day.

Ernst looks to me and nods. 'The tactic of *Schwerpunkt*.' *Encirclement*.

Yes, and that too is part of the historical pattern. To draw us in, surround us, and then . . . eliminate us.

'There are differences,' Ernst says after a moment. 'Peter's deliberate devastation of the countryside is a complete one-off in terms of the scale of the thing, but the principle's the same.' Ernst gives a little laugh. 'The Russians learned it from the Tatars, actually.'

'Really?'

'Yes. It was in the May of 1687. A Russian army of one hundred thousand men, under Golitsyn, had marched south to take on the Great Khan and end the persistent Tatar raids into Russian territory. They had travelled down the Poltava road, as fate would have it, and as they approached Perekop, so they saw that the whole of the horizon ahead of them was filled with smoke. The Tatars had burned every living thing ahead of them. They struggled on for a while, but quickly realised they'd have to turn back. No battle was ever fought, but the Russians lost over forty-five thousand men, nearly half their force. The experience taught them a useful lesson though.'

'And that was it? The first time?'

'Urd no. If you really want to trace it back to source, you'd have to look to Fabius.'

'Fabius?'

'The legendary Fabius Maximus, the Roman dictator who fought Hannibal. Or rather, *didn't*. You could say he originated this form of warfare. His tactic was to retreat before his enemies – in his case the Carthaginians – destroying the land in front of them, while feeding and maintaining his own army, and let them lose men to hunger and disease. Then, when they were finally weak enough, he struck back at them, encircling them, cutting them off from any source of reinforcement or resupply.'

'And then eliminating them.'

'Right.' Ernst pauses, looking at me questioningly. Thus far he's enjoyed making the historical parallel, but he has suddenly understood that it's to a purpose. 'So how does this help us understand what's going on right now?'

I hesitate, then launch in, aware that the boys are listening to every word.

'Think about it. About the Russians, I mean. What if they're doing what they always did? Destroying their own land in front of their enemy? Drawing us in, deep into their territory, then turning on us. Only, what if they're doing it in Time?'

Ernst stares at me, surprised. But I can see that he likes the idea. But does the analogy hold? Is that really what Yastryeb is up to?

Ernst is looking thoughtful. 'Maybe,' he says finally. 'Only how would they go about that? How – when we can jump out of there any time we want – could they form an effective *Kessel*? How could they surround us when we won't let ourselves be surrounded?'

'I'm not sure,' I answer. And that's true, only I'm beginning to get the vaguest glimmer of an idea. 'By doing exactly what they're doing at Poltava and destroying their own history bit by bit, by drawing us in, perhaps by encouraging us to help in that destruction. And then trapping us in ruined cul-de-sacs of time.'

Ernst, however, seems anything but convinced by the idea. 'But why would we do that if they were already doing the job for us? Hecht would *never* risk the agents.'

'He's already lost five.'

Ernst's mouth opens then closes again. 'Yes, but—'

'Don't you see?'

'See what?'

'How hard it would be for Hecht *not* to respond . . . not to risk at least some tentative action to try to gain advantage of the situation. After all, it's what his whole being is trained to do. To see the historical cusps and react to them. For him *not* to react . . . it's almost impossible.'

Ernst looks worried now. 'But he *must*. If that *is* what they're doing.'

'Yes,' I say. Only I'm remembering now that look on Hecht's face, the silent dismissal, first of Freisler and then of myself. Decisions. Even now, Hecht is making grave decisions.

Scorched earth . . . And I think of the *Kessels* at Stalingrad and Poltava, and of the thousands of French soldiers dying of cold and exhaustion on the road to Moscow, and I wonder, just for an instant, whether that is to be our fate, too. Whether, when the time comes and the snows begin to fall, we too will be found wanting.

222

In the real history – the history we know – events go like this.

It is eight in the morning, on 17 June 1709, Charles's twenty-seventh birthday, and – as is his habit – he has ridden out to inspect his men and their positions, a few miles south of Poltava, near the village of Nizhny Mliny. The Swedes and Cossacks are drawn up along the bank of the Vorskla, facing the Russians across the river. As Charles rides along, within musket range of the Russians, one of his Drabants falls from his horse, shot dead in the saddle.

Unconcerned for his safety, Charles rides on, then turns his horse to climb the bank, turning his back contemptuously on his enemy. At that very moment, a Russian musket ball strikes his left heel, piercing the boot and travelling the full length of Charles's foot, smashing the bone and leaving by the big toe. Charles grunts with pain, but carries on, gritting his teeth and finishing his inspection as if nothing has happened. Yet when, three hours later, he tries to dismount back at camp, he passes out from the pain.

It's a bad injury, one that Charles almost dies of. Coming just nine days before the decisive battle of Poltava, it proves critical in that Charles, his army's chief strategist and good-luck totem, will not be there in person on the battlefield.

But history has changed. This time, as Charles climbs the bank, the musket balls whizz harmlessly past the young king, and as he looks back contemptuously at the Russian lines, he does not see his unknown 'nemesis', lying there among the trees where the river makes a turn, his head blown off.

But I, sitting there on my horse among the honour guard, waiting for the king to rejoin us, have seen it all: saw the man appear from nowhere and, at an arm's length, shoot the Russian sniper dead before vanishing again. As clear an instance of time assassination as I've ever seen.

So do we leave it at that, or do we intercede? Do we attempt to change it back?

I have a strong sense of them waiting there for us in the wings, a gut feeling that if we sent someone in to try to change things back they would simply ambush them, picking off our agents one by one until we ceased to exist. In my mind I can picture the massive firefight that would result, there among the trees, and know that however good we are, they would outnumber us three, maybe four to one and kill us all.

What's more, we could use whatever weaponry we chose to use, but they would only respond in kind. No matter how much we upped the stakes, they'd top us, as if it were some crazy game of poker in which we held the losing hand. Three twos against four aces.

I turn my horse and make to ride away, only as I do there is a massive explosion behind me, back where the dead assassin lies. My horse bucks wildly, then calms, and I look up in time to see Charles, staring across the water at the huge pall of smoke and steam that's rising from the crater in the riverbank, a look of astonishment in his eyes.

He's wondering, no doubt, what unearthly form of mortar could have made such a huge hole, yet as the water rushes in, boiling and steaming against the super-heated earth, I, at least, understand what it is. A message. To me. To let me know that they know I'm there. And the thought chills me, because once more I don't understand their motives, only that they're taunting me.

223

Hecht is far too calm for my liking.

'But they know I'm in there,' I say, repeating it to him. 'It's as if they know something. As if they're mocking me.'

They know I'm dead, is what I really mean. *Know it and want to keep reminding me of it.*

'Or were just removing the evidence,' Hecht says.

Only why? It's not like the Russian sniper was one of their agents . . . Or was he? Is what we're witnessing second thoughts – some huge change of mind on Yastryeb's part? Has he suddenly decided *not* to back Peter, but to put all of his considerable influence behind someone else? Menshikov, perhaps? It's possible. I mean, I've always wondered about Menshikov, wondered if he was one of their agents, that is, because his origins are veiled to say the least. If he is, then it makes a kind of sense, because it's far easier to directly control one of your own men than seek to influence such a powerful and headstrong young man as the six-foot-seven Peter.

Only it doesn't *quite* make sense, because Peter doesn't seem to do much wrong as far as the Russians are concerned. Indeed, I'd go so far as to say that he fulfils the same function in their history as Frederick in ours. Without him, well, there *is* no Russia.

At least, that's how we've been reading it all along. But what if we're wrong? What if there's some other path their history can take?

'*Maskirovka*,' Hecht says quietly, and Freisler, sitting just across from me, smiles and nods.

It's an old Russian term, a catch-all concept, covering deception, camouflage, and all manner of operational security. Yet what kind of *maskirovka* would be worth losing Poltava? It might seem obvious, but we keep returning to this: *what possible advantage could be gained by seemingly losing it all?*

I want to find that out, only Hecht isn't going to let me.

'I've changed my mind,' he says, fixing me with his grey eyes. 'I'm sending Freisler in. You're too prominent, Otto. For some reason . . .'

He doesn't say it, but I can guess what he's alluding to. My escapade on the river with Krylenko and the *staritskii*, the laser gun.

'But I—'

Hecht interrupts me. 'You'll stay here, Otto. *Okay?* Then, more gently. 'We'll use you. Don't worry. But not yet. Not until we find out a lot more about what's going on. What our two agents were duelling about, for a start.'

I go to open my mouth, then think better of it. It's a woman, I'm sure. What else could be that important?

'So what do you want me to do?'

Hecht reaches down, then hands across two files. Print-outs. 'I want you to read these. And then I want you to go and see Kirchoff.'

'*Kirchoff*? But—'

'You'll see him. And afterwards you'll come back here and we'll talk. Okay?'

It's *not* okay, and I want to protest, only Hecht seems insistent.

I stand, then bow smartly to him, as a soldier bows to his commander. And then I turn and, without another word, walk over to the door and step through.

224

Kirchoff! What the fuck does he want me to see Kirchoff for? There's nothing wrong with me. Nothing *mentally*.

But first the files.

Only when I get back to my room, it's to find Ernst there, sitting on my bed. He wants to talk. About Katerina and Kolya and – most of all – about what happened back in Krasnogorsk.

Only I don't know what happened. Not yet, anyway.

Ernst looks fragile and nervous, but that's how he is these days, and the news that Katerina and I somehow died back there has not improved his condition. Perhaps he even blames himself. But

I'm not going to be sucked into speculating about the situation, not until I know a hell of a lot more than I do right now.

I change the subject. Ask him what he makes of Poltava and the changes the Russians have made. He makes me go through them again, one by one, then shakes his head, just as mystified by it all as I am.

'It makes no sense,' he says. 'Absolutely no sense.'

'I know. Only it must. *Somehow.*'

'And the changes up the line?'

'Are devastating, so Hecht says. Russia, well, there *is* no Russia, in effect.'

Ernst considers that, then looks at me again. 'We haven't got it all,' he says. 'There's something missing. Something that makes sense of it all.'

'Sure,' I say. 'Only what?'

Ernst gestures to the files I'm holding. 'What are they?'

'Files on our agents. The two who were in there.'

'And they're among the five who are dead?'

'Yes. As of now.'

'Do I know them?'

I nod. 'Neipperg's one of them. The other's Stein.'

'Ah . . .'

We were in the Garden with Josef Neipperg. He's of our time, so to speak. He shared a lot with us. And now he's dead. For now, anyway.

I sigh, then sit beside Ernst on the bed, handing him Stein's file. 'And there's another thing.'

'What?'

'Hecht wants me to see Kirchoff.'

Ernst's head comes up quickly. He meets my eyes, then, embarrassed, looks away. He licks at his lips, then asks. 'And what do you think of that?'

'I think it's a shit idea.'

Ernst is quiet after that. Too quiet.

'*What*?' I ask.

He looks to me. 'I think you should. After what happened. It must have been quite a shock, seeing yourself like that. Not to speak of . . .'

Of Katerina.

I let out my breath. 'I don't need to see Kirchoff. I don't . . .' I stand, then throw the file down angrily. 'What the fuck is Hecht up to? I mean, why summon me back if he doesn't think I'm capable mentally?'

'That's not what he's inferring.'

'No?'

'No. But you're not a machine, Otto. And it must have hurt. It must have . . .' He looks away, then visibly shivers. 'I can't imagine, I mean, what I'd have felt. I've never loved someone that much, Otto. I've never, well, never been that lucky.'

I stare at Ernst, seeing him suddenly. Seeing how lonely he is. How incomplete.

Sitting, I put my arm about his shoulders. 'You think I should see him, then?'

Ernst turns his head and looks at me. His eyes are smiling, yet there's still the same pain in them, behind it all. 'I think you need to.'

'But if Hecht finds out about Katerina . . .'

'Hecht won't. Kirchoff won't tell him.'

I almost laugh at that, only Ernst is in earnest. 'He *won't*,' he says again, this time with emphasis.

'How do you know?'

'Because he knows already. Because I told him.'

The files don't tell me much, only that they're both good agents. Solid, reliable men. Men you could trust with your life.

No wonder Hecht is worried.

I'm about to get washed and changed, ready for my session with Kirchoff, when young Horst pays me a visit.

'So?' I ask. 'What's the news on our friend Kolya?'

He hands me yet another folder. I open it, then frown. 'Is this it?'

'That's it.'

'But—'

'I was looking for the best part of a month, subjective. Twenty-seven different sites, in eleven separate epochs, and that's all I could find. It's like, well, if I didn't know better, I'd say that our friend Kolya had set about destroying any clear links.'

'What do you mean?'

'I mean that his ancestors keep going missing. Boating accidents, fires, sudden disappearances, journeys where they set off and never come back, even straightforward abductions. If it made any sense, I'd say he'd gone out of his way to kill his own ancestors. Only . . . how would *he* survive without *them*?'

I look down once more at the almost empty folder. 'You're serious?'

Horst nods.

'So what does Meister Schnorr think of this?'

'He thinks you should come see him again. He thinks . . .' Horst smiles, then bows his head politely. 'No,' he says. 'I'll let the Meister tell you himself what he thinks.'

And so I find myself again in that long and narrow room, seated beside old Schnorr as he taps an entry on to the pad and the screen lights up.

'These are the lines we've traced. The six entries we began with, and the thirty-two we subsequently traced.'

'Thirty-two, but I thought—'

'We were lucky with five of them. Five out of thirty-two. Says it all, don't you think?'

'Says what?'

'That our friend Kolya is tampering. Removing people from the timestream. Hiding them away somewhere.'

I laugh. It's a ridiculous idea.

'You're not concentrating, Otto. *Think*. We know he can travel through time. He'd have to, to bring the corpses of you and the woman into the timestream *you* inhabited. If he can do that, then maybe he's found a way of "tagging" his own ancestry. Of being able to move them through time somehow, removing them from their places in history and tucking them away somewhere.'

I am staring at old Schnorr now, open-mouthed. 'Even if he could, why in Urd's name would he want to?'

'To protect himself? To stop someone killing him further up the line by assassinating one of his ancestors?'

'But . . .'

'It's only a theory, but take this into account, if you will. Every single one of those ancestors that we tracked down and who subsequently disappeared, every one of them, I repeat, *without exception*, vanished in such a way that they left no trace.'

'No *trace*?'

'Bodies, Otto. There was a distinct lack of bodies. Of bones and graves and, well, piece it together yourself. What is the likelihood of that? In fact, what is the likelihood – within one ancestral, genetic line – of all of this happening?'

I open my mouth to answer, then close it. Because I realise suddenly that old Schnorr is right. At least, right in his broad reading of events. As for the detail . . .

'How do we find them?'

Old Schnorr laughs at that. 'You go back. See for yourself. Work out how they were taken and where.'

'But—'

'They must be somewhere,' he goes on. 'Somewhere *safe*. Like this, maybe . . .' And he gestures to the walls of Four-Oh that surround us.

'But didn't Horst—'

The Meister interrupts me, for once unusually stern. 'That's not Horst's job. He's a researcher, not an agent. You want to find out what your friend Kolya is doing, you do it. After all, it's *you* he killed.'

I stare at him a moment, then look to Horst, noting the young man's embarrassment. Then, knowing at some deeper level that he's right, I bow, first to Schnorr and then to Horst.

'Forgive me. But you can tell me where to look?'

'Where *and* when.' And, now that the moment has passed, old Schnorr smiles again. 'Intriguing, eh? Makes you wonder just where he actually comes from, doesn't it?'

Only I think I know. I think another piece of the puzzle has just fallen into place.

227

I'm keen to get started, to track down Kolya and the ancestors who haven't yet disappeared, only Hecht has other ideas.

'Freisler's seen one of their agents,' he says, looking up from behind his screen. 'In the Swedish camp. I want you both to go in there and take him. Question him. Find out what you can.'

It's not the time to argue, to say that there are more important tasks. I bow my head, then hurry to the platform where Freisler is waiting for me. He hands me a pack and a weapon – a tranquilliser gun, I note, made to look like a 'replica' from the age – and then steps up.

I watch him vanish, then take my place on the circle. It's only then, as I look about me at the room – at the concentric circles of desks that surround the platform, and at the women, seated at their posts – that I realise how intensely I'm being watched. Which is strange, because I've never had that feeling before, never had this sense that, somehow, all of their hopes rest on me. Or maybe I'm just imagining that. Maybe, in these tense and uncertain times, they feel this way about every agent who ventures out into the darkness of the Past.

I turn, looking for Zarah, and see her there, at Urte's station, leaning over the smaller, younger woman, whispering something to her. She looks up and, seeing that I'm watching her, smiles and gives a wave. That too is unusual. But I've barely time to register it when I'm there suddenly, among the bushes at the edge of the camp, the cold night air swirling about me. Freisler is three paces distant, his back to me, looking in at the activity around one of the campfires.

I step alongside. Putting a finger to his lips, he points, indicating a soldier just to the right of the others, sitting with his back to a massive log. The man is dressed in the bright blue uniform of Lewenhaupt's infantry, but even at this distance I recognise him.

'Svetov,' I say quietly.

'Yes,' Friesler whispers back. 'Arkadi Svetov himself.'

I confess that this once I really *am* surprised. Svetov is their chief agent up the line in the twenty-fourth century – in the Age of the Mechanists. Even Dankevich takes orders from him. So what is he doing here, playing the infantryman on the evening before Poltava?

And I realise something else. He must have been *in situ* for some while, because these Swedish soldiers – their 'shock troops', famous for their use of cold steel on the battlefield – have been together the best part of a dozen years and more, and while Svetov won't necessarily have had to have been part of it quite that long, he would most certainly have needed to be one of their comrades for a year or two simply to win their trust. These elite Swedish regiments do not recruit passing volunteers. Thus, to see him at his ease among them tells me a great deal. The Russians have been planning this a long, long time. They've had their agents in place all the while, waiting for us, setting their traps.

Of which this, perhaps, is one?

I can't let myself believe that. Can't start getting paranoid about them knowing our every move. I mean, how could they? Even *I* don't know what I'm about to do.

No. They were just lucky, intercepting our agents in that fashion. Hard work and numbers, that's what it was. Yes, and sharp eyes, too.

I look to Freisler, wondering if he's got any kind of plan. We can't march straight in there, that's for sure. I'm about to ask, when Freisler turns to me.

'Just stay beside me,' he whispers. 'You take the Swede.' He taps my gun. 'In the neck. I'll take Svetov.'

I'm about to ask what's happening when one of the Swedes gets up and, slinging his rifle over his shoulder, calls across to Svetov. My Swedish is poor – dialect Swedish, anyway, which this soldier speaks – but it's clear it's their turn to patrol the camp perimeter, and as the two of them move out from the circle of the firelight, Freisler and I shadow them.

I do as Freisler does, taking his lead, obeying his silent gestures without question, moving through the darkness of the trees until we come down into a kind of gulley, at the foot of which is a clearing and a narrow stream. We are to the right of the other two, just behind them yet no more than ten paces distant as they emerge into the clearing.

We hear a sharp exhalation of surprise, and I see that the two are faced by a loose semi-circle of men, all of whom point weapons.

Freisler. Five times Freisler, and all of them grinning.

I don't need to be told. This is the moment. Even as I raise my gun, I hear the whizz and soft smack of Freisler's dart thudding into Svetov's neck. My own hits the other man an instant later.

Svetov's hand, half raised to touch his chest and jump to safety, falls limply away as he slumps, the drug taking immediate effect.

Beside him the other guard topples like a dummy and lies still.

Freisler looks to himselves and nods, and one by one they vanish, leaving only us there beneath a sliver of a moon, the stream rushing and gurgling not five yards from where we stand.

'Come on!' Freisler whispers urgently. 'We've twenty minutes before they'll miss him.' And, crouching over Svetov, he rips the man's shirt open then takes another capsule from his belt, slots it into the dart-gun and fires it – ungently, I feel – into Svetov's chest.

While the antidote is taking effect, we jointly haul him up and, as I hold him up against the trunk of a birch, Freisler secures him with special cord, tying his hands behind him, his legs and arms bound tightly so he can't escape.

Svetov's a big, blocky man, in his forties now, with longish flaxen hair that's groomed in the Swedish style, and a face that's both hard and handsome in an unorthodox way. As the antidote kicks in, Svetov lifts his head lazily and makes the kind of noise a waking sleeper makes, an incoherent slur of half-words. And then his head snaps up, his eyes coming suddenly clear and sharp.

'*You*!'

I smile. We've only met once before, when we were both young and inexperienced, but I recall his animosity towards me. It was a long time ago subjectively, and the years seem to have mellowed him, for he stares back at me now with what seems almost like respect.

'What do you want?'

'I want answers,' I say. 'And I don't care what we have to do to get them.'

He looks down, avoiding my eyes. 'Okay. What do you want to know?'

I look to Freisler, surprised. It's not what we expected. Svetov is supposed to be a real tough nut. Not a man to offer up anything.

'I want to know what your role was here. Why you were slotted in where you were, in Lewenhaupt's infantry. What was the reason for that?'

'I don't know.'

'Come on,' Freisler says with quiet menace. 'Save yourself the pain . . .'

'No . . . I'm serious. I don't know. I wasn't told.'

'Who do you report to?' Freisler asks, moving up close, his face a hand's length from Svetov's.

'The Master.'

'Yastryeb, you mean?'

But he doesn't answer that.

'So what's the plan?' Freisler asks. 'Why are you making all these changes? Why are you fucking with your own history?'

Svetov smiles at that, and Freisler slaps him: a vicious, stinging blow.

'I asked—' Freisler begins.

'And I heard,' Svetov answers aggressively, pushing his face almost into Freisler's.

'Well?' I ask, after a moment. 'Are you going to answer?'

'I *don't know*,' he says, with an exaggerated deliberateness, turning his head to look at me. 'I *wasn't told*.'

'I don't believe you,' Freisler says, drawing his knife. 'I think you know everything. I think—'

'I think you're full of shit!'

Freisler punches him hard in the stomach. I wince, feeling the blow. When Svetov's got his breath again, I crouch, and, looking up into his face, ask, 'Why are you doing this? Why are you undermining Peter?'

He spits blood – significantly, away from me – then meets my eyes.

'We aren't.'

'You *aren't*?'

'I said *we* aren't.'

'Then who is?'

'I don't know.'

Freisler explodes. He slams his fist into the side of Svetov's head.

'Don't play fucking games!'

Only maybe Svetov is telling the truth. Taking Freisler's arm, I draw him away. 'I think we should change tack,' I say quietly, so Svetov can't hear. 'Find out what he *does* know. He must be in contact with other agents. You know how things are. There must be *some* word – if only rumour – as to what's happening.'

Freisler broods on it, then nods. There's obviously bad blood between he and Svetov from somewhere in the past, but that doesn't concern me right now. I want to know why Svetov – one of their most senior operatives – has been kept in the dark by

Yastryeb. Because that makes no sense, unless Yastryeb for some reason doesn't trust Svetov.

And if that's so, then why not simply kill him?

Freisler turns back to Svetov. The Russian eyes him warily, like he suspects another blow at any moment, but Freisler merely stands there, hands at his sides, studying Svetov, as if to unravel him with his eyes.

'So what *do* you know?'

Svetov laughs. 'Oh, that's subtle. Real professional.'

Freisler ignores that. 'You know what? I could dissect you, if I wanted. Take you apart bone by bone. Draw the nerves out of your flesh like fine wires. I know how. Only I'm not sure the effort would be worth it. You clearly don't know enough. And what does that tell you? Where does that place you in the bigger picture? You're a big man, Arkadi. No foot soldier, you. But here you are, playing a sleeper's meagre, lonely part, being fed scraps of information while clearly something big is going on. How does that make you feel?' Freisler smiles. 'I'll tell you. It makes you feel shut out. Snubbed. Or is it worse than that? Is this a kind of . . . exile?'

Svetov's eyes flare. Not much, yet enough to show that Freisler has struck close to home. 'The master would not do that.'

'No?'

'No.'

'Then why are you here? What possible reason could there be to use a man of your talents so . . . *cheaply?*'

Svetov looks away. That clearly stings, as much as any blow. No doubt he's brooded on this. Only I can see he has no answer, only his hurt, his growing resentment.

Freisler sees it, too, because he hones in on it. 'You see, we have a problem understanding just what's happening here. Why your master should waste so many men buggering up his own history.

Why he should expend so much time and effort doing our work for us.'

Svetov is silent, but his eyes smoulder. It's as if Freisler is articulating his own innermost thoughts. In fact, he probably wants to know why even more than we do.

I interject. 'He told you to be patient, didn't he? To trust him, no matter what.'

Svetov looks up at me, then looks away.

'It's all right,' I say. 'You don't have to tell me. I know how difficult it must have been. I can see it. The two of you alone. Him telling you that he had a special task for you. One that – on the surface, anyway – was not merely unglamorous, but made little sense. Something that would make sense, *only when the time came.*'

His eyes come up briefly, and I know I've got it right, but he still won't answer.

'I know how hard that can be, Arkadi. Know because I've been there.'

'You don't know *anything.*'

It's a cold, hard statement that makes me reassess things. I've got part of it, but not all. So what have I missed? I take a chance. 'Does the name Reichenau mean anything to you?'

Freisler turns and stares at me, but I press on.

'*Michael* Reichenau? Do you know anyone by that name?'

Svetov shakes his head.

'What about Kolya?'

Svetov shrugs, as much as he can. 'Kolya's a common name.'

'Not *so* common.'

'Common enough. I know three at least, across the ages.'

It's enough to make me wonder whether one of them is my Kolya, but I don't pursue it. Not now, anyway. And he doesn't seem to be hiding anything. But we're not getting anywhere being so obtuse.

'The agents Yastryeb sent in—'

'What agents?'

'The ones who ambushed our men.'

'I don't know anything about that.'

'No?'

'No.'

'But you know that things are going wrong here? From the Russian point of view, that is.'

Svetov's voice is almost contemptuous. 'I know my history.'

'Then why is Yastryeb allowing it?'

For once his silence – combined with the look on his face – suggests not resistance but an inability to answer. Svetov *doesn't know*. And he burns to know. To understand what's going on. And again that makes no sense.

I look to Freisler. 'What do you want to do?'

It seems an innocent enough question, but Svetov watches us both with concern. The fact that he can't answer makes him value-less to us. Yet we can't just let him walk away. And even if his colleagues jump right in and change time, bringing him back to life, it's never easy dying.

Because you can never be absolutely sure. Not when things are happening that you just don't understand.

This once, however, Freisler surprises me. Reaching down, he takes another capsule from his belt – like the others, but yellow-banded – and fits it in his gun. Then, without a word, he presses the mouth of the gun to Svetov's chest and fires.

Svetov twitches violently. He looks to me pleadingly, then jerks again and falls limp.

It's an eraser. I know by the colour of the capsule. Svetov will remember none of this. He'll wake up with a violent headache and a gap in his memory that he'll fill with speculation. Only he won't jump to find out why, because he's a sleeper. Yastryeb has told him to stay.

It's not a permanent solution, because the first time he meets another agent he'll tell them what happened and they'll investigate. Only it'll buy us time. Time, maybe, to take another of their agents and question *them*.

Only this is feeling less and less right. Less and less like the Russians have a clue what they're doing.

Which leaves me thinking one thing.

228

'Reichenau,' I say, before Freisler can say a word. 'It has to be Reichenau.'

Hecht looks to Freisler, who just shrugs.

I might be wrong, of course. I might be barking up completely the wrong branch of the World Tree, only if the Russians don't know and we don't know, then it would seem that there has to be a third party involved somehow, and the only third party I know – the only one with a platform of their own, if Gehlen is right – is Reichenau.

But how do we find that out?

The answer is we don't. Because Hecht is not convinced. He wants me to go in again, only this time back six months. He wants to drop me in alongside our two sitting agents and find out first hand what's going on.

'What if they're waiting for me?'

'The Russians or Reichenau?' Hecht asks.

'Whoever. What if they've done what they did to Burckel? What if they've surrounded them with so-called "friends"?'

'Then let's put you in there at a distance from them. You can watch them for a while. See whether the situation looks clean. *Then* you can go in close.'

'Okay.' But I'm asking myself why Hecht wants to send *me* in, and why he hasn't done this already? He could have spared an agent for the task, and it seems such an obvious thing to have done. So why has he waited?

Is he losing his touch?

Looking at him, I dismiss the thought. Hecht looks as sharp, as in control, as ever. So there must be a reason. He must have a game plan, even if he's not sharing it with me.

Which makes me think of Svetov and Yastryeb.

Hecht looks up at me again. 'I want you to go and see Zarah to work out the details. Oh, and while I think of it, Meister Schnorr wanted to see you. Says he has news of your friend Kolya.'

'Ah . . .'

Freisler looks to me questioningly, but I'm not about to explain. Besides, I want to ask old Schnorr a few questions of my own. Things that have been nagging at me since our last little talk.

229

Old Schnorr welcomes me in, then, dismissing his assistants, locks the door and turns to face me again.

'What I'm about to tell you, you must tell no one, understand me, Otto? It is a great secret. One that I have sworn to keep. One which, well, one which I have had to seek special permission to share with you.'

'From Hecht?'

'Urd no. The Meister must be the last to know of this.'

That shocks me.

'Oh, I know how that must sound. Only . . . take a seat, Otto. There's a little story I must tell you. A story from the days when Meister Hecht and I were young. When we were both *Reisende* like yourself.'

'Wait,' I say, not wishing to be rude, but conscious that unless I get a word in now, it might be some while before I can. 'Why mustn't Hecht know. Is this—'

'The story,' old Schnorr says, and gestures towards the chair again. 'The story will explain it all.'

I sit and wait, as old Schnorr seems to gather up his memories, his eyes, resting in that old, deeply lined face, seeming to take on a strange, youthful clarity.

'It was long ago,' he begins, coming closer, his hands drawing lines in the air as he speaks. 'One hundred and fourteen years ago, to be precise. Four-Oh years, that is. As I said, I was a *Reisende* back then, based in Swabia, in the middle of the twelfth century.'

'Barbarossa,' I say, grinning with surprise. 'You were assigned to Barbarossa!'

'I was indeed,' Schnorr answers, his eyes smiling at the memory. 'And a grand place and time it was to be, I can tell you. Why, my young blood thrilled to be there alongside that heroic figure. And heroic he truly was. Only, well, my companion back there did not share my view. My fellow agent was, how shall I put it, more than a little sceptical about the Emperor.'

'*Sceptical?*' The idea shocks me. For I too have met with Barbarossa and rode with him on campaign, and a more honest and admirable man I've rarely met. If Nevsky is one face of kingship, then the Emperor Frederick the First, known more commonly as Frederick 'Rothbart' or 'Barbarossa' – 'red beard' – is the other: one of the few men to whom the epithet 'heroic' fits naturally.

'By the way, I saw you once,' Schnorr says. 'At Gelnhausen, in the north. You would not have seen me, of course. I stood at the back of the Hall, in the shadows, but—'

Again, I am astonished. 'You were *there*? When Frederick made me a companion?'

'I was there. But to the matter in hand, *my* companion. He was based in the castle of Staufen, Frederick's favourite castle, in the south of his domain. I guess you'd say he was a sleeper. As such he saw much less of Frederick than I. But there was a reason for that. You see, he had shown these tendencies before.'

'Tendencies?'

Schnorr looks down, as if searching for the right words. 'Tendencies to, well, to *disagree* with policy. To question things. To . . .' Schnorr sniffs. 'In short, he put the Meister's nose firmly out of joint, and as a result was sent to Staufen to kick his heels. Under my supervision, of course.'

'His name?'

'Oh, you don't need a name, Otto. If I tell you his name, you might let it slip some time. And then Hecht would know.'

'Hecht was Meister back then?'

'Urd no. It's like I said. Hecht was a mere *Reisende* then. Being groomed, no doubt, but an agent like the rest of us. No, Hudner was Meister then. Irmin Hudner. A good man, if unimaginative.'

I stare at Schnorr, realising suddenly how little I know of our history, how centred my knowledge is in the Now.

'Anyway,' he continues, 'things came to a head. My companion argued openly with Frederick over some trivial matter . . . about how Frederick treated his servants – as if servants should be treated like nobility! – and I had to jump back and sort things out. It was easily changed, but Meister Hudner had had enough. He called a special meeting of the Elders – even Gehlen was wheeled in, in his sealed tank of course – and they decided to rescind his authority, in effect, to ban him from travelling in the ages.'

'I see. And what did he do?'

'He appealed. Asked for exile.'

'Exile?'

'In the past. In nineteenth-century Prague, as it happens. He had been there and liked the place. Met a woman, it seems. Maybe part of it was due to that, but anyway, the Elders met a second time and agreed. Hecht, it seems, made a special plea for the man.'

'They were friends?'

'Oh, like brothers. Like you and Ernst, so I understand.'

Too like us, I think, only I don't say that.

'So they allowed it?'

'They did. And there he is, to this day. Or should I say, there he was. He's dead now. Time-dead. Only, of course, you can always go back and see him.'

'Fine. But why should I want to do that?'

'Because he's met Kolya.'

I stare at Schnorr. 'You *knew* this?'

'I found it out. While you were with Freisler, back at Poltava. Or should I say young Horst did. He observed Kolya visiting our exiled friend.' Schnorr smiles. 'You should thank the boy sometime, Otto. He clearly wanted to do his best for you.'

'I will,' I say. But my pulse is racing and my brain . . .

'Forgive me, Meister. You say I should go and see him. Only, how? If Hecht is not to know, then—'

'The women,' old Schnorr answers, then wanders past me, going to his desk. 'Go ask the women. Tell them what you need. And tell them . . . tell them Hecht is not to know. They'll understand.'

Making my way back to my room, my head is in a spin. Tell them *not* to tell Hecht? It's unheard of. Hecht knows everything, surely? But Schnorr spoke as if he knew what he was talking about.

And it's only when I'm back in my room, the door closed behind me, that I realise that, distracted by what old Schnorr was telling me, I forgot to ask him what I meant to ask.

I call him straight away, but he's gone. Young Horst is there, however, and – after thanking him – I ask *him*, staring down at his face in the screen.

'It's been bothering me,' I say. 'This business of Kolya kidnapping his own ancestors.'

'In what way?'

'It's just . . . I don't see what use it would be. I mean, they're all taken *after* they've passed on their seed, right?'

'Right.'

'Then what use *are* they? Surely he needs to protect them *before* they pass on their seed, not after? To make sure that his genetic line remains unbroken.'

Horst smiles. 'Agreed.'

'Then . . .?'

'Don't you see it? They're his *expendable selves*. They've served their purpose genetically. Therefore he can use them. To protect the others. To ride shotgun, if you like, down the years.'

I laugh. 'Is *that* what he's doing?'

'It looks like it. I didn't see it at first, but . . .'

'Can I come over?'

'Of course.'

'Then wait for me there. I'll be ten minutes.'

230

Only I'm not. Because there's been another development. Freisler has come back from Poltava to announce that there's to be a parley. Peter himself has offered to meet Charles on the morning of the battle, to discuss a possible peace.

From Peter's point of view it makes a lot of sense. Now that history's been tinkered with, the odds are stacked high against

David Wingrove

him. But why on earth should Charles want to make a deal with Peter when he can crush him on the battlefield?

And he wants to crush him. To inflict the maximum humiliation on his rival.

'It won't happen,' I say.

'Not as things stand,' Hecht says. 'But you're supposed to be meeting Charles, aren't you? The night before the battle, alone in his tent.'

I laugh. 'You think I can persuade him?'

Hecht shakes his head. 'No. But you could kill him.'

I look down. It would not be the first time I've been used as an assassin, but I don't feel good about this. I don't feel . . . *right*. And it has nothing really to do with Charles, who's a murderous little bastard at the best of times. Besides, they'll only change it back. They're bound to.

Whoever they are.

I meet Hecht's eyes. 'Is that what you want me to do? Kill him?'

'Maybe. But not yet. There's time and plenty to deal with Charles. First we need to find out what's happening with our agents.'

Hecht's very calmness makes me think that he knows something. It's such a contrast from his earlier urgency that I'm pretty much convinced that something's happened to make him feel more relaxed. Only what?

'Go and see Zarah,' Hecht adds after a moment. 'She'll brief you. Then report back to me once you know what's happening. And Otto . . . take no silly risks, okay?'

'Okay.' And I bow my head and hurry off to do his bidding.

Zarah's waiting for me in the prep room next to the platform. As ever, she is immaculately groomed, her uniform smartly pressed, her hair freshly brushed and tied back from her face.

'So?' I ask. 'What do I need to know?'

She hands me a thick winter coat and gloves and a large sealed envelope. I look down at the envelope, then back at her. 'Do I open this now or later?'

'Later. When you're back there.'

'And?'

'Our agents are staying at an inn to the north of the town. Next door to the stables, close by the river.'

'Which is *where* precisely, and *when*?'

She answers in a deadpan. 'Baturin. November 1708.'

'Baturin! In *November!* But . . .'

'That's where they are. And when.'

I swallow. 'Shit!' On the third of November, Baturin will be taken by Menshikov's troops and the ancient Cossack capital burned to the ground, not a single person spared.

But Zarah only smiles. 'You'll be all right. But remember. Open the letter the moment you've jumped through.'

'But *Baturin* . . .'

'Things have changed,' she says.

'Anything else I need to know?'

'No. Read the letter. It's all in there.'

I put on the coat, pull on the gloves and embrace her. '*Starke,*' I say, pressing my lips gently to her forehead – 'strength' – then turn and make my way to the platform.

231

One moment I am standing in the brightness of the circle, the next in darkness, mist swirling around me, snow beneath my booted feet.

I am on a bridge, the water flowing dark and powerful beneath me. To my left an oil lamp burns noisily, its flame gusting in the night wind, melting the snow that falls on the bridge surrounding it, yet as I turn, looking to my right, my mouth opens in surprise.

This isn't Baturin, this is Prague! For there, not twenty paces distant, is the unmistakable wedge-like shape of the Bridge Tower. I am on the Charles Bridge, above the mighty Voltava, in the ancient capital of Bohemia.

And I realise instantly what has happened. Old Schnorr has had a word, Zarah has arranged it and, even as I tear open the envelope, I half know what to expect.

There's a thousand Czech krona – in tens and twenties – and a single sheet of paper. Unfolding it I find handwritten on it a name – Jakub Schikaneder – and an address – 11, Rasnovka. And there, at the foot of the page are old Schnorr's initials and a date – 4 December 1892.

Rasnovka, if I remember correctly, is in the Jewish quarter, to the north of the Old Town. Twenty minutes' walk at most. And though I don't have much Czech, they speak enough German here for me to get by. Prague at this time – indeed, at any time – is a very cosmopolitan place.

I set off at once, making my way under the great gatehouse and past a dozing guard. The gas lamps are lit, burning dimly in those tall but narrow thoroughfares, yet the streets are virtually empty. The dark metal of the tramlines shows through the snow that covers the cobbled surface, but of the trams themselves there's no sign. I've no clue what time it is, but it must be late. Very late.

Flurries of snow blow into my face as I make my way through, and as I walk I ask myself where I've heard the name Schikaneder before, and whether I'll recognise him somehow, perhaps by some familiarity in his face.

The Old Town square is empty, the two great gothic towers of the Church of Our Lady before Tyn silhouetted against a bright full moon, which rests like a giant pearl on the cushion of a blue-black cloud. The sight is magnificent and I turn and smile, looking about me, understanding in an instant why he should choose this place for exile.

I hurry on, heading east along Celetna. At the Powder Gate I stop, hearing the bell toll three, then stand aside as a coach and horses flashes past, throwing up slush and snow in its wake, the driver leaning over his horses, cracking a short whip, while his master, a big, heavily bearded man in full opera dress, sprawls out, snoring in the back.

In the silence that follows I walk on, my footsteps muffled by the snow, but I've gone less than a dozen paces when someone calls out.

I stop and turn, then wait as the man comes out from beneath the gate tower. He's a soldier of some kind, a guard maybe, or a policeman, his gun slung over his shoulder, and he's clearly not happy to see me there, making him stir from his warm guard box.

This is an age of anarchists and revolutions, and anyone out this late is suspect, especially someone dressed as oddly as I, in the clothes of a different century.

He barks something at me in Czech and I answer back politely in German, giving it a faint Austrian accent.

'I'm sorry,' I say. 'I'm a stranger here.'

Thinking that I'm a countryman, he softens his manner, speaking now in German.

'Hold there, friend. What business have you out at this hour?'

'My coach lost a wheel,' I say, 'coming in on the Pizen road. I had to walk. My friend Karl, he lives in Rasnovka. I'm going there now.'

'Rasnovka?' he says, frowning and coming closer, so that I can make out his pale blue eyes, his balding pate and snow-streaked beard. 'But that's in the Josefstadt. He lives there?'

'Karl's a poor man,' I say. 'He can afford no better. But I've come to change his luck.'

And, knowing the ways of officials of this age, I slip the man a ten krona note, and he beams and touches his cap and bids me a very good morning.

232

Rasnovka is a long, broad street, forming a dog-leg from south to east, just one block from the river. The fourteenth-century Church of St Castullus stands at its southern end, candles burning in its vaulted entrance, and in the snowbound dark it seems the warmest spot in that bleak, forbidding place. This is the very edge of the Josefstadt, the Jewish Quarter, and is some way from the seven ancient synagogues that serve this town within a town.

I look about me, taking in the fact that there are no phone lines strung across the street, no aerials or dishes, reminding myself that this is just before the Modern Age begins, before radio and television and mass communications. They have trams and trains, but that's about all. This world is still, in essence, medieval, and maybe that's why Schikaneder has camped out here, on the edge between the old world and the new.

At least, that's my guess.

Number eleven is a tall, grey house of five storeys, its façade stern, almost anonymous in its regularity, heavy shutters pulled across the windows. There's not a glimmer of light from within and I'm beginning to think I might have to find lodgings for the night – in Wenceslas Square, most likely – when I note that there's a side gate and what's clearly an alleyway running between the houses.

I push at the gate, which is taller than me and in need of a fresh coat of paint, and find myself in a dark and narrow space. In the moonlight I can see trees at the back of the house – a garden, possibly – and make my way through. It's as I emerge, out into the open space at the back of the house, that I hear someone opening the shutters to one of the windows, high up, at the very top of the house. A pale light spills down.

I step back, looking up, careful not to trip over anything in the half dark, and find someone staring down at me, as if I'm expected. And maybe I am. Maybe old Schnorr has been here before me, seeking Schikaneder's permission. Yet why at this ungodly hour?

'I'll come down,' he says, quietly but clearly, then vanishes back inside. I wait, and in less than a minute, he appears at the back door, a heavy black cloak draped about his shoulders, a candle held out before him in an elaborate silver holder. He's a tall, dark-complexioned man, with a full dark beard and long hair falling in ringlets in the Jewish manner. But what I'm most aware of is his smile, which is guarded, sardonic.

'Come, Otto,' he says. 'Come in out of the cold.'

233

I study the back of him as we climb the narrow stairs, surprised to find so young and vigorous a man. His hands are strong and finely made, his hair a deep and lustrous black.

But why surprised? Schikaneder is still a youngish man. He'll not die for another thirty years.

The stairs seem endless, the candle flickering wildly ahead of us, throwing shadows everywhere. And then, suddenly, we're at the top, the door to his rooms open before us, a fire burning brightly in the grate that greets us as we step through.

It's a warm and welcoming room, lit by three pretty glass-cased gas lamps that hang from the ceiling rose. A huge, pillow-strewn settee fills the right-hand wall and a thick, Turkish-looking rug rests underfoot, covering most of the floor. There's a silken Chinese screen, and two other chairs – one of them a plush-looking armchair – and, on the mantlepiece, a menorah, a nine-armed Jewish candelabra, made of polished silver.

Going across, Schikaneder pulls the window down, then folds the shutters across. That done, he turns to face me.

Jakub Schikaneder is a man of pale and distinguished features. He's of medium build with a prominent nose and chin, a heavy, almost sensuous mouth, and deep, attentive eyes. Brown eyes. Eyes that seem, at the same time, warm and critical.

Yet the abiding impression I have of him is that he's ill. Physically ill, that is. Consumptive, maybe. Or is it only the gaslight that makes him seem so; only the stark contrast between *his* looks and, say, for instance, Seydlitz, or one of the other young Teutonic 'gods' we send out among the ages? He seems too refined to be a German, too southern. No wonder he chose to play the Jew back here. He looks the part.

And I mean no slur by that. The Jews of Prague are renowned not merely for their industriousness and intelligence, but also for their creativity. The young Franz Kafka, eight years old in this year, lives but a mile from here. Nor is he the only one. My beloved Rilke was born and lived here – indeed, maybe lives here even now. For this is the time to be, the place to be if you are young, and creative, and Jewish.

And even if you're not . . .

But I don't pursue that yet. Don't look into what point he might be making by his choice.

'You have the money?' he asks.

Taking the packet from my coat, I hand it to him. 'It's ten short,' I say. 'I had to pay the watchman.'

He nods. 'Tea?' he asks, slipping the packet into the deep pocket of his cloak.

'Tea?'

'You know, a cup of tea with a drop of brandy, perhaps? To keep the chill away.'

'I . . .' Impatience almost makes me blurt out my question about Kolya, but, seeing how he's watching me, I smile, realising that he's waiting for me to relax. 'Thanks,' I say, then half turn and gesture to the settee. 'May I?'

'Please do. Make yourself at home.'

His German is rusty, like he doesn't use it much.

Or chooses not to.

I sit and wait, looking about me, enjoying the small details of the room, my attention captured by one of the paintings on the wall beside the screen. I stand and, walking across, study it close up.

The dominant colour of the canvas is a faded cream that's almost grey. Sky, sea and sand are each mere variants on that washed-out shade. To the bottom left, a girl lies limply on her back on the sand, her head tilted back, her eyes closed. Beyond her, resting just above the horizon, a pale and hazy sun spreads a faint wash of light across the desolate sea. The only other detail is a large pale brown rock, to the right of her, that rests there impassively, like the skull of a great dinosaur, its reflection in the shallow water casting a dark stain across that corner of the painting.

The girl's right arm lies stretched out away from her, like she's sleeping. Like Ophelia she lies there, dressed in a diaphanous gown of white, the only sign of life in that bleak landscape. Only she's dead.

I turn to find Schikaneder standing there, a blue china cup in each hand, looking across at me.

'You like it?' he asks, handing me a cup.

I turn back. *Do I?*

'I guess,' I say. 'Its mood . . .' Its mood disturbs me. But I don't say that. 'It's very . . . *melancholic*.'

'And real. It's what I saw. That awful, bleak sun. And the rock.'

'You?'

He smiles. 'It's what I do. I'm a painter. Or didn't Meister Schnorr mention that?'

'I know only that you were a friend of Hecht's.'

'And that I was a rebel, yes?'

His smile coaxes my own. 'I was told something like that.'

'Well, it's true. I never did like the way they did things at Four-Oh. Too damn sanctimonious for my liking. Or am I saying too much. Are you . . .?'

'Sanctimonious?' I hesitate, then. 'I don't know. Maybe.'

'Then clearly not.'

'Why?'

'Because you can see it in yourself. The rest of them aren't even conscious of it. Even when you point it out to them.'

He sighs, then sips from his cup and smiles. Already I like him, even if he paints what I consider melancholic kitsch.

'You know what the worst thing I did was?'

'No?'

'I laughed at him. At Hudner, I mean.'

'You *laughed* at the Meister?'

'I couldn't help it.' He looks past me at the painting. 'All of that crap about empires and great men and turning the map black or red or whatever colour . . . it's all a nonsense. It's individuals that count. He could never see that.'

Maybe not, but I can see already why the Elders wanted him out. *Opinionated*, that's what Hecht would say, if he said anything. *A wild card.* Yet as a man out of the loop, he seems likeable enough.

'You don't agree,' he says, when I fail to answer him.

'I'm a *Reisende*,' I say, keeping it simple. 'I report to Meister Hecht.'

Schikaneder looks down, a sudden, thoughtful cast on his

features. 'Of course . . . I forgot. Hecht's Meister now.' Then, 'Are you hungry?'

'Hungry?' I think about it, then shrug. 'Yes, but—'

'Wait there,' he says, putting his cup down and heading back towards the kitchen. 'I've some leftovers . . .'

Eccentric, too, I think. Then I recall what he said about laughing at Meister Hudner. It's unthinkable. You might want to kill the Meister, perhaps, if you'd been 'turned', but not laugh at him . . .

I can almost hear Hecht's voice. *A dangerous man to have in the ranks. A threat to morale . . .*

Schikaneder returns, offering me a plate on which is a large wedge of pie, a good three inches thick, and a fork.

'Rabbit and mushroom,' he says. 'Fresh from the country.'

I take it, then look to him. 'Don't you miss it? Being a *Reisende*?'

'Sometimes . . . but not what we did. Or tried to do, rather. War by other means, as Frederick called it. It seemed rather . . . *arrogant* of us. Not to speak of its futility.'

'Ah . . .' And I realise at that moment that I've another Burckel here.

'But it wasn't only that,' he continues, perching himself on the arm of the settee. 'I was amazed they didn't get bored with the whole charade. I mean, year after year.'

I put the plate down beside me on the settee. 'Why so late?'

'For your visit?'

'Yes. You were expecting me, so old Schnorr must have arranged it for this hour.'

Schikander smiles. 'I'm a night owl, Otto. I like darkness and rain and . . . Come. Let me show you.'

He takes me through the bleak, ramshackle kitchen, up a narrow flight of stairs, and into another room at the very top of the house – a work room – finished canvases stacked against the far wall, a camp bed against the wall to my right, its ruffled, paint-spattered sheets pulled back. To the left, a half-finished canvas rests on an easel. Above it, a large, square, four-pane window is set into the sloping ceiling. The moon sits in the top right panel of the glass, boring a perfect white hole in the dark of the sky.

It's a typical artist's garret. Depressingly so.

The painting on the easel is of a harbour at nightfall, the faintest line of sunlight on the horizon, the sky turbulent, the sea a great restless swell, the whole thing grey-green and hazy, the two solitary figures at the harbour's edge, their backs to us, dwarfed by the surrounding elements.

Again, it's melancholic. If *this* is how he sees things . . .

I look to him. Staring at his own canvas he seems sad suddenly, as if he sees himself reflected in those tiny figures. *Not consumptive, no. Manic-depressive.*

'Has it changed, Otto? Or does the War grind on?' His eyes meet mine briefly and he seems to shudder. 'You don't know how much I hated it. The Game. The "Us and Them" nature of it. Their cheap and shoddy justifications for the madness we were part of.' He pauses, then says, 'I think I would have killed him, if I'd stayed.'

'The Meister?'

He nods. 'Better that I'm a painter, eh, Otto?'

I sip at my tea, tasting the brandy, letting it warm my throat as I wait for him to continue. Because that's why I'm here. To listen to him. To find out what he knows.

'They're going to pull all of this down, did you know that? Four years from now. The whole of the Josefstadt. All, that is, except for a few key buildings, the synagogues, naturally, and the Old Jewish cemetery. I'll have to move, of course, but . . .' He realises he's rambling, and smiles an apology. 'But you've not come to hear any of that, have you? You want to know about Kolya.'

'I do,' I say, but I feel suddenly uncomfortable, standing there in that room. The unmade bed, the unfinished canvas . . . it all seems far too intimate somehow, though I can't say why. It's like he's on display here, his whole self. 'Look, can we go back through?'

'Of course.' He senses my discomfort, and a little of his warmth for me drains away. He wanted me to see, to understand who he is and why he's that way, and in a way I've rejected what he's shown me, not overtly, by contesting it, but covertly, by not embracing it.

He wants me to say, 'Yes, I *see*, I *understand* because *I* feel that too'. But I won't play that game. I won't indulge him, even if he has information that I really need. Because I don't believe what he's saying. I don't believe that the 'Game' has no purpose. I *can't* believe it. For if there were no 'Game', no 'War' through time, there would be no Katerina and me. And where would that leave me?

And so we sit once more, he on the armchair, I on the settee facing him, eating rabbit pie as he begins to talk of the old days, when he too was a *Reisende*, of St Petersburg in the time of Catherine the Great, and of a chance meeting in a tavern by the Neva.

Another story. But one which is crucial to it all. To the 'Game', ironically, even if Schikaneder himself doesn't realise it.

234

'I didn't know what he was at first. I thought he was time-bound, just another citizen of that age, if an exceptional one. It was only later that I began to piece things together. After I knew. After I'd found out.'

Schikaneder pauses, staring across the room. There's a sudden intensity to him, as if he can see what he's describing.

'The first thing I noticed was his eyes. Extraordinary eyes. I've never met anyone who seemed to burn so much with life. Most people were afraid of that. They avoided him, considering him a threat, even mad. But he wasn't. Quite the contrary, in fact. There never was a saner man – a man more addicted to reason – than Kolya. He was quite young at the time – in his early twenties, I'd guess – but even then there was something about him. A driven quality. Not quite obsession, but not far from it. And something else. An inner resentment, I guess you'd call it. A bitterness at the world. Later on I discovered that his mother had died when he was five. His father, well, he'd no idea who his father was . . . not at first, anyway.'

'In what capacity did you meet him?'

'It was that first day I was there. I'd jumped in to the Sleutelbourg, – you know, downriver, to the east of the city – and got a ferryboat up to St Petersburg. I hired a room at one of the dockside inns, and that's where I met him. He was staying there too. That evening he sat near me at supper and engaged me in conversation. I liked him, and the next day – as I say, by "chance" – I ran into him again. He had advertised for skilled workmen, and I'd gone along, not knowing it was him, to see if I could get a job. He was building a new settlement, off in the marshes to the north of the city. The rates he was offering were good – in fact, the best you'd find anywhere in the north – and there were a lot of people interested. The place was packed. They were queuing out the doors. And there, at the centre of it all, was Kolya, seated behind a stout oak table, those eyes of his assessing each man in turn and either dismissing him with a shake or giving a terse nod of acceptance.

'That was odd, and I should perhaps have guessed it then. The way he asked no questions – nothing at all about how skilled a man was, or even what skill he had – just a look and a shake or a nod.'

He smiles. 'Later I understood, of course. It was a time-paradox. What he'd been doing was to jump forward and see who he'd hired and how good they were, before jumping back and hiring them in the first place. Some, of course, were never hired, but the good ones . . .'

'He was definitely jumping through time, then?'

'Yes.'

'And he hired you because he knew you, right?'

'You might call it chance or coincidence, but I don't believe that. I met Kolya because Kolya wanted me to meet him. He knew who I was and what I would be, and he also knew that I would tell nobody about him. Until now.'

My mouth opens. 'But—'

'I didn't know that. Not then. It took me some while to work it out. But that's how it was. How it *is*, you might say. For here we are.'

'So what precisely were you doing in St Petersburg?'

'Establishing an identity. Doing what we *Reisende* often do, and bedding down into an age. I can't be sure, considering what happened, exactly what Meister Hudner had planned for me – whether it was to try to assassinate the empress, or become her latest lover, or what – but it doesn't really matter. All that matters is that Kolya found me.'

'Are you sure of that? That *he* found *you*?'

'Quite positive. There's no mistaking it. As for *why*, well, that's less clear. Only that it has to do with you, Otto Behr. And with a place called Krasnogorsk.'

I go cold. 'Who told you about that?'

'He did. Though not until a lot later. But let me tell you this in the sequence *I* experienced it.'

Schikaneder goes through to the kitchen and returns with a bottle of red wine and two glasses. He pours, then hands me one.

'It was like this. Kolya had bought a large plot of land to the north-east of St Petersburg, on what they called the Finnish shore. Larger craft couldn't sail there because of the sands, which at low tide prevent any form of navigation, but at high tide some of the smaller galleys could make their way across. There, just across from Peter's island fortress of Cronslot, Kolya was building his own small town. A town that, to all intents and purposes, was a fortress to match Peter's. My first sight of it, from out in the bay, was also the first time I found myself questioning just who Kolya really was and what he was up to. Until then I'd thought him an exceptional man, perhaps, but not unusually so. But suddenly, seeing what he was up to, I began to ask myself whether he might not be an enemy agent.'

He smiles. 'I thought that for some while. But even then I ought to have known. The signs were there from the start.'

Schikaneder leans closer. 'It seemed such a strange place to set up his own little kingdom, right there within sight of the tsarina's palace. It was just as if he was inviting someone to come along and ask him what the hell he was doing. Only no one ever did. Perhaps his tactics were perfect. Perhaps the one place you *don't* expect to find such a place is right there, directly alongside the very centre of power.'

'Such a place?'

'Let me explain. It wasn't just that the place *looked* like a fortress, with its high stone walls, its guard towers and its massive, heavily defended gate, it was the feel of the place. There were barracks for the workers just north of the site, and armed guards supervising the work. And Kolya wasn't just building outward to the north of the river frontage, he was building *down*. Some of the men he'd hired were miners by profession, and they were busy day and night excavating deep shafts and long, broad tunnels directly underneath the fortress.'

'And no one knew this was going on?'

'No one. Not the Russians, nor us . . . and certainly no one from Catherine's administration. At least, if they did, they were keeping very quiet about it.'

'But it must have been seen from ships passing along the central channel.'

'Certainly. Seen and noted. But it was on all the maps. Kolya made sure of that. Only it was marked as a government cannery.'

'So what was it for?'

'First things first. When I arrived – when I stepped off the boat and on to the dockside, that is – Kolya himself was there to greet me. He showed me round. He was rather proud of what he'd built, but he was, he said, taking it further.'

Schikaneder pauses to sip at his wine. 'That was one of the things that surprised me, that threw me off my guard, I guess. The fact that he was so open at the start. I think I understand now why he did it, because he knew he didn't have anything to fear from me. Because, of all the German agents in the field, I alone wouldn't tell Meister Hudner. And because—'

'Because he knew you would end up here?'

Schikaneder nods, and I can see that even now, even after spending years brooding on this, that that fact still sobers him. That Kolya knew, right from the start. But then this is Time, and someone who can master Time and use it flexibly can find out many things denied to the time-bound.

'He showed me it all, that first day I was there. Made me his assistant. Told me the plan.'

'The plan?'

'As I said, let me tell you it as it happened. It was that evening. We were sharing a bottle of wine, as now, in Kolya's rooms at the top of the central tower. It was like a great keep, an ancient baron's tower, only Kolya had had huge windows built, modern windows of thick glass that gave him a view across the water, to west and south and east. An enormous fire was burning behind us in the massive fireplace, and the servants had been dismissed. That's when he told me.'

'About the plan?'

Schikaneder leans across and fills his glass again, then offers to top mine up. I nod my thanks and hold the glass out to him.

'It was to be an academy,' he said. 'His job was to find recruits, mine to train them.'

'And you *agreed* to that?'

'Not at once. I wanted to hear more. So I asked him in what way he meant me to train them.'

'And what did he say?'

'That he knew who I was and what I did, and that he wanted to use what I knew to make changes.'

'Changes?'

'He said he knew how I felt. Knew I was dissatisfied. Oh, and other things. The most personal insights. It was like he'd studied me, but from the inside. Now I know how he did it, but back then . . .'

'What do you mean?'

'I kept a journal. When I first came here, to Prague. I wrote it all down. Everything. Not just what I did, but how I felt and what I thought about things. Then one day the journal went missing. I'd kept it in the drawer in my room, but he must have come here when I was out. It's the only way he could have known those things.'

'And Meister Hudner and the others . . . what did they think was going on?'

'As far as they were aware, I was working at a cannery. Keeping a low profile and waiting for instructions.'

'And Kolya's offer?'

'I thought about it for a few days, then went back to him.'

'He knew, of course, what your answer was.'

'Of course. Kolya always knew everything before he did it. He didn't like surprises. If something came out wrong, he'd jump back and change it, get the right result.'

'Like us, then, and the Russians—'

'Yes, only not for a cause. For himself.'

'Didn't you ask him who he was working for?'

'I did, and he asked me why it mattered. Whether there was any real difference.'

'You weren't tempted to jump out of there? To go and tell Hudner what was going on?'

'No. Why should I? I mean, I was intrigued. I thought, well, I thought maybe this was what I'd been searching for all along. A different approach.'

'Only . . .'

'Only Kolya wasn't interested in what *I* wanted. His only concern was that I'd pass on what I knew.'

'About Four-Oh and how we do things?'

'Yes.'

'And you gave him what he wanted?'

He nods.

I sit there in silence, stunned by the depth of his betrayal, wondering whether this chain of events is linked somehow to my death up the line. Whether that too began a century and more ago.

Yet even as I think that, I realise that I'm looking at Time in completely the wrong way. It didn't have to happen a hundred years ago. It could have happened yesterday. In fact, for all I know, Kolya isn't even born yet. He could be jumping back from somewhere in the future, and until we know that—'

'When did all this happen?'

Schikaneder shrugs. 'I'm not sure. Some time in the 1770s. The women will know. It'll be in the log.'

'Which will have changed.'

'I guess . . .'

His nonchalance exasperates me. 'Haven't you *any* idea where he comes from?'

'Your guess is as good as mine.'

'Yes, but what would *you* say? You spent time with him.'

Schikaneder considers that: 'Twenty-fourth century. The Mechanists.'

'Why?'

'Just the odd word or two. Things he let slip when he was relaxed. Jargon stuff.'

For the first time I feel I'm getting somewhere. 'And his friends?'

Schikaneder laughs. 'Kolya didn't have friends. Just acquaintances and people who worked for him. No one was allowed to get close. He's very single-minded. Or maybe that's not the word. Self-centred, more like. In fact, I've never met anyone quite so self-centred as Kolya. I've watched him. He'll set up whole new timelines and then destroy them, simply to achieve a single aim. He's not like us in that respect. He's profligate with Time.'

'Ruthless, you mean?'

'Totally. I don't think the man understands remorse.'

'And was Kolya the only name he used?'

'Never anything else. He didn't even have a surname. At least, I never heard one used.'

'How long were you with him?'

'Four months. And you know what? I still don't know what he was doing. I know what he took from me, but what he did with it . . .' Schikaneder drains his glass. 'I only know what he *said* he was doing.'

'And what was that?'

'Making a nest for his cuckoos. Those were his words. A nest for his cuckoos.'

236

There's more, but it only confirms what I already know, and as dawn breaks, Schikaneder slips on his cloak and walks me back to the Charles Bridge.

I'm not sure what I feel about the man now that I know what he did. His exile seems far less glamorous than it did – more a question of expedience, of saving his skin by getting out and keeping his mouth shut – yet he still cuts a romantic figure as he stands there in the first light, cloaked and booted, his long dark hair swept back by the morning's breeze. And when he offers his hand, I take it.

'Good luck, Otto.'

'Thanks.' And, touching my chest, I jump.

Zarah's there as I come through. 'Are you ready?' she asks.

'No. Give me a moment. I need to see Meister Schnorr.'

I can see she's not happy, but she nods. 'Okay. But not too long. If Hecht sees the log there'll be some explaining to do.'

'Thanks . . .' And I hurry off.

Old Schnorr is alone in his rooms. He looks up, surprised to see me, but before he can say a word, I confront him.

'Did you *know* what he was? What he *did*?'

The old Meister removes his glasses and rubs at his tired eyes.

'Our friend, the artist? I know he was unreliable.' He replaces his glasses and stares directly at me. 'Why? What *did* he do?'

I tell him, and old Schnorr whistles – he actually whistles – with surprise.

'Why was he allowed out there?' I ask, strangely more angry now that the man himself's not there, now that I'm not within the circle of his charm. 'I mean, unreliable doesn't come close. The man's a traitor. He sold us all out. And for what? Because he was bored.'

Schnorr sighs. 'I know you must find it hard to understand, Otto, but there were less of us back then. Our friend Schikaneder was an extremely talented young man and it made little or no sense to discard him just because a few of us thought he was eccentric. They'd spent years training him up. It was no easy matter to throw all that away, and besides, Hecht was his champion. If there was ever any trouble, Hecht would intervene. Three, maybe four times he interceded on his behalf, persuading Meister Hudner not to ground him but to persevere, to put up with his eccentricities until he came of age. But he never did.'

'So what do we do now? Do we tell Hecht?'

'I think we have to. Only not just yet. Leave this with me for now, Otto. Go to Baturin. Do what you must do. When you're back we'll reassess things. As for Schikaneder, keep what you know to yourself for now. Don't tell anyone. Not Ernst, nor Zarah, not anyone, understand? The less people who know . . .'

I nod, trusting to his experience. Besides, I need time to think before confronting Hecht, because there's still the matter of saving Katerina, and if Hecht takes charge he might consider that a low priority.

Zarah is waiting for me back at the platform. She can see from my face that something's happened, but she's wise enough not to ask – or maybe she thinks she can find out from Meister Schnorr.

Whichever, she's silent as she hands me my pack, her brief smile as I ascend on to the circle, the only sign of engagement with me.

And then I'm there.

237

Baturin is a town in turmoil. Ten days ago, the local Hetman, Mazeppa, leader of the Ukrainian Cossacks, fled with two thousand of his men to take sides with Charles of Sweden against his sworn master, the emperor Peter of Russia. The town is fortified and guarded; three thousand of Mazeppa's men remain to defend it. Huge stores of food and powder are stacked within its storehouses. But the Russian army is approaching and Peter's most trusted general, Menshikov, and his cavalry are about to encircle the town. It is only a matter of days before an assault begins.

Our two agents are here somewhere, monitoring the situation, only, to be frank, it doesn't interest me. If it were my choice I would not be here but pursuing Kolya, wherever he is, trying to unravel that thread of time in which he has killed my love and me. My every instinct cries out to hunt him down and change our fate. Instead I am here, in Baturin, doing Hecht's bidding.

The broad and dusty streets of Baturin are busy as darkness gathers, mainly Cossacks and their women, their bright clothes and boisterous manners giving the evening a carnival air. Yet these will all be dead two days from now. The Russians will put Baturin to the sword as an example to the rest of the Ukrainian Cossacks. More than seven thousand will be slaughtered. And whoever survives that savage blood-letting will perish in the flames that will leave this ancient stronghold a wasteland of ashes.

I am looking for an inn called the Goat of Marmaris. Finding it, I settle on the quay some fifty paces distant, letting my feet dangle above the water.

There's food in the sack, made to look like the food of this age. There's also a bag of coins and a knife. I slip the knife into my belt, then, pretending to idle, watch the comings and goings.

It's a good half hour before the first of our agents arrives, looking about him warily as he enters the inn. He doesn't see me sitting there in the shadows, but I see him clearly – see the troubled look of him, the way he ducks furtively inside.

Body language. Sometimes it says much more than words. Here is a man with problems, a man almost breaking under the pressures of his life.

A moment later another hurries up, a woman this time, her face veiled. She too stops to glance around before ducking inside, and I know without needing to be told that I have struck gold: that this, whatever it proves, is at the heart of it.

Casually, I stand, looking about me idly, as if barely interested in what anyone else is doing. Yet in that brief and casual survey I become aware of something: I too am being watched. Off to my left, at the mouth of an alleyway, a young Arab boy is studying me with an interest beyond the mere casual.

I'm trained too well, of course, to let him know that I know he's there, and walk slowly, almost lazily across to the inn. Stopping close by I pause to urinate against the wall, and note his long shadow, cast by the low and setting sun, move past my own.

I wait a while then duck inside, into warmth and shadow and the almost suffocating stench of fat and grease and old cooking. It's very gloomy and it takes a moment for my eyes to grow accustomed to the lack of light, but they're not down here anyway, and, guessing that they've gone up on to the roof terrace, I climb up and join them.

It's a mild night for November, but even so, they are alone up there, the two of them, on the far side of the terrace, in one of the corner cubicles. I walk across and stand there at the edge of the terrace, well away from them, though from the look of them they've barely noticed that I'm there.

I look out into the evening, seeing the low sprawl of the ancient town spread out below me, the flicker of fires beyond the river, where the various Cossack *voiska* – or 'hosts' – have their camps just outside the city walls. It's a glorious, clear night, and the sky is littered with stars. An almost perfect night.

I take a seat at the side. There's no sign of the Arab boy, and that worries me a little, but after a few moments a girl – a serving maid – appears. A pretty young thing with an air of toughness about her – as well she might be, having to deal with Cossacks day after day.

'You want to order?'

'Just some wine,' I say, and place a silver altyn – worth three copeks – in her palm.

She smiles and hurries away, and I turn back, looking across at the two who are playing out their little drama.

They are facing me almost, their faces barely inches apart. She has discarded her veil, to reveal a head of lustrous dark hair and a face that, if not beautiful, is certainly handsome. What's more he is holding her hands – both her hands – with a tenderness that's unmistakable. This pair are lovers.

Yet even as I watch, something happens. He says something, chiding her perhaps, and she moves back a little, annoyed. He leans towards her, his head tilted slightly, and says something more, his voice so low I can't catch more than its pleading tone. But whatever it is, it clearly upsets her, for she pulls back sharply, abruptly freeing her hands. She stands.

He looks up at her, anguished now, his hand reaching out for hers, trying to soothe her, only she won't be soothed. And though

I can't make out what she says to him, I know – if only from his face – that it's sharply critical.

He looks down, a sudden hopelessness in his face. 'You *won't* then?'

'No.'

And as she says it, I see what it costs her to say that single word, and wonder what it is she won't do, and why it taxes her so. But he's suffering. There's a haunted look of despair now in his eyes.

He stands, staring at her one last time, then, without a glance back, walks away.

I watch him leave, then look back at her, seeing how she stands there still, unmoving, looking down at her hands as if imagining them again in his. And then she gives a little shudder and a tear rolls down her cheek.

I look away, then look back, wondering if I should go across, when suddenly I am aware of someone in the chair beside me. The Arab boy.

'You want her, master?' he asks, very quietly. 'Ten copeks and she's yours. Yours until the dawn, to do with as you wish.'

I turn and stare at him. His eyes are smiling, as if they understand me. For we are both *men*, after all.

I fish in my pocket for a coin and bring out two silver altyns and a copper grosh – eight copeks worth in all – and hand them to him. 'Eight. And that's all you're getting.'

He nods. 'I'll bring her to your room, master?'

'No. Arrange a room here.'

'A room would be extra, master.'

I look at him sternly. 'A room is in the fee.'

His eyes hold my own barely two seconds and then he looks down and nods again. 'As you wish, master.'

And as I watch him go across to her, I wonder what I am getting myself into, for she's a whore. Our agent's lover is a whore.

As I step inside, I can smell her perfume in the air, the same cheap perfume that whores in this and every century seem to wear.

She lies there in the candlelit gloom, naked on the bed, her charms, such as they are, exposed to me. Oh, she's pretty enough, her breasts full enough, her hips broad enough, to please any man. Only I'm not here to be pleased. I'm here to find out what's been going on, and why our two agents here have fucked up badly.

'Get dressed.'

She stares at me in disbelief. 'What?'

'You heard me. I want to talk with you.'

She sits up, looking across at me with a perplexed, almost petulant expression. 'You don't want me?'

'I don't want you.'

And it's true. I may be a man, and it might be some while since I last had sex, but I really *don't* want her.

'What are you, a *castrati*?'

Think what you like. But she's annoying me now. How could one of our *Reisende* have fallen for *this*?

'Get your clothes on. Before I beat you.'

I have no intention of beating her, but I don't want to waste any more time. If I can find out what's going on here, I can get back to more serious matters. Like saving Katerina.

'You a man's man, eh?' she says, as she begins to dress. 'You like boys, yes?'

'I have a wife.'

She laughs. 'You think I'd make a living if only single men came to see me? Why, I'd starve. Married men, they are the worst sinners. Everything they can't do at home, they want to do here, in my bed.'

'And your friend, from the inn? Your lover? What does *he* like?'

Mention of him sobers her. She looks away, her face colouring, as if I've just slapped her.

'Is none of your business.'

'Is very much my business. He's one of *my* men.'

She looks up at me, surprised, but then recovers. 'You're lying. He is his own man. He tell me that.'

'I could have him killed. Like that.' And I snap my fingers.

She stares at me a moment, seeing the hardness in my face, then gives a nod.

'So who are you?' she asks quietly, coming across to me, her breasts still uncovered.

'Get dressed and then we'll talk.'

239

'So how did you meet him?'

'Aaron? I met him back in Bobovichy, six months back.'

She sits cross-legged on the bed, looking up at me as I pace slowly back and forth. Now that I've had time to study her, I'd say she was Greek, or Turkish, maybe. Her dark brown eyes and full lips have something of the Romani about them. It's not a face to launch a thousand ships. And yet I remember the tenderness with which our agent touched her. The love.

'He was a client, then?'

'At first. But he was kind to me. Bought me meals. Treated me special.'

I nod, as if I understand. And maybe I do. It can get lonely in the ages, and Aaron – Lothar Rieber, in reality – is but a man.

'And his partner? Was he a client, too?'

'His partner?' She feigns ignorance.

'Come on, you know who I mean.'

'Another of your men, eh?'

But I don't answer that, merely stare back at her, awaiting her response, and finally it comes – a shrug of the shoulders.

'He's bad news, that one. The things he likes to do . . .' She raises her eyebrows, then, with a sigh. 'That was what it was about . . . earlier.'

'He sleeps with you?'

'If you can call it that.'

'And Aaron doesn't like that?'

She hesitates, then nods.

'He asked you not to, right?'

At that she grows indignant and her hands fly up expressively. 'He has no right, telling me who I should go with! How am I to live?'

'Have you no other skills?'

She laughs. 'None to earn me what I can earn doing this. Besides, I like what I do.'

'And Aaron? He likes it?'

Her face changes. 'He hates it.'

'Then marry him.'

She stares at me, astonished, and then she dissolves in laughter. '*Marry* him! What, and starve like some peasant's ill-fed dog? Don't be a fool! Besides, he's said himself more than once that he can't promise me a thing.'

'He said that?'

'Clear as day. Says he's waiting for instructions. From *you*, no doubt!'

'It's true.'

Her face clouds again. When she speaks next, the fire has gone out of her. 'Then I was right to say no.'

I walk over to the window and pull back the rough hemp

curtain an inch or two, looking down at the street outside. It's filled with Cossacks and their women, making the most of these last few nights of peace. Behind me, I hear her sigh. I turn back, to find her watching me.

'Are you sure you don't want me?' she asks, arching her body slightly, seductively.

I walk across. 'My wife, Katerina, she is young and beautiful. She makes love like an angel.'

'An angel, eh?' And it's said wistfully. 'Such a shame. You're a handsome man.'

'Otto,' I say. 'My name is Otto.'

She reaches out and lays her hand flat against my groin. I do nothing, and after a moment she removes it – the same hand that held her lover's hand so gently but an hour past.

A whore, yet not a bad woman.

'The other, the bad one, what is it he asks you to do?'

'Don't ask,' she says, as if I should imagine the very worst. 'Just don't ask.'

240

A simple triangle, then, after all. The woman a whore, one of the men a sadist, the other a tender lover. All in all, a tragedy waiting to happen.

Simple, yes, only it doesn't feel right.

I track down Rieber's partner, a man named Edmund Koeler. I have met Koeler several times before now, but never really made a connection. Now I pull rank, ordering him to tell me everything.

We are in his room, talking as he gets ready for the evening ahead. A single candle burns in a stand on the corner table. In its flickering light I watch him button up his shirt.

'I should have reported him,' Koeler says angrily. 'He knows the rules.'

'Maybe. But couldn't you just use another woman?'

He turns on me. 'Why should I? She's the best in Baturin. The best in the whole of southern Russia, if you must know. The things she does.'

I sigh. 'Okay. Listen to me. I'm ordering you to back off.'

'*Ordering* me?'

'I have Hecht's warrant to do whatever's needed. He sent me in to sort this mess out.' I pause, then say, 'You want to know how it ends?'

'Tell me.'

'You kill each other.'

'We . . .' He falls silent, shocked by that. 'Shit! How do we . . .?'

'A duel. You both are hit, and die.'

'Urd protect us!' He looks down a moment, then. 'You've seen this?'

'Freisler did.'

He lets out a long breath. 'And Lothar, does he know?'

'No. And I'd rather he didn't.'

Koeler fastens the last button then turns to me. 'Okay. I'll back off. But have a word. He's getting too involved with the woman. And what is she? A common tart, who'll do a trick with anyone for the right fee. What kind of woman is that to fall in love with?'

I can see, both from his words and from his face, that he has lost all respect for his partner, and that too is dangerous.

'What exactly are you doing here?' I ask.

'We're pursuing someone. Lothar thinks he's one of their agents, but it's odd.'

'Odd?'

'I can't make out what he's up to, or why. The Russians . . . usually you can tell what they're up to. But this one . . .'

'You're sure he's one of theirs?'

'We've seen him vanish, then reappear. And he's not one of ours, so . . .'

'Where is he now?'

Koeler smiles. 'I'll take you there. It's where I'm heading myself. But be careful. These Cossacks can be touchy people. One wrong word . . .'

I'm not sure what he means, but I throw on my coat and go along with him, heading out into the night once more.

241

There's a big open space – used as a marketplace during the day – between the river and Baturin's main gate, and it's there that they've gathered in their thousands, this fierce, bold tribe – if you can call this hotch-potch of unconnected peoples that – the men ruggedly handsome in their shaggy fur hats, their long, heavy-lined cloaks, their soft leather boots and cross-belt bandoliers, the women dark and defiant, in colourful long dresses and fur-lined cloaks. Huge braziers are burning brightly, throwing up sparks into the night. To one side are the tents of blacksmiths and armourers, and next to them a dozen and more merchants, selling their wares from carts. Vodka, of course, is in plentiful supply. Above all, there is the sound of balalaikas and from time to time a glimpse of shirt-sleeved men dancing the *gopak*, kicking out their legs to the whirling rhythm of the music. Everyone, it seems, is happy. You would not think this was a town under threat.

Koeler seems to know where he's going and I follow him through the press of bodies until we come to the river. The boats of the Zaporozhian Cossacks are tied up here, and they've formed a small town of their own on the bank, their tents crowded together along the shore. But they're not what we've come to see.

'Look!' Koeler says, gesturing towards the far corner of the square, where, visible now through the crowd, is a raised platform, upon which stands a massive fellow, a good seven feet tall if he's an inch, his bared chest and arms rippling with muscles. On a pole at each corner of the platform is a blazing torch, the warm light glistening off the big man's shaven skull. He's barefoot, wearing only baggy Cossack trousers, but his face has the fierceness of a wild bird.

'Is that him?' I ask Koeler quietly.

'Urd no. But our friend likes to come and watch him. Wait a while. He'll be here. You never know, you might recognise him.'

And so I wait, watching as the big man takes on all-comers, one after another, some of them fighting to amuse their friends, others to try to win the purse, others simply from pride or an excess of vodka. But all of them suffer the same fate: lifted by the seat of their pants and thrown down into the dust beside the platform to the roared approval of the crowd.

I've almost forgotten why we're there, when Koeler nudges me. 'There,' he whispers. 'To your left, just behind the fat one in the red cloak.'

I look.

'Well?' Koeler asks. 'Anyone you know?'

'No.'

But that isn't entirely true. I *have* seen our friend before, only I don't know where or when. All I know is that – in profile, anyway – he looks familiar. Very familiar.

'Shame,' Koeler says quietly. 'Still, there are other ways to find out who he is.'

'What do you mean?'

279

'I mean to follow him this time. Find out where he goes, who he sees. I thought you might help me, seeing as you want to sort this out.'

But our friend doesn't seem to be going anywhere. For the next hour and more he watches the platform, amused, even shouting out at times, as the big man continues to defeat every challenger.

I'm growing a little tired of the sport, when suddenly our friend makes off, as if at some signal, and, nudging me again, Koeler takes off after him, keeping back a little way. I follow, moving out left, but keeping the fellow in sight.

We move away, out of the crowd, into a long, dark alley that runs parallel to the river. I've almost caught Koeler up when, looking past him, I realise that our quarry has vanished.

Koeler has stopped, waiting for me. 'There,' he says in a whisper. 'That building to the right. That's where he went. You climb up, I'll go round the back.'

It's a small, two-storey building with a surrounding wall. The shutters are closed, but there's a chink of light from one of the rooms at the top

'Well?' Koeler asks.

I could argue, but I don't. The adrenalin is pumping and I want to find out what our friend is up to as much as Koeler does. If he *is* a Russian and he *is* meddling . . .

And then I see him vividly in my mind, running towards me, dagger drawn, meaning to stab me.

Only that was a dream, because there never *was* a Lishka, and even if there was, Katerina and Lishka and I were never attacked.

So why do you remember it so clearly if it never happened? And why is he – the assailant from the dream – here now?

As Koeler slips away round the back of the building, I climb up on to the top of the surrounding wall, then haul myself up on to the flat roof, dropping down on to the terrace. Voices drift up from the room below. And I almost let it wash over me, only I realise suddenly that they're speaking German – *Mechanist* German.

I kneel, then put my ear to the ground, listening.

Two voices, one of them – again – familiar, only I can't place it. And then a third, much deeper, with no trace of Mechanist jargon in it, speaking a stilted, awkward form of German, as if it isn't their natural tongue. What they're saying makes little sense: something about a meeting, but so unspecific as to be useless as information.

I straighten up and look about me. There's a raised hatch on the far side of the roof, leading down, I hope, into the room behind where our friends are. Quickly, quietly I make my way across, then lean out over the back of the roof. Koeler's down there, by the back door. He looks up at me and gives the coded signal to go in, which I return, only I'm hoping he's got something better than the knife I'm carrying. But I'm going in anyway, even if I have to jump straight out, because I want to know now who's down there and what they're up to, because none of this feels right.

This isn't the way the Russians usually operate. And besides . . . *why are they speaking German?*

Is this something Hecht's not told me about . . .

As I pull the hatch open and slip into the darkness, I feel the faintest glimmer of anger at Hecht for not confiding in me more. For not *trusting* me. I thought I was his *Eizelkind*. That it was I who was being groomed to replace him. Only now I'm being shut out. Denied information. Made to go in blind, as now.

I cross the room in darkness, the door just ahead of me, faintly rimmed with light. I stand before it, listening, but there's only silence, and when I throw the door wide open, I find an empty room.

I step inside. There's the stub of a cigar still smouldering in a shell-like metallic ashtray on the low table to my left. There are three chairs, and on the other side of the room, a sturdy wooden bureau on which a book lies open.

I am about to step across and see what it is, when the air between me and the bureau shimmers faintly and a figure materialises.

The figure has its back to me so that I cannot see its face, but I know who it is without needing him to turn. It's Reichenau. That awful, double-skull of his gives it away. Shocked by his sudden appearance, I hesitate a moment too long, and he is gone again, the faintest scent of ozone in the air.

I walk across and look down at the bureau. The book is gone. I'll never know now what it was or what significance it had. That is, unless I jump back into the room when all of them are there.

The idea tempts me, but just then Koeler comes into the room, his gun drawn.

'Gone?' he asks.

'Gone. Three of them. German-speakers.' But I don't say anything about Reichenau. That nugget I'm keeping for Hecht. Because this is my proof, if I needed it, that Reichenau's involved somehow.

Yes, but why here, in Baturin? What could he possibly want in a dump like this?

It needs an answer, but not just yet. Instead I make another decision.

'We're pulling out,' I say. 'You, me and Rieber.'

'What, *now*?' And he looks horrified at the suggestion, like I'm being totally unreasonable.

'Just as soon as we find Rieber.'

He stares at me, then, thrusting his gun into his belt, turns away. 'Shit!'

I could, of course, jump out there and then, and get Zarah to activate the platform and bring the two of them back automatically, only I don't know what Rieber is doing right now, and if he's in company, then I don't want him just disappearing. That *would* get back to Reichenau.

'Where would he be right now?' I ask.

'With his whore, I should think.'

'Where else?'

Koeler glances back at me, still angry. 'How should I know? I'm not his keeper!'

Only he is. For that's how we operate in Time. And that, for me, is as good a reason as any to get these two out of here at once. Things have gone badly with this operation, which is, after all, only designed to keep history on track. These two are minders, not makers of new historic pathways, but they've fucked up, and it's all to do with their inability to get on.

Maybe Reichenau found that out. Maybe that's why he's here, where we're weak. Only how did he do that? How exactly is he monitoring our operations, if that *is* what he's doing?

Or am I just being paranoid? Am I attributing the man with knowing too much?

One thing I do know. His presence just now in the room has thrown me badly. Has made me question everything about our operations.

I even think I know what the book was, though I can't be sure – only that it looked the same size and colour and . . .

And there were pictures on each page. Large pictures that might have been photographs.

Like the book his so-called daughter handed me that time.

I go cold. I look to Koeler and he's still simmering with anger. 'Where will he be?' I ask a second time. 'Have you *any* idea?'

'He has a room,' Koeler says quietly.

'What? Separate from you?'

Koeler nods.

'Urd save us . . . Take me there, now.'

Cossacks. There's nothing in Baturin in November 1708 but Cossacks. And not even any of the important ones. Mazeppa's fled to Charles, along with most of his important hetmans.

So what in Urd's name would Reichenau want in Baturin?

Dead men, maybe. Or men who would be dead, if he didn't take them. Men who weren't in the future genetic history of the world? Yes. But why?

What is he up to?

All this is going through my head as, silently, Koeler and I walk back through the dark and dirty streets of Baturin to where Lothar Rieber has his billet.

Koeler knows I'm annoyed with him, and he probably also knows that he'll be in big trouble with Hecht when he gets back to Four-Oh, but he's also angry with me, and as we arrive at the inn where Rieber's staying, Koeler turns on me.

'It's *Rieber* who's fucked up!' he says angrily. '*Rieber* who should be sent back! If he'd not been so fucking stupid with the girl . . .' He looks down, trying to control himself, then looks back at me, speaking more calmly. 'Leave me here. Please, Otto. I know so much. I'm so close to finding out what's going on. Take Rieber, sure, but send me in another partner. Someone more reliable. I'll do the job. Hecht knows I'll do it. Only don't close this down. Not yet. Please.'

'Okay,' I say calmly. 'I'll think about it.'

Only I won't. I've made my decision. Just as soon as I have the two of them alone, I'm jumping straight out of there and then getting Zarah to pull them back. I can't trust either of them any more. They've lost it. I can see that now. And when agents lose it . . .

We go inside, through the packed bar and on up a set of stairs at the back of the big room.

Rieber's not in his room, but I know he'll return. There's nowhere else to stay. And so Koeler and I settle down, he on the chair, I on the bed, waiting silently, each with our own thoughts.

And finally he comes.

'Edmund?' And then he sees me and his eyes widen. 'Otto? Otto Behr?'

'Lothar . . .'

And I jump. Back to Four-Oh. Back to Hecht, and Zarah, and trouble . . .

243

Hecht looks up at me from behind his machine. 'So?' he asks.

'He's there,' I say. 'Reichenau. He was in the room in Baturin. I saw him.'

'Did he see you?'

'No. I was behind him. He took the book, then jumped.'

'Book? Which book?'

'I'm not sure. But it must have been important.'

Hecht looks past me at Freisler. 'See if you can find out what it was.'

Freisler nods, but he doesn't leave. He wants to hear what I've got to say.

'They were speaking German,' I say. '*Mechanist* German. Two of them, anyway. The third . . .' But I don't get to say what the third was speaking. Hecht lifts a hand.

'Okay,' he says. 'You've done well. You should rest now. Go and see Zarah. I understand she's arranged something.'

A rest? I almost say something, but Hecht's giving me that 'don't question it' look, and I feel Freisler's hand on my shoulder.

285

'Come, Otto,' Freisler says. 'The Master needs to be left alone now.'

That's strange, for I've hardly begun. But I've learned not to question things. Not openly, anyway.

Freisler comes with me, but before we get to the platform – while we're still out in the connecting corridor – he turns to me. 'You want to know what's going on, don't you?'

I laugh. 'Of course I do. I'm rushed in to try to sort things out and then . . . nothing.'

'That's not entirely true. We sent you in again.'

'You sent me in?'

'You went and met Charles, in his tent, on the night before the battle, just as you were supposed to.'

'And?'

'It was a trap. You died. So we changed it. Made sure you didn't go.'

'How?'

'We sent you somewhere else. Or, should I say, *are* sending you.'

'Then Hecht knew about Reichenau already?'

'Not until you told him. But that was last time. This is second time around.'

I see. Only I still feel a little angry at Hecht's lack of confidence in me. Angry that he's left it to Freisler to explain, as if I'm no longer in the loop.

'Why is he doing this?' I ask, half knowing that Freisler is the wrong man to ask; that if anyone should want me shut out, it's probably Freisler.

'Doing what?'

'Excluding me. Keeping me in the dark.'

Freisler smiles. 'Hecht is the strategist, Otto, not you or me. You must see that. We're just the foot soldiers. Skilled, true, but foot soldiers nonetheless. Hecht alone sees the big picture. That's how it is and always has been. He is the Master. So leave it to him. He knows what he's doing.'

Hearing him say that I feel a little foolish, because I'd trust Hecht with my life – and in fact have done, many a time. So why question him now? If he says I need a rest, I probably do need a rest. Only . . .

'Okay,' I say. 'A rest. But afterwards I want to know everything – everything *you* know, that is.'

'Sure,' he answers. 'Whatever you want to know. Now go. Zarah's waiting for you.'

244

And not just Zarah, but Urte and Inge and Leni. A regular little welcoming committee.

'Where's my pack?'

'You won't need one,' Urte says.

'And my clothes?'

Zarah studies me a moment. 'Those will do. You can change when you're there.'

'So where exactly . . .?'

Urte puts a finger to my lips. 'Just go.'

And so I find myself, less than thirty seconds later, standing on a broad dirt track between two stands of pines.

I have no idea where this is or when, only that it's a fresh, warm day.

Birdsong echoes in the stillness.

I turn, looking back, but there's nothing, and I begin to wonder if Hecht hasn't, perhaps, planned this; whether, in fact, I'm exiled, stranded in some uninhabited time-stream.

And then I hear it. The sound of a saw.

I walk towards the sound and, after a while, a long, barn-like building comes into view, a great stack of wooden beams piled alongside. Two men – peasants by the look of them – stoop over a big, double-headed saw, drawing it back and forth across a massive pine trunk that's spread across two large trestles.

I walk on. Coming into view just beyond the barn are other buildings: *izbas* mainly, but also a smithy, several workshops, another two barns, a church with a small blue cupola, and there, where the land climbs to the left, part hidden by the trees – a larger, better-built home – a proper two-storey *dacha*.

Russia. I am in Russia.

From the position of the sun, it's mid-afternoon, or perhaps mid-morning, but as I walk on, someone appears at the door to one of the workshops – a keen-eyed man in his middle years with long dark hair and a neatly trimmed dark beard. Wiping his hands on his carpenter's apron, he looks across at me, squinting into the daylight, then breaks into a beaming smile.

'Meister Otto!'

It takes me a moment to recognise him, for he's a good ten years older than when I last set eyes on him, but then I laugh aloud and, hastening across, wrap him in a great hug.

'Alexander Alexandrovich!'

'Oh, Meister, it's so good to see you! Why didn't you tell us you were coming?'

'I wanted to surprise you.'

But in that moment I have realised something; if Alexander is here, then maybe, just maybe . . .

'Katerina?'

'The mistress? She's in the house. But wait . . . the cart. You must see the cart.'

'The cart?'

'The one you ordered built before you went away. It's finished.'

He turns and gestures towards the workshop, wanting to show me, but I interrupt him.

'Later, Alexander, I promise. But first . . .'

He bows, embarrassed. 'Of course. Stupid of me.'

'Come,' I say. 'Walk with me, Alexander Alexandrovich.' And I place my arm about his shoulders as we walk up the slope, following the path.

He wants to tell me everything that's happened since I left, but I tell him no. I don't want to know. Not yet.

And as I walk up that path towards the *dasha*, I feel something that I haven't felt for years. Fear, and an incredible sense of anticipation.

Stopping, I turn to him. 'Will you wait here, Alexander? It's just . . .'

'Of course . . .'

And so I walk on, alone, until I'm standing before the door, in the shade of a trellis that skirts a well-tended garden. The house is silent. The only noise is the sound of a woodcock calling and the distant sound of sawing. And then I hear something. Children's laughter followed, a moment later, by a sound I'd begun to think I'd never hear again. Katerina's voice.

I push through, into the long, deeply shadowed hallway. There are coats and smocks hanging on the pegs to my right, and piles of boots and shoes of all sizes, while to my left there's an open door, and through that door . . .

My voice fails. I try to call her but I can't.

Katerina is as beautiful as ever, yet I realise that she has aged. Ten years? Fifteen? Only she is even more beautiful for that, her figure fuller, her hair longer and more lustrous. She is in blue, of course, her favourite colour, and as she turns towards me so her laughter turns to awed surprise. And then she shrieks and runs to me.

I tremble as she comes into my arms, as her mouth seeks mine and we embrace as if a thousand years have passed. As well they might have. Only it feels like the very first time I have kissed her; as if the years lie ahead of us not behind. And as I draw back from that kiss and see my eyes reflected in the darker pools of hers, I understand why I have felt dead these past few weeks, for to be away from her is to be away from life itself.

'I've missed you,' I say, my hand touching her neck, my lips gently meeting hers again.

'Not as much as I missed you.'

'I thought you were dead.'

'Dead?'

'Urd protect me, look at you . . .'

My blood is pounding and I want to take her there and then, only I realise suddenly that there are others in that great, airy room. I look about me, stunned, realising with a shock just what I've walked into.

Katerina laughs and leans in close, whispering in my ear. 'You'll have to wait.'

But for once I barely hear her. Taking Katerina's hand, I move back a little from her, staring at each of the five young girls in turn, my astonishment making them giggle. They think it's a game, but it's not. I have never, in all my days, had such a shock.

I look to Katerina. 'Are these . . .?'

She looks at me, then at them, and back at me, sudden understanding coming to her eyes. 'Sweet Mother of God, you mean . . .?'

'The first time,' I say, my voice an awed whisper.

She stares at me a moment longer, then, swallowing, takes charge of things.

'Girls . . . come and welcome your father home. Natalya, you first. And be polite now. Remember what you learned.'

And the first of them – the image of Katerina, only twelve, thirteen at most – gets up from where she sits on the window seat and comes across. She is dressed, like all of them, in a simple white cotton smock, against which her long dark hair falls in a cascade of glorious ringlets. Just looking at her takes away my breath, for this is my daughter. These are *all* my daughters.

She gives a little bow, then, smiling broadly, says, '*Welcome home, papa,*' in perfect German.

I laugh, delighted, and look to Katerina. But the best is to come, for, reaching up, Natalya holds my neck, gently making me bend down to her, so that she can place a kiss there on my cheek.

A tear rolls down to greet her kiss.

Next is Irina, nine and a tomboy like her mother. After her comes Anna, seven and shy. Martha, five, proves the actress of the family, curtseying low and giving me a cheeky wink, while the baby, Zarah, three years old, refuses to approach me, holding on tight to her mother's skirts. I pick her up and, by staring at her sternly and then making a face, force her into laughing.

My girls. My beautiful, unthought-of girls. And as I stand there, surrounded by them, looking from one to the next, I vow that I will do everything in my power to protect them. That I would give my life a thousand times over to let them live and be happy.

For I'm not a stupid man, and in that strange, wonderful moment of sublime and utter bliss, I am aware that such joy has its darker side, and that now, more than ever, I am vulnerable; that I have become in that instant a hostage to Fate and Time and, best and worst of all, to Love. A dark and overpowering love.

I wake beside her in the night and, rolling over on to my elbow, look down at her shadowed form. She is naked, the thin cotton sheet covering her legs and stomach.

I feel like waking her, simply to make love to her again, only I'm loath to disturb her sleep, for she looks so peaceful, so very happy in her dreams.

I blow a kiss, then gently climb from the bed and walk over to the window to sit there on the sill, looking out across the valley towards the village and the barn. This is mine. Everything I see, and more besides. Cherdiechnost. My estate, purchased in my name. My little foothold in the realms of time.

Untouched, I think, and wonder how that's so, for I know the Russians have targeted me elsewhere. But this feels safe, and yet dreamlike, for everything I want is here. Everything and more.

Throwing on a gown, I walk silently through, looking in at their bedrooms. Natalya and Irina share a room just down the hall. Next door are Anna and Martha, and in a small room, on her own in a hand-carved cot that I'm sure is Alexander's work, is my darling Zarah. I stand above her, looking down, in awe at her childish beauty. She lays on her side, her hair messed up and sweaty in sleep, her tiny thumb in her mouth, and I know I am in love – just as much in love with her and her sisters as I ever was with her mother. Yet how can that be so? For what I feel for Katerina swallows worlds. So how can there be room for more? And yet there is. Room for each one of these five small treasures.

I wipe my eyes and turn. Katerina is in the doorway, watching me. She smiles, then comes across, unembarrassed by her nakedness. Her breasts are pendulous and heavy, the nipples hard.

'Come back to bed,' she says. 'We've catching up to do.'

I smile, then briefly turn back, looking down at my baby-child again. 'I should have known.'

'Known?'

'How beautiful they'd be. So like their mother.'

I turn back, meeting her eyes, and find a look there that I've not seen before. Not just love for me, but . . . I don't know. It's hard to say what it is exactly, only I know that she would not be anywhere else, or with anyone else, than here and now, with me.

I reach out and take her hands and draw her gently close. 'You know what?'

'What?'

'I think I'm dreaming.'

She smiles. 'Then keep dreaming, Otto. Don't ever stop.'

246

Alexander Alexandrovich is sitting on a tuft of grass outside the front door, waiting for me as I emerge early that next morning, looking much as though he's been there all night.

I grin at him, amused by his enthusiasm, then throw out my arm, pointing towards the workshop.

'Come, then, Alexander! The cart!'

His face lights and he leaps up, hurrying to be at my side as we walk down the gentle slope towards the barn. It's a beautiful morning, made all the more so by the fact that I am here and now, Katerina asleep in my bed, my children . . .

I stop dead, looking to my companion, a broad grin on my face.

'*You* have children, Alexander.'

'Yes, Meister?'

'Do you love them?'

Alexander blushes, then nods reluctantly, as if it is unmanly to speak of such things. Yet this is new to me – totally outside of my experience. Yesterday I had no children, but today . . .

Today the whole world is transformed. Made fresh and new and bright and full of promise.

I laugh, in such good humour that I decide, there and then, to hold a feast, that very evening.

'Meister?'

'Yes, Alexander Alexandrovich?'

He gestures towards the workshop. 'The cart?'

And so we go and see it, and a fine piece of work it is, for which I reward him. Only I don't stay long, Returning to the house, I wake Katerina and ask her who I should see to arrange the feast.

Dressing quickly, she summons the steward, a short yet muscular man named Pavlenko. Igor Pavlenko. He is extremely pleased to see me, grinning like an idiot, yet when I tell him what I want, he is instantly serious and claps his hands and has a dozen peasants running about within minutes, each with a whole list of things to do.

'Your father,' I say, turning to Katerina again. 'We mustn't forget to invite your father.'

Her face clouds, and for a moment I think I've made a real gaffe, that he's dead. But it isn't that.

'He's out of town,' she says. 'He went to Tesov three weeks back. He'll be so disappointed when he finds out he missed out on a feast.'

'Maybe he's back. It's not that long a journey. Four, five days at most. I'll send someone to see if he's home.'

But Katerina's not so sure. 'He'd have come over, if he were back. He always does. Why, he almost lives here these days. The girls spoil him so.'

I smile at that. At least I've made my father-in-law happy. And that, in Russia, is no small accomplishment.

'Let's send someone anyway, just to be sure. And your mother . . .?' I stop, knowing that this time I *have* made an error. 'I'm sorry,' I say gently. 'I didn't know.'

She pushes the door closed, then turns to me. 'We need to talk,' she says, very matter-of-factly. 'If you're not to make . . . elementary mistakes. You need to know what's been happening.'

I reach out and hold her a moment, feeling her face against my shoulder. 'When did she . . .?'

'Six years back. It was winter. She was very ill. A lot of people were. There was a poor harvest that year. Anyway, we thought she'd pulled through, only . . .'

For a moment we hug, saying nothing, then I kiss the top of her head. 'I'm sorry. I really liked her.'

She smiles up at me sadly. 'You were at her funeral. You know, it's really odd, all this. It's happened before, but . . . not like this.'

'I'm out of sequence, huh?'

Her smile broadens. 'Very much. That business with the girls . . . What *did* you feel?'

I stare back into her eyes. 'It was like the first time I saw you. I was . . . *overwhelmed.*'

She kisses me. 'You're such a good father to them. Or will be.' She grins. 'Back in the past.'

'And in the future, too, I hope.'

Yet it has to be, surely? For them even to exist must mean I've been there, in that past, which for me, of course, is still in the future.

I speak to Alexander Alexandrovich, and he harnesses a horse to the new cart and sets off to bring Razumovsky, if he's there, and – so he says – to give the cart a good 'test'. Only when he says 'test', he uses the German word *versuch*, meaning 'experiment', and it makes me wonder what other little seeds I have sown in this place.

While he's gone, I sit with Katerina in the kitchen, talking, enjoying the attentions of my daughters who, one by one, come down from their beds to slowly fill that big, sunlit room.

But let me pause. Even to *have* a kitchen is this age is something. For this is, remember, the thirteenth century, and nowhere, outside of castles and palaces and monastery refectories, do they have such things as kitchens. Cooking over an open fire's the thing. But I have brought a degree of innovation to this place. Nothing that can't be found somewhere in this age, of course – nothing anachronistic – but it is certainly unusual, and the servants love its 'sophistication', its 'modernity' and take pride in working here.

Those servants now appear as if from nowhere to prepare breakfast, and like Pavlenko, they are delighted by my return, embracing me and clapping my back heartily or gently touching my cheek – this from the older women – so that after a while I begin to feel like the Prodigal Master, even though they might as well be strangers for what I remember of them.

At Katerina's prompting, I ask them questions, and soon I begin to get a feel of the close-knit web of lives that exists in this place.

By now, Martha is encamped in my lap, her head against my shoulder, the simple physical presence of her there – her childish warmth – making me feel drowsy. And on *her* lap is one of the seven cats we own – Nikita, it appears – a fat, grey animal that looks as if it's swallowed an extremely large rodent.

Just after midday, Alexander Alexandrovich returns, the cart filled with overflowing crates and baskets and stoppered pitchers. They're from Katerina's father, and the news is that he's home from Tesov and coming along later. And there's more . . . only Alexander Alexandrovich has been sworn to secrecy by Razumovsky.

'Go and work, Alexander,' I order him, knowing that unless I do Katerina will pester him until he gives up his precious knowledge. 'I'll see to the cart.'

He hurries away, relieved.

I look to Katerina. 'What do you think? What could he possibly have brought back from Tesov?'

The answer's obvious to us both. Tesov is north-east of us – a trading post that specialises in only one thing.

'Furs!' she says excitedly. 'He's bought the girls their own furs!'

But we're going to have to wait and see. There's much to do, and we've barely finished getting things ready – setting out the great trestle tables in the main field – when Razumovsky arrives in his troika, even as evening falls.

He's not alone. As he steps down, he turns and puts out his hand, helping down a young, blond-haired woman of a startlingly pale complexion. She gives a frightened smile and pulls her dark furs tighter about her.

A slave, I think. *He's bought himself a slave to keep his bed warm at night.*

And who can blame him? Only I glance at Katerina and see the guarded, almost hostile expression in her face, not to speak of the troubled looks on the faces of my girls, who have formed a line beside her, waiting to welcome their *dyedooshka* home.

But Razumovsky seems oblivious to these undercurrents. Striding towards me, he embraces me, almost lifting me from my feet.

'Otto! So *good* to have you back! Travel is clearly good for you! You look a good five years younger than when you set off!'

And, releasing me, he turns and puts an expansive arm out towards the pale young woman. He is drunk, of course.

'Katerina, Otto, girls . . . Please welcome my wife, Birgitta.'

Drunk, yes, and stupid. Stupid not to realise what waves this whim of his will cause. Insensitive, too, but that's his style. In that, I think, he's *typically* Russian. Katerina's indrawn breath is audible, yet her father seems not to hear it. But she is not alone in being shocked. The girl is barely twenty, if she's that, a good ten to fifteen years Katerina's junior – and she will have to call her 'mother'.

Before he can say another word, I grab his arm and drag him through, into the house, slamming the door behind me.

'Your *wife*?'

Razumovsky grins. 'Isn't she beautiful?'

I want to punch him. 'Can't you see what you've done, Mikhail?'

He stares at me, puzzled.

'Did you even begin to think what Katerina would feel, putting that woman – that *child* – in her mother's place?'

'Otto?'

'And your granddaughters? Did you think what this would do to them? How *upset* they'd be?'

'But—'

'No.' And I'm furious now, having worked myself up into a rage. 'All you thought of was your dick!'

Razumovsky opens his mouth, then closes it again, considering my last statement.

'She is good, Otto. A good woman. Her mother—'

'Her *mother*?'

He lowers his voice. 'Her mother was my lover, you understand, in Tesov. I would go and spend a month with her, every summer, these past five years. But this year she died. Her daughter . . . I promised to look after her.'

'Look after her, fine, but *marry* her? Bring her into your *home*?'

I'm conscious that I'm shouting, and that my voice is probably carrying out on to the porch, where Katerina and my daughters and half the household staff are standing, listening. I make an effort to calm myself, but I really am outraged by what he's done.

298

'You dumb-arsed Russian bastard!'

Razumovsky is astonished by my outburst. He shakes his head, then, unexpectedly, roars with laugher.

'You think this affects anything, Otto? You think Katerina would *allow* it? No, I am only being kind to the girl, and besides . . .' his voice drops to a conspiratorial whisper, 'she is a real wildcat beneath the sheets.'

I try to stare him out, to make him feel ashamed of himself, but Razumovsky has no shame. He shrugs, then turns his back on me, searching beneath the worktop for a flask of something. He emerges a moment later, clutching a flagon of red wine and, uncorking it, takes a mouthful.

'So how was your trip, Otto?'

He has forgotten. Barely ten seconds have passed and he has already dismissed what I've said to him.

'That woman—'

'Is a goddess,' he says, wiping his hand across his beard.

Walking past him, I throw open the door. The porch is empty. They have all gone. I turn back.

'Mikhail . . .'

He staggers out, clutching the flagon. 'Yes, my boy?' And he puts his arm around my shoulders.

I cannot stay angry. Razumovsky is what he is, and he's probably right about Katerina. Only he has done this family harm by marrying the girl.

He looks about him at the empty porch, a look of comic astonishment on his face. 'Where *are* they?'

'In the great field,' I say. 'You know, the feast?'

'Then lead on,' and he takes another, longer drink from the flagon then wipes his hand across his beard again, belches manfully and grins at me. 'It's so *good* to be home, don't you think?'

299

The moon is full, stars scattered like a basketful of jewels upon the velvet dark. At the far end of the field, which has lain fallow since last autumn, they have dug a trench, ten yards long, two wide and two deep. They have lined it with logs and built a massive fire, which burns at the centre of a great square of trestle tables.

Razumovsky is right. Being home *is* good. Better than good. I sit at the head table, Katerina beside me, my girls to either side, my people – eight hundred *muzhik*, peasants, that is, and twenty household staff – gathered at the nearby tables, eating and drinking in the fire's fierce blaze while our own musicians – five men and a boy – pound out a relentless melody.

It is only now that I understand what I have built here, for Cherdiechnost is not just an estate, it is, in its way, a little kingdom, an experiment in living. Oh, I'm not claiming I am the only 'good' master in this age, yet the context of history adds weight to what I've done here. There are no slaves here, for one. Every last man, woman and child on my estate is free – their freedom bought under the ancient process of *barshchina*, in this instance for three full years' service on the land, the product of which has been ploughed back into the estate, to build the smithy and the storage barns, the workshops and, almost unique in this age, the crafts school. In that respect and others, this place is something new. For I have given the people here the chance to live happy, fulfilled lives, not lives of misery. To earn their little place upon God's earth. There's great pride here in what we've achieved, and as I look about me I see how they glow with the force of living.

How strange that is. I do not know these people, and yet I know them like my own pulse, the very beat of my heart.

There are eighteen of us seated at the long table. Katerina and my girls and I make seven. Across from me sits Razumovsky and his pale young bride. To his left is my master carpenter, Alexander, his stout little wife beside him, head down as she tucks into her meal. Further down the table is the head of the crafts school, Yuri something – I have forgotten already – and his assistant, who I'm told will shortly be his wife. My steward, Pavlenko, sits uncomfortably to my left, two places down, his tall, thin wife beside him, smiling constantly at everyone. I say uncomfortable, but it's difficult to make the man rest and enjoy the meal, he is so keen to do his duty.

My daughters are to my right. Across from them sit three more guests, the blacksmith, Kleist, his Russian wife, and the priest, Iranov.

Kleist is a taciturn man. A Saxon, from a small village near Osnabruck, Kleist has the look of something *made* – hammered out on his own anvil, perhaps – he is so very still in himself. Asked a question, he will take a good minute or two to consider every aspect of it – as if inspecting a blade he has been beating out for imperfections – before answering. Fortunately, Father Iranov more than makes up for the smith in terms of volubility, talking constantly, ten to the dozen, as they say, such that it's a surprise to find his plate cleared, his mead cup empty.

Father Iranov is a good fellow. A kind, funny, and deeply reasonable man. I found him – so Katerina tells me – in an inn in Suzdal', lamenting his loss of faith. After an evening in his company I recruited him, built him his own stone church, and, more to the point, the crafts school. Not that he found God again. Far from it. Just that I persuaded him that a man of good character could often be a better priest than a man of rigid beliefs. And besides, I didn't *want* a proper priest, not one of the meddlesome kind, anyway, though a priest I had to have.

Iranov, you see, is our 'buffer' – our very own 'pretend' priest. Were he not here, the Metropolitan of Kiev would appoint one to be his spy and chide us – maybe even punish us – for our godless ways. As it is, Iranov plays at being priest. And everyone's kept happy. Whatever, he certainly looks the part, with his huge belly and his bushy black beard.

Seated across from me, his pale bride silent at his side, Razumovsky raises his mug and grins. 'They love you, Otto! Look at them!'

'And so they should,' Katerina says, with mock indignation. 'There's not a fairer nor more generous master between here and Kiev!'

Father Iranov nods. 'Nor one who's better travelled!'

If it's a dig at me, it's delivered with a smile; but it makes me wonder just how often I've been away across the years.

A good deal, probably, unless I've badly neglected my duties to the *volk*. But it makes me wonder just how much I can ask Katerina. Last night . . . I yawn . . . last night there was no chance to talk. I smile. Or no desire to. Being back in her arms was enough. But now I'm curious.

She *knows* about my future. Could tell me precisely what happens and where and when and how, and that – so we *Reisende* have had drilled into us since we were boys – is dangerous knowledge.

And yet I'm tempted. Tempted to ask her just what I've told her across the years.

For I must have told her something.

She leans close. 'What is it, Otto?'

'Not now.'

Her eyes search mine. 'All right. But no secrets. Remember? We tell each other everything.'

'*Everything?*'

'You agreed.'

'Did I? When?'

She smiles. 'Any time now.'

'Any . . .?'

I see that she's ribbing me, and smile.

She looks down at her plate. 'Did you know I was betrothed once, before I met you?'

'Kravchuk, you mean?'

'No . . . to a boy named Peter. A local boy. He died of the pox six months before the wedding. He caught it one day and was dead the next. It almost killed us, too. My father . . .' She looks up, meets my eyes. 'You can imagine. To have a daughter and not to see her married, that is a poor fate for a father. And then you showed up.'

After Kravchuk, I think, and begin to understand why for the first time.

'Don't be angry with your father,' I say, taking her hands. 'He must be lonely.'

She almost smiles. 'I'm not, only . . .' Her eyes move away, then back to mine. 'Can't you change it, Otto? Slip back in time and . . .?'

'No,' I say firmly. 'I can't.'

She's about to argue further when a great squeal goes up from my girls and, almost as one, they climb down from their places and hurry towards a cloaked figure who has appeared on the far side of the fire.

I watch through the flickering glare of the flames as they crowd round the stooping figure – a woman, it seems – greeting her like they'd greet an aunt. But they have no aunts. Katerina is an only child.

'Who's that?' I ask Katerina quietly.

'That's Jamil. She's helps me look after them.'

That surprises me, as does the name. It's Eastern. But their love of her is unmistakable. Two of them hold her hands, and the other two press close as they come round, approaching our table. Yet as her face comes into view, I have a moment's confusion so profound that for a moment I am certain that I must be dreaming, for I last saw this woman – this *Jamil* – naked on a bed in Baturin, three hundred and fifty years in the future.

I stand, watching as they bring her to me.

She smiles, a shy, almost embarrassed smile, then bows her head. 'Meister . . .'

'You have a twin,' I say, as she straightens. 'Someone I met on my travels.'

Even in the half-light, I see the shock in her eyes, the way the blood drains from her face, and then she looks down. When she looks at me again her eyes are moist. 'I *had* a twin, but she was taken from us – abducted – when I was just eight years old.'

I don't know whether to believe her or not, but if she's lying she's a superb actress. For a moment I think of Old Schnorr and repeated faces, and ask myself whether this could just be a coincidence, yet the more I think about it, the more certain I am that she's a time agent – a Russian – and know that I need to jump out of there just as soon as I possibly can.

To check up on her. To make certain I'm not just being paranoid about this. Because the likelihood of her being in both places by chance is almost zero.

Twins . . . I don't believe she ever had a twin.

'Forgive me,' I say, addressing those about me. 'I need to take a pee.'

And without another word I stride off towards the trees.

248

Hecht is busy, so I leave matters in the more than capable hands of Zarah, who promises she will give me my answer, and tells me how and where I'll find it. And so, less than a minute after I've left the table, I return.

Jamil has taken a seat beside my father-in-law. As I sit again, she looks at me strangely, wondering, no doubt, just what's going on in my head.

Reaching beneath the table, I find the envelope exactly where Zarah said I'd find it, placed there that afternoon by one of our agents, long before the feast began.

I open it and slip the single sheet of paper out.

Katerina is looking at me, her eyes narrowed. 'Otto . . .?'

Finished reading, I fold the note and slip it into my pocket, then reach across and, lifting my beer mug, stand to make a toast. 'To Cherdiechnost!'

The toast is echoed with a great roar from every side. 'To Cherdiechnost!'

Jamil is quiet, however, and when I go round the table and crouch beside her, she almost flinches.

'I'm sorry,' I say quietly. 'I didn't mean to waken any ghosts, only I really did see someone, so like you as to be . . .'

She looks at me, her dark eyes the same as her twin's, and yet so different, so free of any subterfuge. 'Where was this?'

'Baturin,' I say. 'Down south. Among the nomads. She . . . she worked in an inn there.'

'And you think it was her?'

'I don't know. Maybe. Only . . .' I sigh, then look away, struck by the impossibility of explaining the situation to her. Because from what we've learned, Jamil *did* have a twin, and she *was* abducted from her village when the two girls were eight. Only from there the trail goes cold. The girl simply disappeared. Until, well, the rest you know. Our two agents and the whore and—

I'm surprised that I hadn't guessed that she too was an agent. Only why should I? What single clue did I have? Nor did it ever occur to me that one of theirs would play the whore. But then, why not?

Jamil is staring at me. 'Meister, do you think I could find her? Do you think—'

I interrupt. 'Baturin is a long way from here, Jamil. A woman travelling alone, it would not be safe. Besides, I don't think she's there any more. When I went back to look for her, she'd gone.'

The look of disappointment – of dismay – on Jamil's face, almost makes me relent. Only there really is no point in her travelling to Baturin, for even if she made it there safely, her twin would not be there.

'Couldn't we send someone? To try and find her? I have money, I—'

I gently take her hands. 'Jamil, I wish I'd never said a word, only when I saw you . . .' I harden my tone the slightest bit. 'Your sister is lost. Accept that. You could search for her the rest of your life and never find her.'

'But *you* found her. And you weren't even looking.'

It's hard to argue with that. Harder still to hold her hands, and look into her pleading eyes and tell her no. And so I compromise.

'Look. This is what I'll do. Next time I travel south, I'll look for her. I'll ask in every town I visit. Now that I know . . .'

Gratitude shines in her eyes. Without warning, she kisses me full upon the lips, and for the briefest moment, I have a vision of her twin, lying there on the bed in Baturin, naked in the candle-light, her every charm displayed.

Flustered, I move back away from her, relinquishing my hands. 'Jamil, I—'

She flushes with embarrassment. 'Oh, Meister, I'm so sorry, only . . . you made me so happy. The thought of my twin sister . . .'

I sigh, knowing now for certain that nothing but sorrow can come of this, and rue having said a single word to her.

As I sit down again, Katerina leans close, speaking quietly to my ear. 'What was that, Otto?'

'Nothing,' I say, though the fact that Jamil's twin has vanished from the time-stream is a mystery that neither Zarah nor our agents can explain. 'Nothing at all.'

249

That night, in bed, I turn to her and ask, 'What do you *know*, Katya? When I've been here before, what have I said?'

In the soft glow of the candle, her face changes, becoming suddenly defensive. 'You told me not to tell you. You told me that an evening would come when you would ask, and that however much I was tempted, I was never – and you made me swear it on our children's lives – *never* to tell you a single detail of anything that had happened outside the boundaries of this time and place. I was not to say anything about . . . your travels.'

'I told you that?'

'Yes.'

'Then I guess I had good reason.'

'You did.'

'You know that for a fact?'

'I do. I even know why. But I'm not to say. If I did, well, it would change things. You wouldn't do what you have to do. And if you didn't . . .'

'Whoa, hold fire there. If I told you, that's enough.'

But I sense now that there's a shadow behind everything I do and say. That it's all prefigured somehow, set hard into some complex, closely interwoven loop. Only I can't even ask her that, for if I do things will change. And not, from Katerina's hints, for the good.

Then why is she suddenly so sad? Why are her eyes filled now with sudden tears?

'Katya?'

But she doesn't answer, simply douses the candle and pulls me down beside her, making me hold her as she trembles in my arms.

250

The next morning we set up a trestle table outside the front door of the *dacha*, and wait as the villagers assemble from all over the estate. Every *bol'shak*, or head of household, is gathered, along with those craftsmen who were recruited in the last six months and are as yet unmarried. They wait patiently in a long line, conversing cheerfully in the spring sunlight, as Pavlenko checks each of the cloth packets for a second time.

Further off, in a huddle near the huts, the rest of the *muzhik* – the peasants – are gathered, looking on, or at least, those that have managed to get out of their beds after last night's carousing.

Katerina leans close. 'I'll tell you who each is as they come to the table.'

I'm glad she's there, for this would have been an ordeal without her. There's scarce six faces that I know among them, yet they all know me.

I glance at her. 'We do this how often?'

'Twice a year. We would have done it a week or so back, only you were still away.'

I nod, then, seeing that Pavlenko's ready, gesture for the first of them to come forward.

'This is Semevskii,' Katerina says very quietly, so I alone can hear. 'He has two unmarried sons and a young daughter. He's a field worker, from the north village.'

As Semevskii – a tall, gangly man, with twisted brown teeth – comes to the table, I put out my hand and grasp his firmly. 'Semevskii,' I say, smiling at him warmly. 'How's your little princess?'

And so it begins. As Pavlenko hands me one of the cloth packets, I have a brief word or two, then hand it to the man, who quite literally tugs at his forelock and bows then walks away, grinning like a fool.

Or is that unfair? Because Semevskii and all the others queuing here have every reason to grin. For here, on this estate, the workers are not merely free men, they are common shareholders in our venture, and this ritual is no less than the giving to them of their half-yearly share – an equal share – of the profits made. There are a set of books, open for any one of them to inspect, of what's been produced, what used, and what sold on to the merchants of Novgorod. And a good little trade it has proved to be. Looking through the books this morning, I was impressed not only by Pavlenko's neatness and efficiency at keeping records, but by the industriousness of the peasants and craftsmen of Cherdiechnost.

'This is what *you* made,' Katerina said earlier, when I'd asked. 'It was hard at first, making them understand how it worked, and there were a few rotten apples to be got rid of, I can tell you, but eventually they began to see how by pooling their resources they could not only produce much more, but begin to diversify. They built the workshops and the mill, the smithy and the pottery, and, when things were really bad, we got through because you'd had the foresight to make them store some of the grain and keep it against hard times.'

Hard times . . . it's hard to think that these happy, well-fed peasants have ever had hard times, but so it is. And as they come to the table, one by one, each to take their share, so I begin to feel very good about what I've done here.

'Puskarev,' Katerina says, yet as Puskarev comes forward I laugh in amazement.

'*Puskarev?*'

He grins, his teeth like pearls in his dark, African face. 'Meister?'

'It was his owner's name,' Katerina says in a whisper. 'You bought him at the slave market in Novgorod and brought him back here, *remember?*'

And she gives me a little nudge as she says the last word.

'Puskarev,' I say, and because she's given me nothing more on the man, I ask, 'Are things well with you?'

'Fine, *danke*,' he says, and gives me a beam of a smile, as if to let me know just how highly he regards me.

As he turns away, I look to Katerina. 'I didn't see *him* at the feast last night.'

'That's because he wasn't there. He was in town, with four of the other men, delivering the *tamga*.'

'We pay that?'

'Everyone pays. Or risks the anger of Prince Alexander.'

I give the smallest nod. This is a little kingdom, and you don't need to have that much imagination to see how difficult it must have been maintaining this, because, for all my innovations, this land is still a wilderness, and to defend what one has built takes a strong arm and a will of iron. And endless vigilance.

I turn to her again. 'Was there ever a time when it might have failed?'

'Plenty of times. But we always came through. You taught us that. How to endure. How to protect what we had. How to plan against the future.'

'I did?'

And there are suddenly a hundred questions I want to ask her, but already there's another of the men before me, and as I shake his hand and hand him his packet, the truth of the situation suddenly hits me.

'This is it!' I say to her excitedly, laughing with surprise. '*This* is the moment when I decided to do it!'

She stares at me, puzzled.

'Don't you see? It's a paradox. I set all of this up – worked hard at it for year after year – all because I saw, just now, what could be achieved.'

'But that's—'

'Time,' I say. 'Non-sequential time.'

251

Let me tell you what I think. The fact that Jamil's twin is a time agent is of profound significance. As is the fact that she has vanished from the timestream, now that she's drawn my attention. But is that the *only* reason for what the Russians attempted at Poltava? To taunt me? To let me know that they know about this place, this little haven of mine?

If so, it would be a first. To target a single time agent – which is all I am, after all – and create whole new timestreams, just to let me know I'm being watched.

And not to kill me.

It doesn't make much sense, only there is no other explanation.

You see, if Jamil's twin – the whore of Baturin – is a time agent, and it's fairly clear she is, then the fact that Jamil is here, in such a sensitive position, minding my children, cannot be mere coincidence. Because they don't work like that. They would not take her and train her and introduce her to me, unless . . .

But there I stall. Unless what? Do they plan to 'switch' her? Is that it? At some future date will Jamil be replaced and my girls find themselves at the tender mercies of a trained killer?

It's possible. More than possible, in fact. Only they must know I'd think of that.

So maybe that's it. Maybe they want to undermine me, to make me feel insecure, here where I should feel most safe.

Warfare by other means. Psychological warfare.

Let us assume, then, that that is what they aim to do. To make me paranoid. To make me fear those closest to me. Well, there's an easy answer to that: send Jamil away. Remove the doubt by replacing the tutor.

Which is what they'd expect me to do?

Katerina finds me as dawn breaks over Cherdiechnost, sitting up on 'the hump', a grassy hillock raised some hundred metres or so above the surrounding countryside, the estate laid out like a map below me, the lake to my left, the main settlement – part-hidden by the trees – to my right, the blue cupola of the church shining brightly in the sunlight.

'Otto?'

'I've been thinking,' I say. 'About Jamil and her twin.'

She sits beside me. 'The girls won't be happy.'

'I'm sorry . . .?'

'You'll have to send her away. If she stays . . .'

I nod. She's understood. Has thought this through the same way I've thought it through.

'I'm sorry,' I say. 'If there was any other way.'

We're both silent for a time, looking out over the fields. In the early morning light the shadows are long, the lake in darkness, the forest lining the length of its northern shore, the north village just beyond, over a stout plank bridge.

'How long are you staying this time?'

'I don't know.'

'Last time . . .' She stops, looks down, then plucks a blade of grass and puts it to her mouth.

'Go on . . .'

'Last time it was a whole year. I began to think . . .' She sighs. 'I began to think that might be it. That you'd *always* be here. But I should have known, after what you'd told me.'

I ought to be annoyed with her, but I'm not. It must be hard not telling me. 'A whole year?' And I can't help but smile, thinking that that's to come. That it's fated. Because I know now that I'm in a loop, and not just any short-term loop, but a big one. One that covers whole years of my life, something intricate and complex.

Only why? What's happened to 'the Game'?

'So how many times . . .?'

'Have you stayed here?' She considers, then says, 'Fourteen times.'

'And this?'

'The fifteenth.'

That makes me think. I have five children and the child mortality rate is high in this Age. For all five of mine to have survived is rare, bordering on exceptional, which makes me think that maybe I've 'cheated' – brought things back from Four-Oh, perhaps, to help against disease and childhood maladies. Only I can't ask. Nor can I ask her if Hecht knows I'm here. But he must do, simply for me to be here, mustn't he?

Katerina is looking at me, her dark eyes concerned. 'It must be hard, living as you do. Sideways, backwards, any way but straightforward.'

I reach out and touch her neck. 'Maybe. But it has its compensations. Without it, I would never have met you.'

She doesn't smile. This time she's sad. 'Maybe that's the problem. Maybe that's why it's all so hard.'

Only it doesn't seem so. Sometimes it feels so easy I forget, losing myself, becoming an entirely different man, and maybe you'll argue that that's my job, only how am I serving the *volk* by being here? If I think about it at all, it feels like I'm stealing time from them. Shirking my duties. Indulging myself at their expense.

But mostly I don't think about it. I shut it out. Thus three months pass like a dream. A golden, summer dream. And then, on the day before the harvest, I seem to 'wake' again, and finding myself so, wonder what's so different about the day. It's not anything that's happened, just an instinct – a sense, if you like, of hyper-alertness that I've come to trust over the years – the time traveller's equivalent of an adrenalin rush. Yet there's no time to dwell on it.

The work party is waiting for me in the new field – thirty strong young men, stripped to the waist in the dawn's early light, ready to begin. Pavlenko is there, too, to help supervise, only today I decide I'll work with the team, and I send Igor away, knowing that, with the harvest looming, he has more than enough to occupy him.

The new field is an encroachment on the forest to the north of the estate. We cleared the space four weeks back, cutting down the trees and burning them. Their ashen stumps litter the clearing. Our task now is to uproot what remains of them, and clear the field of rocks and stones, ready to plough the earth and seed it with a winter crop.

I smile to myself as we set to, working in a line, the metal-cast wheelbarrows – made to my specifications – behind us. There's a real enthusiasm for the task, because these young men know that the more fields we have, the more crops we raise, and therefore the richer every last one of them will be. It's not an attitude you'd find anywhere else in the northern lands where bare subsistence farming is the norm, but we thrive on it, knowing that the markets in Novgorod will take whatever we can produce.

The soil itself isn't good – it's a poor, grey soil, nothing like the rich dark soil of the steppes – but a mixture of potash and manure helps raise its fertility, as does the practice of letting each field lie fallow every third growing season.

This is no Eden. It's a hard land. But these are hardened men, well up to the challenge. I work at one of the charred stumps, digging around it, then, using the spade as a lever, bring it up out of the ground, clods of earth thrown up as it comes free. Throwing the spade down, I crouch and, lifting the heavy stump, carry it across and drop it into the barrow with a ringing sound.

Three of the younger men – hardly more than boys – are on duty, wheeling the full barrows over to the cart, where two more load them on, ready to take them over to where we're laying down the foundations for a new stretch of wall. Nothing is wasted here.

And as we work, we talk, or sing, moving slowly, patiently across the field as the sun climbs the sky towards midday, when we stop and, satisfied that we've cleared a good half of it, make our way back to the north village where the women have prepared us lunch.

Tomorrow is a special day in our calendar, and much of the talk in the field has been about it. Tonight, as the sun begins to set, Anna Efimenko, an old widow from the south village, renowned for having lived a peaceful and virtuous life, will light a candle in front of the icons in her house and bow before them, then, avoiding being seen, she will sneak out to the fields and harvest the first three sheaves, there in the darkness, where the 'evil eye' cannot see her. She will bind them together and, after praying to the old gods, return to her house and extinguish the candle.

That done, all will be well. The harvest can proceed with the blessing of the gods.

Leaving the young men to wash and change, I return to the *dacha*, where Katerina is packing a basket for the picnic I promised the girls.

As I stand at the sink, naked to the waist, sluicing myself down, so I study myself in the glass. I am, I know, a changed man. Changed by my children, certainly, but also by the people of this place, this 'Kingdom out of Time', as I like to think of it. About my neck, on a simple leather cord, hang ten tiny silver hammers of Thor – a gift from Katerina. My arms look bigger than before, heavily muscled, my hands callused from manual labour, my flesh burned dark by the sun, my face covered – for the first time in my life – with a thick dark beard.

I put my hand up to my face to feel the growth, and find Katerina watching me in the glass, with that look on her face that's becoming slowly familiar to me and which I'm sure is mirrored in my own – a hunger to see and to remember, to store up for the days to come when we'll be apart.

'What happens?' I asked her, weeks past, late in the evening, when we were alone, the girls asleep in their beds.

'What do you mean?'

'When I leave . . . back to Four-Oh. How do I . . .?'

'You just go. One moment you're there, the next . . .'

'You mean I just vanish, wherever I am?'

'No. It's at night, mainly, but once . . . Once I was standing with you, among the trees, hand in hand. And then you were gone, you just weren't there any more. That was the worst time.'

'But mainly . . .'

'I wake and you're gone. And I know you've gone back. I can feel it.'

I remember nodding to her, unable to find the words, as I nod to her now and look away.

For just the thought of it breaks my heart.

The children – boys *and* girls aged six to thirteen – spend each morning of the year, festivals and Sundays excluded, in the three big, high-ceilinged classrooms of the crafts school. There, besides obtaining a solid grounding in the skills they'll need to become good farmers, tanners, livestock breeders, carpenters or whatever else, they learn their numbers and basic literacy. Enough to allow them to hold their own at market and no more. It's far from a complete education, but that would be wasted on them, not because they're incapable of learning more, but because it would be a burden, living in these backward times. This is the thirteenth century, after all, and a *muzhik* is still a *muzhik*, no matter what's in their head. Moreover, outside of Cherdiechnost, such 'embellishments' are unwelcome in citizens of their lowly status. The boyars of this age want their peasants subservient and dumb. They don't want an educated sub-class. In fact, were it known what I'm doing here, they'd probably try to burn the crafts school down.

The peasants themselves recognised this from the start and, of all my innovations, this was the hardest to push through, especially my insistence that the girls too should get their chance. But little by little I made them see the benefits and now they glow with pride to think that their children will be better than themselves.

Even so, it's a fragile thing, and I wonder just how long it will survive me. The powers-that-be – of Church and 'State' – depend almost entirely upon the ignorance of their subjects. The last thing they want is for the *muzhik* to start thinking for themselves.

Hecht would not approve. He would argue that I am setting myself up against the flow, building dams when I should be building rafts that float easily and unopposed down the stream of events, and part of me agrees. It's even possible that I'm storing up trouble. Only *I* am master here, not Hecht, and if this small estate is my lot – the only chance I'll have to 'play' at being 'lord and master' of a thousand peasants – then I'll play with a serious intent. That is, *to make a difference to the lives of those I touch here.*

I watch from across the stream, as, to the ringing of a bell, the children spill out from the big wooden schoolhouse, boisterous and loud after being cooped up all morning in their hot and stuffy classrooms, keen to get out into the fields and help the adults.

My own three, of course, are among them, better dressed, perhaps, but not ostentatiously so. Like their father and mother, they have learned to fit in, not to play high and mighty. For we are family here. Households and estate. And there is no stronger bond.

Seeing me, they shriek and run towards me, crossing the plank bridge in leaps and bounds, Irina the first to reach me.

'Papa! Papa! Are we really going to have a picnic?'

'We are!' I say, picking her up and swinging her round, even as the other two rush up to me. 'We're meeting Mama on the hump. Look . . .' And I turn, letting them see, not a quarter of a mile distant, the sight of Katerina and three of the servants carrying the big basket-woven hamper by its handles, making their slow way up the slope.

Just beyond them, to the left a little, and set back among the trees, is the wooden frame of a half-completed house, and as we look, so my father-in-law, Razumovsky, steps out into the sunlight and, seeing us, lifts a hand in greeting. He has sold up his business interests in Novgorod and moved in with us, much to the girls' delight.

'Go on,' I say. 'Go to your mother.' And they rush off past me, half turning to blow me kisses as they go.

The feeling I woke with has faded. Hard work and sweat and

the company of my fellows has subdued it – *blunted it*, one might say – but it is still there, at the back of my consciousness and in the pit of my stomach, like a tingling that doesn't tingle, or a sound just beyond the range of hearing.

It's what we travellers sometimes call '*a sense of the presence of the frame*'. The frame being the no-space dimension that both surrounds and is embedded within every other; that same medium through which we travel every time we make a jump.

Sometimes it manifests itself in a strange sense of unreality. A feeling that the world is a simulacrum, generated merely for the purposes of the Game. At such times it's easy for the inexperienced *Reisende* to make mistakes, to think that the timestream that they're in is somehow less real than that from which they've come, and that their actions therefore have no consequences. Or none that matter. Symptoms include taking bold risks, being cavalier with one's own safety and, perhaps worst of all, telling someone in that world precisely *who* and *what* you are.

You'll smile, for I have done all of these things. Only I have had a reason for everything I've done. No, I'm talking here of a kind of random activity akin to drunkenness. A kind of letting go.

The cloth is laid down on the grass, the picnic spread out by the time I get there.

Katerina greets me with a brimming mug of apple juice, freshly made that morning.

It's cool and refreshing and I drink it down in one, handing her back the empty mug then wiping my mouth with the back of my hand. Seeing it, she laughs. 'You are becoming more Russian by the day!'

To some extent it's true. Down to the clothes I wear: the leather shoes – more moccasin than shoe – the plain cloth trousers and my cotton smock. I have indeed gone native. Why, I even slur the simple Russian words I use, like I was born here in the north of Rus'. But I still think like a German.

I grin, then look past her, to where the girls – all five of them, including the baby, are playing a kind of skipping game with a rope. I watch them for a while, a strange inner stillness settling on me as I study their happy, shining faces, the way their long hair jumps in the sunlight. *Slow it down*, I think. *Let me see it clearly. Let me remember this.*

But I understand now, with the full force of experience, just how transient this is. Like all such moments, it's gone almost as soon as it's there, for this is what it's like to be time-bound. The days and hours and minutes flying by, and no returning . . .

I look down, choked suddenly, not really knowing why. Katerina reaches out and touches my cheek. 'Otto . . .?'

I meet her eyes. 'It's okay. It's just . . . I'm happy.'

She nods, and I see she understands. 'You feel it too?'

Perfect, I think. *Perfect that she understands me so.* 'It won't happen yet,' I say. 'I'm sure it won't . . .'

Only I'm not sure. This feeling . . . it's like someone is making decisions for you somewhere else in Time. Moving you. Placing you somewhere else on the board.

'Let's not spoil the day,' she says and smiles. 'Come. Sit down. There's chicken pie and ham. Whatever you want.'

But what I want isn't possible. What I want is to stay here for ever and never leave.

254

It is late in the afternoon, the youngest, Zarah, asleep in my arms, when Anna runs up from the fields where she's been playing and calls out to me. 'Is it true, Papa? Is Jamil returning for the harvest?'

I look to Katerina, alarmed, but she shakes her head. 'No, Anna, it's not true. Jamil went home, to Belarus. You know that.'

'Who told you this?' I ask, sitting up straight. 'Who has been spreading such rumours?'

'Young Tikhon, you know, Tikhon Ignatev. He said he saw her in the marketplace in Novgorod.'

Katerina has gone pale. Ignatev is one of Alexander's apprentices in the carpentry shop, a sober, hard-working young man, not given to wild flights of fancy, and he *was* in town with Alexander yesterday.

I turn to Pavlenko, who is seated with his family nearby. 'Igor, go fetch young Tikhon! Quickly now!'

The steward hurries off. While he's gone, I hand Zarah over to Katerina, then gather the rest of my girls about me and speak to them.

'Listen,' I say. 'This cannot be Jamil. It can only be her twin, and she is a bad woman, an *evil* woman. If you ever see her, here on the estate, you must tell me at once. And you *must never go with her*. Not ever, understand? Not even if she claims to be Jamil!'

I have frightened them. Little Martha bursts out crying, while both Anna and Zarah look close to tears. But this is necessary.

'I know Jamil would never hurt you,' I say, gentler than before, 'but her sister . . .'

Razumovsky, who has been napping, now wakes and sits bolt upright. Seeing his girls in tears, he frowns at me and gives a roar. 'Otto! What's going on?'

'It's Jamil's twin,' Anna says, before I can speak. 'She's a witch! Papa's said we're to run away if we see her!'

I would laugh at her childish distortion, only it's far too serious a matter. If she *is* here . . .

Then why would she show herself?

I turn, my hand going up to touch the necklace of tiny silver Thor hammers about my neck as if to reassure myself, and see young Tikhon running full pelt up the slope towards me, the portly Pavlenko trailing in his wake. The men and women have stopped their labours in the fields to stand and watch.

Breathless, he stands before me. 'Meister?'

'Jamil. You saw her?'

Tikhon gasps for breath, then nods. 'Yes, Meister. She smiled at me. But we didn't speak.'

'Are you sure it was her?'

'Or her twin.' And he smiles, as if it's a joke, but that's not his fault; he's not to know.

'What was she doing?'

'Doing, Meister? Why, shopping, I guess. She had a basket.'

'And you saw her . . . what? Once? Twice?'

Tikhon shrugs, then scratches his head, as if to aid his thought processes. 'Three, maybe four times? Every time I walked through to Master Jablokov's workshop, there she was!'

'Thank you, Tikhon.' And to impress him that he's not in trouble I take a copper denga from my belt-pouch and hand it to him. It is a day's wages and more. 'Now go,' I say. 'I'm sorry to take you from your work.'

He beams. 'It's okay, Meister. We'd finished anyway. Master Alexander—'

Pavlenko says it for me. 'Tikhon, you can go.'

Embarrassed, he bows, then turns and walks away. But watching him go, I feel cold despite the heat of the late-afternoon sun, for there is nothing accidental about this. This has been done to remind me just how vulnerable I am.

A man alone, he can cope with such threats, but a family man, with children . . .

Katerina touches my arm. 'We'll be okay . . .'

'Will we?'

I meet her eyes, knowing that I have never felt so defenceless. Because I know what they are capable of. How they might materialise, at any time, in any place. Heartless assassins who'll kill a child without compunction then fade back into the air. What good are walls or locked doors against such adversaries? How can one defend against their careful, calculated schemes?

Urd help me, I think. For there is nothing I can do. Nothing. And that is a dreadful, debilitating feeling. It makes me feel sick, *poisoned*.

Only maybe that's what's intended. To wound me. To weaken me and make me less effective.

I take a long, calming breath, conscious how everyone there on the hump is watching me, taking their lead from me. And I know, in that instant, that I cannot be seen to be weak, no matter what I feel inside. Those bastards think they have me, but that's far from the truth. For I am fated to return here, to live here and have children.

All that is in *my* future.

I smile and look about me, exuding confidence, making them smile just to look at me.

'It's all right,' I say. 'We'll post guards. Keep watch against her, and if she comes . . .'

'We'll slit her throat,' Razumovsky says, drawing his knife theatrically, making the girls give little squeals of delighted horror.

I nod. *If you're quick enough. If you can cut air.*

I open my mouth, meaning to say more, when a cry goes up from the fields below us and, turning, I see what it is. Horsemen – a dozen or so of them – coming across the plank bridge from the north village.

As the leading horseman draws up ten feet away, I realise that I know him, that I met him in Moscow, when Katerina and I were there, years – *or was it months?* – ago.

He is one of Prince Alexander's bodyguards – his *oprichina* – and he and his men must have ridden out the eleven miles from Novgorod to see us. His horse – a grey – is lathered, and as the man addresses me, it pulls back its long head, as if it longs to gallop more.

'Are you the owner of this estate?'

I stand defiantly before him, my arms across my chest. 'What if I am?'

Men are coming up from the fields now, hurrying to reach me, wanting to hear what's said and to take their place behind me, facing these strangers who have trampled our crop without a second thought. They carry sticks and scythes and other makeshift weapons.

There are eleven horsemen in all, armed warriors, rough blankets thrown across their horses' backs, their packs slung over the horses' rumps. With their topknots and loose clothes, their short swords and spears, they look like nomads, yet these are the highest authority in the land: they represent the Prince.

Hearing the tone of defiance in my voice, their leader scowls at me, then leans over his horse's neck to spit. Then he looks at me again, contempt in his eyes. 'You owe the Prince your duty.'

'I owe him nothing. What was due has been paid. Every last kopek.'

'So you say. But word is that this is a rich estate and that you have . . . *underestimated*.'

Men are still coming up from the fields. Already there are sixty or so behind me, and more are joining them every second, but the horsemen seem barely aware of it. The men behind me are, after all, only *muzhik* and would run if it came to real swordplay. At least, that's what these rogues are thinking. And so it normally is. Only these are my *muzhik*, and we have been through hard times together and fought off many adversaries. This is not the first group of men to venture out from Novgorod to demand what isn't theirs.

And yet I don't want any trouble. Not if I can help it.

'What do you want?' I say, keeping my voice hard.

Their chief turns, looking about him, assessing what he can sting us for. I know now that he doesn't recognise me, and though it may be a fault in his memory, it is probably because our meeting happened elsewhen, in another timeline.

I have met him, but he has never met me. Until today.

When he turns back, he finds me smiling, and that clearly puzzles him. Maybe he thinks I plan to cheat him, for there's a little movement in his eyes – a moment's recalculation – and then he names his price.

'Two thousand kopeks.'

There is a collective murmur from behind me: part astonishment, part anger. The figure is exactly what we've paid already.

My smile remains fixed. 'That sounds very reasonable . . . if you are a *thief*, or a Tartar-lover!'

Anger flares in his eyes. He draws his sword and kicks the grey forward, yet as he swings the sword, I duck beneath it and effortlessly ease him from his horse's back, bringing him down on to the grass with a bump.

It's a manoeuvre meant to hurt his pride more than his body, and as he gets up, so I move back slightly, circling him. I am unarmed, but I don't need to be, not against this one.

He picks up his sword and faces me. His men hold back, watching to see what happens. If I'd attacked him – hurt him, or disabled him – they'd have been on me in an instant, but this is now a matter of pride – of face – and so they wait to intervene, expecting him to punish me for my impudence.

But he's more wary now. The fall has bruised his confidence. Even so he has the sword and I'm unarmed. There can only be one end to this. This time he doesn't swing indiscriminately, but jabs. Only, to his amazement, I reach past him and, putting my hand over his sword hand, twist it sharply, snapping the wrist.

He cries out as the sword falls away, and as he does, so two of his men spur their horses forward only to fall from their mounts, dead, heavy arrowheads buried between their shoulder blades.

I look past them to where Alexander and three of his apprentices stand, bows in hand, then to the fallen captain.

'Take your little gang of thieves and go! And tell Nevsky that the next time he tries to rob honest men, he had better bring an army, not a gang of bungling fools!'

He glares at me through the pain, then, shrugging off the helping hand of one of his men, hauls himself to his feet. 'You do not know what you have done.'

'No?' I smile. 'Novgorod is a long way from Moscow. Tell your master that. And tell him . . . tell him I shall have vengeance for what he did at Krasnogorsk.'

That puzzles him, but his puzzlement lasts only a moment. If he could, he'd kill me where I stand, yes, and burn the estate, even if it meant not collecting the *tamga*. But he can see this is no ordinary situation, and now that two of his men are dead . . .

He has the two corpses lifted back on to their horses and secured there, then, ignoring his own pain, clambers back on to his own, holding the rein in his left hand, his right pressed against his chest.

He snarls at me. 'Next time I see you I will kill you.'

I am silent, but from behind the horsemen, Alexander's voice rings out. 'Shall I kill him, Meister? Shall I put an arrow through his eye?'

I could order it. I could have them all slaughtered, right here and now, only . . .

Only what? I ask myself, realising that for once I'm not thinking. If I let them go they *will* come back, without question, and maybe Nevsky too at the head of his little army. Whereas if we kill them now, maybe someone will think they were waylaid, by a robber band maybe or . . .

Or whatever. The point is that it would take Nevsky some while to find out what happened to his little band, even if he asked in Novgorod. And by then . . .

I turn and look to Katerina and my girls, then give the order. 'Kill him, Alexander. Kill them all!'

256

We take care of our wounded, then 'bury' the strangers in the deepest part of the lake, their bodies weighed down with stones, their horses with them. That upsets the peasants more than the killing of the men, for the horses were fine animals.

'Maybe so,' I say, sharing their unease, 'but if anyone from town should see us riding such fine beasts, word would quickly get back to the Prince, no?'

I say that, but word will get back somehow, at some time, for it's not easy keeping such a big secret – not when there are so many of you, and many of those weak-minded and loose-tongued. But that's not the point. The point is to make it hard for Nevsky, to give me time to prepare for his coming. For I know for a certainty he'll come.

I expect the girls to be shocked, but only the two youngest seem affected.

'They've seen worse,' Katerina says, her eyes reassuring me, letting me know she doesn't blame me for what happened.

'Yes, but you know what will happen now?'

'Nevsky will come, with *all* his men.'

'Then we must be prepared.'

She nods, a half smile on her lips.

'Good,' I say. 'Then gather all the *bol'shak*. We have much to discuss.'

257

I have Alexander make a map, and on it I mark what needs to be done: where to build the stockades and watchtowers, where to make the water traps and conceal the secret caches of weapons. I mark where we need to place angled stakes, to defend against Nevsky's cavalry, and where to construct stone walls. And more, much more.

It's a lot of work, especially with the harvest to be brought in, but there's ample time before Nevsky comes from his base in Moscow. It will be spring at best before he can get here. Besides, there's no lack of commitment from the men. They've seen what Nevsky's men are capable of, and they know the choice facing them. It's stay here and fight or run away, and they have invested far too much of themselves into this place to run.

It's a matter of pride.

The feeling that I woke with has returned, as if the weather is about to change. But the day remains hot, the sky a perfect blue, and as the evening falls, I put my mood down to the day's events: to the visit from Nevsky's men, and the return of Jamil's twin. That last particularly disturbs me, and when we're finally alone in bed, Katerina asks me what I think is going on.

I reach out, touching the copper ash leaf that hangs about her neck that I had made for her that time by the smith in Belyj, then shrug. I'd like to have an answer, only I don't, because the more I think about it, the less I understand.

'Are you *sure* she's an agent?' she asks.

'Yes.'

'Then why hasn't she struck before now? What is she waiting for?'

Good question. And I can only keep returning to my first thought. To weaken me. To undermine me. Only she could do that just as well by making a move, by attacking one of my children.

I get up and walk through, looking in at their doors, checking on them for the fifth time that evening.

As I return Katerina looks up at me, her dark eyes seriously concerned. 'What can we do?'

'Nothing,' I say, feeling sick at the thought. 'Until something happens. Then . . .'

'Go on,' she says quietly, reaching out to take my hand as I sit beside her on the bed.

'Then I'll jump back. I'll see Hecht. Explain things.'

And get his permission to act, I want to say, only I'm not half as confident as I'd like to be that he'd give it. That he'd understand. That's why I keep hesitating. That's why I've not laid it bare before him. Because I'm not sure what his response would be. And it matters. More than anything I've ever done.

We make love, and afterwards we sleep. And then, somewhere in the night, I wake to find a shadowed figure standing at the foot of our bed, looking down at me. Yet even as I sit up and cry out, it vanishes. But I know it was there.

Katerina sleeps on, sated, oblivious.

I get up and walk over to the window, then sit there on the sill, looking out across the moonlit fields. A cold sweat covers my body, and my heart is hammering wildly in my chest. It's an awful feeling. Truly awful. For I was never taught how to cope with something like this; never bred to feel this much. And I realise I am frightened. For the first time in my life, I am scared stiff, because I don't know what to do or how to act to preserve this life I've carved from Time.

Stolen, Hecht would say.

But why not? Why can't *I have this? What harm am I doing anyone?*

Only I know Hecht's answers without asking for them. I am changing things. Muddying the timestream. People are dead who should not be dead, while others are alive who never should have lived. And then, of course, there's Nevsky. For what we've done here today will affect what Nevsky does, and Nevsky's central to it all.

As ever, I have made too many ripples. I have been noticed. Just as when I fired the *staritskii* that time and blew a hole right through Krylenko's forehead.

The memory of it sobers me. Hecht won't be pleased. How could he understand?

I've broken every rule, after all. And me his *Eizelkind* . . .

Katerina stirs, then wakes. Seeing me at the window, she sits up and rubs her eyes. 'Otto?' she asks wearily. 'What is it?'

I want to explain to her. To tell her what a mess I've made of things, and that none of this was *meant*, only even as I make to form the words, it hits me like a sudden storm centred on my chest, and the whole world dissolves about me. The last thing I recall is her eyes and the sweet roundness of her mouth as she stares at me in shock.

Back. Back to Four-Oh.

The room's familiar, the shadows known from other days. Above Meister Hecht, the Tree of Worlds glows brightly in the dark, as his long fingers dance across the keyboard.

My hand goes to my neck, feeling for something that's no longer there. Only I don't know what.

Hecht is brusque, as if there's too much playing on his mind for him to worry about *my* state of mind. Not that I really feel anything, unless this emotional numbness counts, this absence of feeling.

He looks up and his grey eyes narrow, noting my sunburned skin, the thick growth of beard.

'I've a job for you, Otto. Mid-thirteenth century. You know the period and you know most of the major players, so that's not a problem. As far as strategy's concerned, it's a simple infiltration, for reconnaissance purposes. Here.'

He hands me a file. I flick it open and read the opening paragraph, then look to him.

I find it hard to speak. For some reason my head is full of dialect Russian. Even so I frame the words with care, for all that the German feels strange on my tongue.

'You want me to become a knight? A Teuton Knight?'

Hecht meets my eyes. 'A Brother, yes. I thought it was time. Have you a problem with that?'

'No, Master . . .'

'Then go to.'

Zarah is waiting for me in my room. As I step through, she comes across and, taking my arm, looks deep into my eyes, like she's a doctor, examining me.

'Are you okay?'

I hesitate. 'I'm not sure, I . . . What you gave me . . .'

'Was just a blocker. To ease the transition. You had a hard time in there. I felt, well, I felt you needed a little help. To get over it.'

'Over it?'

It's all very vague. As I said, I feel numb. Not physically numb, but like there's something I ought to remember, only I can't.

'How long will it last?'

'A while. It'll wear off, eventually. We've not erased anything, if that's what's worrying you.'

It wasn't. In fact, right now pretty much nothing worries me. Even the thought of becoming a Knight-Brother, which at any other time would excite me is just, well, *information*.

Zarah smiles, then pats my shoulder. She's looking at me strangely, and I don't know why, but I let it pass.

'Okay,' she says. 'I'll help you get ready. Only listen . . . When it does come back . . .'

There's a strange movement in her face, a hesitation, such that, even in my state of numbness I ask her, 'What?'

'Just that there are reasons. Explanations . . .'

I don't know what she's talking about. Reasons? Reasons for what? Only I'm not motivated enough to ask.

Blockers, eh? I think vaguely, as Zarah begins to help me dress. But that's the beauty of blockers, they screen out everything, even the need to question what in Urd's name I should want to forget.

Part Nine

The Gift of an Owl

'Their view; it is cosmic. Not a man here, a child there, but an abstraction: race, land. *Volk. Land. Blut. Ehre.* Not of honourable men but of *Ehre* itself, honour; the abstract is real, the actual is invisible to them. *Die Gute*, but not good men, this good man. It is their sense of space and time. They see through the here, the now, into the vast black deep beyond, the unchanging. And that is fatal to life. Because eventually there will be no life; there was once only the dust particles in space, the hot hydrogen gases, nothing more, and it will come again. This is an interval, *ein Augenblick*. The cosmic process is hurrying on, crushing life back into the granite and methane; the wheel turns for all life. It is all temporary. And these – these madmen – respond to the granite the dust, the longing of the inanimate; they want to aid *Natur*.'

– Philip K. Dick, *The Man In The High Castle*

Smoke drifts across the battlefield, temporarily obscuring the scenes of carnage. For that briefest of instants only the sounds remain: the awful, hideous screaming; the pitiless roar of the cannons; the sound of metal clashing against metal, the shouts and the whinnied shrieks of horses.

Zorndorf. I am on the battlefield of Zorndorf, the scene of Frederick's most disastrous defeat. But Frederick himself is safe. Thanks to us, the great man lives, and Nemtsov, Dankevich and Bobrov – Russian agents, sent in to prevent us saving him – are dead. Only Gruber now remains. Gruber, one of our own. A traitor.

Breathless, I look about me. Ernst is okay, and Freisler. And there, not twenty yards away, is Frederick, mounting von Gotz's pale grey horse. Safe now.

I turn back, looking for Gruber. At first I don't see him, but then I do. He's also down, lying there on his back, groaning.

I walk across to him.

Gruber stares up at me, blood and spittle on his lips. The wound to his chest is a bad one. He's been burned deeply, and he's ebbing fast, but as he sees me he smiles, as if he's won.

'Here,' he mouths, and I kneel, leaning close to make out what he's saying.

'Your Katerina . . .' he says, then coughs. 'The Russians know . . . Cherdiechnost . . .'

And so he dies. But I feel a fist of ice about my heart. They *know*? Urd protect me, let it not be true!

260

No more delays, I tell myself. *It's time to see Hecht. Time to tell him everything.*

Only Hecht's not in his room, and no one knows where he's gone, so I go and see Ernst.

Ernst is bathing, washing the blood and sweat of the battlefield from his tired body, a happy man now that he's ventured out in time again.

I talk to him through the frosted glass. Or try to. Because Ernst wants only to speak of the battle we've just fought; of saving Frederick, and killing the Russians. It's only when I raise my voice, repeating what I've said, that he finally takes it in.

'Gruber said the Russians know. About Katerina. And Cherdiechnost.'

Ernst's head appears around the glass, eyes shocked. 'They *know?*'

'Yes. That's why I have to tell Hecht. I have to go back there and get them out of there.'

Ernst cuts the flow of water, then grabs a towel. 'He won't like that.'

'Then I'll persuade him. Make him see that it's in our best interests.'

Ernst looks at me as if I'm mad. 'He'll ground you, like he grounded me. Then where will you be?'

'Where will I be if I don't?' I can hear that I'm pleading with him now, but I can't help it. 'I don't exist without her. And my girls . . .'

Ernst stares at me. 'Girls? You mean you and Katerina had children, and you didn't *tell* me?'

I feel ashamed. 'I'm sorry. I should have told you. Before I went to Christburg. There just wasn't a good time to raise the subject.

336

And then there was Seydlitz's Barbarossa project, and the fall-out from that . . .'

Ernst pulls on a long tunic, then turns to me again. 'Urd save us, Otto! This changes things. Hecht will *never* allow you back there! It's bad enough you had a woman – but *children*! It wouldn't surprise me if he went in personally and erased the whole of that timeline.'

'But that's it. He *can't*. I'm in a loop, and a long one, at that. I go back there, sometime in my future. That's when I have them.'

Ernst whistles.

'So what do I do? I can't just leave it. You know I can't. She's my life, Ernst. You of all people should know that.'

Ernst sighs. 'I know. Only Hecht won't see it that way.'

'But he must do. I mean, it was he who let me go there. To Cherdiechnost. To the estate. He sent me there, for a break.'

'Hecht?' Ernst stares back at me sceptically. 'Are you sure?'

'Well, Zarah was the one who actually sent me back. But she acts on Hecht's instructions. He knows everything she does. It's all in the record. If he *didn't* know . . .'

No. It's not possible. I've seen Hecht's 'Haven' for myself. Seen how he keeps track of it all. He and his brother.

Ernst touches my shoulder 'You've not told this to anyone else, have you, Otto?'

'No one.'

'Then let's go and see Zarah. Take counsel with her. If there's a way, she'll know it. Besides, if you *are* in a loop, maybe she knows something about it.'

Maybe, I think. After all, they knew where to check for me. That figure at the end of my bed must have known the lay-out of my house extremely well to jump in so accurately.

'What if she says, "see Hecht".'

'Then you go see Hecht. But not until you must. Not unless you're really desperate.'

261

On my way, I remember something Zarah said to me, months ago, when I first came back from Cherdiechnost. Before Christburg and Operation Barbarossa and that whole bloody business at Zorndorf. Something about there being reasons. Explanations.

I want to know now what they are.

Zarah greets us and takes us through to a large room I've never been in before, an anteroom at the back of the platform. She seems to be expecting this, and that too is somewhat disconcerting. She makes us sit, then paces up and down nervously, talking all the while, like she's giving a lecture.

'I knew you'd come. I knew at some point you'd work it out.'

I make to speak, but she doesn't let me. It's like she has to keep talking or she'll never get said what she has to say.

'It must have become obvious to you long ago, but we're sure of it now. At least, as sure as we can be.' She pauses, glancing at me, then carries on. 'It's like this. The rules of engagement have changed, Otto. The Game itself has changed. It was little things at first. Things that didn't quite make sense, perhaps because we were reading them as old-style phenomena, interpreting them under the old way of thinking. Why, even Gehlen missed it at first. But slowly, bit by bit, we began to glimpse what it was.'

She stops, looking directly at me. 'Something's happened, you understand. New equations, possibly, or new technologies, further up the line. Put simply, the ceiling has gone. Agents are coming back from the future. Hecht was the first, at least, the first we knew about, but there have been others since. Ours *and* theirs.'

'So how does this . . .?'

'Wait, Otto. Hear me out. That's where Hecht is now. Up the line. Trying to work out just what's going on.'

'But if he's already met himself . . . well, he must know, surely?'

'Not everything. In fact, not much outside the bare bones, really.'

'But . . .'

My mind spins, like all of the gears have come loose. They must come from no-space bunkers like this one, surely? Because nothing else exists up here at the end of Time. It was all destroyed. Or is that the old way of thinking?

'Does Hecht know?'

Zarah meets my eyes. 'About the estate? No.'

'No?'

'We thought it best not to trouble him. We thought . . .' She sighs. 'Okay. Here's the bottom line. We've done a deal with you, Otto. Upriver. We help you and you . . . you help us.'

'Impossible.'

'No. It's true. You help train us. The women, I mean. Show us how to operate in Time. For our part—'

'Wait a minute,' Ernst says. 'You're talking about going behind Hecht's back. You're talking about out-and-out treason.'

Zarah stares back at us. 'That's not so. We were always loyal. Loyal beyond the call of duty. But things are about to change. You could say they *have* changed, already. You see, Hecht . . .' She swallows, then forces herself to say it. 'Hecht is about to die.'

262

We travellers are used to change. It is the medium in which we exist. We work night and day to promote it. Only . . .

Some changes are much bigger than others. Harder to accept.

Hecht's death, the thought of it fills me – fills all of us, I'm sure – with dread, for Hecht is our 'Father', our Helmsman. He steers our no-space ship through the timestreams. He is the Guardian of the Tree of Worlds. Our Master, and not just in name.

Was that what he came back to tell himself? That he was going to die? If so, what preparations did he make? Or is that a paradox? Can one ever be prepared for death?

Not only that, but . . . did he tell himself how futile it would be to try to evade his fate? Was that why he broke his own rule and met himself?

And what significance does it have for us?

A new Master, for sure. But who? For who, of all of us, could possibly step into his shoes? Who, for Urd's sake, has been trained?

Freisler, perhaps. Only Freisler would be a disaster. For a start he's not got the respect of the *Reisende,* many of whom hate the man. No. There would be war – civil war – if Freisler took command.

Who then?

No. Don't even say it. I'm not ready. I don't know enough, not a tenth enough, to step into his shoes. Besides, after all I've done – after all the rules I've broken – it would hardly do for me to put on the Master's cloak. How, after all, could I look a fellow agent in the eye and tell him he has strayed, when, I know for a certainty that my very existence in the future flouts those same rules I would be sworn to uphold?

It can't be me. Not Master in Hecht's place. Not now. Not even if, perhaps, he meant it ultimately.

Then who? For there's no other candidate.

'Do we have much time?' Ernst asks, breaking the long silence.

Zarah looks to him, her face pale and troubled. 'A month. Thirty-seven days, to be precise.'

340

'But if he knows . . .' I begin. Then, with a shock, I understand the relevance of the timing. 'New Year's Day,' I say quietly. 'New Year's Day, of the year 3000.'

'That's right,' Zarah says. 'The new millennium.'

We both know that it isn't. Not technically. But someone does. Someone thinks the date significant enough to kill Meister Hecht on that day.

'Do we know . . .?'

'Nothing,' she says. 'Hecht won't say. Only that he can't prevent it.'

'But that's ridiculous!' Ernst says. 'Anything can be changed. That's what we've been taught, haven't we? And if we know in advance . . .'

'He won't allow it,' Zara says, something in her face telling me that she's already argued this one out fiercely with Hecht himself.

'Then do it anyway!' Ernst says fiercely. 'Thor's teeth! Are we to stand here, hands bound and weapons sheathed, while the finest of us is taken?'

'You'll do as the Master says,' Zarah answers. 'It is his explicit order.'

'But—'

I know how Ernst feels. It feels like giving up, like, well, like a kind of suicide. Because if he knows and doesn't act . . .

I stand up abruptly, throwing my chair back away from me, sheer exasperation propelling me to the door.

'Where are you going?' Zarah asks.

'I'm going to find Hecht, and I'm going to ask who killed him.'

'And if he tells you?'

'Then I'll track him down and kill him.'

341

Only it's not that easy. I wait there by the platform for two hours, and then a third, and still he doesn't come.

Eventually I go back to my room, but only after making Zarah promise to summon me the instant he returns. I don't want to sleep, but, lying there, tiredness overwhelms me and I succumb.

I wake, to darkness and to silence, thinking about what Zarah said. And not just about Hecht, but about the 'deal' I'm supposedly going to make – no, that I *have* made – up the line somewhere. The rest of it doesn't surprise me quite so much, because for some time now I've suspected that things have changed. It's only the how that bothers me.

New equations, she said; *new technologies*.

Ernst's voice breaks the silence. 'Otto. I need to see you.'

I sit up and, sensing my movement, the lamp comes on. 'What is it?'

'Hecht's back,' he says, his voice sounding clear in the air. 'Only before you go and see him, you need to know a few things. I've been talking to Zarah.'

I stare across the room thoughtfully, then get up and walk across.

'Otto?'

I hesitate a moment, then press the pad. The hatch hisses open. Ernst is standing there. He gives me the briefest smile, then moves quickly past me. As the door hisses shut again, I turn to find him staring at me strangely.

'What?'

'It's you, Otto. You're the one the Elders choose to replace Hecht. Only . . .'

'Only what?'

'It's unclear. I mean, they've only just begun to piece it all together, but something happens. And then you're gone.'

'Gone?' I laugh. 'But I can't go. I have to be there. The loop.'

'As I said, it isn't clear. They're finding out more about it by the hour. They've agents coming back all the time now. There's a lot of conflicting stuff, but the reports are consistent in one respect: you aren't there.'

'They've looked for me, then? Followed me? Seen where I went, what I did?'

'No, it's . . . it's apparently not that easy. It's like, well, it's like you step outside of things suddenly. One moment you're there, the next . . .'

I frown at him. 'What do you mean?'

'I mean, the machines stop tracking you. One moment you're there, a pulse on the screen, like every other *Reisende*, the next . . . nothing! Not a trace of you. Like you've vanished from the Game.'

'Or died . . .'

'No. Zarah was quite adamant about that. There's a distinct signal pattern when an agent dies. It's not instantaneous, apparently. It takes an instant or two for the body to shut down, for the focus to stop sending back its trace. Likewise if the focus was cut out of your chest . . .'

I look down. 'Maybe I was nuked. That would be pretty damn instantaneous.'

'Yes!' Ernst laughs, then recollects himself. 'Sorry . . .'

'It's okay. So what *does* she think happened? Where does she think I went?'

'That's it,' Ernst says. 'They've none of them a clue.'

'And Hecht? Does Hecht know any of this?'

'Why don't you ask him? As I said, he's back, and he wants to see you.'

264

I don't know how many times I've gone to see Hecht in his room, but this time it's different, as different as it could get and remain familiar. Different because I know now that in thirty-seven days this man will die, this man who has been central to my life for almost half a century, who has shaped and guided me and always – *always* – been there, like a rock at the centre of it all. Or, better yet, like the still, strong trunk of a tree rooted in Four-Oh.

His manner is no different. He looks up as I enter, his grey eyes taking me in and weighing me up at a glance, while his fingers continue their quick, precise movements across the keyboard.

'Sit down, Otto. Sit down and tell me what's on your mind.'

I sit. But as for what's on my mind . . . I hesitate, not knowing what to say first or even whether to say it.

I look back at Hecht and see that he's watching me, his fingers fallen still. 'All right,' he says quietly. 'Let me guess. You want to know if I know? Correct?'

I swallow, then nod.

'The truth? I didn't. Not until an hour back. It was quite a surprise. It seems I misjudged you. I thought you . . . *cooler* than you are, better dominated by reason. If I'd known . . .'

'Go on,' I say. 'If you'd known . . .'

He meets my eyes again, his own colder than I've ever seen them. 'You would *never* have gone back. But what's done is done, eh? And not to be undone.'

I go to speak, but he raises a hand to silence me. 'Six hours ago I'd have been angry. Very angry. Six hours ago . . .' He pauses then gives a strange little shake of his head, an uncharacteristic gesture. 'No matter. We're tied in now. Locked tight. Things have to be.'

'I don't understand.'

His eyes harden. 'Don't you? Then for Urd's sake work it out! Just think what you might have done!'

'Done?'

I know what I have done. Only nothing so dramatic, surely, as to deserve this tirade?

'You of all people, Otto! My *Eizelkind . . .*'

I feel awful, letting him down, but less awful than I would if I did nothing. If I left Katerina and the girls to perish.

'I *have* to do this,' I say. 'They are my family.'

'Family, yes, but not your *volk*. They're Russians, Otto. *Russians!*'

'They are my blood.'

'They could *never* be your blood.'

For all he's said about the last six hours having cooled his temper, anger burns in his eyes now. And something else. A kind of hatred. If he could, he'd have me killed for what I've done, and that knowledge sears me. I thought I was his friend, as near a son to him as I could be, but it clearly isn't so. Or isn't now. I have been cut adrift by him. Disinherited.

Or so he'd have it, only he's soon to die, and I will become Master in his place. All of this is preordained. *Locked in tight*, as he terms it.

He stands, then walks away from his machine into the shadows. But I am not dismissed. Not yet.

'Anyone else, yes, any one of them . . . but not you, Otto. I'd never have believed it of you. But I was wrong. My judgement was fatally flawed. There were clues, right from the start, and I chose to ignore them. Chose to trust you, rather than question you, thinking you somehow a different, a more *trustworthy* man than you are.'

That hurts. I go to speak again, but he denies me. Talks through me.

'What makes it worse is that you had them all in on it with you. Zarah, Urte, Ernst . . .'

I look down. 'I couldn't help it. Her eyes . . .'

Hecht turns and shouts. 'Damn her eyes! And damn you for falling for her! What were you taught, Otto? Not to meddle, that's what!'

'*Meddle*?'

'What else would you call it?'

'Love. I'd call it love.'

Hecht laughs bitterly. 'Love? Lust, more like! Romantic claptrap!'

I want to argue, but I know there's no point. Hecht has never been in love, so how could he understand? I stand, meaning to go, only he won't let me.

'No, Otto. It's not that easy. You can't just walk away. Not while I'm still Master here. I've *jobs* for you.'

As the echo of his voice fades, so I wait, head bowed, my back straight, at attention, as if nothing has changed between us.

'Yes, Master.'

He walks across, then circles me slowly, as if he's inspecting me; as if he wants to know how a traitor looks. At least, that's how it feels, for my whole self squirms under his penetrating gaze.

Only I won't say sorry. Not for loving Katerina.

'1952,' he says. 'That's where you're going. Berkeley, California. There's someone there I want you to locate and get to know.'

'I don't know the era.'

'Not a problem. We have an agent there already. You'll be working with him.'

'Was that where you went?'

He doesn't answer, merely circles me again.

'Don't fuck up,' he says.

'No, Master.'

'Then go. Maria has the details.'

'Maria? But . . .'

'Zarah has been suspended from her duties until further notice. Now go. Oh . . . and Otto . . . you will report back directly to me. No one else. *Understand?*'

'Yes, Master.'

'Then go.'

265

Berkeley, California, June 1952. America before the fall. Before the great war with China that would destroy them both. It's an era I know almost nothing about, but my contact, Matteus Kuhn, is something of an expert. He's been here more than eight years now, fitting in, getting to know the place, the time.

I jump in at night, into what seems a curious mixture of barn and garage, as if the one has been half converted into the other. It's transitional. Three of the walls look original, the fourth made out of sheets of corrugated metal. An old car lies in the shadows to one side, most of it covered up by a big green tarpaulin, but one sleek, black wing is showing, a thin-rimmed tyre exposed to sight.

There's all sorts of junk here, stacked up against walls, in boxes, and on shelves to one side, like the detritus of a whole age has washed up here in this godforsaken building, but there's also a kind of loft, at the back of it all, and as I turn and look, so I hear the faint fluttering of a nesting bird.

I see the overlarge eyes shining down on me from out of the darkness and smile. An owl.

I move carefully through and step outside into the back garden. It's huge, maybe one hundred feet by fifty, the lawn cropped close, the whole thing surrounded by a high, slatted wooden fence. Across the way is the house itself – a medium-sized two-storey building with a sloping roof, its windows unlit, the back porch in shadow.

I look about me at the neighbouring houses, their windows shining with electric light, then pause a moment, listening, hearing the sound of cars – automobiles, there are no fliers yet – on the freeway nearby.

I sniff the air, the all-pervasive scent of petro-carbons filling my nostrils, the defining smell of this age. It's a warm, balmy evening – typical of the San Francisco area, I later learn. Matteus is out, but it doesn't matter. I've got a key, and his absence allows me to go in and have a poke around before he gets back.

Hecht's given me no idea why I'm here or what I'm looking for, which makes me think that maybe he's sent me here simply to get me out of Four-Oh and thus out of his sight, only the date seems familiar.

I walk across, letting my impressions of the time slowly settle. This is the best time for an agent, usually, the most exciting. But not this time. This time I can't help but think that my family's back there, stranded in the thirteenth century, easy pickings for a Russian assassination squad. Imagine how that feels. Then imagine again. Because you can't. You can't even begin to imagine how awful it is. I bury it deep, then get on with the job.

I fit the key into the back door, then slip inside, into darkness. It's a kitchen. There's a door in the corner, to my left, the edge of which is rimmed with light from the hallway beyond. In the faint light I can pick out a number of crude household appliances: a standing cooker with a hob, a small refrigerator, and in the far corner a washing machine. There's an old-fashioned sink with a drainer, on which is placed a single plate, a single cup.

It all looks old and shabby. Objects from a world in transition. A world of evolving forms. A world about to undergo violent and radical technological change, not to speak of the overwhelming effects of overpopulation.

I freeze, hearing noises from the next room. Voices. I listen a moment then, as a burst of music sounds, I understand. It's one of their devices: a radio, I think it's called.

I step through. There's carpet underfoot, a hideous mustard- and red-diamond pattern. A single coat hangs on a peg on the wall by the door, full-length black leather, like a Gestapo officer might wear. A staircase leads up.

The sounds come from the room at the front. I walk across and look inside. There's a standing lamp in the corner to my right. In its light I see that the room is empty, the curtains drawn. The radio is near the door, on a cabinet against the wall, a chunky thing in a walnut case, shaped like the window of an ancient church. The semi-circular dial glows faintly. Beside it there's a funereal-looking box with a heavy lid, the purpose of which I can't guess. I step inside. There's a big lounger against one of the walls and a matching armchair and, on a low table on the far side, by the window, a television set.

I crouch in front of it, studying it, amazed by its crudeness. It has the look of something that could sustain enormous pressures; that you might find at the bottom of the ocean. The screen itself is tiny – no more than nine inches corner to corner, the maker's name on the façade just above the knobs. *General Electric Company*.

I straighten up. Behind the TV set is an alcove filled with shelves of books. I study their spines, then pick one out at random.

The Owl In Daylight.

I put it back, frowning. There's something wrong about it, but I don't quite know what.

The voices on the radio drone on: something about a man named Steinbeck and a place called Salinas.

I turn slowly, taking it all in.

Nothing here. Nothing . . .

I go out. Go upstairs. A bedroom. A bathroom with a toilet. A small study. I go in and stand there.

Notebooks. A strange machine, the casing green with three rows of keys, a single letter on each one.

A typewriter, I think, the knowledge dredged up from somewhere.

I walk over to the desk. Besides the typewriter there's a filing tray made of bright blue plastic. In it there's a stack of paper. A manuscript. I flick through it. Fiction or fact? It's hard to tell. Nothing leaps out.

There's a notebook, just to the left of the typewriter: a small thing, six inches by three.

I pick it up, open it. Names and addresses.

Abendsen, Hawthorne . . . Anderson, Poul . . . Atley, Greg . . .

I flick through. *Nothing*.

Or nothing I know. Not yet.

I put it down, and as I do, so I hear a car pull up outside. A car door slams. A moment later there's the sound of a key turning in the lock downstairs.

I go out on to the landing.

He steps into the hallway. Matteus Kuhn. Or, as he's known here, Matt Caldecott. As I know already from his file, he's a short, balding man. Not like a German at all, at least, not what you'd expect from a *Reisende*. Which is maybe why Hecht chose him for this assignment.

He sees me and almost double-takes in shock. 'Who the fuck . . .?' Then something kicks in in his memory. 'Otto? Otto Behr?'

I go down and shake his hand. 'Hecht sent me,' I say. 'I'm here to help you.'

It sounds weak, and it is, but he accepts it at once. It's as if Hecht has *blessed* it.

He leads me through into the living room and shuts the door, then smiles at me, clearly pleased to have me there. 'What century are you based in?'

'The thirteenth,' I say. 'And the eighteenth.'

'So this is . . .?'

'Different.' I gesture towards the box beside the radio. 'What *is* that?'

'A gramophone.'

I'm no wiser. 'And that's a radio, right?'

He's grinning. He knows he's going to enjoy this. 'Right, though technically it's a wireless.'

'Wireless?'

'Yeah.'

His American accent is strong. It's not so much a drawl as a kind of roundness to the way he pronounces the words, together with a kind of laziness. I can see that I've either got to learn it fast or play the visiting German. Matt's cousin, maybe. Or an old friend . . . Only even as I think it, I realise that there's going to be a problem with that.

America and Germany were enemies right up until seven years back, and if Matt and I are old friends, then he'll have some explaining to do. We need to come up with a cover story fast.

'Look,' I say. 'Have you arranged anything for tonight?'

'Sure. I've some friends coming over. Buddies of mine.'

'Buddies?'

'Uh huh. You'll like them. Phil's a writer, and—'

'Hold fire. There's things we need to sort out. Like who I am and where you know me from.'

Some of the excitement goes from his eyes. 'Right. Sure. I guess being German isn't exactly flavour of the month right now.'

'But I am. So what's the story?'

He thinks a moment, then smiles. 'Okay. I got it. You're a professor, right? And you've been over here since '33. You've got Jewish blood and you got out while you still could. Before Kristallnacht and the camps.'

'Right.' Only I'm not a hundred per cent sure. 'What if someone asks me about all that?'

'You can bluff your way?'

'The facts of it, sure. But that's not what I mean. I'm not sure I know what I ought to be feeling about it. And if I've been here since '33, wouldn't the accent have gone by now?'

'You'll be fine. These yanks expect a German to sound like a German. They're comfortable with that. As for the rest, well, who's going to challenge you?'

And I do have that number tattooed on my arm, after all. The worknumber from the twenty-eighth century. That could easily pass for something different.

'D'you want a drink, Otto? A beer maybe?'

I smile. 'Sure.'

And while Mattheus goes off to get me one, I lift the heavy lid of the gramophone and look inside.

266

'But that, surely, *is* the point,' Phil says, pointing his beer at me as if for emphasis. 'If Hitler *hadn't* split his forces, if he *had* gone straight for the jugular – Moscow – then he'd have won! Europe would have been Nazi, and the USA would have stayed out of the war, and you know what? We'd have been just as happy dealing with them as we are with our present trading partners! Happier, probably, seeing how damn efficient they are. Christ! I can even see a scenario in which we went in on *their* side, against the Brits. I mean, we've been looking since the turn of the century for any excuse to weaken the Brits and split up their empire. Why, we almost came to blows, back in the twenties, when the Brits were training up the Japanese navy!'

Phil is standing by the TV, looking down at us as we sit there, listening. Phil's not what you'd call a handsome guy, but he's got a nice smile and a graceful manner. Matt says he's twenty-three, but, with his slender frame, he looks even younger, despite his receding hairline. He's wearing a red wool shirt and jeans that are a bit too short, and scuffed Oxfords, but what strikes you most about him is his eyes. Intense green eyes. I like Phil. He's an interesting man. Unlike Matt's other buddy, Greg, who sits there, nursing his beer broodily, like he's afraid to offer any kind of opinion.

Greg's a big guy. He could easily lose four or five stone. Matt says he's a glimpse of the future of America in that respect, but what he means by that evades me.

'I still don't see it,' Matt says, picking up on Phil again. 'Russia was just too big. So let's say the Nazis *did* capture Moscow? Just how long would they have held it? How long would it have been before Zukhof launched a counter-offensive and took it back?'

'Damn fine soldier, Zukhof,' Phil comments, glowing warmly at the thought of the man. 'Pity he put Stalin's nose out of joint. Yeah, and he sure paid for that. Stalin sacked him as commander-in-chief in forty-six, just as soon as the war was won. His reward for being more popular than the great leader, eh?'

It's a perceptive comment, for Stalin, like Hitler, did not – *does not?* – tolerate rivals.

'Zukhof was lucky,' I say. 'At least he got to live. Stalin's usual style was to have the man killed, then give him a state funeral!'

'You speak as if he's dead,' Phil says, his eyes narrowed as he looks at me.

'I doubt if he'll last another year,' I say. 'Rumour is his health is bad.'

The fact is I know that Stalin dies next March.

'So what do you do, Otto?' Phil asks. 'I mean, what do you teach?'

'History,' I say, and we both laugh.

'I like history,' Phil says. 'But what was it like? In Germany, I mean, before the war? Was it stifling? Claustrophobic?'

'One breathed hatred,' I say. And I can say it with conviction. For while the Nazis are *volk* – that is, they're on *our* side in the Game – it's one of my least favourite periods of history. In fact, they're odious bastards, if you want the truth.

Phil nods. 'Here it was, well, it was like no one wanted to know. There was scarcely anything in the press or on the radio. It was like a conspiracy. A conspiracy of silence.'

'All 'cept Phil,' Greg chimes in, with a real southern States drawl. 'Phil liked to keep us *all* informed.'

I look to him, then back to Phil, wondering just what the connection is, just why these two are friends.

But Phil's looking at me, questions in his eyes. 'So what's your specialty?' he asks. 'What period?'

'Frederick,' I say. 'From 1742 to 1786. You know, Prussia . . . the Seven Years' War.'

'Leuthen,' Phil says. 'Rossbach . . .' He hesitates, then. 'And Zorndorf?'

'Excellent!' I say, delighted that he knows. 'The three great battles that assured the survival of Prussia and made Frederick's reputation!'

'Never heard of the man,' Greg mumbles, but I'm conscious that Matteus is watching me, a certain glow in his eyes, for Frederick is, as I've said before, our hero, and Matteus knows I've met him.

'That's *real* history,' Phil says and nods. 'Real heroism. To take on the three greatest powers of the Age – France, the Austrian Empire and Russia – and defeat them, one after another, in the space of ten months.'

'Against all odds,' I say, and all three of us – Phil, Matteus and I – nod and smile, like we're talking about some all-conquering baseball team.

Real history . . .

'Hey, wouldn't it be great,' Phil says, his green eyes wide and excited, 'if you could go back there. See it with your own eyes. *Live* it! Christ! That'd be something!'

'Yes,' I say, and I'm almost tempted to tell him, just to see what his reaction would be. Only I don't.

'What do *you* do, Phil?' I ask. 'I mean, aside from reading history books.'

267

They finally go just after midnight, leaving Matteus and I to the silence of the house. As Matteus clears away the plates and glasses, I follow him about, talking.

'I liked him. Phil, that is. He's an interesting guy.'

Matteus smiles. 'Isn't he? But wait. I want to show you something.'

He takes things through to the kitchen, then returns a moment later, a sphinx-like smile hovering on his lips.

'What?'

'Just wait. You'll be surprised.'

I watch him lift the lid of the gramophone, pushing it right back on the two metal extenders, then reach in and, with both hands, lift out the internal mechanism. He puts it aside, then reaches in again, this time with his right hand, removing what looks like a thin silver tile, twelve inches by twelve, covered in mesh. But I know what it is. I've seen one before, in the late twenty-first century. It's a tri-vi player.

'I thought . . .' I begin, then fall silent. Matteus is breaking rules here, but he knows that, so either he's got dispensation for this, or he's smuggled it in.

He puts the 'player' down on the table, next to the diminutive television set, then tugs on the catch holding the mesh. Immediately the mesh flicks up to form a wafer-thin square three feet by two, that rests horizontally on top of the player.

Matteus's smile broadens. He takes a tiny silver disc from his pocket and slips it into the slot. Then, stepping past me, he reaches out and switches off the overhead light. There's a second or two of darkness and then the air above the mesh lights up.

'It wasn't made in 3D,' he says, 'but it's a good conversion job.'

Music sounds, echoey, haunting, vaguely oriental. As words form in the air and scroll upwards, so the music changes, becoming nastier, more threatening, in line with what's written in the air. Something about robots – Nexus 6 replicants – and advanced genetics.

'What is this?' I ask, as the screen fills with a nightscape of a city, great fiery flares reaching into the sky. But Matteus doesn't answer, just lets it run.

Los Angeles, I read, *November 2019*.

'But that's—'

'It's a movie,' he says. 'Just watch.'

I sit on the lounger. Matteus comes and sits beside me, control in hand. The music is beautiful. The city looks like Greater Berlin eight centuries from now. And then an eyeball fills the screen, reflecting the scene.

There are two great ziggurat-like buildings in the distance. A flier makes its way towards them.

I watch, totally absorbed, as the action begins. A psychological test. A murder. Cut to Deckard, sitting in a sushi bar . . .

We watch maybe half an hour of the film, then Matteus jumps it forward.

'But . . .'

'We haven't time,' he says. 'I want you to see the rest, or some of them. They made over forty, eventually.'

'About Deckard?'

'No. But by the same guy. The guy who wrote the original stories. These were the first, though. These set the standard.'

I'm still confused. But now there's something else on the screen.

'What's this one called?'

'*Total Recall*. It was massive when it first came out. The guy who plays the lead – Schwarzenegger – was the biggest thing in Hollywood at the time.'

'Hollywood?' And then I get it. 'Oh, right. The place they made most of the movies.'

We watch it for a while, and then he jumps it forward again.

'This one was made about twenty years later. It's called *Minority Report*.'

We watch ten, maybe fifteen minutes of it, then I take the control from him and pause it.

'Okay,' I say. 'I've seen enough. It's good. But why are we watching it?'

In the half-light from the paused frame, Matteus looks at me and smiles. 'Because it's Phil's stuff. He's the guy who wrote it.'

I'm stunned. '*Phil?*'

Matteus stands, then switches on the light. Everything seems dowdy and old-fashioned after what we've been watching, like it's some kind of inferior reality.

'That's why I asked for this posting. So I could meet him. Become his friend. You see, this was my period. This is what I've researched since I was fourteen years old to the exclusion of all else. 1939 to 2020.' He grins. 'These are remarkable times, Otto, but the most remarkable thing about them was their ability to dream, to create powerful, dominant fictions for their time. And Hollywood . . . Hollywood was where it all came out of.'

He turns and crouches over the player, folding up the mesh.

'And Phil?'

Because I still can't believe that Phil wrote all of the stuff I've just seen. That it all came out of his head.

Matteus laughs. He seems half drunk. When he turns his head and looks at me, his eyes are on fire. 'I stumbled on Phil. Discovered him by accident, almost. In fact, I didn't make the connection at first, but then, when I did, I searched out everything I could about him. Made *him* my life's work.'

'And Hecht approved of this?'

He lifts the player and carries it across to the empty gramophone box. 'Hecht didn't know. Besides, he wanted someone here. Someone who knew the culture and the times, so he didn't ask what my motive was. He was just glad I was ready to step in.'

'But you said you *asked* to be here.'

I watch him drop the player into the bottom of the box, then reach out for the bulky inner mechanism of the old-fashioned gramophone. He eases it into the casing, then drops the lid.

'Here in Berkeley, I mean. And he agreed. He didn't mind where I was, as long as I was here, in the western United States in '52. As long as I was *in situ*. In fact, I've been here since '44. Story was I was invalided out of the armed forces. But it gave me a chance to meet Phil. I used to go along to the record store where he worked, the Art Music Company on Telegraph and Channing. We used to talk about Beethoven and Wagner—'

'You say *worked*. Has he quit that?'

'He was fired from it last December. Fell out with his boss.'

'Ah . . .' Which again surprises me. He seems such a mild-mannered man. 'And he's been writing ever since?'

'He's always been writing. But now he does it full time. He's sold a couple already, but, well, this is it, you see. This is where it begins. In the next year and a half he's going to write and sell more than sixty stories!'

It seems a lot, but who am I to judge? 'Those movies we saw . . .?'

'They make them later, from the eighties onward. That's when he becomes *really* popular. After he's dead.'

'And you . . .?'

'I wouldn't tell him a thing. I know the rules. Only . . . it's exciting, Otto. To be near the man. To be his friend. To be able to talk to him the way I do.'

I nod. It's how I feel about Frederick. And Peter, come to that. Only those are supposedly great men. Phil . . .

'I know how it looks,' Matteus says. 'But there are great men and great men. And Phil, truly, is a great man. You'll see. Even now, well, he just thinks in ways other people just don't think. That's what marks him out. His ability to look at things askew. He's a shaper, Otto. What he imagines now, well, fifty years on, the rest of the world will catch up. That's what I mean about him. He's a visionary. A pure fucking visionary!'

I'm impressed by Matteus's enthusiasm. 'You think he'd make a good agent, then?'

Matteus laughs. 'Too fucking right!' Then, more quietly. 'That's one of his themes, you know. Time travel. You should talk to him about it sometime. Why, you'd think the guy had actually gone and done it.'

I'm quiet a moment, thinking about that, and then I nod. It's after two now, and I haven't slept in over two days. 'Matteus . . .?'

'Yes, Otto?'

'Let's talk some more in the morning. Right now I'm tired. Right now I could do with some sleep.'

But the truth is, when I get into my room, I find I can't sleep.

For all Matteus's enthusiasm, I can think of only Katerina and my girls.

I sit there on the edge of my bed, staring down at my hands, a kind of awful numbness descending on me. It's a terrible, helpless feeling, like I've abandoned them, left them to their fate. I want to jump back and confront Hecht – to shout at him and vent my anger and frustration – only what's the point? It's like Ernst said; he'd only ground me. Lock me up and throw away the key. No, there's nothing I can do back there to change things. Which only makes it worse.

I hear an owl call in the darkness outside and, standing, go over to the window.

There's a tree at the far end of the garden, just to the side of the barn-like garage, up against the fence. As I watch, the owl launches itself and swoops, plucking the dark shape of a mouse from the lawn.

I watch it climb, then settle on the fence, beginning to pick at its prey, to kill it, then eat it whole.

'*Katerina*,' I say softly, my breath clouding the glass. '*I will come for you. I promise. Just don't die. Just don't any of you fucking die before I come.*'

268

Matteus drives a Tucker Torpedo '48. It's a beautiful car and cost him $2,450 new. When I ask him where he got the money from he says he 'won it on the gee gees', as if that makes any sense. It's the kind of car you drive if you want to attract attention to yourself, a big, two-ton, gas-guzzler with a 5.5-litre engine mounted above and behind the rear wheels with a top speed of 110 miles an hour. Preston Tucker, who came up with the idea, only ever produced fifty-one of his Torpedoes before he was investigated for securities fraud violations, otherwise his might have become a household name. But the Torpedo is a fine legacy, especially in gold, which Matteus's is. I like the white-rimmed tyres, too, and the padded white interior. It's a classy machine, unexpected in this age.

We drive over to Phil's house, in West Berkeley. He lives at 1126 Francisco Street, across from the elementary school, in what Matteus says is 'the shabbier part of town'. The property itself looks old and run-down, the kitchen tagged on as an afterthought. There's no garage, but there's a nice fig tree in the front yard. Music plays from an open window. Bach's *St Matthew's Passion*.

Matteus has disappeared inside. He said he was only going to be a moment, but ten minutes pass before the door opens again.

It's Phil. He wanders over to the car and, as I wind down the window, leans in to shake my hand.

'Hey, Otto, how are you? You wanna come in for some coffee?'

He hasn't changed since the other night, and looks as if he could easily have slept in his clothes. His hair's uncombed, and he's yet to shave, but his smile is welcoming.

'Sure,' I say. 'Sounds good.'

It feels strange, just leaving the car there, unlocked, at the roadside, but that's very much of this age, too. Crime happens, sure, but you can still leave things unlocked, mostly.

We go inside, where I'm surprised to find a pleasant, Greek-looking young woman, with long dark hair and a nice, warm smile. This, it turns out, is Kleo, Phil's wife, and that surprises me a little because I didn't see Phil as a ladies' man, let alone married.

Kleo sits me down and pours me coffee, and, while Phil talks about Bach and the art films he's been to see recently at the Cinema Guild down on Telegraph Avenue, she potters about the kitchen, humming to herself.

Phil, it seems, has the whole of the *Matthew Passion* on record. He goes out of the room, and returns a moment later, with what looks like a huge black box-file, which I realise holds twenty heavy black discs – each about ten inches in circumference. Gramophone records, it appears, 78s. They can only store about three minutes on each side of the thick black wax discs, and I look to Matteus in amazement before handing one of them back to Phil.

'Cutting-edge,' I say, but Phil doesn't seem to hear me.

'Listen to the quality of that,' he says, referring to the disc that's playing. 'Mind, in the future, it'll be a lot better. They'll have little gaseous pills, which you'll pop in a tiny glass bowl, and there'll be the whole of Bach on that pill. Every last little thing he wrote. And you'll be able to talk to the glass and ask it for your favourite, and it'll play it by resonating the air and—'

'*Phi-il* . . .' Kleo says, with a pleasant, sing-song intonation. 'Be kind to our guests. They're probably not into all that stuff of yours.'

'No?' Phil looks to me.

'There'll be new technologies, sure,' I say, nodding and smiling back at him. 'After all, it's the machines' turn now.'

'What d'you mean?' Phil asks, suddenly very serious.

'To evolve,' I say. 'That's what the war was about, in one sense. Rapid technological evolution. Why, technologically we probably advanced about three or four decades in the space of a mere five years.'

Phil nods thoughtfully, taking it all in, then he turns abruptly and looks to Kleo.

'Matt's talking about taking a trip, Kleo. Out to Nevada. Him and Otto. They want to know if I'll go along with them.'

It's the first I've heard of this, and I look to Matteus.

'That's right,' Matteus says, giving me an 'I know what I'm doing' look before turning back to Phil and Kleo. 'It'll take three days there and back.'

Kleo smiles. 'S'okay with me. You want me to pack a bag for you, Phil?'

'Would you?'

'Sure. I'll go and see my folks while you're away. It's been a while.'

Phil turns, looks to Matteus, then to me. 'Then that's that. When are we off?'

269

We're heading east on 120, high up, on the very roof of the world, it seems. Big Oak Flat is behind us, Yosemite up ahead, ten minutes' drive at most. It's late afternoon and the sun is low, shining in through the back window. Phil has been asleep the last hour or so, snoring loudly in the back.

Matteus is driving, one hand resting lazily on the wheel as we climb the slow gradient through this magnificent country. We're heading into wild country and the sky is a pure and beautiful blue. The road is empty, like we're in the only car in all creation.

The radio plays softly. Nat King Cole and Bing Crosby, Al Martino, Sinatra and Guy Mitchell. The popular music of the time, cloying, romantic, but unintrusive. It washes over us as the miles pass.

Matteus glances at the fuel gauge, then looks at me. 'It's low. We'll need to stop for gas again.'

'This thing *drinks* petrol.'

'Yes, but she runs beautifully, don't you think? Besides, it's only money.'

That irks me. As a *Reisende* I find it irritating that Matteus uses Time to make such cheap gains.

'Is it true what you said? That you *gamble*?'

Matteus grins, oblivious of my disapproval. 'If you can call it that. I mean, why not?'

'You shouldn't. It might draw attention.'

'Only if I get caught. And that's not likely. I never place a bet twice in the same place.'

'What do you use?'

He smiles. 'The form guide for '53.'

'What if someone should find that?'

Matteus pats the small bulge in his shirt pocket. 'Always keep it here.'

I'm silent a moment, then: 'Where exactly are we heading?'

'Mineral County.'

'And where's that?'

'Over the border.'

'So why didn't you tell me about this before?'

He glances at me, surprised. 'I thought you knew. I thought that's why you were here. To make this trip.'

Which makes me thoughtful.

'Otto?'

'Yeah?'

'Why are you so sad?'

I look to him; see how he's looking at me. 'Am I?'

'Sure. Never seen a man look sadder. Like you lost something, or some*one*.'

He's quiet a moment, then. 'D'you want to talk?'

'No.'

'Well, if you do . . .'

For a while he just drives. Then, seeing a gas station up ahead, he slows and pulls over to the right, gliding up to the pumps.

It's twilight now, and as the attendant comes across, I find myself thinking about Katerina once again, and the girls. While I'm here no time is actually passing. Not where they are. I could be 'away' for years and not a second would have passed back there in Cherdiechnost. Theoretically I could jump back the instant after I jumped out. Only I know somehow that that just isn't going to happen. Why? No reason. Just a feeling. But so strong a feeling that it makes me wince.

Matteus looks to me, concerned. 'Are you okay?'

'I think I need to use the bathroom,' I say, climbing out, even as the blond-haired attendant smiles a howdy at Matteus and begins to unscrew the petrol cap.

I pee, then come back, standing there across from the car, looking past its sleek golden form at the sun-bathed mountains in the distance, the red-streaked clouds and the blacktop, which stretches away for miles in either direction, the view unhindered. There are mountains up ahead. It's a landscape of exposed soil and rock, and at any other time I might be moved by its raw beauty, only – *America . . . what the fuck are we doing in America?*

I can't see any kind of connection. Hecht has sent me here to exile. I'm sure of that now, a captive – like Matteus – to trivia and this lesser kind of reality.

Matteus is talking to the attendant about the car, telling him where he bought it and a little of its history. As I walk up, the guy turns and smiles at me. He's tall, blond, a regular storm trooper, if ever I saw one. Unmistakably so.

Whose side were you on? And just how did you get hold of an American passport? What deals did you have to make?

As we drive away, Matteus chuckles, and I ask him why.

'Our friend back there . . . he could easily pass for a German. He has the look.'

'He has . . .'

Matteus is quiet for a time, then, like I've asked a question, he says. 'You want to know, don't you?'

'Know what?'

'Why I chose *this* car and not some other.'

I shrug. In truth, it makes no difference whatsoever, but I ask anyway: 'So why did you?'

'I almost bought something else. A '48 Lincoln Cabriolet. The Lincoln's a beautiful car, more expensive than this and a convertible, and before that I was going to buy a Cadillac, an Eldorado, that's another beauty, especially in a pure white trim. Only, well, this was the one. It had everything. Those others, they're good cars, fast, reliable, *powerful* cars, only . . . this is the one I knew they'd talk about, the one that'd make people ask questions.'

'And that's *good*?'

'Well, it ain't bad.'

'You know what I'd buy if I had the money?' Phil chimes in, surprising us both by the fact that he's awake. 'I'd have bought a '51 Mercury Kustom Carson. Kustom with a K, that is. Most beautiful car I've ever seen. The kind of car a movie star might drive. The one I saw was blue. An ethereal blue, with a pure white top and white wheels.'

Matteus is nodding slowly. 'Beautiful car, I agree, but it's the rarity of the Tucker that sold me. That and the story behind it. Hey . . . anyone know what kind of engine drives this beauty?'

Neither Phil nor I know, so Matteus carries on. 'It's a converted six-cylinder helicopter engine, that's what! Ex-army surplus. The original was air-cooled, but Preston Tucker adapted it, made it water-cooled. That's what gives it its oomph. One hundred and sixty-five horsepower . . . that's seventy-five horsepower more than a Chevvy!'

Phil whistles, impressed, but I haven't a clue what Matteus is going on about. Nor do I care, really, only it is a very comfortable car, and of all the means of transport I've used across the centuries, this is one of the most stylish.

'So,' Phil says after a moment, 'what *is* this place we're going out to see?'

'It's a research facility,' Matteus says, staring straight ahead through the windscreen. 'Belongs to a private company. A big pharmaceuticals firm.'

I'm surprised, but Phil just nods. 'So what's your interest in it?' he asks, leaning forward over the back of my seat. 'You work for their rivals?'

Matteus laughs. 'You could say that.'

'And you're checking them out?'

'Right.'

I want to take Matteus aside and ask him what he's doing, only now is not the time. But I'm convinced of one thing now: sleeper agents aren't reliable. Being alone in hostile territory for such a length of time isn't a good thing. They develop quirks, eccentricities. Risk-taking eccentricities. Like the gambling.

The miles pass. The light fades and an intense darkness swallows up the world, the triple headlights of the Tucker cutting a broad, crisp swathe of light ahead of us as the blacktop vanishes beneath our wheels. This is wild, open country with little else other than mountain and tree and rock. A wilderness, hostile to man.

There's hardly any traffic on the highway. In fact, we've probably not passed more than two or three hundred cars in the whole of the journey east.

An innocent time, I think. *Everything open, up for grabs. Before the crowded, overpopulated years. The years of misery and suffering. The years of unchecked genetic experimentation. Before it all went wrong.*

'How much longer?' I ask.

Matteus glances at the milometer. 'We're about fifty miles from the border now so . . . another fifty on top of that?'

'Which gets us where?' Phil asks.

'Hawthorne.'

'Hawthorne, eh?' Phil says. 'Same as your friend Abendsen?'

'That's right.'

'Nice name. I should use it sometime. It's the hardest thing, you know, names.'

'Yeah?' But I can hear that Matteus is only half interested.

'Yeah,' Phil carries on, oblivious. 'Give your characters the right names and they take on a life of their own. Give them something wrong – something that doesn't fit – and . . .'

'Phil?'

'Yeah, Matt?'

'You ever handled a gun?'

I blink with surprise, then turn to look at Phil. He's suddenly got a strange look on his face. As well he might, because he's alone in a car with two guys, miles from anywhere, and we're talking about guns.

'No . . . why?'

'I just asked, is all. There'll be guards, you see.' Matteus pauses, then says, 'Just in case.'

'I don't need a gun,' Phil says, and there's an edge to his voice.

Matteus turns and grins at him. 'Hey! Only kidding!'

Phil's face wrinkles with relief. He grins back at Matteus. 'You fucker . . .'

'Hey, ain't I?'

And so we sail on through the night, the dark, sculpted wilderness of Yosemite surrounding us, the radio playing quietly, Hawthorne, Nevada getting closer by the minute.

270

We book in at a motel on the edge of town, one room with a big double and a single. Matteus and I share the double. Phil wants to talk some more, but Matteus is tired after the drive and

I'm not feeling much like talking, so while Matteus and I get some sleep, Phil puts the radio on low and lies there on top of the blankets, fully clothed, stretched out, his hands behind his head.

That's how I find him when I wake, just after dawn. Matteus isn't there, and when I ask, Phil gestures with his head towards the door.

'He went out, half an hour back. Said he was going to try and find a map.'

'Right . . .'

But that too disturbs me. It all seems so casual. So unprepared. And bringing Phil along – what's that about?

I walk through to the bathroom and begin to wash at the sink. As I do, I hear the volume of the radio go up a notch or two. There's a snatch of some corny Country and Western song, and then Phil changes the station. A man's voice drifts from the next room.

'. . . unlike most yew-fologists takes a sceptical viewpoint. He argues that . . .'

I turn, looking back at Phil. 'Yew-fologist?'

'UFOs,' Phil says, turning the radio down. 'Unidentified Flying Objects. Country's nuts about 'em. There's aliens in the skies and reds under the bed!'

I smile. 'Reds . . . like in Russians?'

'That's right.' Then, a glint of curiosity in his eyes. 'You been away somewhere?'

'You could say that.' I sluice my face, then grab the towel and wipe myself dry. 'I've been in Europe. Observing the reconstruction.'

'All right . . . I wondered about the accent.'

'So these ufologists . . . what exactly do they do?'

'Spread rumours. Frighten people. Scare the living shit out of them, to tell the truth. As if some advanced alien race would be interested in us!'

I walk through and stand there, looking at him. 'I thought that's what you did? I mean, write about that sort of thing?'

'Fact that I write it, doesn't mean I'm dumb. Doesn't take a genius to work out that it makes no sense at all. I mean, if they were in our skies, we'd know about it. They wouldn't go skulking around, appearing before a few hillbillies here and a few hillbillies there, would they now? As for abductions . . .'

'Abductions?'

Phil sits up, looks at me squarely. 'Aliens abducting people from their cars on deserted highways, doing tests on them up in their mother ships and then dumping them back on the highway in nothing but their vest and socks. Don't you *love* that image?'

Phil chuckles, enjoying himself.

'So you don't believe any of that.'

'No sirree. It's all a crock of shit, if you ask me. If aliens have the technology to travel light years to get here, they aren't going to skulk about and hide their light under a bushel, metaphorically speaking. They wouldn't need to. Whether they were nasty or nice, they'd take the direct approach – Washington DC, I reckon, directly over the White House – either with all guns blasting or with a whole flying saucer full of doves. Pretty white doves with two heads a-piece . . .'

Again he laughs, and this time I laugh with him.

The door opens. It's Matteus. 'You guys having fun?'

I turn and smile at him. 'We're talking UFOs.'

'UFOs?'

'Sure. You got the map?'

'Best I could get. Two inches to the mile. Said we were thinking of prospecting.'

'Prospecting?'

'Yeah, There are lots of mines in this region. Have been for over a hundred and fifty years. Before it was a state, even. Thought it would give us an excuse if the local sheriff's department stopped us. I bought us some hard hats, too, and some other stuff, just for cover.'

'So what's the plan?'

'Thought we might drive as close as we can to the place, leave the car somewhere it won't be seen, then go and sniff about.'

'Can I ask you something?' Phil says, that concerned look back in his face. 'Is this going to be dangerous?'

Matteus looks at him straight. 'If it were, I wouldn't have brought you. We're just going to have a little look, that's all. See what we can see. But first off, let's go and grab us some breakfast. I don't know about you two, but I'm starving.'

271

There's a big wire fence, maybe ten feet tall, stretching away into the distance on both sides. Beyond it there's nothing but sand and rocks and the odd patch of vegetation, and, in the near distance, a big escarpment of smooth, weather-sculpted rock. There's no sign of a facility. But that doesn't daunt Matteus.

'It's in there,' he says. 'Trust me. I know.'

'You know because you've seen it?'

'It's there, I promise you. Just wait a second. I'll go back to the car and get the cutters.'

As Matteus walks away, Phil looks to me. 'How long have you two been friends?'

'A long time. We were at school together, back in the homeland.'

'Matt's a German?'

'Didn't you know? His full name is Matteus. Matteus Johann.'

Phil turns, watching Matt as he walks over to the car and lifts the hood. 'That makes sense of a whole number of things,' Phil says quietly. 'His ambivalence to the war, for a start.'

I nod, but say no more. But I know one thing: just as soon as this trip is over, I'm jumping back and changing things. I'm going to make sure that next time we come here Phil isn't with us.

Matt's back a moment later, a big pair of bolt cutters in one hand. He walks over to the fence, then, taking a grip, begins to cut through the wire, link by link. It takes about two minutes. He kicks the cut section of wire inward and is about to throw the cutters down when I stop him.

'No. Keep those. We may need them if we don't come out this way.'

'But the car . . .'

'We'll find the car.'

Matteus hesitates, then nods and looks to Phil. 'You ready, Phil?'

Phil doesn't look sure; but then he nods and, before Matteus can stop him, ducks through the gap and over on to the other side of the fence. Matteus and I follow.

'Which way?' Phil says, keen now that he's taken the first step.

Matteus stops and, handing me the cutters, takes the map from his back pocket and unfolds it. He studies it a moment, then points to our left – to the west, if I've got my directions right.

'There. It ought to be just beyond that outcrop there.'

'You've been here before?'

'No. But this is where it is. You-know-who said it was.'

Hecht, he means.

I'm surprised that there are no surveillance cameras, no guard towers or patrolling jeeps. It seems too quiet. It can't be that important if it's this easy to get in, can it?

Or maybe that's it. Maybe if the security were tighter – more prominent – then people would be more curious. Especially the locals. Even so . . .

It takes us a full ten minutes to cross the open plain and reach the cover of the rocky escarpment. It's like a scene from an old western – the kind where the baddy flees and gets holed up in a canyon and has to shoot it out, and when I say that, Matteus excitedly tells me that this is precisely where they film all of that TV and movie stuff – here and hereabouts.

Phil, however, is quiet. Too quiet, I think. Like he's suddenly regretting his earlier bravado and wishes he was back in the car.

Matteus gets out the map again and, checking that he's where he thinks he is, folds it again, tucks it into his back pocket, and begins to climb, making his way between the boulders up the steep, dusty slope. We follow. Halfway up we rest, looking back at the way we've come. You can't see the breach in the fence from here, nor any sign of our passage.

Matteus has a knapsack on his back. Shrugging it off, he opens it and reaches in, bringing out a heavy water bottle. Uncapping it, he drinks, then passes it to Phil.

'Where is it?' I ask.

'We should see it soon. Just over the brow.'

Phil takes a long swig and hands the bottle back. He wipes his mouth then frowns. 'We aren't trying to get inside, are we?'

'*You* aren't,' Matteus says. 'I want you to stay outside and keep watch.' He dips into the knapsack and brings out a whistle on a string. 'Anyone comes along, you blow this, twice.'

Phil takes the whistle uncertainly. For all he knows we're spies. Russian spies, perhaps, or East German, which is just as bad.

Matteus caps the bottle and slips it back into the sack, then slings it back on to his shoulder. 'Okay. Let's go.'

Matteus is right. It isn't far away. But even he's surprised how strangely futuristic it looks, staring down at it from half a mile distant.

'Weird,' Phil says, shaking his head. 'That doesn't look like it comes from our age. That's real Buck Rogers stuff!'

Matteus puts down his binoculars, then hands them to me. It's like he either hasn't heard Phil, or Phil is no longer important.

'What do you think?'

I put the glasses to my eyes and gently adjust the focus. From a distance it looks big and circular and shiny, like a grounded flying saucer, but through the glasses you can make out that what makes it appear so shiny are whole concentric rows of solar panels. Whatever else it is, it's energy efficient, and that alone marks it out as something from the future.

I trail the glasses across the roof, looking for an entrance of some kind, then jerk back.

'Thor's teeth!'

'*What*?' Matteus says. 'What is it?'

'There's a plaque,' I say. 'With the company name on it and a symbol – like the sign for infinity.'

'The lazy eight.'

'You know?'

'There was a mine here by that name. It's how it's marked on the map.'

'Right.' But I'm remembering where I last saw that symbol. It was on the pendants around the necks of the two Russian agents that got blown up by Seydlitz and Kramer, after my failure in Christburg.

Yes, and the same symbol was on the flyleaf of the book of Russian folk takes Hecht had on his shelf. The lazy eight with the two arrows pointing towards the centre.

The exact same symbol as is on the building down below, brazen and open, like they don't care who sees.

Or don't think anyone will?

'So?' Matteus asks. 'What does it mean?'

'I don't know,' I say, as if that's true, but my pulse is racing now, because in the second or two between seeing the symbol and working out where I last saw it, I have my answer.

Only it can't be possible. Surely?

'We need to get inside,' I say.

'Right.'

'Only . . .' I lower the glasses. 'I think you should stay here with Phil. If I don't come back . . .'

Matteus stares at me, about to argue, but right then the matter is decided for us. Far to our right, where the fence is breached by a gate, behind which are two sentry boxes and a traffic barrier, a little cavalcade of four big black sedans has drawn up.

We watch as about a dozen guards emerge from the boxes either side. They're carrying heavy armaments, and as each car draws up, one of the guards looks inside while the others stand back, guns trained.

As the first car moves through, I expect it to travel on the half mile to the installation, but it pulls aside and waits, its engine idling, while the next car is processed, and only when all four have been examined and okayed, does the little convoy roll on, the four big black cars like a funeral procession.

At least, that's the impression that comes to my mind. Death. This has to do with death.

As the cars pull up on the far side of the dome-like building, I train the binoculars on the leading car. More guards have emerged from inside the building – unarmed this time. Not so much guards, it seems, as attendants. Going to the back door of the first car, they open it and begin to help the occupants out.

Five of them in all, no, six, stepping out into the bright desert sunlight; each of them dressed in white, prison-like attire. Men and women, blinking up at the brightness.

'They're cuffed,' I say.

The other cars are emptying out now. I train the binoculars and see that their occupants are wearing the same white one-piece uniforms, and that every last one of them is cuffed.

'What the fuck is going on?' Matteus asks quietly. 'I thought—'

'Experiments,' Phil says. 'There've been rumours.'

We both look to him.

'Rumours?' Matteus asks.

'Yeah,' Phil says, nodding to himself. 'About prisoners. Rumour is they offer them parole in exchange for their participation in medical tests. *Experiments.* Things the courts won't let them do legally. Things they can't do on rats and dogs. Things they need *humans* for.'

'New drugs,' Matteus says. 'It makes sense . . .'

But I know better. And even if I don't know exactly why they're there, I *do* know who's behind this now. Reichenau.

Matteus looks to me. 'You still want to go in alone?'

'No. I don't think we should go in at all. I think we should get out of here. Before we're seen.'

'But . . .'

'But what?' I look to Phil, then back to Matteus. 'There's only one way of getting in and out of there safely, and I think you know what I'm talking about. But I don't think Phil here's ready for that information yet, do you?'

Phil's face wrinkles. 'What information?'

'Nothing,' Matteus says defensively. 'Tricks of the trade, that's all.'

'So you two *are* agents.'

'Of a kind,' I say, and glare at Matteus, angry at him for having put us in this situation. Down below the prisoners have been led inside and the big sedans are slowly turning, making their way in tight procession back to the gate.

It's hot, even in the shadow of the rocks. Matteus passes the bottle round again. This time I sip, then pour some over my brow and sluice my face. That done, I look to Matteus again. 'You know what I think? I think we ought to find out where those sedans come from. Ask a few questions. Discover just who's making the deals. Going in there . . . that isn't an option.'

Matteus, I can see, wants to argue. He wants some action. But even he knows it would be stupid to try. Not if there *are* armed guards and only one way in and out of the place. Nor can we jump in – not with Phil looking on.

'Let's head back to the car,' I say. 'Circle round north where those gates are, and stop off at a few of the towns heading east, find out if they saw those sedans passing through.' I pause, then. 'Is there anything marked? You know . . . a prison?'

'Nothing,' Matteus says.

'You're sure?'

'Absolutely.'

'Where *is* the state penitentiary?'

'I don't know. Carson City, maybe? Wherever it is, it's not on this map.'

I turn back, staring at the building, trying to work out what's the best way to tackle this situation. The desert's empty now, no sign of the sedans.

I'm about to turn back, to give instructions, when there's a sudden pulse, like a compressive bending of the air, emanating directly from the centre of the building, and a feeling like the air pressure has just changed, making my ears pop.

In fact, everything feels strange. I have an impulse to speak, but before I can, before the message goes from my brain to the muscles of my mouth and throat, everything goes black – an intense, impenetrable blackness.

For a count of three, that's all there is. It's as if the air surrounding me has congealed. And then, like someone's switched the light back on, we're back as we were.

Only not, because all three of us fall instantly to the ground, as if we're puppets and our strings have been cut. There's a moment when we just lay there, stunned by what's happened, and then Matteus laughs in amazement. Not only he, but all three of us, are now sporting a two-day growth of stubble.

'Christ!' Phil says, close to babbling. 'What *was* that? Did we all fall asleep or something?'

Time, I think, getting to my feet and beginning to brush myself down. *They're manipulating time.* And then I realise what that means and look to Matteus.

'Urd's breath . . . it's a platform!'

272

We drive back through Hawthorne in silence, the radio off, each of us locked in his thoughts. In fact, it's only when we hit Bridgeport and Highway 395 that Phil finally leans forward and, addressing Matteus, says, 'So who are you guys? Are you agents?'

'Agents?'

'You know. Government.'

'Kinda,' Matteus says. But I'm not comfortable having Phil there. Not now that I've thought about it. I want to talk this through, only that's not possible with him in the car. Or is it?

'There's this man,' I say. 'He's a, well, I guess you'd call him a revolutionary. Name of Reichenau. He runs a sect called the *Unbeachtet.*'

'The unnoticed,' Phil says, surprising me again.

'You know the word?'

'I know the club, back home in Berkeley. You think there might be a connection?'

'I think it's worth checking out.' I pause, then say, 'D'you think you could take us there, Phil? Tonight, maybe?'

'Sure,' he says. 'Only not tonight. It doesn't open midweek. Just weekends.'

Silence falls again. We drive on a mile or two, then Phil sits back and, smoothing his hand through his new growth of beard, asks casually, 'So what's with the sudden darkness and the beards and . . .' He laughs. 'If this is some weird dream, then it's really feels fucking real. I mean, I can smell the leather upholstery, hear the swish of the tyres on the road, the way the engine turns over, real smooth and quiet . . . You don't normally get that kind of shit in dreams, do you?'

'No . . .' I hesitate, then. 'You want to know the truth?'

Phil laughs uneasily. 'I'm not sure that I do. Not if it's like the rest of it. Oh, and what's a platform?'

Matteus looks to me.

'Pull over,' I say to him. 'Let's talk about this.'

Matteus slows, then turns the wheel, cruising over to the right, stopping on the gently canvered embankment. He switches the engine off, then looks to me again.

'So?'

'I've decided what we're going to do. We're going to change it. I'll jump back. Make it so he never came on this trip.'

'What?' Phil says, leaning forward. 'What are you saying? *Change* it?'

'Are you sure?' Matteus says.

'Yeah. I've got to go and see Hecht anyway. He'll want to know. Unless you want to end it here?'

Phil looks twitchy at my suggestion that we're going to 'end it', but I smile at him reassuringly. 'We're not going to harm you,

Phil. Only you're right on one count. This *is* some weird shit. You see, we're from the future.'

Phil stares at me for a full five seconds, and then he roars with laughter. 'Great! The way you said that, your face . . .'

'No, Phil, it's true. What you saw earlier – the platform – is one of the means by which we travel through time. Only that wasn't one of ours. You see, we're the good guys. We're the Germans.'

273

It takes a long time to convince him, and even then I'm sure Phil thinks he's dreaming or imagining this. That someone's slipped him some experimental drug – like the prisoners in the desert facility – and he's living some strange alternate reality.

Driving through Yosemite doesn't help, because there's a sense in which the magnificent scenery is just sliding by, like some elaborate backdrop.

'It explains a lot,' he says. 'I mean, like how you know so much about history. Frederick and Hitler and . . .'

'Barbarossa . . .'

'Yeah, Barbarossa.' Phil stretches his arms out in a yawn, then smiles. 'One thing puzzles me, though. Why me? If you wanted to keep things secret . . .'

'Because this is your territory,' Matteus says. 'This is the kind of thing you're going to write about. Time travel and changed realities.'

'Only you guys actually live it, is that right?'

'Right,' I say. 'Feel the beard. How else did that get there?'

'Well, maybe I just fell asleep. Maybe you guys drugged me. The water in the bottle, maybe that had some hallucinogenic drug in it.'

'But we *all* drank from the bottle.'

'Then maybe we all went through the same experience.'

I smile. 'Maybe.' Then, remembering something, I reach across and, unbuttoning Matteus's shirt pocket, make to remove the form guide from it.

'Hey . . .'

'It's okay. We're going to change it back.'

Matteus relaxes, lets me take it. I hand it to Phil. 'Next year's. You could make a million following that.'

Phil takes it, studies the cover, then flicks through, his eyes wide, his mouth open. 'Is this for real?'

Matteus gestures behind him. 'There's a *San Francisco Chronicle* under the seat there. Check the racing results for two days back.'

We wait, while Phil finds the page in the paper, then checks the results against the entries in the form guide. 'Holy shit!'

I reach across and take the guide from him. 'Only Matteus isn't supposed to do that. It's against the rules.'

'The rules?'

'Yeah. We're what you call *Reisende* – travellers – and there's a code we're supposed to live by, only some of us don't. Some of us cut corners.'

Matteus makes a face. 'And some of us are so straight-fucking-laced . . .'

Phil sighs. 'Jesus, but this is—'

'Amazing,' I say, but I make the word sound so ordinary, so mundane, that he stares at me, as if seeking some explanation for my lack of enthusiasm.

'It's what we are, Phil. How we live. Slotted in here and there throughout time. Making changes. Fighting the Russians. Trying not to die or to get too involved with the people we have to deal with.'

'But it sounds such—'

'Fun?' I'm silent a moment, then. 'Look, this is how it's going to be. I'm not going to change things yet. I'm not . . .'

'Wait a second,' Phil says. 'Just hold on there. What do you mean by *change things*? What precisely are you going to change?'

'It's simple. I jump back, to the day before we met. And I make sure that we don't meet. So none of this happens. This whole time-line gets erased. This trip, the evening with Greg, meeting Kleo at your house . . . none of that will have happened.'

Phil nods. 'I see. And I'll not remember any of it?'

'Not a single fragment. The only one who'll remember anything is me, and that's because I'll have effected the change. It'll be me who'll go back.'

'Uh-huh . . .' Phil considers a moment, then. 'You couldn't write some of it down for me? Like, it would be a real help, with my stories, I mean . . .'

I laugh. 'Phil . . . from what I've seen, the last thing you need is help.'

274

It's dark by the time we get back to Phil's house, and Kleo, hearing the car, rushes out, her face lit up in a big smile, seeing Phil home safe.

'Remember,' I say to him. 'Not a word. We've got a deal, right?'

'Right,' he says and, giving us a wave, puts his arm around Kleo and heads back indoors.

'He'll tell her,' Matteus says. 'Ten dollars to a nickel he'll tell her.'

'What if he does? They'll neither of them remember. Not once we've changed things.'

'Yeah, but what about Hecht? You plan on telling him?'

'You?'

'No.'

'Then it's our secret. Another rule broken.'

Matteus smiles. Then, remembering what we saw, he asks, 'So who's Reichenau?'

'Let's get back,' I say. 'I don't know about you, but I could do with a stiff drink.'

'Sure.'

We drive the rest of the way in silence, and it's only once we're back indoors, drinks in hand, that we take it up again.

'So?' Matteus says, perching himself on the armchair just across from me.

'Reichenau's someone I bumped into, up the line, in the twenty-eighth century. He kidnapped Gehlen and stole his time equations.'

'A Russian?'

'With a name like that? No. A German, as far as we can make out. But not one of ours.' I pause, then add, 'He's a very distinctive man.'

'How so?'

'He has a double skull.'

'A double . . .?' And then Matteus sees it. 'A *doppelgehirn*?'

'That's right.'

'Shit . . . Must make it hard for him to blend in outside of his time zone.'

'Sure. But it doesn't stop him. I saw him again in Baturin, in the eighteenth century.'

'And now here?'

'Right.'

I stare down into my glass for a second or two, then look back at him. 'What did Hecht say, when he gave you the instructions? How did he know that something was out there?'

'Hecht didn't say anything. He sent a messenger. Young guy, name of Haller.'

'Haller? But Haller's . . .'

'What?'

'Never mind. You were saying . . .'

'Haller said you'd be coming, and that I was to drive you up to a place in Nevada. He gave me the map reference and told me I might need some cutters and other stuff. Beyond that . . . Well, I don't think even *he* knew what was there.'

I nod, considering things. 'So someone was there before us. Someone *knew* what we were going to see. So why send *us*? Why not send in a hit squad? Blow the place to kingdom come?'

'Maybe Hecht's tried that. Maybe this Reichenau has out-manoeuvred him.'

'Then why not tell me that?'

Matteus shrugs. 'You tell me. I thought you were in thick with him.'

I look down.

'Oh, it's like that, is it?'

'There's a woman,' I say. 'Katerina, back in the thirteenth century. I . . .'

I meet his eyes and see he understands. 'Shit,' he says gently. 'I'm sorry. And Hecht won't let you . . .'

'No. That's why I'm here. As punishment.'

'Are you sure? That doesn't sound like Hecht to me.'

'Hecht's about to die.'

Matteus's eyes bulge. 'Hecht? No, no he can't be . . . He'd stop that, surely?'

'It's a done thing,' I say. 'Locked in tight. Part of a loop.'

Matteus seems to deflate before my eyes at the news. 'Urd protect us . . . Who will . . .?'

'Take over? Me. But then I go missing.'

'*What?*'

'Like I said, it's all locked in. Unchangeable. Only there must be something I can do *outside* of the loop. Some way I can affect things.'

Matteus nods thoughtfully. 'Maybe that's why you're here. Maybe *that's* why he's not given you explicit instructions. Maybe he's cutting you the slack you need.'

'Maybe. Only I can't see how that helps. So there's a platform here. What difference does that make if we can't get inside and use it?'

'Who says we can't?'

I shrug. The truth is, even if I could get to use Reichenau's platform, or disable it, then how does that help? If things can't be changed, then . . .

Make another loop. A second, different loop.

It's vague, unformed, but the best I can come up with right now. Only I'm not telling Matteus, nor Hecht come to that. Talking of which . . .

'I'd better go see him.'

'Hecht?'

'Yeah.'

'Why?'

'To report back.'

'But you don't know anything. At least, nothing that he doesn't know already. Why don't you wait? See what Phil comes up with.'

'Phil?'

'The club, dummkoff. *Unbeachtet.*'

It makes sense. 'Okay. But as soon as we've found out . . .'

'We change it. Agreed.'

'Good.' And I smile at him and raise my glass, because I find I like Matteus after all, cut corners and all.

The owl wakes me, its call intruding into my dream, making me start awake and go to the window to look out. It's after three and the moon is low in the black, cloudless sky. Pulling on my jeans, I go downstairs and out on to the back porch, then stand there in the shadows, silently watching as the owl swoops and hunts, ignoring my presence.

Downed and beautiful it is, its curving flight so graceful, so *perfect*, that I wonder why I have never noticed it before. For a moment it's at rest, its great yellow eyes blinking slowly, regularly, in the darkness.

Like the owl in the film, I realise. *What was it called? Ah yes*, Blade Runner . . .

I go inside. For owls there is no passing time. Life just is. Time – the measurement of time – is a human thing. A product of consciousness. Without consciousness . . .

I go into the living room and, lifting out the innards of the gramophone, set up the tri-vi again and sit there in the darkened room, the sound low, watching the film.

I'm at the part near the end, on the roof of the building as the rain pours down and Deckard lies there, his hands broken, Roy Batty crouched nearby, when I grow conscious of Matteus in the doorway, looking past me, watching intently.

It's beautiful. And when Batty makes his speech, I find myself suddenly so moved by the words, so *engaged* with what he says, by the dignity he shows, and by his consciousness of loss, that a tear rolls down my cheek.

I look to Matteus and he smiles. 'That's something, huh?' he says softly.

'But that's *us*,' I say. 'That's how . . .'

I stop, choked up, unable to say more.

'I know,' Matteus says. 'So maybe now you understand?'

I nod, then look back, yet as the film comes to its close, I'm conscious that something has just happened to me. What it is, I don't yet know, but I feel different somehow. Changed.

Matteus kills the signal, then walks across and switches on a lamp. 'Coffee?' he asks.

I nod, but my mind's elsewhere, set off by Batty's words, chasing down roads, down timestreams I have long forgotten.

I've seen things you wouldn't believe . . .

276

Unbeachtet turns out to be a jazz club in a big, three-storey dark-brick building in a run-down part of town. The Tucker causes a real stir among the black guys gathered on the sidewalk just outside the club, and while Phil and I wander across to the ticket office, Matteus stands at the centre of a group of them who want to know more about the car and even, perhaps, have a poke around in the big six-stroke engine in the back.

'Who's playing?' I ask Phil, as we wait for the girl behind the grill to stop talking to her girl friend and serve us.

'Sonny Rollins,' Phil says. 'He plays tenor sax. He's been working with Miles these past few years . . .'

'Miles?'

Phil stares at me like I'm an idiot, then shakes his head. 'Christ, man, you *are* from the future! Miles, Miles Davis. *Birth of the Cool*? You heard of that?'

The girl finishes talking, turns and smiles at me. 'How many?'

'Three please.'

'Make that eight,' Matteus says, putting his hand on my shoulder. 'We're going to treat my friends here.'

The girl looks to me, one eyebrow raised.

'As the man says,' I say, and dig out another twenty-dollar bill.

'Hey, that's a fine thing you're doing, man,' one of them says.

'A real friendly thing . . .'

Inside it's dark, gloomy to the point of being dungeon-like. Waitresses move between the tables like wraiths, while a fug of cigarette smoke makes it hard to see across the room to the tiny stage where there are a number of musical instruments: a drum kit and a piano, a stand-up double bass and, against a silver stand, a big tenor sax.

'Two tables,' Matteus says to a passing waitress, 'and some beers. Eight beers.'

I grab his arm and pull him close. 'What's with your friends?'

'They're regulars,' Matteus says. 'They know this place. You want to find out a few things, well, here's your chance.'

I release him. I thought he was messing about, playing the big man, but it makes sense. Good sense. We settle, near the stage and the beers arrive – opened bottles, unpoured. I look to one of the guys.

'Otto,' I say, putting out my hand.

'Rudy,' he answers, smiling broadly, his teeth flashing a brilliant white as his hand wraps about my own. It's a firm, generous grip. Welcoming.

'You a regular here?'

'Every week, man. Don't miss a show if I can help it. Not if I can afford it, anyway.' He grins. 'Speaking of which, it's much appreciated man. You're a real dude.'

A real dude, I think, and smile at that, then clink my beer bottle against his.

'They get good acts here?'

'*Good?* They's the *best*, man. Take Sonny Rollins. Ain't but one sax player as good as him, and he's playing *with* him tonight!'

I clearly look non-plussed, so he adds. 'Jackie McLean, man. Like I'm talking . . . *hot*.'

'He's that good?'

'That good and some,' says one of Rudy's mates, who introduces himself as Ben.

'You're not a jazz fan, then?' Rudy says, leaning a bit closer so I can hear him properly.

'Classics,' I say.

'Well, you gonna *see* a classic tonight.' And he laughs, and it's so warm that I find myself joining in.

We drink beer, talk, and then finally the band comes on. It's okay, but somehow I don't connect with the music. Don't *understand* it. There's a lot of improvisation going on, and I can see – and hear – that they're all fine musicians, Only . . .

Only it doesn't connect.

At the break I get up and, on the excuse of going to the john, wander round the back of the club, seeing what I can see. Most of the doors are labelled 'Staff Only', and when I try the doors they're locked. There's a staircase goes up into darkness and I'm tempted to follow it, only right then two men step out of an office to my left, and I'm about to explain that I'm looking for the toilets when the words freeze on my tongue.

The one on the left – a tall, red-haired, plumpish man, wearing a trilby – I've never seen before, but his companion, to the right of him, I've met on three occasions at the least.

Heinrich!

He clearly doesn't recognise me. Or, more likely, hasn't actually met me yet. But I'm surprised to find him here. I knew he worked for Reichenau, but I'd never have guessed he was a 'traveller'.

'Yes?' he asks, seeing how I'm staring at him. 'You want something?'

389

No one else would recognise it, but there's a distinctive accent there. A twenty-eighth-century accent.

I'd like to know what you're doing here and why? But I don't say that. I smile apologetically. 'I'm looking for the rest room . . .'

'Wrong way,' he says, pointing back the way I've come. But there's a slight inquisitiveness in his eyes now. Maybe it's a response to the slight Germanic traces in my accent. Or maybe he's just curious why I'd be here, in what's clearly the staff area of the club.

'You enjoying the music?' he asks, reaching out to touch the arm of his companion, as if to hold him there a moment longer.

'Not much. I'm a Beethoven man, myself.'

He laughs at that. 'Me, too. Only I can't book *him* . . .'

I smile at the joke, but my eyes have caught a detail. On the chain about his neck is a tiny silver pendant. The lazy eight. The infinity sign with the two inward-pointing arrows.

Connections, I think. *But why here? Why now?*

I turn to go, then turn back. 'It's Otto,' I say, holding out my hand. He takes it, smiling again, giving a gracious little nod of the head.

'Henry,' he says. 'A pleasure to meet you.'

'And you.'

And then I leave, making my way back through to the main body of the club, making sure as I go not to touch anything, knowing that if I can preserve whatever trace he has left of himself on my palm, that we might yet have a chance of tracing where he originates and maybe finding out just when and where he first encounters our friend Reichenau.

Hecht is hard to read. Is he unimpressed by what I've got to say, or does he simply know it all anyway? If he does, he keeps that to himself.

'But now that we know where the platform *is* . . .'

'We've tried,' he says. 'If we make any kind of aggressive move against it, he simply changes its location. Goes back in time and builds it somewhere else. That's why I sent you in without any warning. So you could see it for yourself. See what we were up against.'

'But surely . . .?'

'He seems to know our every move, even before we make it. It's like he's tracking all our agents.'

It's a devastating thing to say, only Hecht says it without the faintest trace of emotion.

'He can't be.'

'No,' Hecht agrees. 'And yet he does.'

'So what do we do?'

'We? You, you mean. I'm about to die, remember?'

Again, it's said almost factually, almost without bitterness. As if, in the short while I've been away, Hecht has come to terms with it.

Like Roy Batty, I think, only the comparison is strange. The two are so different.

'You want me to go back?'

'Yes.'

'And do what?'

Hecht's steel-grey eyes never leave mine. There's no expression in them. For all the animation in them, they could be camera lenses. 'That's up to you. *You're* making the rules now.'

I'm making the rules? But before I can query that, something strange happens. The Tree of Worlds, which has been glistening overhead, shimmering faintly in the dark, now seems to shiver, as if a strong wind has passed through its branches.

I look to Hecht. 'What does that mean?'

'Change is coming. Major change.'

'Your death . . .?'

'Is part of it, yes. My time is done. The Game is almost over now.'

'But how can it end?'

'Nothing is for ever, not even the Game, it seems.'

'But, Master . . .'

And now something breaks in him and he stands and turns away, stepping back into the darkness, such that for a moment he seems almost to have vanished. But he is there still. If I squint into the shadows I can still make out his form.

'I didn't mean to fall for her.'

'No. But you did.'

'Then it must have been *meant*.'

He turns back, angry now. '*Must* it? Or was it simply self-indulgence?'

'No. Compulsion. I'll not deny it. But can't you see? Before here there was nothing, no meaning, no substance to my life. Oh, there was the Game, but—'

'Listen to yourself, Otto. Listen to what you're saying. See how far you've strayed. Urd protect us from such error!'

I am silent for a while, then I stand and make my way to the door. There is no more to be said. I can be Hecht's man now or I can be my own. Even so, I cannot leave without apologising.

'I'm sorry. I must be a great disappointment. All of your hopes . . .'

And now his voice *is* bitter. 'You don't know, Otto Behr. You simply do not know. The long years, the careful planning.

And you destroyed it all. Removed the glue, the binding, leaving the pages to blow away in the wind. What *damage* you have done.'

I leave, subdued by his bitterness. Only I wouldn't change a thing. If I had to destroy a dozen Games, I would do it for her.

Maria is there at the platform. 'How was he?'

'Bitter. He blames me for everything.'

'He doesn't understand.'

Her words surprise me. '*Understand?*'

'He's never loved. Not a person anyway. Ideas, tactics, strategies – those are his loves. And fine loves they have been, only they're not human.'

'Then why . . .?'

'Why obey him? Because he is the Meister. Because there was no alternative. Until now . . .'

'Then what has changed?'

'You have, Otto. *You* have.'

278

The musicians have started the second set when I return. Both Phil and Matteus look up from the table as I squeeze between them.

'You okay?' Matteus asks.

'Yes. I went to see Hecht.'

'And what did he say?'

'He says I'm on my own.'

'Ah . . .'

Matteus turns away, watching the musicians. For a time he says nothing, then, touching my arm, he gestures towards the back of the room. 'You want to go?'

'Yes.'

He turns to Phil. 'We're gonna go. If you want to stay . . .'

Phil hesitates, then shakes his head.

We shake hands around the table and say our goodbyes. A minute later we're outside, on the lamp-lit street. The two young boys who have been 'guarding' the Tucker for Matteus grin broadly at the sight of him, then scurry forward to be paid.

A dollar apiece, I note.

'Okay,' Matteus says once we're all inside. 'Back to my place?'

We stop at a liquor store on the way and buy some more beers and a bottle of single malt Scotch, but I'm barely aware of the transition between car and house, because my mind's working away busily, trying to connect what I know. Trying to make sense of all the disparate pieces of information I now have.

Reichenau is here, or has been here. Certainly his man, Heinrich, is. But what they're up to is still a mystery. Why, for instance, run a jazz club? And what were they doing with those cuffed prisoners at the facility in the Nevada desert? Were they being *sent* somewhere?

And what's with the pendants? The lazy eight? Is this some kind of cult?

Matteus and Phil are in the kitchen, talking. I go through and stand there, watching them a moment.

'But that must be strange, I mean, really strange,' Phil says, speaking animatedly, using his hands. 'I mean, one moment you're in a place and it's just trees and open fields and a river, maybe, and the next—'

'Mile-high buildings of steel and concrete.'

They both turn to look at me.

'That's just how it is,' I say. 'I've seen Moscow when it was just a trading post. And Berlin . . . Berlin was just a tiny wooden fort on a turn in the river, forest on every side. And then, a full thousand years later, there it was . . . a giant sprawl of *kunstlichestahl* – "false steel" – filling the north German plain . . . five billion people crammed into its levels.'

Phil's mouth has opened in wonder, but I can see from his eyes that there's still a part of him that's unconvinced, that thinks that maybe we're a pair of con men, inventing all this shit just to impress him.

I look to Matteus. 'I think we ought to show Phil a thing or two. Prove we're not talking total horse shit.'

'You want to?'

'Sure. I think we ought. As friends.'

Matteus shrugs. 'Okay . . .'

We go back into the living room and while Matteus sets up the tri-vi, I pour myself a finger of Scotch and settle back.

'Jesus . . .' Phil says, as Matteus sets the tri-vi down. 'What the fuck is that?'

'The future,' Matteus says, and I can see from the gleam in his eyes that he's imagined this moment more than once.

'But what . . .?'

'It's tomorrow's TV.'

He laughs. 'Then it won't work.'

Matteus looks sideways at him. 'Why?'

'Because there won't be any signal.'

Matteus smiles and produces the tiny silver disc. 'It's all recorded. On this.'

He hands it across. Phil studies it, amazed. He's used to big, heavy black wax discs, and this, this is barely the size of a coaster, and not half as heavy.

'Jeeze . . .'

I smile. 'The best is yet to come, Phil. Slot it in the hole there and sit back. I think you're going to enjoy this.'

I've seen this before – not often, but once or twice – where a man has been shown his future, his achievements. But rarely have I had such pleasure as when I tell Phil that what he's seen is *his*, that all of this weird, fantastic shit came from out of *his* head. That *awes* him. Only Matteus then tops my moment by bringing a big cardboard box full of old paperbacks down from his study and handing them across to Phil. Scruffy little books with garish covers.

'What the . . .?'

He takes one out and stares at it agog, and then another, and another . . .

And more, many more, every last one of them bearing Phil's name. I watch as he opens them up, one by one and flicks through, reading the odd paragraph here, the odd line there, and nodding to himself.

'Yeah,' he says finally. 'Yeah . . .'

Matteus is grinning. 'You believe us now, then, Phil?'

But Phil has gone very still. He's staring down at the pile of books in front of him and slowly shaking his head.

'You're wrong,' I say, making him look up at me.

'Wrong?'

'About this. It isn't a dream. It's real. Those are your books, Phil. From the future.'

Only I'm thinking – *How did Matteus get them back here? He'd have had to have had them copied. Made from his own DNA.*

And why would Hecht permit that?

Phil, however, is still bemused. 'But this can't . . .'

'Can't be real? Why not? The platform, the beards we grew . . . the tri-vi, Matt's form guide for '53, and now these. What more have we got to show you, Phil?'

Phil has been crouching on his haunches, now he stands, wiping dust off his hands, the dust, perhaps more than the books themselves, convincing him with its detail.

'It's just, well, there might be other explanations. I mean this
. . .' He looks from me to Matteus, then back to me. 'Well, it's a
bit far-fetched, wouldn't you say?'

'What have we got to do, Phil?' Matteus says. 'Take you
there?'

His voice comes almost as a whisper. 'Could you?'

'No,' I say. 'You'd need one of these.' And I open my shirt and
show him the neat, long-healed scar, and explain to him about
the focus, and how it works, and that, more than anything, finally
convinces him.

I pour him a Scotch, then sit there, watching him sip from his
glass and chuckle to himself, picking up one book after another
and shaking his head in amazement.

Then, suddenly, an idea occurs to him, and he looks to me.
'Hey, do you think, well, do you think I could show these to Kleo?
I mean . . . if it's all going to be changed back anyhow . . .'

'I don't know,' I say. 'But not now. Later, maybe.'

Phil nods and looks down. Then, speaking slowly, he asks. 'So
what happens to me? I mean, apart from writing all of this shit.
Do Kleo and I have kids? Do we . . .?'

He looks up and finds me staring back at him. 'No,' I say. 'I'm
not telling you. Even if we're going to change it all back, it isn't
good for you to know.'

'But—'

'No. End of discussion.'

And I stand and leave the room before he can read anything
in my face, because I know things – things that Matteus has told
me about Phil's future, and especially about his four wives – that
I don't want Phil to even guess at.

Besides, it's late now – gone two – and I'm feeling tired.

'You'd better go, Phil,' I say, coming back into the room. 'Kleo
will be worried.'

He chuckles. 'Kleo will be asleep.'

I look to Matteus. 'You okay to drive?'

'Sure. I'll take him.'

But Phil seems anxious suddenly. 'Otto?'

'Yes, Phil?'

'How long have I got? I mean, knowing all this stuff? How long before you change it all back?'

'A couple of days?' I shrug. 'I don't know, Phil. Until we've worked things out.'

'But what if you *don't* work things out?'

I smile. 'Don't worry. It's what we do. What we're good at.'

Only this once I'm not so sure. This once I wonder whether we've jumped ourselves into a corner.

279

Sleep comes, with dreams of Katerina – not, this once, of Katerina as a lover, but as the mother of my children. In the dream I watch her from close by, yet it is as if she doesn't see me there. She is dressed in white, a bright red cloth beneath her, in a field of grass so green it almost hurts the eyes, while about her our children dance and play, carefree and happy, their long dark hair flying out in billowing clouds.

In the dream I laugh delightedly, then grow conscious of someone standing just off to my right. I turn, and there's Phil, an art pad under his arm. He smiles at me, then walks across and settles next to Katerina. She smiles at him as if she knows him, and as he opens up the pad, so my eldest, Natalya, sits down next to him, on the other side to her mother, and asks him what he's doing. Taking a pen from his pocket, he begins to draw, holding the pad so she can see. From where I'm standing, I can't see what he's doing, but I know what it is anyway.

Of course, I say, or think I say, then wake, a sheen of sweat covering me.

The owl calls. *Ta-woo*, it says. I lay there silently, looking to the window, and once again it calls, with a low, clear *Ta-woo*.

280

I have Matteus stop outside the art shop near the campus and go inside, returning a moment later with a large art pad, like the one in the dream. We're on our way to Phil's, and this is something of a detour, but not much. Besides, it's a fine morning, and it's nice to be out, nice to feel the warm breeze flowing in through the open windows of the Tucker.

I am feeling better than I have for weeks. Happier. More confident. Why? I don't know why. I just am.

As we pull up outside of Phil and Kleo's, I turn to Matteus and, even before he's switched off the engine, say, 'Leave the talking to me, okay? There's something I want Phil to help me with, and it might take a little while.'

Matteus gives me a strange look. 'Why?'

Should I tell him? I decide not to. 'Trust me,' I say. 'I know what I'm doing.'

It's what I've said to Ernst before now, and Hecht. The same kind of thing that's got me into trouble several times. Only this once I've a hunch that if anyone can come up with an answer, it's Phil. That – I'm sure – is what the dream was trying to tell me. That was why it connected my family with Phil. And what was Phil doing? He was drawing diagrams on the art pad. Lines and loops. Time diagrams, I'm sure of it.

When we knock, Kleo answers the door. Phil's still in bed, sleeping off last night.

We tell her not to wake him, and settle in the kitchen with coffee.

I like Kleo, and I'm sad that Phil isn't going to stay with her too long. She's the best of his women. The only one he could have made a real go of it with. But I don't tell her that. I simply smile a lot and gently flirt with her in the way a woman likes – nothing aggressive, but enough to flatter her ego a little. I'm not used to it much, but Kleo's warmth makes it easy, and I can tell she likes me. In the end she cooks both of us breakfast, and we're busy eating it when Phil finally emerges, yawning and stretching and looking even more like he could do with a good shave.

'Hi,' he says in his 'just-come-wide-awake' fashion. 'You been here long?'

'Twenty minutes,' Matteus says through a mouthful of hash browns. 'Otto's got a job for you.'

It's not how I wanted to introduce things, and I have asked Matteus to let me do the talking, but what's done is done.

'A job?' Phil asks, taking a seat, then smiling up at Kleo as she places a steaming cup of coffee in front of him.

'Yes,' I say, giving Matteus a sharp look. 'I need you to help me plot something out. A storyline, you might call it.'

'Uh-huh?' Phil looks interested. 'Anything particular?'

I look down, take a sip of my coffee, then meet Phil's eyes. He's watching me very intently now.

'I thought we might go to the park. Talk there.'

Phil waits for more, but I'm silent, watching him, and after a while he shrugs. 'Sure. Whatever . . .'

I look to Kleo. 'Are you okay with this, Kleo? I mean, we're taking your husband away from you a lot . . .'

'S'fine,' she says, giving me one of her special smiles. 'You all be back for supper?'

I look to Phil, then to Matteus, and nod. 'Sure. About seven, if that's okay? We'll bring back some wine. Make an evening of it. Just the four of us.'

She likes that, and as if to show that perhaps she'd like to kiss us all, gives Phil an especially sweet kiss on the top of his head, and momentarily lays her hand across the top of his shoulders.

Phil smiles up at her. 'Thanks, hun . . .'

And, seeing it, part of me aches to take them both aside and tell them never to give up on each other, never to let go. But for them, the future mustn't change. It has to be. To make him what he is. To bring us here. For he, I'm sure now, has the answers. He, if anyone, can tell me how to get outside the loop.

281

Phil is staring at me, shaking his head.

'Christ!' he says. 'So you just raised the gun and shot him?'

'Between the eyes,' I say. 'Burned a hole right through his skull. To pay him back for what he did to her. For what I'd *seen* him do.'

We are sitting on a bench in the middle of the local park, talking about Kravchuk.

Matteus is silent. This is all new to him, too, but I can see how he's looking at me differently now. Not disapprovingly. Or, at least, I don't think so. If anything, it's with sudden understanding. As if he knows now why I'm sad. Why I've *been* sad.

But he's not said a word yet, critical or otherwise, just listened.

I've been talking for the best part of six hours now, spelling it all out, telling it, if not in direct chronological order, then certainly in a way that makes best sense of it all. I've told him about the Teuton Knights and about Seydlitz's scheme to change the outcome of the Second World War. I've spoken of Frederick and the DNA-based snuff box that saved his life, and of the defection of our agents to the Russians. And then – because it is integral to all else – I've told him about Katerina and our times together, of how I fell in love with her and broke every rule in the book simply to keep her, and I can see that he likes that. But I tell him also of Reichenau and Kolya, and of Ernst suspended like a tormented angel in the glade in the forest, trapped by the time-anchor. Of the mile-high battlements of Asgard, and of the great physicist, Gehlen, and of King Manfred and his gigantic kin, oh and many other things.

And when I've done, he questions me, making me expand my story, or clarify this point or that, and still we haven't done. 'I need to write it all down,' Phil says. 'I need . . .' And then he grins, sudden understanding coming to him. 'The art pad . . .'

I nod. 'But you mustn't tell Kleo. Or if you do, say it's part of a book we're planning to write together.'

'So what exactly do you want from me?'

I glance at Matteus, who has been silent longer than I've ever known him be, then look back at Phil. 'There's one other thing I haven't told you. We're going to die. Katerina and I. Kolya is going to capture us and kill us. I know because I've seen it. He showed us our own corpses. It's foreordained. In a loop, if you see what I mean. Only, maybe there's a way round it. Some way of circumventing the loop.'

'Looping the loop,' Phil says and gives a little laugh before he turns serious again.

'Sorry . . .'

But I smile. 'No need. *You* didn't kill us. But you might – just might – be able to save us.'

That evening I move in with Phil and Kleo, Kleo making up a bed in the spare room Phil uses as a study. Matteus wants to stay, but I tell him to go back to the club and see if he can find out anything more about who owns it and what goes on there – apart from the jazz, that is. He doesn't like it. He thinks he's being sent on a fool's errand, but I need some time alone with Phil.

Kleo makes us sandwiches and brings us beers, but otherwise she leaves us alone, and slowly Phil begins to make sense of what I've told him, asking me question after question until he's got the sequence of events right, writing down events on the big art pad and linking them with arrows. It takes him three or four attempts, but finally, some two or three hours into the process, he looks up at me and smiles.

'There,' he says. 'Those are the intrusion points. Wherever I've put an event in a circle, that's where it links off into the future – to some further event which has yet to happen.'

I study them, one after another, then nod, impressed by Phil's grasp of things. I've not had to tell him twice how it works. And when I tell him that, he laughs and stands up and, going over to his shelves, searches about for a while, then comes back with a dog-eared copy of a magazine called *Astounding*. On its predominantly green cover is a picture of a man, standing in front of a great blue hoop of air, from which two identical copies of himself emerge, one to either side of him. Above the central figure's head, over the date – October 1941 – is the story's title, 'By His Bootstraps' by Anson MacDonald.

'Read it,' Phil says. 'It might surprise you.'

MacDonald, it turns out, is a guy called Robert Heinlein – another science-fiction writer and one of Phil's heroes – and the story deals with time paradoxes. I learn that Heinlein also wrote a story called 'All You Zombies', about someone creating copies of himself in time, but before Phil can give me the complete history, I stop him and make him attend to the problem in hand. *My* problem.

'Well,' Phil says, grinning now. 'The solution's easy. The problem is knowing precisely *when* to use it.'

'What do you mean?'

'I mean, you can die and not die, simply by copying yourself along a single timeline. Have two of you and two of Katerina go into the situation that kills one of each of you.'

'So we have to die?'

'Sure. That's already happened. It's in the loop. But you can come out of it and move on *after* that, and this is how . . .'

And Phil proceeds to draw me a diagram. In it, Katerina and I jump in to join up with ourselves at a point we've already been to, somewhere in my future, but in a timeline that approaches the moment when Kolya captures us and kills us. Two of us are captured and killed, the other two *see* us being captured and killed. We – the surviving couple – then move on to an instant beyond the moment where our other selves are killed, and then jump back, to the precise moment we jumped into this mini-loop, only at a slight distance, so, as Phil says 'you can observe your other two pairs of selves moving forward into the timestream that leads to Kolya.' Which means, in effect, that there are three of each of us at that single point in time: two already there, two jumping in, and two observing the process. And there need to be six, Phil explains, for the maths of it to work – because otherwise we get stuck in the loop in an infinite regression. Four have to move on down the line to encounter Kolya. But two must be left to jump right out of there, having witnessed it. Two *have* to move forward, otherwise we keep going back to the moment we began in an eternal, unbreakable cycle.

I study it twice and then a third time, and then I laugh at its simplicity and elegance.

Only . . .

'How will we know *when*?' I ask him. 'How will we know what point to jump in at?'

'Ah,' Phil says. 'As I said, that's the problem. And as yet, I'd say, you haven't got an answer. Not until you find out more about Kolya.' He shrugs, then. 'Maybe you should go back, to Krasnogorsk, I mean, trace him back from there. See where he comes from. Find out what went on before that moment with the cart.'

Again, it's so obvious it startles me. But I know why I haven't considered it before now because there's always been the barrier of Hecht. But now that's gone. Or will have, soon. And when *I* am Master . . .

'Phil, you don't know what this means to me.'

Only, when Phil meets my eyes, I realise that he does. And when he reaches out and hugs me, I hug him back, manfully, like I'm hugging a brother knight.

283

It's after three and I'm thinking of calling it a night and getting some sleep, when we hear the Tucker pull up outside. Phil lets Matteus in, and I can see at once that he's excited. But, conscious that Kleo is in the house, I pull the door to, then tell him to speak quietly.

'I've got our lead,' he says, eyes gleaming.

'Reichenau?' I ask, my heart pounding suddenly.

'No, Kolya. He's here, in West Berkeley. I've got an address.'

'*Here?*' Phil looks dumbfounded.

'Sure. We could go there now. It's only . . .'

'No,' I say. 'Right now we get some rest. Tomorrow we'll go over there. Check things out.'

'But—'

'Another night won't make a difference. And we need some sleep.'

Matteus desists, but he looks disappointed. He's clearly hurried back with his news, hoping to see some action. But it'd do us no good to go sneaking about at this time of night. And besides, I want to sleep on this, because it doesn't make a lot of sense, both Kolya *and* Reichenau being here. If they are.

I find out all I can from Matteus, then send him home. Phil wants to talk some more, but, grateful as I am to him, I send him off to bed. Then, alone in the room, I jump back to Four-Oh.

Maria is there, along with what looks like a night-shift. Most of the machines are untended, and I wonder what that means. Are all of our agents back here in Four-Oh?

But I'm in a hurry. I ask Maria what scope I have, and she tells me that as long as I stay in '52 I can go where I like. I thank her, then go and track down Old Schnorr. He's sleeping, but one of his assistants wakes him and he gets up and comes to greet me, pleased to see me. 'I've found one,' I say. 'Either Kolya or one of his ancestors. In California, in 1952. I wondered if you had any information.'

Old Schnorr settles himself before his machine, pulls at his beard a moment, then looks up at me, a half smile on his lips. '1952, eh? I can't remember anything, but we'll check.'

I wait, and a few moments later he looks up at me again. 'No. Nothing. Nothing in our records, anyway. Mind, there is a gap of one hundred and eighty years between 1847 and the next sighting in the 2030s. You want me to send one of my young men back to find out?'

'No. It's okay. I'm going back there myself. I'll find out what I can and let you know.'

I thank him and am about to leave when he calls me back.

'Otto, I had this made up for you. But you don't have to read it all now. You can take it with you. It's made from your DNA.'

'Ah . . .'

I take the folder from him and bow my thanks.

'Oh, and Otto . . .?'

'Yes, Meister?'

'Is it true . . . about Meister Hecht?'

I hesitate, then nod. 'I'm afraid so.'

'And nothing can be done?'

'It seems not.'

But now that he's raised it, I'm beginning to wonder. If I can get myself out of the mess of dying – if I *can* – then why can't I pull the same trick for Hecht?

Why not? But right now it's Kolya I'm interested in. Kolya who I want to find.

284

I jump in just after midnight, some three hours objective before I'm to find out the news about Kolya. It's a big house and dark, not a single light to be seen in any of the dozen or so windows. The long, broad street is empty, the only sound the noise of a distant train. Across from me two of the big mansion-like houses show scattered lights, but there's no sign of anyone.

I walk across the front lawn and make my way round the side of the building. The garden's neat, the grass trimmed, everything in its right place. Moonlight falls on an affluent, well-ordered house. I go to the French windows at the back of the house and look inside. The curtains are open, giving me a view of a wealthy, suburban room. A big couch, a TV – bigger than Matteus's, though not by much – and a huge rug. Minimalist, one might say. Or underfurnished. No sign of children.

I turn back, looking about me at the garden. No swings, no slides, no scooters, or anything a child might use. It makes me think of what Old Schnorr said to me, about Kolya kidnapping his past selves once they'd produced their link in his ancestral chain. Maybe that's what this is. Only how is Reichenau involved? Because he must be involved somehow, especially as his man, Heinrich, is working at Kolya's club. What is that deal? Is Heinrich *watching* Kolya? Has Reichenau placed him here for just that purpose?

There's a single door at the back of the house. I try it, but it's locked. I think of breaking a glass panel and letting myself in that way, then I notice that there's an open window, one floor up – which I can easily reach if I climb up on to the top of the porch.

A minute later and I'm inside, in what looks like a guest bedroom. Again it's spartanly furnished, like the minimum of effort has been made to make it look normal.

I walk across and pause a moment to listen. Nothing. I try the handle, then curse. It's locked. I jump out, then jump back the other side of the door, emerging in a deeply shadowed hallway. I take a moment to accustom myself to the gloom, then move down the hallway towards the stairs. There are doors off to either side, every one of them closed. I try them, one after another and find that they're all locked.

Why? I ask myself, and the answer comes at once. *To delay. To slow someone like me down if necessary.*

Yes, but why?

That's part of my trouble. I haven't got a handle on Kolya yet. I've only got what Old Schnorr has told me, about protecting himself through Time, and that seems a trifle . . . how shall we say . . . mad?

The use of acute intelligence to an utterly illogical end.

I go downstairs, hearing nothing, not even the tick of a clock. There's thick carpet beneath my feet wherever I go and not even the smallest creak of a floorboard, as if someone's been very careful to attend to such details. Even so, I feel that there's something here. Why have this house for no reason?

Downstairs the doors are pushed back, the rooms open for inspection. There's a massive kitchen – state of the art for this time – and a ballroom of sorts. There's a study, and two reception rooms, and a bathroom and, tucked away beyond the study, a small room with mirrors on the walls. Floor-to-ceiling mirrors.

The study intrigues me. The drawers to the desk are locked, of course, but there's nothing on the desk itself, not even an ink jotter. As for the shelves of books, they're fakes. Just fronts. Pull out a section of fake books and it's like an old Hollywood set, nothing behind the surface.

So who is this for? Who is this meant to impress? *Who comes here?*

But I'm convinced of one thing now. There's no one here. Not now, anyway. I'm about to jump out of there when I decide I'll make a mould of the one of the desk locks. I jump out, jump back.

I'm partway through making the mould when I hear a car draw up outside. I freeze, then crouch beside the table, expecting the front door to open at any moment, but there's nothing, and when I peer out through the drawn curtains at the front of the house, it's to see a car parked across the way, outside one of the neighbours' houses.

I go back to the study, finish taking the mould, then jump straight out.

Having had the key made, I ought, perhaps, to have jumped straight back in. Only I needed a break, to sleep, for one thing, but also to read Old Schnorr's file and let my impressions of the house settle. And so I go back to my room, in Four-Oh, returning to Phil's just before dawn.

Phil's clearly having trouble sleeping, because as soon as it's light, he brings me in a coffee.

'So what's the plan?' he asks, hovering in the doorway.

'We visit Kolya's house.'

Phil hesitates, then: 'Who *is* this Kolya?'

I pick the file up off the floor and throw it across. 'That's what we know. Only there are a few gaps.'

Phil, who's flicking through the pages, smiles at that. 'There are *always* gaps.' He pauses. 'Is he dangerous?'

I nod, remembering how he looked. 'I'd say so. And obsessive, which is always a bad sign.'

'And, of course, he kills you.' Phil laughs, as if that's funny, and then he adds, 'Maybe that's why he was so mad.'

'What do you mean?'

'When he made the swap, with Prince Nevsky. You said he was mad with you. That his eyes smouldered like he really hated you for something. Well, maybe that's why. Because he killed you and you still survived.'

I stare at Phil. 'You think so?'

'Shit! *I'd* be mad!'

That's true. So maybe it's worked already. Maybe all of this is part of the loop as well.

I sip at my coffee, then look up. Phil's looking at me strangely. 'What?'

'Just you,' Phil says. 'Just that you aren't what I expected. I don't know what I *did* expect, but not some fucked-up crazy German guy.'

'Fucked up?'

'Sure, Otto. Didn't you know? You're even more fucked up than me. I mean . . . like *degrees* more fucked up.'

'Thanks.'

'Well, Christ. I haven't got any mad monks pursuing me through Time. And I haven't fathered five daughters back in the thirteenth century. And I sure as hell haven't got to work out some way of saving my own ass by jumping back and forth through time so that there's three of me!'

It's true, only I don't like hearing it. Shrugging off the cover, I walk over to the window and, pulling the curtain back, look out into the Californian morning.

'I didn't mean any of those things to happen.'

'No, but they did. And you ought to ask yourself sometime just why they did. Was it all an accident, or was it you, Otto?'

I turn and look at him. He's not accusing me. I can see that. Quite the contrary, the guy actually feels for me. Only his truths are a little uncomfortable.

'I don't know.'

'Of course you don't. We never do. Not until much later. And usually it isn't so important. Only, you *need* to know what you are, Otto. *Need* to know why you're doing these things.'

I know why. I'm doing it for Katerina. Only is that the all of it?

I close my eyes and think of how blue hers are, and see her smile, and I know I would do *anything* simply to be with her. Only is that enough? Does that excuse me fucking up everyone else's lives?

I turn and look to Phil, ready to argue my case, only right then Matteus arrives, the Tucker idling outside.

Timely, I think, and, pulling on my jeans and shoes, go outside to greet him.

We get to the Kolya house an hour later. It looks very different in the daylight. No less imposing, but somehow less mysterious, much more suburban.

The key to the drawer in the desk is in my pocket. Making as if I've never been there before, I climb out of the Tucker and, walking across the grass, go directly to the front door and ring the bell.

The house is silent, empty. Beckoning to Matteus, I begin to walk round the back. Phil waits in the car, looking anxious.

The back garden, too, seems different. It's a sunny, welcoming space in the morning sunlight. Nothing threatening. The window above the porch is still open. Climbing up, I go inside, then reappear a moment later at the back door, opening it for Matteus.

In the light, the house seems abandoned. There's enough furniture left to sell it to a new buyer and no more. The kitchen cupboards are empty and when you reach up to run your finger along the top edge of a door, there's a light coating of dust. Not enough to suggest long dereliction, but enough to confirm what I'd begun to think: that whatever happened here happened some while ago and is done with.

In other words, we've missed the boat.

I'm tempted to jump back three months, simply to find out who was here and what went on, but first I go through to the study and try the lock.

Matteus looks at me strangely. 'Where did you get that?'

I half turn, even as the drawer slides out. 'I had it made.'

I look back, and go very, very still, for there, staring up at me, is a picture of Katerina and I, standing in the sunlight on a jetty, while in the background Fyodor Mikhailovich Bakatin and his three sons pull hard at the oars, making their way back downriver.

Tatarinka, I think, my heart thudding in my chest, my mouth suddenly dry. *That was taken in Tatarinka, seven centuries ago.*

Matteus comes across. 'Otto? Are you—'

He sees what I'm looking at and gives a sharp exhalation of breath. 'Thor's teeth—'

I lift the photo up. Beneath it is another, and another, all from that same long journey across northern Russia that Katerina and I once took. Shots of us on the river, or in this inn or that.

Taken by whom? I wonder, and realise as I do that it must have been a long succession of different people. *Kolya's people?*

Or Reichenau's?

But just what *is* the connection?

I pocket the photos, then dig deeper. There's a map of Mineral County. I show it to Matteus and he grins, like it's confirmed something he suspected. Beneath it is a notebook filled with what look like random numbers.

'It's a code,' Matteus says.

'Probably.' But I know what they are. Coordinates. *Time* coordinates.

And there, at the bottom of the drawer, in a pale cream presentation box – the kind you might use for a pearl necklace – are seven of the lazy eight pendants, their silver forms shining against the plush red velvet.

Silver? Or something that only looks like silver? Because I've got a hunch now what they are, and if I'm right . . .

I pocket them, then close the drawer and lock it.

'Come,' I say, but even as I say it I hear the sound of voices out front. I go through to the front window and peer through the curtains. Someone is leaning into the car, talking to Phil, who looks distinctly uncomfortable.

As I watch, the newcomer pushes back away from the Tucker and, turning, comes quickly across the lawn. A tall, balding man in a long, dark trench coat. There's the sound of a key in the lock, then footsteps on the bare wooden floor of the hallway.

As he steps into the room, Matteus steps quickly up behind him and puts a gun to his head.

Whoever it is, it isn't Kolya, and doesn't bear any kind of familial resemblance to Kolya. He's not anyone I've ever seen before, and from the way he's dressed I'd guess he's an estate agent. The gun terrifies him. He puts his hands into the air, wincing, as if he expects to be shot at any moment.

'Who are you?' I ask.

'I . . . I . . .'

Whoever he is, he's clearly no threat. In fact, he looks as if he's about to pass out.

'Matteus,' I say. 'Put the gun away.'

Matteus removes the gun from the man's head but stays where he is, blocking the door.

'Do you know Kolya?' I ask.

'Kolya?'

'Mr Kerenchev,' Matteus says, using the name of the club's owner.

'Ah, right . . .'

'We're government agents,' I say. 'We're looking for him.'

The man wets his lips with his tongue nervously, then says. 'He's gone.'

'Gone where?'

'I, I deal with his lawyer.'

'You have an address?'

He gives it me.

'Did he have children?'

'Children?'

It's clear he knows nothing. I look to Matteus. 'Come. Let's go.'

We hurry back to the Tucker and drive off. Phil is quiet, brooding, and when I ask him why he tells me.

'That guy knows me. He used to be a customer at the record store.'

'Shit!' Matteus says, glancing round. 'Then . . .'

'We can expect a visit,' I say. Only it doesn't matter. Not now. I've got all I need in my pocket.

286

Gehlen is amazed and delighted. 'How did you know?'

I stare down at the vague, gaseous shape beneath the opalescent floor and shrug. 'I guessed. I mean, I knew they had to have some kind of portable focus, because of the way Reichenau grabbed you from us that time. Only . . .'

'It's from the future,' Gehlen says. 'Way up the line. Such technologies . . .'

The seven pendants are exactly what I thought they were – foci, made not of silver but from their owners' DNA. They are the means by which Reichenau's agents travel through time. It appears that tremendous forces are channelled through each of the circular arms, going round and round at phenomenal speeds, building up momentum until they are released through the facing arrowheads. The resulting controlled collision of particles powers the jump through time.

Gehlen chuckles. A sound like water being pumped uphill. 'You'd think such a thing would simply implode. And it's so delicate and fine . . .'

Gehlen – or his ghost, anyway – is impressed. This thing is so far beyond him that, for once, he's not even jealous.

'It makes you wonder what kind of mind came up with this.'

Or minds. But I keep that suspicion to myself. It's enough to know now what we're looking for. Besides, it must surely make them more vulnerable. To remove our foci our enemies would have to cut deep into our chests, but to remove theirs . . .

That's the unanswered question. Whose *were* these? And why were they in the drawer? Did Kolya take them from Reichenau's dead agents, or were they waiting to be used?

Hecht wants to see me. He wants to know what's going on. He's heard that I asked for an audience with the *Genewart* – Gehlen's gaseous AI – and he wants to know what it's all about, but I'm not sure I want to tell him. In fact, for the first time in my life, I don't hurry to answer his summons.

In the end, he comes to my room.

'Otto?'

He's tense, angry with me. Behind him, I note, is Freisler, like he suspects he might have to use some strong-arm stuff on me.

'What?'

I'm acting like a child, I know, and he could probably ground me, only then he wouldn't get his answers, and as the days diminish he seems desperate for them.

'No need to be impertinent,' Freisler says, bristling with anger.

'No?' But I regret that even as I say it. I bow my head. 'Forgive me, Meister, only—'

'Only you want to see that damn woman . . .' Hecht's grey eyes, usually so cool, flash anger, and then he turns away.

'Yes,' I say calmly. 'Yes, I do. More than anything. Don't you understand? She is my other half. She . . . completes me.'

Hecht turns, about to say something more, but Freisler reaches out, touches his arm, and Hecht steps back. It is Freisler now who confronts me.

'You will have your report on the Master's desk within the hour. If you do not, you will be grounded, your status as *Reisende* annulled.'

I almost laugh. After all, this is what I've been waiting for for weeks now. Only I can't afford to be grounded. Not now that I'm so close.

'What do you want to know?'

Hecht speaks from the shadows. 'What did you find in the drawer of the desk?'

I smile. 'A map of Mineral County. A notebook full of coded numbers. Some photographs – most of them of Katerina and me – and seven pendants, of the same design that was in the frontispiece of your book of Russian folk tales.'

'The sign for infinity with the two facing arrows?'

'That's the one.'

Hecht is himself again, cool and collected. Given these four things, his mind seeks a connection. 'The map I understand. The code book?'

'Time coordinates, I think. Meister Schnorr is looking into it.'

'And the photos?'

'All of them taken on a journey Katerina and I took across northern Russia, between Novgorod and Moscow.'

'Taken by whom?'

'I don't know. But several different people, certainly. And totally without us knowing. Agents, I'd guess. Someone keeping a very close eye on us.'

Hecht nods. 'And the pendants.'

'I gave one to Gehlen – to the *Genewart*, rather – to analyse.'

'And?'

'It's a focus, but of a very advanced kind. Gehlen thinks from way up the line. He was impressed.'

'Gehlen . . . impressed?' Hecht's eyes widen slightly at the thought. 'Made of DNA? Or is there another process involved?'

'Made of DNA. Seven different kinds.'

'So the question is . . .'

'Whose are they, and why were they in the drawer.'

We meet eyes and he gives me the slightest nod of respect.

'You did well, Otto. But next time come to me first. I am still Meister here. For a time . . .'

I feel sorry now. Maybe even a little angry with myself. Only he's still blocking me. At least, I think he is.

'Meister?'

'Yes, Otto?'

'Will you let me go back? To see her? To make sure she's safe?'

'No,' Freisler says. 'Impossible.'

But Hecht speaks over him. 'Okay. But only once you've cleared all this up. Made sense of it. Until then, well, you must be what you were trained to be, Otto Behr. Patient. *Loyal.*'

I bow my head. 'Yes, Meister.' But inside my chest my heart is leaping.

287

'So what did Hecht say?'

Matteus and I are sitting in Phil and Kleo's kitchen. Our hosts have gone out somewhere, and in their absence, Matteus is in an interrogative mood. He's guessed that I went back and, to put him off the trail, I tell him that Hecht was excited about the map.

'He's ordered us back in,' I say. 'He wants us to investigate it further, this time *without* Phil.'

I'm sorry Phil's out because I wanted to rehearse one or two things with him and see what he made of them.

Matteus stares at me a while, then smiles. 'You get some good news, Otto?'

'Good news?'

'It's like a cloud has lifted. You were so tense . . .'

I don't know what he means about tense, but my mood has

certainly changed. Secretly I'm elated by the thought of going back to see her with Hecht's permission, of having everything out in the open at last.

But when Phil returns, the news he brings isn't good.

'The cops came,' he says. 'First thing. Took Kleo and I down to the station house. Made me make a statement.'

He seems to make light of it, but I know how Phil feels about authority. It's the one thing that truly fucks him up.

'What did you say?' I ask gently.

'I lied. Said I wasn't there at the house. That he must have imagined it all.'

'And did they accept that?'

'Not at first. So I asked them, "Was he *robbed*?" and they said no. "Was he *threatened*?" That's when they told me about the gun. Only I must have looked as surprised as I was. You didn't say anything about *guns*, Otto.'

'It was Matteus, wanting a bit of excitement.'

Phil looks at Matteus, not happy with him.

'So what else did they ask?'

Phil looks back at me, his green eyes thinking back. 'Who you two were. Who owned the car.'

'And what did you say?'

'I just lied. Said I was in bed. That their guy must have dreamed it all. Only I don't think the cops are going to leave it be. They let me go but . . .'

'It'll be okay,' I say, using every last drop of conviction I can muster. 'If I have to I'll make changes. But don't worry, Phil. I won't let them trouble you again.'

'Thanks.' Then, remembering something, he grins. 'Hey! I almost forgot! They're showing it! Tonight!' he says, when we don't respond. 'At the Cinema Guild on Telegraph Avenue!'

'Showing what?'

'Eisenstein's *Alexander Nevsky*. You know, the film. They're showing it, tonight, and I've got tickets!'

I stare at him, amazed. 'There's a *film*, about Nevsky?'

I feel I ought to have known, but I didn't. Phil laughs. 'Sure. It's a classic. Not as good as *Children of Paradise*, but the battle on the lake . . .'

Kleo enters, then takes off her coat and steps over to the sink. Phil smiles as he watches her.

'Kleo's going to come along, too, aren't you, sweetheart?'

But she only shrugs, upset, I guess, from having had to go down to the station house.

'What time's the show?'

Phil looks back at me. 'Eight fifteen. But we can get there a bit earlier. Get the good seats.'

I nod, the urge to tell him what I've decided – that I'm jumping back tonight to change things – strong. But I decide against it. There's no point spoiling the evening.

'When was the film made?'

'Thirty-eight. Before the pact.'

He means the pact between Hitler and Stalin. The famous *non-aggression* pact. Hitler's means of buying time to prepare Barbarossa, while Stalin foolishly stripped his officer corps bare with putsch after putsch.

History.

That evening we get to the cinema club just after seven thirty, but already there's quite a crowd and Phil is a little put out that we didn't come earlier. We find some seats. Phil sits immediately to my left, Kleo to my right, Matteus beyond her. Waiting, making small talk, I feel a strange tension in my stomach, and realise it has to do with Katerina, because this is a film about *our* time, set in a time and place I know only too well. I have stood on Lake Chudskoye in the depths of winter, in the shadow of

Raven's Rock where the battle took place. But it's more than that. There's a kind of cruel sentimentality at work here, for no matter how inaccurate this is, it cannot help but remind me of what I've lost.

Kleo places her hand over my own where it rests on the arm of the chair. I turn and look at her.

'Are you all right? You seemed . . .'

'I was just remembering,' I say. 'You see, I was there, in Novgorod, a long time ago.'

How long she doesn't know. I smile and, returning my smile, she removes her hand, but I know now that she's taken with me, and that disturbs me.

When the darkness falls and the film starts, I am surprised by how stilted and old-fashioned it is. It's black and white, for a start, and rather than being realistic it has a distinctly theatrical style. I like the music, yet when I get my first glimpse of their so-called thirteenth-century Russians I can't help but laugh.

'Those clothes!'

There's hushing noises from all sides. I sit back a little in my seat, trying not to react, but when I see the actor who's playing Nevsky, I can't help but be indignant. 'Look how old he is! Alexander was barely nineteen . . .'

'Hey! Can it, buddy!' someone says angrily from the darkness. 'Yeah! Shut it!' another adds.

And so I sit there, silent, watching the drama unfold, keeping my comments to myself. But it's hard. The film's a travesty. The outline of events is vaguely correct, but as for the rest, it's mainly invention and propaganda.

Afterwards we go to a small restaurant two blocks from Art Music, one of the few places Phil likes and will go to, and take a corner table, ordering coffees.

'Well?' Phil asks me excitedly. 'What did you think?'

I'm aware of Kleo there, watching me intently, listening to every word.

'It was . . . *interesting* . . .'

'Yeah? What do you mean by that?'

I smile at Phil. 'You want to know the truth?'

'Sure. After all, you're the expert.'

'Well, to begin with, the film was based very heavily on the *Life*.'

'The *Life*?'

'Of Nevsky. It was written forty years later by a man who never even knew him.

Metropolitan Krill . . .'

'*Metropolitan?*' Kleo asks. 'Is that a Russian name?'

'No, Metropolitan was a title given to the head of the church in a particular region. Kiev had a Metropolitan, as did Novgorod. But Krill was far from his own man. He owed his position and his power to Alexander's first son, Daniil, the ruler of Moscow. As you can imagine, it was in Krill's best interests to keep his sponsor happy, to tell a few lies and build up his master's father. Not only that, but the church at that time needed to build upon the idea of a holy war between Russia and Germany, that is, between the Roman Catholic and the Orthodox church – Rome and Byzantium. Nevsky's victory on the lake fitted the bill perfectly. Only they had to change the facts, if only to make it more heroic than it actually was.'

Kleo looks perplexed. 'You mean, it was all a lie?'

'No. The battle happened. Only not in the way Eisenstein depicted it. For a start, the figures quoted in the *Life* are ludicrous. They claim that over four hundred German knights were killed, along with thousands of Estonians, and that fifty of the Germans were captured and taken to Novgorod. If that were so, then the whole of the Teuton Knights' strength would have had to have been there at Lake Chudskoye, and their defeat would have meant the end – the total collapse – of their crusade in the north-east. That clearly didn't happen. And for good reason. The Brotherhood's own estimate for losses, figures that were borne out by the historical record, was a mere twenty brothers killed and six captured. In fact, some estimates have it that they were outnumbered by the Russians by a factor of sixty to one! So as you can see, the notion of a heroic, against-the-odds victory is a spurious one. The one thing the film *did* get right was that there was a faction in Novgorod who didn't want Prince Alexander to rule them. They knew what an arrogant, haughty, self-seeking son-of-a-bitch he was, and they could do without that. That's why they got rid of him after his victory over the Swedes on the Neva in 1240. Nor was the threat chiefly from the Teuton Knights. The Lithuanians were much more of a threat.'

Kleo is smiling dreamily at me now, impressed. But I'm only just getting into the swing.

'Far from being a defender of the homeland, Nevsky was an out-and-out opportunist. He never looked out for anybody but himself. The film depicts him as standing up to the Mongols – or, at least, being able to set them at a distance – but the truth is he was deep in their pocket. Five times he travelled to see his Mongol overlords at Sarai and at Karakorum. Six months it would take to make the round trip, and he *had* to do it, otherwise the Mongols would have stripped him of his title and set another in his place, by force if necessary. That's how "independent" and "patriotic" our hero was.'

Phil frowns. 'You speak like you don't like the man.'

'You're right. He was a toad. As far from what you saw on the screen just now as . . .'

Only I can't find an 'as'. To my mind, Prince Alexander Nevsky was a traitor to his people. The only reason the Russians keep him in place, I'm sure, is because he fathered Daniil, who in turn spawned a line of Russian kings. But I can't say that, not with Kleo there.

Or so I think. Because what happens next surprises me.

'Did he make a play for her?'

I look to Kleo, who has said the words. She is smiling, her eyes intent on me.

'Pardon?'

'Nevsky? When you met. Did he make a play for Katerina?'

I look to Phil, then back to Kleo, and understand. He's told her. Told her everything.

'You—'

'*Know?* Yes. Phil told me. Phil tells me everything.'

'Then . . .'

She looks up, past me, as the waitress returns with our coffees. We're all silent for a moment until she's gone, and then I lean towards her a little, keeping my voice low.

'Then you know what I am, what Matteus is?'

'Travellers,' she says. '*Reisende.*'

She pronounces the word so perfectly that I know Phil must have coached her the same way I coached him when I explained it all.

'Phil says you have a box full of his books. He says—'

I put a finger to my lips. 'Not now,' I say. 'Back at the house. Let's drink these and get back.'

But Kleo has one further question. 'Phil says you fought with them. The Brotherhood. Were they . . .?'

'Like they were depicted in the film? No. The film's a cartoon in that respect. Pure propaganda. Only . . .'

'Only what?'

'Only that we were better than that. And worse.'

She waits – they all wait – for me to finish. And so I tell them about that summer day on the rocks beside the river, and of that dreadful evening and the raid on the native Prussian village.

'How awful,' Kleo says, her eyes shocked.

'Yes. But the worst of it is that I knew the kind of people that the villagers were. Not individually, but I had stayed with their kind. Seen how good – how innocent – they were. So lacking in ideology.'

Phil makes a little noise in his throat and I look to him.

'That's what kills it,' he says, almost unable to meet my eyes. 'Ideology. It makes men into devils. Even good men.'

I can't argue, and, driving back in the Tucker, I glance in the rear-view mirror, wondering whether they really understand how it feels, and what would happen if we had an accident right now and Matteus and I were to die, and Phil and Kleo carry on into the future, knowing what they know, without it being changed. That's the risk we're taking here. That's why the rules are in place to prevent this from happening. Only, as I'm beginning to realise more and more, I seem to be a one-man rule-free zone. Hecht's right. I'm a wild card. And all of it stems from that moment when I first met Katerina. When our eyes first locked. If I changed that . . .

I'd be as good as dead. And besides, Reichenau would still be alive, and Kolya . . .

Back in Matteus' living room, we get out the tri-vi and show it to Kleo, and then Matteus brings in the box of Phil's novels, and I watch Kleo's face light up like a child's, see how she turns to Phil, holding up one of the books, and how he grins back at her with an 'I told you so' expression. Only I'm conscious suddenly of just what a dangerous game we're playing here, letting them in on all this stuff. And to make it worse, Matteus and Phil start talking about 'the film', and I realise, with a shock, that they aren't talking about the Nevsky, but about the film that will make Phil's name, thirty years from, now: *Blade Runner*.

'You've seen it?' I ask, interrupting.

Phil looks to Matteus and then to me. 'Sure. I—'

'I didn't think it would harm,' Matteus adds. 'We were going to jump back and erase things anyway, and I thought . . .'

I bite back what I was about to say, but Matteus catches my expression and, seeing my disapproval, looks away, blushing.

And so he should, because this is the kind of thing that can leave ripples in the timestream: the kind our enemies might easily pick up on. Then again, who am I to throw the first stone?

'Okay,' I say. 'So what did you make of it?'

'Well, it's difficult,' Phil says. 'I mean, think about it a second or two. The movie doesn't get made till thirty years from now, based on a book I've not yet written, that I won't have written for another sixteen years. A book that's so far ahead of what I'm thinking right now . . .'

Again, I'm shocked. 'You've read it?'

'*Do Androids Dream*? Sure. Matt loaned it to me.'

Just when was this? I want to ask, only it seems I'm too late to prevent it all. I take a long breath.

'So what did you make of it?'

Phil considers a moment, then shrugs. 'The director, Ridley Scott, he changed so much.'

'That's what Hollywood does.'

'Yes,' Phil says. 'I know that, only, the stuff he left out, the empathy box, Mercer, the electric animals, all of the decay and degeneration, the kipple . . . it all had meaning. Profound meaning. I can see that. See what my later self was getting at. Without all that stuff, well, good as it is, it's just an entertainment.'

'Which did you experience first?'

Phil looks to Matteus then back to me. 'The book. Matt was keen for me to experience them in the order they were produced.'

'And? Were the changes good or bad?'

Phil's face contorts as he struggles to find an adequate answer, and then he shrugs again. 'I don't know. I mean, I seriously don't know. As I said, the movie changes so much. And yet, in other ways, it stays true to the original. In its feel, especially. It's like that Scott guy got right inside my head in some ways, whereas in others . . .'

He looks to Kleo, and I can see from her face that she hasn't read the book or seen the movie.

'The characters,' he says finally. 'That's where the biggest changes come. I mean . . . Deckard, in my original, as we see him through JR Isidore's eyes, is "unimpressive". He's a mundane police clerk who, as part of his job, kills androids. Whereas in the movie he's like one of those detectives you come across in noir thrillers. You know, like Chandler's Philip Marlowe or Hammett's Sam Spade, complete with thirties voice-over. And then there's Roy Batty. In my book he barely plays any part in events. I mean . . . Deckard retires him without any real effort, whereas in the movie . . .' Phil shivers. 'Why didn't I think of that? I mean, I really liked what they did with that part of things. The almost child-like quality Batty showed at times, and yet a machine for all that. Ruthless, until the very end, when he lets Deckard live. And then there's that speech he gives. Tears in rain . . .'

'That was Rutger Hauer,' Matteus says. 'You know, the actor who played Batty. It was he who added those lines. They weren't actually in the original script.'

'Really?' Phil considers that, then nods. 'I guess they're simply different things. Different approaches to the same material. But it's a shame.'

'A shame?'

'That all of this will be gone when you leave here, Otto. Erased from my head, like the memories of a ghost.'

'Or tears in rain . . .'

427

Phil smiles at that. 'That's it. I mean, think of it. It would have been nice to have another pass at the novel. To pre-empt the film and get in first. To change it and make it better than it turned out to be. As it is . . .'

He falls silent. I sense that he could talk all night about this, but he leaves it at that. This is weird enough as it is. So I call for drinks and Matteus opens a bottle of single malt and pours four glasses, handing them round. And then we talk, finishing the bottle and opening another, the four of us speaking of times to come and of times that were and of those that might have been. And at the end of it I feel sad, because I've grown very fond of Phil and Kleo, and it's nice – very nice – to be able to be so unguarded, so among friends. But as the dawn comes up outside, I stand and, setting my glass aside, smile and say goodbye, and, right there, in front of them, I step out of the air. Back to Four-Oh. To bathe and sleep and then return . . . to a warm summer evening before I first met Phil.

288

I am back inside the outbuilding, in the barn-like garage at the end of Matteus' garden, looking around me at the junk piled up on every side. It's the evening *before* that first evening I was here, and I've jumped in now to prevent that whole chain of events from ever happening. I'm here to stop Matteus from ever inviting Phil and Greg over, and thus to stop me meeting them and all that followed. Because if I jumped in later – on the same evening – I would be duplicating myself, breaking rules, and I've decided I've done enough of that to last me several lifetimes.

This time I don't hurry. This time I have a good look around, poking among the boxes and beneath the covers to see just what

Matteus has there. And then I hear it. The owl. Climbing the ladder at the back of the building, I slowly, carefully put my head over the straw-strewn edge and look.

There it is, small and grey and downy in its nest, its head tucked in, its eyes closed. I watch, and after a moment it makes a small movement, a slight ruffling of its feathers. Yet it seems to be asleep. I could reach out and touch it, only I know that owls can be fierce when disturbed.

I climb back down and, picking up the container I've brought with me, go outside, beneath the clear Californian sky. If anything, it's a better evening even than the one I remember, the air cleaner, fresher, and as I walk over to the porch, I hear the sound of music drifting out from inside the house. Mahler. His second, the 'Resurrection'. It's the finale of the third movement – the scherzo – *In ruhig fliessender Bewegung*.

I open the back door quietly and slip inside, the music increasing in volume as I step through, trumpets blaring, kettle drum pounding. Typical Mahler.

As I step into the doorway, Matteus looks up from the armchair, shocked to see me there. He puts down his Scotch and stands, reaching out to turn the music down, and then – and only then – his face breaks into a broad grin.

'Otto? Otto Behr?'

I put down the container and reach out to shake his hand. 'Hecht sent me,' I say. 'I'm here to help you.'

So far it's much as we did before, but now I change things, before he can establish a pattern.

'Listen,' I say. 'I've been here before. This is my second time through.'

'Second . . .?' He blinks with surprise, then nods, understanding.

'First things first. I want you to phone Phil. Tell him tonight's off, that your cousin just arrived in town. Tell him you'll pop over in the morning, that you've a gift for him.'

He opens his mouth, making to query all of that, but I quickly interrupt.

'The place in Nevada. We know what it is. And we've got some other stuff, from a house the other side of Berkeley. Stuff we found in a drawer. A map, some pendants, other stuff. I'll explain it all later. But we need to make a trip to see the place again. We need to get inside.'

He nods. 'So what's been happening? What's the news from Four-Oh?'

'Don't ask,' I say. 'All kinds of weird shit.'

Because that isn't why I'm here. Not directly, anyway. I'm here to get Hecht what he wants and then get out of here, double quick. Because there's a woman waiting for me back in the thirteenth century, and five young girls, and . . .

'It's like this,' I say, forcing myself not to think of that, focusing on what Matteus needs to know. 'When I was here before . . .'

289

We could have jumped directly there – jumped in and jumped straight out again – only the drive over to Mineral County will give us time to talk. Time to reacquaint ourselves.

First, however, I want to visit Phil and Kleo and give them the gift I've had made for them.

It's a change – maybe even a serious change, considering how much Phil's life is influenced by such things – but I want him to have it.

We get over to the house just after seven. It's early, but it's a long journey across to Nevada, and I want to get there before the light goes. Putting the container down on the porch, I knock and wait. I don't like waking them this early, but it's likely to be the only chance I'll get to see them. There's no answer, and when I knock again – louder and longer this time – all I can hear is silence.

I walk round the house and peer in. There's no sign of them. Their bedroom curtains are drawn. Through them I can see that the bed's made, the room tidy.

I walk back to the front and call across. 'Matteus . . . They're not here. Do you know if they were planning anything?'

Matteus winds the window of the Tucker down. 'Nothing I know of.'

'Where d'you suppose they've gone?'

He shrugs. 'I don't know. Knock again. They must be there. They're the least adventurous people I know. Phil never goes anywhere. Not if he can help it.'

I go back and knock again, but there's still no answer. I'm about to give up – to suggest to Matteus that we go – when I see the two of them walking slowly up the road towards us, hand in hand.

Phil's smiling, recognising the Tucker, but as he sees me, his face changes, becoming closed, defensive. It's an aspect of him I've not witnessed before, but fits with what Matteus has told me.

Matteus gets out of the car and makes the introductions. 'Phil, Kleo, this is Otto. Otto, my good friends Phil and Kleo Dick.'

I put out a hand and we shake. He looks at my hand, then at me. 'Have we met?'

'No. But I've heard a lot about you.'

Phil looks like he doesn't know whether that's a good thing or a bad. He looks to Matteus, then back at me. 'You fancy some coffee?'

'That'd be nice,' I say, 'but we can't stay. We've got to make a trip. To Nevada. We've business there.'

We're about to go inside, when Phil notices the container. He looks to me. 'Yours?'

'No. It's for you, actually. A gift.'

Phil looks back at me, suspicious now. After all, I'm a stranger to him in this time stream. 'A gift?'

'Sure. For the two of you. Matteus mentioned you liked them.'

'Matteus?'

I smile. 'My cousin, Matt. It's his full name, didn't you know?'

Clearly he didn't. We go inside, into the familiar kitchen, and while Phil makes the coffee, Matteus and I sit there, at the table, making small talk with Kleo.

Phil's strange when he's like this: brooding, like a disappointed child. It's the other side to him, the one I haven't seen, and I'm not sure I like it. Later, so Matteus says, he'll write a novel about his divided self, and call this darker character Horselover Fat, translating the two parts of his name.

As he hands me my coffee, I push the container towards him. 'Careful,' I say. 'It's delicate.'

He sits. 'How do I . . .?'

'That catch there. On the side. Yeah, that's it. Just lift it.'

He does as I say, and the lid to the container slides up. He takes it off, then makes a little noise of surprise. 'Jeeze . . .'

'You like it?'

Matteus, like Phil, is staring at the bird with wide-open eyes. Kleo, looking on, is smiling.

'*Nyctea scandiaca*,' I say.

'A snowy owl,' Phil says, a sudden tenderness in his face. He looks to me, then back at the bird as it preens itself, beak under its wing, its great orange eyes with their dark centres hidden momentarily.

It's beautiful and, of course, a fake, built from my DNA. A copy. But not just any copy. It took a lot of skill to make this bird. Such things won't be possible in this world for a good six hundred years yet.

Phil gives a soft laugh, then shakes his head, as if confused.

'But you don't know us. This . . .' He looks to me, his expression totally different now. 'This is too much. It's too big a gift.'

'You like owls, don't you?'

'I dream of owls. The novel I was going to write . . .' He stops, then turns and looks to Kleo. She's grinning fit to burst.

'Hey,' he says softly. 'It's a wonderful gift. And I thank you, Otto, from the bottom of my heart. This is a gift of true friendship.'

Kleo comes up alongside Phil, looking into the cage. 'What does it eat?'

'Mice.'

We all laugh. They have mice a-plenty in Phil and Kleo's kitchen. Why, they're almost like pets.

'Do I need a licence of some kind?'

It's not something I've thought of, but I don't want to spoil the moment.

'No,' I say, 'but it needs to fly. To hunt. There's a handbook in the bottom of the container. It'll tell you all you need to know.'

And with that it's done. It's time to go. Phil asks us to stay, to share breakfast, but I've finished here. I like Phil and Kleo a lot, but we've a job to do.

We say our farewells and leave, and in the car Matteus asks me how I managed that.

'Managed what?'

'The owl. You must have called in a lot of favours.'

I smile. 'I did. But Phil's worth it, don't you think?'

Matteus grins. 'He is,' he says, and for a while we don't talk, just drive, feeling good about our morning's work.

433

290

It's exactly like it was before: the fence, the massive outcrop of rock, and, beyond it, the facility. Taking the bolt-cutters, I cut through the wire and step through, holding the torn section of fencing back as Matteus eases past. As before, only this time without Phil.

It's early, not even six, and the shadow of the outcrop is long: a dark, broad stroke on the uneven red sand surface. We move into it, into the night's dark chill, hurrying now.

We clamber up, towards the morning light, up over that great hump of rock until we can see the facility, there beneath us, still and silent, its rounded, glass-like surface glittering in the early sunlight.

I've arranged this already. Spoken to Maria. Now I jump back to Four-Oh where she's waiting. I give her my estimates – elevation, direction, distance – and she sends locators in, one after another, studying the screen a moment. And then she smiles.

'Go,' she says. 'Jump straight in there. I'll put Matteus in beside you.'

And an instant later there I am, *inside*, Matteus shimmering out of the air beside me, a long corridor curving away in front of me, a sealed door behind.

I look to him and he nods. We talked this through last night. He knows what to do. At the least sign of trouble he's to jump straight out of here. It's what I've said *I'll* do. Only I've lied to him. I don't intend to leave until I've found what Hecht's looking for. That's why I'm armed. We move quickly, silently, like shadows. If there are cameras here, I don't see them, but there is a door. I hesitate, listening for any sounds beyond it, then put my hand to the door pad.

It opens silently. *No DNA-locks then*, I think. *No retinal recognition systems.*

Everything simple. Like they don't care. Or simply aren't bothered.

It makes me think of what Hecht said. About Reichenau constantly making changes to this. *Relocating* the whole facility time after time. Which speaks of a different kind of mindset to our own. Profligate. Using time plastically. Moulding it to his needs. Not caring what the effects are on the real people who exist in all these worlds.

A different *kind* of game, outside the rules that we and the Russians abide by.

Or did. Because it's all changing. Or so Zarah says.

The room we step into is broad, curved, a series of lockers to our right. I go across to one and open it. Uniforms. Seventeenth century, by the look of them. I open another. More gear. Ancient-looking stuff. Boots and cravats and what looks like women's clothing from some distant century.

I turn and look to Matteus. Judging by the curve of this room we're close to the centre here. There's a door on the far side. I gesture to Matteus to go to it. He goes across, then turns, looking to me, his hand hovering over the door-pad. I nod, and he brings his hand down, and as the door slides open, so he ducks through.

There's a shout of surprise, and, as I cross the room towards the doorway, I get a glimpse of Matteus struggling with someone.

And then he's gone. But I can see across the room now. See the platform and the surrounding work bases. A perfect copy of the one at Four-Oh, only with strangers at the desks. Young men with earnest faces.

They stare at me, alarmed now, seeing the *staritskii* in my hand, knowing it's a weapon. The one who was struggling with Matteus backs away slowly.

'Call Caleb,' he says quietly to someone at the back of the room. 'Code Blue.'

I know Reichenau will change this if he can. Remould it. Unless I can get on to the platform. Because if I can do that, if I can plant the anchor-trace like Hecht wants me to, then we've got him, like a fish on a hook. He can rebuild all he wants, relocate however many times he wants, but we'll still have him.

I move slowly, edging step by step towards the platform, the gun trained on one of them after another, and for a while I think that maybe they're not going to stop me. Then one of them makes a move, maybe trying to distract me and, though I burn him straight through the chest, it's the signal for a number of them to try to rush me.

Matteus went too soon . . .

Yet even as I think it, he's back, standing just behind them, gun in hand, blasting away, buying me precious seconds, cutting a path through them, so that with a leap I make it up on to the great circle of the platform, a flailing arm catching my heel, making me stumble. Even so, I'm there. Yet as I take the warm, tiny little glass and metal device from my pocket, there's a sudden surge of power that seems to grab my chest in a powerful, iron-handed grip. The air solidifies and—

We jump. Not just me, or Matteus, but the whole damn thing. I *know* that feeling. Yet when it's finished, when that cruel, hard hand lets go its grip, I am still there, on the platform, the smell of burned flesh, the moans of the dying still surrounding me.

Elsewhen, but still here.

But how can that be so?

I try to jump, but can't. And when I try again, I almost faint, giddy suddenly, my head like a faulty gyroscope filled with slushing mercury. I stagger and, for a third time, put my hand to my chest and this time – Urd help me – it works!

Away . . . relief coursing through me. Back to Four-Oh. *Home,*

I think, as the platform solidifies about me, as Urte and Zarah reach out to take my arms and help me down. Only as I sit there on the edge of the platform I find that I'm trembling, shaken by what happened.

I look up, meeting Zarah's eyes. 'It jumped. The whole damn platform jumped.'

'I know,' she says, and I can see the fear now in her eyes. 'I thought I'd lost you.'

291

Hecht's looking gaunt. He's never been a fleshy man, only he looks ill now, grey with worry, and this latest news can't have helped.

He sets the report down and looks across at me, the Tree of Worlds shining above him in the darkness. 'You know where you went?'

'2443.' *Neu Berlin . . . in the Age of the Mechanists.*

Hecht's silent for a time, then he stands.

'Is it gone?'

His eyes meet mine, distracted. 'What?'

'The facility? Did he move it? I mean, like before. Did he go back in time and change it all?'

'He didn't have to.'

'But I thought—'

'It seems he's tired of that gambit. Or maybe he's got what he wanted.'

'Which is?'

Hecht sighs. 'I don't know. I haven't a clue what's in that double skull of his.'

'So what now?'

But Hecht doesn't answer. It's like he's suddenly grown old. Or maybe it's just his impending death that casts a shadow over his thoughts, because his grey eyes seem to lack the lustre of former days.

'Do you want me to go in?'

'In?' And then he sees what I mean, and shrugs. 'I . . .' He hesitates, then shakes his head – though I sense it's not in answer to my question. 'He was *there*,' he says, pointing into the air. 'We had a *trace* on him. And then . . . *nothing*. Gone. Like smoke . . .'

And it oughtn't to be possible, because platforms are points of stability, the unmoving focal point to which all else is relative.

Unmoving? No. Let me correct that. Slow-moving. At the rate of a second per second through Time. But in effect . . .

You see, their very stability allows this complex process. For them also to be capable of jumping adds one element of complexity too many. If Four-Oh were not Four-Oh, then how would we get home each time? To what fixed and certain point would we refer?

Only it is, thank Urd. Yet Reichenau has somehow changed all that. Unless . . .

I laugh, astonished that I'd not thought of it before.

'It's not.'

'Not?' Hecht stares at me as if I've gone mad. 'Not what?'

'Not a platform. It's a focus. A big version of what we've got in our chests. Only a mobile version, like the pendants they wear about their necks.'

Hecht almost smiles. 'Yes. That would explain it all. Only why would he need such a thing?'

I can almost see his mind turning over. And then he laughs. A brief little explosion of sound.

'Numbers,' he says. 'Pure numbers. It has to be. A focus, yes. And there was I thinking . . .'

He sighs, then looks to me again. 'In. Yes. You must go in. Find out what you can. What his plans are. Why he needs these mock platforms. Why his man Heinrich is back in 1952. Answers, that's what we need. Answers.'

I nod in agreement. Yet it seems too vague, too unfocused. Hecht usually has a plan, but lately . . .

His future death is killing him. Choking the flow of thoughts and ideas in his head.

'Otto?'

'Yes, Meister?'

'Have you ever wondered about your name?'

'My *name*?'

'Why you were given it. What significance it bears.'

I shake my head. I have never wondered. My name is who I am.

'I gave it you,' he says. 'I . . .' He gestures for me to stand. 'Come. Let me tell you a little tale.'

He walks over to the door and I follow, waiting while he taps the code into the lock. And then we are outside, literally outside, in a walled garden filled with sunlight, on a spring-like day, the air filled with birdsong.

There is a stone bench nearby. Hecht goes across and sits, patting the soft grey stone beside him. I join him there.

He turns, facing me, composing himself. And then he speaks softly, his eyes distant, the faintest smile on his lips as he tells me how I got my name.

'You were always Otto. All of our children are given a first name – what they used to term a "Christian" name – long before they acquire their second names. It's not until a child is five that we bother giving them that, and usually the name is chosen to "continue the line", so to speak. To ensure that the good old German family names don't die out.'

I remember being told this once, by Ernst perhaps, only it has never seemed particularly significant to me. With a system such as ours, it is not possible to follow the old ways, handing down the father's name, generation after generation. This way we ensure our genetic diversity – our *strength* – while avoiding all of the old nepotistic sins of family preference. All the old tribalism. All children are *our* children. All *volk* our *volk*. And I've not questioned that before. Not, at least, until recently.

'Most times there's no more to it than that. A name's a name. Only sometimes I would notice something in a child, and it would remind me, perhaps, of a figure from history, and I would borrow that name and use it on that child. You, Otto, were such a one.'

His smile broadens momentarily as he remembers.

'You were a bright child, but very serious. Adult before your time, so it seemed. And tall. Elegantly so. Such that you seemed, even at four, to have something stately about you, like a young prince. Not that there was anything remotely arrogant about you. No. You were the most polite and sensitive of children. Sensitive of others' feelings, that is. And with your fine dark hair and your elegant stature, I kept seeing reminders of someone I had met, long ago, when I was merely a *Reisende* and not the Meister.'

His eyes meet mine, something of the old fondness in them. 'It was in Stalingrad, in the winter of 1942. I was in the *Kessel* – trapped along with the whole of Hitler's Sixth Army, surrounded by the Russians, with no hope of reinforcements or of our own forces breaking out. It was there that I met him. Behr, that is. Captain Winrich Behr, late of the Afrika Korps. Behr was one of Paulus's most trusted men, responsible for the situation map and for all the facts and figures in the reports sent back to the Führer. He was an impressive-looking young man, with his black panzer captain's uniform and the knight's cross that hung about his neck – like one of those figures from the propaganda posters depicting the perfect Aryan. And so he was. One of Hitler's chosen. Anyway,

General Hube had been sent to see the Führer, flown out of Stalingrad to report personally to the Great Man. Only when Hube told Hitler the truth about the hopelessness of the situation, he could not persuade his Führer that defeat was inevitable. Hitler believed that Hube had been infected by the same disease of pessimism that all his other generals seemed to have caught. He refused to surrender and ordered them to fight on to the bitter end. Downcast, Hube flew back to Stalingrad to tell Field Marshal Paulus the news, and Paulus, at his wit's end, decided to send Behr to see Field Marshal Manstein.

'Manstein, entrenched in his headquarters in Taganrog, down on the Sea of Azov, listened to Behr's report and agreed with Paulus. Behr must be sent to see the Führer, at Rastenburg, at once. And so it was, that very next day, after a long and difficult flight, in the early evening of the thirteenth of January, 1943, Behr was escorted to the operations room of the *Wolfsschanze*, to meet his beloved leader, Adolf Hitler. It was to be a poignant meeting. Behr had been warned, both by Hube and Paulus, how Hitler reacted to bad news; how he would try to manipulate the bearer of ill tidings and persuade both them and himself that only he, the Great Leader, knew the full picture, and that things were much better than appeared. Only Behr did not let the Führer play this trick on him. Requesting Hitler's permission to give his account, he launched in, outlining with a shocking frankness just how bad things truly were within the *Kessel*. How the troops – the *Stalingradkampfer* – were overwhelmed by exhaustion and starvation and the bitter cold. How badly outnumbered they were and lacking in fuel, ammunition and basic foodstuffs. Hitler, for once, listened, impressed by this knightly vision that stood before him. All seemed well, only when Behr had finished, Hitler turned once more to the great map, which was covered in tiny little flags, and claimed – audaciously, but, more to the point, fantastically – that he was preparing a massive counterstroke that would reverse everything and set things right. Behr, looking on, felt a wave of shock pass through him. He had been an enthusiastic advocate of National Socialism, and a fanatical admirer of the Führer, but now he saw through the little man who stood there in front of him, hunched over the map, and in that instant he was stripped of all illusions. He knew then that the great cause he had fought for was based on the beliefs of a fantasist and a madman and that Germany, his beloved Germany, was set to lose not just Stalingrad but the war.'

'What happened to him?'

Hecht looks past me. 'A few days later he was summoned to see Hitler's senior aide, General Schmundt, and questioned closely. Schmundt saw at once that Behr had lost his faith, but Schmundt was sympathetic, however, and decided to take no action against the young man. That said, he could not risk sending Behr back to rejoin Paulus, lest his personal despair infect those about him, so he sent him to join Field Marshal Milch instead, in Melitopol on the Black Sea coast, appointing him to the special staff working to help Fortress Stalingrad hold out.'

'Did he survive the war?'

'He did. And lived to a ripe old age. There's video footage of him in his seventies.'

'And something in me reminded you of him?'

'There was a resemblance, a physical resemblance, but it was more his manner. Something genuinely aristocratic. Princely. He was a knight, in an age that had no need of knights.'

'I see.'

Only I don't, quite.

'But come,' Hecht says, getting to his feet again. 'Let me show you something.'

I see now that there is a wooden door in the end wall of the garden, partly obscured by ivy, and by the bushes that grow densely to either side. Opening it, Hecht steps through, and as I follow him, so I am surprised to find myself in a land of verdant, rolling hills and valleys. Only my surprise is short-lived, for as Hecht stands aside I see them, gathered on the rocks below me by the river, their tiny easels in their laps, and realise with a shock just where I am.

The Garden! Urd save us, I am in the Garden!

'Come,' Hecht says again, reaching out to gently touch my arm. 'You've been waiting all your life for this.'

292

Ernst is surprised to find me in his rooms when he returns from teaching.

'Otto!' he cries, embracing me. 'I didn't know you were back. Where have you been?'

'San Francisco Bay Area, California. 1952.'

'Where the platform was.'

'Yes, but listen . . . you won't believe where Hecht just took me. To the Garden.'

'The *Garden*? No!'

'Remember that day when we went out sketching, by the river, and Hecht joined us, and he had a guest? A tall man, dressed sombrely?'

'Vaguely . . .'

'Well, that was me. The tall man.'

'*You*?'

'I saw myself, Ernst, as a child. Nine years old, I was. And you, you were there too, sitting no further from me than you are now.'

'But why? Why would he do that?'

443

'To show me myself. To explain why he gave me my name.'

Ernst looks puzzled. 'Why did he?'

So I tell him the story, and afterwards Ernst is quiet, thinking things through.

'It must be hard,' he says finally. 'It must make you question everything.'

I stare at him, not understanding, and he adds. 'Knowing that you're going to die. I mean, that you're going to die *soon*, on a certain date. Odin save us, he probably knows *how!*'

'And I become Meister. And then I leave.' I look to Ernst. 'Why would I do that?'

Ernst shrugs. 'Katerina?'

I sigh. I feel I'm no nearer to solving things. No nearer to getting to see her again, to making sure that she's safe. She and my girls.

'So what does Hecht have planned for you?'

'I'm to go in,' I say. '2343. He wants answers.'

'We all want answers. But why you? He could send in a whole squad of other agents.'

It's a good question. And there are others, too. Like why he's not gone for Reichenau's throat. Why – when he knows where he is – he can't pin the bastard down.

'I think Hecht's losing it,' I say. 'His memory is still as good as ever, but . . . he seems to lack *sharpness*.'

'Things have changed,' Ernst says. 'Zarah says there are agents coming in from the future.'

'Yes, but—'

'He knows it's finished for him. That must be devastating. The ultimate failure. To be the father of one's people and to know you won't be there. That it'll stand or fall without you. It must make you question the value of everything you did. Make you take stock.'

I can't argue with that. Only it doesn't seem like Hecht to give up on things. Even if he is about to die, the old Hecht would have done all he could to prepare for that, to set things up for after he'd gone. Simply to let go . . .

'How long has he?' I ask.

'Thirty-one days.'

It isn't long, and no doubt it seems even briefer when you're living it, knowing the sand is running through.

Master of Time, and yet not in control of it. *Subject* to it.

'Zarah will know,' I say suddenly. 'Zarah knows everything. Nothing comes or goes without her knowing about it.'

'Then see her.'

And so I go, there and then, leaving Ernst behind, as I've left him far too often these past months. Only there's nothing he can help me with this time, because if Hecht *is* to die and I become Meister, then the problem's mine and mine alone.

Or so I convince myself.

Zarah, however, is not at the platform but in her room, and when – with her permission – I visit her there, I find her seated on the edge of her bed, her head slumped forward, her face hidden behind the screen of her hair.

'Zarah?'

She looks up, her eyes meeting mine, and I see that she's been crying.

'*Zarah?*'

'He's dead,' she says, and for a moment I've no idea who she means.

'Dead?'

'Meister Hecht. The news came back just now. His brother . . .'

'But I was with him, half an hour back. He—'

I stop dead, recognising the fallacy in what I'm saying. Of course he can be dead, even if I did see him only half an hour back. Thirty-one days, yes. But that's *subjective*. If he went back. Back to the Haven . . .

'Thor's teeth,' I say. 'Are you sure? Dead?'

Zarah nods, and another tear courses down her cheek. I go to her and, kneeling before her, wipe the tears away gently with my thumb.

'How did he . . .?'

'I don't know. But he left something, for you.'

I turn, looking to where she's indicating, and see the slender package on the bedside table, my name – 'Otto' – written in Hecht's neat hand on the brown paper exterior.

So I am Meister now, I think, and am surprised by how calm, how unemotional I am. Hecht is dead and I feel nothing.

I stand and look about me, but nothing seems to go in. Not a single impression sticks. It's like my whole being is in sudden stasis, every sense of mine suspended, my brain numbed by the news. And I wonder if that is normal, or whether that is a failing in myself. And then I remember how I've felt about Katerina, recall that wild, obsessive surge of raw and primitive emotion that she conjures in me, and know that how I feel in this moment is to do with shock.

I go to speak, to say something significant, but nothing comes, and after a moment I just shake my head. And then I remember it – the package – and, picking it up, read my name, mouthing it to the air.

'Well?' Zarah says, calmer now. 'Aren't you going to open it?'

I hand it to her, and, after the briefest glance at me, she slits it open with her fingernail and tips it up, and out falls something bright and reddish-brown, but shiny.

Something made of copper. And as she holds it up, her eyes questioning me, so I feel my heart stop in my chest, like someone's punched me hard.

'Urd save me!' I cry, reaching out to take it from her, bringing the perfect, sculpted copper ash leaf before my eyes, fear gripping me. 'It's Katerina's!'

Part Ten

The Language of the Blood

'The German soul has corridors and interconnecting corridors in it, there are caves, hiding places, dungeons in it; its disorder possesses much of the fascination of the mysterious; the German is acquainted with the hidden paths to chaos. And as everything loves its symbol, the German loves clouds and all that is obscure, becoming, crepuscular, damp and dismal: the uncertain, unformed, shifting, growing of every kind he feels to be 'profound'. The German himself *is* not, he is *becoming*, he is 'developing'.'

– Friedrich Nietzsche, *Beyond Good and Evil*

Part Ten

The Language of the Blood

The German soul has corridors and interconnecting corridors in it, there are caves, hiding places, dungeons in it; its disorder possesses much of the fascination of the mysterious; the German is acquainted with the hidden paths to chaos. And as everything loves its symbol, the German loves the clouds and all that is obscure, becoming, twilight, damp and dismal: the uncertain, unformed, shifting, growing of every kind he feels to be 'profound'. The German himself is not, he is becoming, he is 'developing'.

—Friedrich Nietzsche, Beyond Good and Evil

I want to see Hecht's body. I want to know *how* he died and *why*, and why it couldn't be prevented. And I want to know how Katerina's involved, because if she isn't, then why send me the pendant? More than anything I want to know why I can't go and see her now.

Right now.

I look about me at the four who are seated with me at the end of the long, gleamingly polished conference table. 'Who's Master here?'

'You are . . .'

They say the words in unison, then look to each other awkwardly. Freisler and Old Schnorr, Zarah and, much subdued, my old friend Ernst, looking grey and old beyond his years. Gehlen is there, too, 'looking on' from a flat screen to one side. We're in the Conference Room, the doors locked, *in camera*. A room designed for fifty or more. But there are only the five of us here. Five and a dead man.

'Then why can't I go back?'

Freisler looks to the others, then speaks for them all. 'You just can't. There's too much to do.'

'Then let someone else do it.'

'That's not possible. *You* are Meister now.'

I sense that it costs him something to say it, that he would like to be sitting in my place, at the head of the table. He's about to say more, when Zarah touches his arm and intercedes.

'Things must be maintained. The Game . . .'

Can go hang itself. Only I don't say that. Without the Game there's no Katerina.

No girls. No Cherdiechnost.

'How can it harm? I'll be gone only seconds.'

'Yes, but what if you don't come back?' Ernst says, surprising me. I thought Ernst would be on my side, knowing what he knows.

I laugh, as if the notion is absurd. 'Of course I'll come back. At the first sign of trouble.'

'You'll stay there,' Zarah says. 'You have before. That's why we can't risk it. Everyone depends on you now, Otto. *Everyone.*'

That's hard to take in. That I'm in charge now. The Meister. Dealing with agents, making decisions, naming children . . .

'What if Ernst went in with me? Then, if we got into trouble, he could jump out and you could pull *me* out.'

'No,' Ernst says.

'But why?'

He looks up, meets my eyes. 'Because I couldn't trust myself. You might *persuade* me.'

'Persuade you? *How*? If you were under strict orders.'

'To the Meister, yes.'

I almost smile, seeing his point, only this is too serious to be amusing. 'What if I order it?'

Zarah's ready for this one. 'Then we depose you. Appoint another Meister.'

'Then what good is it *being* Meister?'

'None,' Freisler says coldly, 'unless you take the role seriously. Unless you embrace the responsibility of the job.'

That much is true. I can't act like a child. Not now. Only I must know what's happened to her. *Must.*

'Ernst?'

'Yes, Meister?'

'Would you go in for me? Find out what's happened and report back?'

'Yes, Meister.'

I look to Zarah, then to Friesler. 'Is that okay?'

Both nod.

'Then that's what we'll do. Ernst, you'll report to me in an hour. Until then . . .'

But Zarah interrupts me again. 'Not possible, I'm afraid. There's to be a ceremony.'

'A ceremony?'

'For Meister Hecht. In the chapel.'

'Ah . . . of course.' And I feel suddenly very small and selfish. For a moment I'd forgotten. 'Later, then, Ernst. *Afterwards.*'

'Yes, Meister.'

Old Schnorr is watching me, strangely pensive.

'Meister Schnorr? You have something to say?'

'Not now,' he says, and I note the curious glances that the others give him.

'Then we're done, I guess.'

Only we're not. 'I'll bring in the first of the files,' Freisler says, getting up.

I stare at him, confused. 'I'm sorry?'

'We ought to make a start,' he says, looking to Zarah. 'Don't you think?'

But Zarah shrugs.

'Make a start on what?'

'Reviewing the files,' she says. 'Agents, projects. The whole thing. You're responsible for it all now, Otto, so you need to know what's going on.' She smiles sympathetically. 'That's why we're here. That's why the Elders appointed us. To help you. To ease you in. We're your council. Until you can cope. Until—'

I interrupt her. 'But you know that won't happen. I disappear . . .'

'You forget the nature of Time,' Old Schnorr says, seeming more authoritative, more commanding than I've ever known him. 'You might appear to be with us only for a day or so, even a week, but that time might be *folded in*. You might jump back or jump out. Your time might be stretched. We just don't know. Meanwhile the Elders have appointed us.'

I stand. For a moment they're silent, watching me, looking to see what I'll do. Only I know suddenly that I'll do nothing. Nothing outrageous, that is.

'Not now,' I say to Freisler. 'Later. After the ceremony. We'll make a start then. And Ernst . . .'

'Yes, Meister?'

'Get me news. Let me know that she's all right. I can't function without knowing.'

Zarah is looking down. So too is Schnorr. Only Ernst and Freisler are looking at me, and I have the sense that Freisler is studying me as if to gauge just how reliable I am.

Not at all, I think, and wonder at myself, because Freisler's right. This is no time to be unreliable. No time to be selfish. Right now, the *volk* – the entire German nation, now and for all time – is vulnerable. If the Russians were to learn of Hecht's death . . .

I turn, looking to Gehlen, at the flattened yet familiar face upon the screen.

'Hans . . . what do the Russians know?'

Gehlen is tapped into the mainframe, you see. If anyone knows the overall situation, he – dead as he is – will know.

'Nothing,' he says. 'They think Hecht's alive and well and running things.'

'Then let's keep it that way.' I look to Zarah. 'No ceremony,' I say. 'Our agents aren't to know anything. As far as they're concerned, Hecht is still alive. He's still the Meister.'

'But . . .'

'There'll be time later to celebrate his life. But not now. Now we are vulnerable.'

I look to Freisler. 'Jurgen, have we a project ready to launch?'

'Not ready, Meister, but—'

'Something we can improvise, then?'

He thinks a moment, then nods.

'Then let's do that. Let's distract the bastards.'

Freisler likes that. He smiles. And Freisler rarely smiles. 'Yes, Meister!'

But Zarah, I can see, is still unhappy. I need to placate her over the ceremony.

'Hecht was a great man,' I say. 'We shall not see his like again.'

'He was our Father,' Zarah says. 'Whenever we had a problem, he was there for us.'

I open my mouth, then nod, as if I agree. Only I don't, because I know now what a father *is* and Hecht was never that. No. Hecht was our Meister, pure and simple. Through us he played the Game. And though the Game goes on, things have changed, for *I* am Meister now, and, looking round that table, I realise for the first time what that means.

I have the power to change things. The power to change the way the Game is played.

Only not now. Not yet.

'Zarah, Jurgen, Ernst, leave me now. Meister Schnorr and I have things to discuss.'

And they leave, obedient to my wishes, for I am Meister now and this is my Game.

'Well, Meister Schnorr? What is it?'

Old Schnorr peers at me a moment over his massive spectacles, then, turning aside, reaches down and lifts something from the floor beside his chair. It's an old, satchel-like briefcase – a soft, brown leather bag, worn and ancient, bulging with documents. Setting it on the table in front of him, his fingers fumble at the old brass catches, even as he begins to speak.

'We've been busy, Otto. Very busy. I drafted in two new students to help collate the stuff, but, well, my boys have done me proud. I thought there'd be gaps, even after all our best efforts, but—'

The document he lifts from inside the old briefcase is huge – a good two inches thick and dense with type. He pushes it towards me.

'Kolya?'

'Kolya,' he confirms. 'As complete as we could make it. Seventy-two generations on the father's side. Potted histories, the lot.'

'And no gaps?'

The old Master removes his glasses to polish them and smiles. 'No gaps.'

He replaces his spectacles. His eyes once again look as large as gobstoppers.

'Do we know—'

'Where he's taking them?' Schnorr shakes his head. 'Not yet. Only we're certain he's taking them somewhere. Seventy-two ancestors, and every last one of them disappears without trace the moment the direct descendant is born. Hardly coincidence, eh?'

Hardly. I flick through a page or two, then push it aside. 'So what's the way ahead? How do we *use* what we know?'

Schnorr's smile broadens. 'You're the Meister now, Otto. That's your job.'

'But . . .'

Only he's right. I have to think for all of them now. Come up with the answers. Decide what to do and how to do it.

I need to think this through, come up with a strategy. And not just any half-cocked scheme. Only I've not got a lot of time; not if I'm about to 'vanish' from the screens.

'Meister Hecht wanted me to go in,' I say. '2343. He wanted me to get some answers.'

'Then go.'

'But I thought you didn't want me to go in.'

'If it was the old Meister's wish, then we'll not oppose you. It was only if you went in . . . after her . . .'

'Katerina?'

He nods, a touch embarrassed, and I sense that while he understands, he does not approve. Like Hecht, he thinks I've made a mess of things. And maybe I have, but I am beginning to think it's for a purpose, that what I said to Hecht about it being *'meant'* is true.

Only how to prove that without passing through the loop?

Until I'm out the other side, I can only trust to instinct. And my instinct right now – stronger even than my need to see Katerina and make sure she's safe – is to find and kill Kolya. Time-dead, so he can't come back.

So why not start at the beginning of his story? Where supposedly he's born. In the 2340s.

Old Schnorr has been watching me silently. Now he takes another package from his bag – the same envelope Hecht left for me – and pushes it across.

'We had it analysed,' he says. 'And guess what? It's made of DNA. Katerina's DNA, presumably.'

I tip the pendant from the envelope and pick it up, closing my hand about it, like I have a living piece of her beneath my fingers.

My instinct was right, then. The smith was an agent, put there in Belyj, in that crap heap of a trading post, with the sole purpose of meeting us and getting the pendant into Katerina's care.

Only how did they know what I would ask for? Who found that out and told them?

'One further thing,' Schnorr says. 'We X-rayed it. It might look like an ash leaf, but beneath that superficial form is another.'

'The lazy eight?'

'Exactly.'

So it's a portable focus. But linked to what? *Where does it jump to?*

'She was wearing it,' I say. 'In Cherdiechnost, the evening I left her, when Hecht brought me back here. The question is, how did Hecht get hold of it, and where?'

And there are other questions, too. Like what happened to Katerina when I left her in Krasnogorsk – when I was pulled out of there back to Four-Oh?

Old Schnorr sits there, silent, waiting, I guess, for me to dismiss him now that he's delivered his little surprise. But I've one final task for him. Something to get his young men working on.

'I want you to find her,' I say. 'I want you to trawl time once more for her face. Find out where she went and where she's been.'

Schnorr seems surprised. 'Katerina?'

'Katerina.' And, tearing off the first page of the report, I turn it over and begin to sketch her face.

295

Zarah walks round me, 'inspecting' me, straightening my cloak and making sure I look the part, then nods.

'You'll do.'

But for once I'm feeling nervous as I step up on to the platform, because if Meister Schnorr is right, this is the epicentre. If there are answers to be had, then they're there, in 2343, and that could be dangerous. Especially if Kolya's there.

They've set it all up in advance. Our agents have gone in and established an identity for me, given me a history and a status. Enough to convince anyone should they choose to pry.

I've been to the language lab and had a refresher in Mechanist 'jargon'. Not that I'll probably need it, because the circles I'll be operating within consider it vulgar; just that it would be careless not to.

Everything else I need is in a case that will be delivered once I'm there. As is the custom. For a man of my status – an Inspector of the second rank – would consider it quite beneath him to carry his own luggage.

'Strength,' Zarah says, as she steps behind the screen, preparing to send me back.

I smile. 'Strength,' I say, even as Four-Oh evaporates about me.

And there I am, on a broad, white marble path between tall trees. It's a perfect spring day in Germany and the tiered white façade of the Akademie looms close, beyond the trees, a hundred metres distant.

They are expecting me. Only not today. In the communication from my office, they were told I would be making an inspection on the fifth of April, but I am two days early. But that, apparently, is how we operate at the Ministry. We like to keep them on their toes.

'Can I help you, Master?'

I turn, to find two boys, dressed in what looks like military uniform, their silks predominantly black, each outfit finished off with long leather boots and a sash. They are tall and blond,

457

fourteen, maybe fifteen years old at most, yet they carry themselves with the assurance – nay, the arrogance – of adults.

Oh, and one further detail. On the left side of each of their necks is 'tattooed' what looks like an elaborate Chinese 'chop', in effect, a perfectly square and highly detailed 'bar-code'. This is a 'genetic indent', containing an abbreviated form of the most important genetic details of each of their twenty-six chromosomes. More complex than any fingerprint, it is their distinct identifier in this world, and bears an almost heraldic importance in this society. I have a similar 'indent' on my own neck. False, naturally, for I've no wish to give anyone that kind of detailed information about me, but consistent with the 'indent' kept on the Ministry's files. If anyone bothers to check up on me, that too will coincide.

I look to the elder of the two. 'I have come to see the Doktor. I believe he is expecting me.'

They already know who I am. Can see, from my dress, and from the insignia on the arm of my cloak, what my rank is and thus my status in this acutely hierarchical world. They both give a tight little bow – a curt movement of the head – before one of them responds.

'Then perhaps you would permit us to escort you to his office, Meister . . .?'

He is fishing for my name. I am inclined to smile at this earnest young man, only my status as Inspector does not permit it. Instead I return their bow.

'That would be most kind of you, young Master.'

I am duly deferent, not knowing quite to whom I am speaking. For these cadets – these elite members of the Akademie – are important in their own right, not to speak of their fathers. For the Akademie is where power is bred in this land and at this time. They are taught here how to rule. And the Doktor . . .

The Doktor is the most powerful man of all, for he is the shaper of these powerful young demi-gods. Yes, and in more than one sense.

We walk on, the two boys flanking me, their curiosity kept in check. They want to ask me why I'm there – what has gone wrong this time, and who it affects – only the strict rules of the Akademie insist that the Doktor's business is his alone, until – and if – he should wish to share it.

We pass through a massive – almost medieval – gateway, the ten-metre-high thick wooden doors pushed back, past a row of blue-uniformed guards and into the massive entrance hallway, its cerulean blue domed ceiling a good fifty metres above my head, the twin eagles – symbol of Germany throughout the ages – displayed in giant mosaic on the perfectly circular floor.

Power. It all speaks of imperial power. Of a brute strength that, in its way, is as sharp-eyed and ruthless as the eagles of its chief motif.

I know my way, yet I let them lead me, up the broad, curved marble stairway to the left and into a corridor built, like all else, in the imperial style, wide and high-ceilinged, with massive pillars to either side.

We march with almost military precision to the end of that corridor where, framed by imposing pillars and a lintel of heroic proportions, a studded, leather-faced door of equally massive size faces us, two guards stood before it, dwarfed by the portal they defend. Unwavering they stand there, as, above the lintel, a camera eye turns to study me.

And then a voice sounds. 'Meister Scholl. Please come in.'

If he is surprised, his voice does not betray it, and, as the guards step aside and the giant door swings slowly back, so I turn briefly and give the slightest nod of thanks to the two young cadets, knowing I will doubtless see them again.

The Doktor's study is huge. Tall shelves of books fill every wall.

His massive desk and equally imposing leather chair are a good twenty paces from the door, beside a window that would grace a cathedral, which offers him a view down on to the main quadrant.

I walk slowly across, and as I come closer, so he rises from that great nest of a chair and, unsmiling, comes round the desk to greet me, his hand outstretched. I grip it and bow, then step back.

'Herr Doktor.'

'I was expecting you,' he says. 'For the fifth read the third, eh?'

And, when I look up and meet his pale grey eyes, I see that my early arrival has merely confirmed what he believes of the Ministry: we are little more than petty bureaucrats; an irritation rather than a threat.

'So?' he says, pointing to a chair facing his own, one which in its starkness, its simplicity and sheer *smallness* serves to emphasise – if emphasis is needed – the disparity in status between he and me. 'What is it *this* time?'

I go to the chair and, waiting for him to resume his own seat, squat uncomfortably on its edge.

'Forgive me, Herr Doktor, but it is a matter of some delicacy. There have been reports. Anonymous reports, I hasten to say, and unconfirmed as yet. But the Ministry would be seen to be failing in its duty if—'

He interrupts. 'Reports of *what*?' And the steel in his voice – the contrast with his polite, if unsmiling greeting – is stark. The Doktor is, surprisingly, a small man. If he is five six, then that's flattering him. And he's bald, too, and portly. But commanding. There's no doubt of that. Like Napoleon, he commands the very air about him.

I hesitate. 'I would rather not say. As I said, it is a matter of extreme delicacy and—'

'Bugger delicacy! Have we another damn traitor in our midst?'

I am silent, as if considering what to say, and, impatient now, the Doktor rises from his chair and, pressing his hands palm down on the edge of his desk, glares at me angrily.

'*Well?*'

'An accusation of this nature—'

'There! I knew it! Some worthless *klatsch* opening their *unterentwickelt* mouth and spreading foul rumours about one of my lads! *They're* the ones you should be investigating, not us!'

I note the word he used: '*unterentwickelt*'. Underdeveloped. It is one of the foulest insults one can offer a man in this society.

'Forgive me,' I say, lowering my eyes and – as I've practised often in preparation for this role – adopting a pedantic, bureaucratic mode, 'but the rules of the inspection must be followed to the letter. I would dearly like to share such information with you, Herr Doktor, yet to even hint at the true nature of the accusations could, as we know from experience, do irreparable damage to the young man concerned.'

The Doktor sighs heavily, then sits. 'So what you're saying is that you want to interview them *all*, is that it?'

'Not *all*, Herr Doktor. A random sample will do.'

'Random as in *including* our so-called traitor?'

'Of course.'

'You know this is our busiest time, with the examinations coming up?'

'It cannot be helped, Herr Doktor. Were it not so important a matter . . .'

He takes an exasperated breath, then, speaking so politely that it seems rude, 'So what will you require?'

'A room, with a bed and a desk.'

And I know, without fear of contradiction, that it will be the smallest room the Doktor can find, with the shabbiest desk and the most uncomfortable bed. For we are enemies, when it comes down to it, the Ministry and the Akademie, and the Doktor

461

resents our intrusion even as he grudgingly acknowledges the necessity.

'It will be as you wish,' he says, and I smile and thank him and rise from that small, uncomfortable chair and, with a parting bow, leave the great man's presence, pleased to have cleared the first hurdle unscathed.

296

The room is small and bleak, a monk's cell, reminiscent of a dungeon, the walls bare, the bed unmade – rough sheets, a thin blanket and a single pillow stacked neatly on the thin, unsprung mattress. The desk is smaller than I could have imagined – barely large enough to work on – while in the corner stands my case.

I turn to the boy – an eight-year-old – who escorted me and nod. 'This will be fine. Thank the Doktor for me.'

The thought of thanking the Doktor clearly terrifies the boy, but charged with this duty, he bows low and scurries away with almost indecent haste.

They know, I think. Already rumours are circulating from boy to boy, their speculation fuelled by a distinct absence of fact.

Indeed, there is no fact, for this investigation, like my presence there, is a complete fraud: an imaginary peg on which to hang an imaginary coat. But it will suffice. It will allow me access, and access is what I need.

Access to Kolya's mother. For she is here. I have only to find her.

Shutting the door, I walk over to my case and, lifting it, place it on the bed. Crouching, I study the lock, relieved to see that it's untouched, the smear-seal untampered with. Then, taking the pulse-key from my pocket, I touch it and the mechanism springs open with a double-click.

There's an unused notepad, made, like everything else, of my DNA, together with a detailed list – running to eighteen pages – of the students at the Akademie. Beneath those are a single change of clothes and a basic dictionary of twenty-fourth-century *ge'not*. Tucked into a pocket at the side is a detailed map of the locality and, in a small, sealed box, are various drugs. Right at the bottom – and it's the bulkiest item by far – is the file on Kolya, which I've yet to properly look at. And other, personal things, Katerina's pendant among them.

Five days, I'm giving myself. Time enough, I hope, to find some clue as to who Kolya is and why he's doing what he's doing.

I remove the notepad and the list and place them on the desk, then fasten the case again and slide it beneath the bed. Then I make the bed and, that done, go to the door and call for the guard.

The man comes at once, bowing low before me. 'Master?'

'Where do I wash?'

He shows me and I shower. But, returning to my cell, it is to find a stranger there – an adult, not a boy, wearing a meister's robe.

'You'll need a chair,' he says, before I can ask his name. 'I guess you didn't ask for one.'

And he smiles, which confuses me, because he seems so unlike his superior, the Doktor, and yet so similar.

'I forgot,' I say, 'Herr . . .'

'Haushofer,' he says, offering his hand. 'Klaus Haushofer. And before you ask, I've been assigned to you as your liaison officer.'

He seems on the surface of things a pleasant man, his charm expressed physically in the soft roundness of his face, the bluff ordinariness of his features. He seems a man without airs. Only this is an age of 'airs', of precise – one might say *exact* – social placement, and I wonder just how real his jovial nature is.

He looks about him and shakes his head disapprovingly. 'No, no. This won't do. They take the Doktor's instructions far too literally. Something basic, he said. But this isn't basic, this is spartan.' And again he looks to me and smiles. 'I'll arrange something. But tell me, are you hungry?'

Which is why, five minutes later, I find myself in the refectory, beneath a high ceiling of ancient wooden beams, several hundred students seated at tables nearby, as Haushofer arranges for a servant – a mute, I note – to bring us our meals.

He is sat beside me, leaning in towards me conspiratorially as he speaks in a half whisper. 'I would have taken you to the masters' dining room, only I thought you might like to see how the boys live. Get an idea of how social – how *regimented* – their lives really are.'

And so it seems, for there is very little noise, very little of the boisterous behaviour one might expect from such a large gathering of young men. Oh, there is talk at the nearby tables – mostly, I should think, of who I am and what in Urd's name I could be investigating – but it is restrained, *kept within limits*.

I turn and look about me, conscious of how uniform they all look. Some have black hair, some red, but the predominant colour is ash blond, cut in the same close-to-the-head style, like the brother knights.

Eyes meet mine briefly and look quickly away, for they know who I am and what power I might have over their lives. Only they don't look scared. Hostile is what they look, like a family having to put up with an unwelcome guest.

Haushofer is watching me, even as he chews his bread. He smiles, then nods to indicate the insignia on my arm.

'You're not one of the Bremen crew, then?'

I could take exception to that word, '*crew*'. It is, after all, a kind of slur on my profession, only I sense that that's perhaps what he wants. To exude friendliness while sniping at me all the while. I let the insult pass.

'No, I'm from Breslau, actually. And before you ask, I've not been sent because of any local connection. We take turns to investigate such matters. It prevents *favouritism*.'

There! A tiny dig back. A suggestion – if only slight – that they might try to influence things here at the Akademie. To use their connections to pull strings.

And what connections they have. Why, there is barely a senior official in the whole of Greater Germany who has not passed through the Akademie.

But Haushofer does not react. Unless his smile is a reaction, which I doubt. His tactic, it seems, is to be as pleasant to me as possible – to seem to be my friend, to act informally in my company, and by that means to elicit information. Only it won't work. Because I *haven't* any information. And because I'm not here to play *his* games. I'm here to find Kolya.

To that end, I study the women who are working behind the counter. As far as I know, Kolya's mother wasn't a cook or a serving woman, yet what we know of her is sufficiently vague to make it worth my while to check. Haushofer notices the direction of my glance and, leaning closer, asks me if I would like one of them sent to my room.

I don't answer, merely stare back at him, and after a moment he shrugs, as if it is my loss, and I begin to understand just how they operate here.

Corrupt, yes. Of course they are corrupt. Because power *is* corrupt. And what they teach here – what they live and breathe and, so it seems, *eat* here – is power.

When the meal comes, I eat in silence, letting Haushofer make the small talk. I learn he has a wife and two sons, oh, and a daughter. He almost forgets the daughter, for what use is a daughter in a world such as this, except to be a *hausfrau* and bear children? *Male* children, preferably. And little by little I come to hate the man with an intensity that I daren't show, even though I know he expresses merely the common opinions of his age.

Mechanist opinions. Views from a Mechanist world.

Yes. But what do I mean by that?

Mechanism is the philosophy of this age. It is a belief that destiny is genetic. That individuals are not important of themselves, only as an 'expression' of race. Just as each separate gene is integral to the chromosome of which it is a part, so each individual, they argue, is integral to the race. For the Mechanists, people are simply gene-machines, to be fine-tuned and brought towards the 'median', which is the ultimate goal.

That fine-tuning begins within the womb, and continues throughout childhood and, in some cases, through to old age. For some, like the early Guildsmen, it involves physical alteration – the beginning of that painful system of surgical adaptation that finds its final flowering, if it can be called such, in the twenty-eighth century. For most, however, it is a slow and complex process of genetic 'shaping'. Of modest alterations to what is already – as they see it – good genetic stock. Aryans, of course, for we are talking eugenics here, after all. And here, at the Akademie, we are at the very epicentre of that process. Here, in the Herr Doktor's skilful hands, young men of promise are engineered into perfect specimens of the *volk*, shaped both in mind and essence. *Enhanced*, as the terminology would have it, their chromosomes cleaned up.

And while the men are bred for excellence, the women are bred to produce more men, the best men they can. That, according to the Mechanists, is their role in this life. As it was under Hitler. As it is – and I recognise the flaw – in Four-Oh. The German way, you might say. Not *Mother* Russia but . . . the *Father*land.

Only now, with girls of my own, I have a different view.

I push my plate aside and am about to take a sip from my glass when an alarm begins to sound – a pulsing buzz that has an immediate effect on the boys. As one they rise and, in a silent, orderly fashion begin to troop out of that great hall. Haushofer touches my arm, and we make our way out too, the boys giving way to us. Out into the great open space of the main quadrant where already the boys are lining up in their years and classes, boys and masters spilling out into the sunlight in a leisurely yet businesslike manner.

As Haushofer and I walk across, I look about me, seeing how the surrounding buildings go up into the sky, tier after white sunlit tier, like gigantic steps leading up to Heaven. All except the building behind us – the administrative building, from which we've just emerged – which squats beneath the others, topped by its huge, almost Byzantine dome.

We climb a short flight of steps that leads up on to the raised stage-like area, joining the massed ranks of the masters. As we do, I look up, beyond the long ranks of boys, to the great leaded window in the far building, and see the unmistakable figure of the Doktor, standing beside his desk, looking out over the scene.

The alarm pulses and pulses and then stops.

The Doktor turns abruptly and leaves the window, emerging a moment later at the top of a set of broad marble steps that lead down into the quadrant. As he does, so total silence falls.

He moves slowly yet purposefully between the ranks, a small man, dwarfed by these fine specimens of German youth, yet there is an authority to his manner that is unmistakable. As he joins us on the platform, every eye is on him, every one of us in that quadrant waiting to hear what he, the Doktor, will say.

I watch him from a distance of no more than ten feet, and see the pride that's in his eyes as he surveys his protégés: four thousand of them in all, from the vulnerable-looking, almost babyish six-year-olds to the eighteen-year-olds, whose confidence and physical perfection makes them seem like statues turned to flesh.

There's a long pause, while he surveys his domain, and then he turns and looks to me and, to my horror, puts out an arm to indicate my presence. And in that instant I realise that all of this has been contrived for this purpose – so that the Doktor can address me, publicly, before the whole Akademie.

'Gentlemen,' he says, his voice booming across that packed space. 'As you know, we have a guest from the Ministry staying with us for a day or so. Herr Scholl. *Inspector* Scholl, should I say. I just want to take this opportunity of asking you all to cooperate fully with the Inspector while he's here. After all, we have nothing to hide.'

It's hard to convey the disdain with which he utters those final words, only it surprises me that laughter – mocking laughter – doesn't follow. But there is only silence. Conscious that every eye is on me now, I bow low, as if the Doktor has somehow praised me, yet I know that I make the gesture only because I am at a loss this once, and that some kind of response is called for.

For a moment the Doktor's steely gaze remains fixedly on me, and then he turns away and, lifting his hands, claps them once, at which signal the boys turn and begin to file back into their buildings, as if this has all been rehearsed.

Which no doubt it has.

I turn and look to Haushofer and find him watching me thoughtfully.

'Okay,' he says quietly. 'Your room should be ready now.'

297

Haushofer is as good as his word. My new room is bigger and better furnished than the last, only there's one snag: it's situated in the servants' quarters, directly above the kitchens, which means that not only is there noise, all day and a good part of the night, but that everything in the room is permeated by a stale cooking smell.

It is another insult, of course, and not a subtle one, but I ignore it. Besides, poor as my quarters are, they are – though Haushofer doesn't know it – perfectly situated. Where better, after all, to begin my search for Kolya's mother?

Haushofer leaves me, surprised that I'm content. There's no lock on my door, but my case is locked and I can't believe any of the servants would intrude, and so I decide to tour the servants' quarters.

Walking down the great stairwell I am glanced at by passing servants, but nothing more. They can see who I am, and assume I am on official business. And so I am, in a sense. Serving the *volk*.

And when you find her?

I'm not sure what I'll do. Question her, probably. Find out what she knows of Kolya and his father. If she'll talk. But that's where the drugs come in, to *make* her talk. If she's reluctant.

And then?

The object, I guess, is to kill him. Time-dead. Only if he's as clever as Schikaneder claims he is, then that might prove more than a little difficult.

I go from corridor to corridor, up stairs and down, looking in rooms and nodding to myself, as if satisfied. Only there's no one who resembles her. But then, as I'm about to give up and go back to my room, I glance out of a window and think I see her, walking slowly across a courtyard between buildings, carrying a pile of fresh white linen. Yet even as I make my way towards the door, about to pursue her, the two young men who first greeted me out on the great marble pathway – Gunsche and Sanger, I have learned – appear as if from nowhere and, intercepting my course, beg me to accompany them. Haushofer, it seems, needs to see me again, to discuss something.

And so, leaving my quarry, I go with them, not without looking back – in time to see her disappear beyond a door that's swinging closed.

Kolya's mother, blithely unaware of her own significance in Time, carrying my nemesis in her belly.

298

Haushofer's room is close to his master's, the Doktor's – within hailing distance certainly – and I notice that even though he wishes to talk to me 'in confidence', his door remains open, no doubt to answer any summons from the great man.

Right now, Haushofer sits at his desk, signing some papers. On the wall behind him hang three portraits, the President, the Guild Master and the King, the last of which depicts that same long-limbed and pale, despairing creature I last saw four centuries from now, encased in glass.

King in name alone, I think, wondering what Haushofer would make of where that particular genetic experiment would lead. That is, to Manfred and the *Adel*. And I find myself feeling sorry that I won't have a chance of meeting Manfred's ancestor, because it might have been interesting to learn just what it felt like to be the first of such a line.

Gunsche and Sanger leave, having delivered me, but not before I glimpse an exchanged look between them, a kind of smirk. I ought, perhaps, to be above it all, but I find that their arrogance – their naïve assumption of superiority – gets under my skin, and I decide, even before Haushofer has said a word, that the two boys will be on my list of interviewees.

'Well,' he begins, pushing the papers away and sitting back lazily in his chair, his fingers laced together behind his neck, 'now that you've settled in, I thought we'd have a word about procedure.'

'Procedure?'

'Yes. As you intimated to the Doktor, this is a delicate business and we'd prefer it if we could make it as minimally disruptive as possible. The Doktor suggests – only suggests, mind – that twenty boys be chosen, from a range of years.'

'It is our usual practice—'

'—to question more than that, I know. Only there have been a number of recent investigations and they have had the effect of . . . *unsettling* the boys. Of undermining them, one might almost say. And not *just* the boys. The families, too, have been affected. The stress of having their children under suspicion.'

'There is only one boy under suspicion—'

Haushofer raises a hand, palm outward, in a conciliatory fashion. 'I understand that, Herr Scholl, only we have had to use our not inconsiderable influence to prevent some of the parents taking the matter up directly with the Ministry. Now, you and I are both realists, Otto. We understand that the relationship between Ministry and Akademie is, well, let us say *strained* and leave it at that. But I feel it would be in both our interests to come to some more *amicable* arrangement.'

I almost laugh, because Haushofer wants to make some kind of deal, and, though he doesn't know it, I am the last person he ought to be approaching, fake that I am. But I can't tell him that. I have to act as if I *do* have influence, however small. That is, until I have what I've come here for.

I lean forward slightly. 'You talk of *undermining*, Herr Haushofer. Have you ever thought what would happen if we acted as you suggest and accommodated such . . . deals? It would be chaos. Germany would rot and fall. And then what? Where would the

Akademie be then? No, Herr Haushofer, we must not relax our standards one iota, nor for a single second. It is our duty. To the race. To the *volk*.'

Haushofer sighs, then changes his tack. 'You have a list?'

'A list?'

'Of the boys you wish to speak to.'

'I will provide it. Tomorrow, first thing.'

'Good. But Otto . . . be careful how you tread.'

I look surprised. 'I am safe here, no?'

The question takes him aback. 'Of course. I wasn't suggesting . . .' He pauses, then, leaning closer, says. 'It is not the Akademie you have to fear, Inspector, but, well, as I hinted before, there are those who feel that the Ministry is exceeding its authority . . . being too zealous.'

I am curt, my voice cold. 'The powers of the Ministry are granted by the President himself.'

'Yes, yes, but—'

'But nothing,' I say, standing, bringing the discussion to a close. 'Now forgive me, I must begin my preparations.'

Only back in my room I find myself pondering what Haushofer said. It wasn't clear, but he seems to be suggesting that a group of influential men – men with sons at the Akademie – are, in some fashion, plotting against the Ministry. How that affects me I'm not sure, but it might be best to find out a little more. To jump back to Four-Oh and find out what we know. Only I'm not going to try to kid myself that that's the real reason. I want to go back because I need to know what Ernst has to say. Whether Cherdiechnost is safe, and Katerina . . . I stand, then look about me. The case lies open on the bed. I ought to close it, perhaps and lock it, only I'll not be gone more than a few seconds.

Maria is on duty at the platform, filling in for Zarah. She tells me that Freisler wants to see me, and that he's in Hecht's old rooms.

Freisler looks across at me as I step through. With the lights up bright, the room looks very strange – so bare and bleak, despite the shelves of books. The Tree of Worlds seems dull and pale, the vaguest presence in the air. Its natural medium, I realise, is darkness.

Freisler is not alone. Two of our younger agents – Haller and Ripke – are there with him in the back room, filling plastic crates with Hecht's belongings. Seeing me, they pause and bow their heads respectfully, reminding me yet again that I am Meister now.

'What are you doing?'

'It's your room now,' Freisler answers, coming to the doorway. 'We were preparing it for you. The books . . . you must tell us what you wish to keep. If you want, we can—'

I interrupt. 'Has Ernst been back?'

Haller and Ripke look away, busying themselves with their work. Freisler nods, then comes across. 'He came back an hour past,' he says quietly. 'I saw him myself. He said all was well. *Peaceful*, he said.'

'Where is he? Can I speak to him?'

'It's okay. He went back. To keep an eye. He said he would jump back directly if anything was wrong.'

'Ah . . .' The flood of relief is incredible. I feel lighter suddenly, less burdened.

Reaching out I briefly touch Freisler's arm. 'Thank you. But listen. I need to be briefed. About the political situation back where I am. I need . . .'

And I tell him what I need. And Freisler nods and says he'll get on to it right away. Then, reminding me, he asks, 'The books?'

I look about me, remembering how they were arranged, in four distinct sections. 'Keep everything that's pertinent. That might be of use. The discarded timelines . . . send those to the library. No, to the linguists, they'll have more use of them.'

'As you wish, Meister.'

'And Jurgen . . . keep an eye on Ernst for me, will you?'

'Of course, Meister. Now let's see if we can't get you that information you need.'

299

As I stand on the platform, waiting to jump back, I find myself thinking about Hecht and the Haven, and wondering whether I'll have a chance, once this is over, to go there.

That is, if I can get there. If Zarah knows how.

And even if we can't . . . surely Hecht's brother will know enough to contact us, to jump here, maybe, and lead us back. Or is he dead, too? Was that where it happened? Back in the distant past, among the Neanderthal?

But this is unhealthy speculation. I clear my mind and signal to Maria. And then I jump. Back to my empty room in 2343.

Only it's not empty. Even as I materialise, I see a figure there – male, bulky, definitely one of Kolya's 'brothers' – crouched over my case. But before I can reach out and grasp him, before I can leap on him or swing a punch, he is gone and I am alone in the room again.

I sit down on the edge of the bed, shaken by the encounter. Because it's like Hecht said before he died. Kolya seems to know everything. It's like he knew precisely when I wouldn't be there, and exactly how long he had. And that's impossible.

No. It really *is* impossible.

Only he's done it somehow . . .

It makes me think of some tiny insect, crouched upon the back of a much larger beast, its feeding tube sunk deep into the flesh of its victim, whose sheer bulk makes it unable to turn and see its tormentor, let alone strike back. That's how this feels. Like Kolya's behind us all the while, on our back, sucking away at us. Only why? What has *caused* all of this?

Because there has to be a cause. Even in a fucked-up, non-sequential medium like Time, there still has to be a cause. Something to set it all off. Because nothing happens in a vacuum. Absolutely nothing.

I stand above the case, looking blankly down at it, still stunned by what's happened. I know what he's taken without needing to look. The Kolya file. And it strikes me – especially in view of what Schikaneder told me – that we've done Kolya's work for him: traced all of his direct-line ancestors and saved him the bother. Only this once *sequence* would seem to work against him, because he had taken his ancestors out of history *before* we found them.

Only, I recall, we *didn't* find them. It was their absence that alerted us, not their presence.

So is that what he's doing? Defending his own personal time-line throughout Time, using his 'expendable selves' to do so?

It seems the most likely scenario? But why? Who is he defending himself against?

Not against us, I'm sure. The Russians, then? Maybe. Only I'm not sure how I'm going to find that out.

I close the case and lock it, then sit there on the bed, staring into space, trying to come up with something – an explanation, a first cause, a reason for this madness.

But nothing. What Kolya is doing makes no sense at all.

And I realise that I've been here before, at this impasse with logic – back when I was crossing northern Russia with Katerina, making my way with her to Moscow and the odious Nevsky. Then, too, it made no sense. Instinct alone got me through. And even then, I had to die. And I know for a certainty that it's all linked in. That the agents coming back from the future, Reichenau, Kolya and my death – and maybe Hecht's death, too – are all part of the same complex loop. And strangely, the linking of it all comforts me, because, though it makes no sense right now, I know – at that moment – that it will. When I know enough. When all the pieces fit. When all the loose ends are traced and tied.

And for the first time that day I smile, remembering what Freisler said. That Katerina is okay. And, smiling, I jump back to Four-Oh. Only to see Old Schnorr this time, to pick his brains about this latest twist.

300

But what Meister Schnorr has to say only makes me fearful once again.

'I know,' he says, when I tell him about the stranger in my room and the stolen file.

'You *know*?'

'Yes, he sent me a note.'

And just the way he says it makes me sit up straighter, as if I'm about to be given bad news.

'Go on.'

'It seems he's tired of my young men poking about in the past. He's begun to hurt them. The note . . .' Old Schnorr swallows, a sour expression on his face. 'He had it branded into Horst's back. Two of his "brothers" cut Horst's shirt from his back and held him down while Kolya applied the iron.'

'Why didn't Horst jump?'

'They'd drugged him. Questioned him thoroughly. Then Kolya sent him back.'

'Sent him back?'

'Horst didn't jump. He couldn't have done. He passed out. And we didn't bring him back, so . . .'

I give a shivering breath. 'So what are you going to do?'

'I'm going to do precisely what Kolya's asked me to do, and back off. I don't want any more of my boys hurt. That is . . . if that's okay with you, Otto?'

'Of course. But why has Kolya suddenly taken this tack?'

Old Schnorr removes his glasses and wipes them. 'Obviously he needed us to find out the information in the file. But he's got that now, and I guess he doesn't want us snooping around any more. We've served our use.'

'What if we ignore him? What if I send agents in? Maybe try to snip off the line at some point?'

'You could try. But my guess is that he'd anticipate that. Somehow he knows what we're going to do before we do it.'

Again, it's impossible. He can't know that. Unless . . .

'He's upriver,' I say, suddenly certain of it. 'He's sitting up ahead of us in Time and responding to our moves as we make them. He doesn't know *before* us, it only looks that way from where we are. He's making changes retrospectively. Twisting time to suit himself.'

'Maybe,' Schnorr says, 'but how does that help us if we're stuck back here in the present?'

'I don't know. But Zarah said something about our agents – German agents – coming back from up the line. If we can make contact with them somehow . . .'

I know. It sounds vague even to my ears. But I recall that moment back in the room in 2343, and the feeling of certainty I felt – about all the pieces falling together slowly – and I know that has to mean something. Kolya isn't invincible, after all. He's not a god. And even if it seems like he has the jump on us at every turn, there must be a way of catching him out. He must have a weakness. Everyone has a weakness.

Only I have no plan, and as Meister that's bad, because they're all looking to me for a plan – a way of proceeding. I look to Old Schnorr and shake my head.

'I don't know,' I say. 'I . . . I just don't know.'

'Then go back. Finish what you were doing. If it's in the loop, it'll have meaning.'

Now that does make sense. *If* it's in the loop.

'You think there's something there to find?'

Old Schnorr shrugs. 'Meister Hecht thought there was.'

Maybe. Only towards the end Hecht seemed far from focused.

'What if I find her?' I ask. 'Do I kill her? Do you think he'd let me kill her?'

'I doubt it. But that's your call, Otto. *If* you find her.'

301

And so I return again, to my room in 2343. Only I don't sleep well. At the back of my mind I'm half convinced that Kolya is going to jump in there while I'm asleep and slit my throat, only I know he won't, if only because I've yet to have my children – yet to spend all of that time at Cherdiechnost. I'm *guaranteed* that time, and so I'll live through this. Or so I read it. But when finally I get some sleep, I'm plagued by dreams, and by one nightmare in particular where I'm back in Cherdiechnost, at night. Nevsky is there, hauling an empty cart – the same cart as held Katerina and my corpses – smiling at me toothlessly, while he points to a painted wooden sign that reads 'Krasnogorsk, 1000 verst.'

So that I wake, sheened in sweat, even as the dawn peeks through the curtains at my window.

Haushofer greets me gruffly. He looks like he too had a bad night, and when I hand him my list, his temper worsens.

'Sanger! You can't pick Sanger! Sanger's father is Minister of the Interior!'

'I know that.'

'Then you'll choose someone else. Some other boy.'

'But I want to question Sanger.'

'It's out of the question.'

'What if Sanger's my suspect?'

Haushofer stares at me in shock. 'You mean . . .'

'No. I *don't* mean. Only I must have free access to everyone. There can be no exceptions. It doesn't matter whose father is who. If you wish, we can take this matter up with the Ministry directly.'

It's not what I want – in fact, it's the very last thing I want, because if they start asking who I am we're in trouble, but Haushofer doesn't know that. He's silent a moment, and then he stands. 'But *Sanger* . . .'

'You have a room prepared?'

Haushofer hesitates, then nods. Some of his brash confidence has been knocked off him by my intransigence. 'I'll need a viewer. And a file on each of the boys. Medical files, too. Nothing kept back. We need to be *thorough*, after all.'

Haushofer glares at me. It's almost as if I've suggested something indecent. 'We will protest,' he says. '*Officially*.'

'Good,' I say, and stand. 'In triplicate, I hope.'

His eyes narrow, a certain hatefulness revealed in them now. 'You would do well not to make enemies, Herr Scholl.'

True. But not in the sense he means.

The room they have allocated me is in a building on the edge of the campus, overlooking woodland. It's a fairly standard room, with an old-fashioned blackboard running the length of one wall and maps and portraits of various historical figures – Arminius, Barbarossa, Frederick, Bismarck, Hitler and Gelthardt – suggesting to me that they teach history here normally.

I've had the room cleared – all but for a single desk and two chairs. On the desk are my files and a 'viewer', which will allow me to read and interpret the genetic indents on the boys' necks. Much is made of this in the Ministry, and if what I'm doing here's to be accepted as standard procedure, then I need to comply. Besides, I find it all rather interesting, for these people believe with an almost absolute faith that what is encoded in your genes determines who you are and what you'll be. Ironic, considering the tampering that's done here at the Akademie. The *enhancing*, should I say. For it's also a belief in some quarters that money – and power, of course – can make up for certain genetic . . . *deficiencies*, we'll call them.

The Akademie, so I'm reliably told, has become expert at papering over such genetic 'cracks' and making the best of 'substandard' genetic stock. In other words, of making sure that certain bloodlines – certain families – remain in power.

A new twist on a very old tale, you might think. And rightly so.

The boys – six of them for this morning's session – are sitting in the anteroom next door, waiting on my summons. Haushofer is with them, sitting facing them, as if to remind them by his stern and unrelenting demeanour just how they ought to behave. Seeing them thus, as I passed through the room, it struck me that I have seen few smiles and little laughter since I've been here, as if the seriousness of the business of the Akademie – the manufacture of perfect servants for the State – does not permit any element of joviality or fun. The boys are like patients, to be cured of any 'sickness' of triviality they might possess. To be honed and sharpened and finally released, tools to be used by Greater Germany.

No wonder some of them break.

And I know to an extent just how they feel, for it was how we too – we who survived the dark times and were raised in the Garden and in Four-Oh – have been nurtured. Raised to duty. Raised to believe that it was genetics that distinguished us from those lesser men who did not survive. Raised to consider ourselves an elite, supremely talented, the natural end of all the universe's striving. As if nothing would come after us. As if we were *it*, the pinnacle.

I examine the first of the files, them, clearing my throat, call out the name. 'Stefan Kaunitz.'

Kaunitz is twelve but tall for his age, dark-haired and fine-featured. As he appears at the door and bows to me, I stand.

'Close the door and come across.'

He seems nervous – as well he might – but his social training covers it well. When he sits, he sits with a straight back and a raised chin, and his grey eyes meet mine unflinchingly. I almost smile. He would make a fine *Reisende*.

'Stefan. You understand that this interview will be completely confidential, and that whatever you say here will be between you and the Ministry alone?'

'Yes, Meister.'

'Good. Then relax a little. My questions cannot harm you, not if you have been true to the Fatherland.'

There's the smallest movement of the head, almost a nod, but Kaunitz doesn't relax. If anything he seems more tense. His eyes flick to the viewer and then back to mine.

'Your father,' I say, not even glancing at my notes. 'His work means that he travels a great deal, no? Have you ever travelled with him?'

'Sometimes,' he answers quietly. 'In the summer months.'

'And does he confide in you? Tell you what he's doing and why?'

This time Kaunitz hesitates before answering. 'Sometimes.'

'There's nothing wrong with that. Fathers *should* confide in their sons. But what you learn . . . do you keep that to yourself?'

'Of course, Herr Scholl.'

I nod. 'Good. And friends. Do you have any close friends outside of the Akademie? People from home, perhaps?'

'My brother,' he begins. 'Only he's here at the Akademie, too. But when we're home . . .'

He stops, as if he's said too much.

'Go on.'

'We hunt together.'

'Ah, good. And are you a good huntsman?'

'My father considers me so.'

Looking at the boy, I can imagine it. They probably own a large estate – it's not in the boy's file – with woods and ancient tracks. Stocked, no doubt, with the latest products of the Reich's labs. Beasts that died out centuries back and have been genetically re-created: black bear and wolf and wild boar. Creatures that are embedded deep in the Germanic psyche.

'Your sisters?'

'Yes, Herr Scholl?'

'Do you like them? Do you have much to do with them when you're at home?'

I can see by the puzzlement on his face that this isn't the kind of question he was expecting, but I am intrigued by this young man. If I *have* to question him – and I must if I'm to maintain my cover here and buy myself the time to find Kolya's mother – then I might as well satisfy my own curiosity.

His eyes look inward momentarily, troubled by something. 'We ... see one another rarely. I'm here most of the time and, well, they have their duties in the household, and . . .'

He falls silent, as if he has said enough, and in a way he has. I understand young Kaunitz, for there was a time when I was much like him and would not have questioned how things are, only I wonder how a whole race can function in this fashion, denying half of its own living being, emphasising only one facet of its dual nature.

'I need to look at you now,' I say. 'If you would come round and stand beside the viewer.'

Kaunitz does as he's told, and for a time I am silent, examining segments of the indent's code and jotting down my observations.

I am not trained for this, of course. It is a subtle skill and while I can get by – I know my genetics, after all – what I glean from the exercise is barely worth knowing. He's healthy and will live long, providing he avoids the assassin's bullet. For this age, no less than any other, has its terrorists and trouble-makers. Its dissenters.

'Good,' I say finally. 'Be seated.'

Kaunitz waits as I finish writing, and when I look up at him again, his eyes seem less defensive than they were. He thinks it's almost over, and were I interviewing him in earnest, this is when I would ask my most damning questions. Now, when he's most vulnerable and least on his guard. But I am done with Kaunitz. There's nothing wrong with the boy. In any age he'd be a fine young man. It is the system, not him, that's at fault, even if the poor boy cannot help but be part of it.

So it was under the Nazis.

I dismiss Kaunitz, then, feeling I need something less anodyne, decide to spice up my morning. Walking over to the door, I glance at Haushofer, then, pointedly turning away from him, face the eldest of those seated there.

'Gerhardt Sanger. Come. It's your turn now.'

303

It is late evening before I return to the room above the kitchens. I'm mentally tired and know I've put too much into the sessions. But, fake as they were, it was hard not to. Hard to buck my own nature and do only half a job.

Fifteen interviews I managed. One third of those scheduled, and some of them – like those for Sanger and Gunsche – really hard work. Sanger I found particularly difficult, because, I suspect, he wrong-footed me at one point. I asked about his mother, and his face changed, as if I was deliberately taunting him. Anger flashed in his eyes.

'My mother's dead! If you read the file you'd know that! They tried to kill my father, but they got her instead. Fragments of bone were all they found, along with what remained of the flier . . . Russians.'

The bitterness with which he said that final word remains with me even now. I apologised, of course. There was little else I could do. And while I still dislike the young man, I understand him a little better now. As all of them.

For that, more than anything, is what this day has turned out to be. A day of understanding. I find I have learned far more about this age in this one day of private interviews than I'd ever grasped by studying the histories. Observing these young men – seeing them struggle with the questions I slowly, bit by bit, devised for them; questions which challenged their conditioning – I finally came to terms with what, on a human level, this age is about.

Seated at my desk, looking out across the twilit courtyard down below, I find my mind making links across the ages. This 'new' scientific system of belief ... how does it differ from the old workings of Faith? In what respect do the two diverge?

In practical effects, not at all. Be they priests or geneticists, both exude a cast-iron certainty. They positively glow with belief, while their flock, be they 'lost souls' or 'gene-machines', display varying degrees of 'faith'. Some – those boys in the middle age range, particularly – are troubled that they don't believe enough – that they have vague, disquieting doubts. Can it really all be put down to blind chance and billions of years? Or is there some shaping force? Some conscious, underlying pattern to it all?

It's a curious reversal, and from such musings a new 'faith' will unfold in time. But not yet. Not for a century or more.

Changing tack, I think of why I'm really here. Of Kolya and what he's up to here. Kolya certainly knew what *I* was up to earlier, and that probably means he knows my every step while I'm here in 2343, even before I take it.

Yes, but I'm not going to let that stop me. Because this leads somewhere. To Krasnogorsk, certainly, but not only to there. And he can't know *everything* about me, surely? He can't know *every* single move I make. Because to do so he'd have to be in the room with me, watching me, seeing what I do.

The thought encourages me. Kolya may know the broad outline of events as far as I'm concerned, but he doesn't know the fine detail. And maybe Phil Dick was right. Maybe Kolya *was* angry that time because he knew I'd found a way to stop him killing me. Time-dead, that is.

But most of all I'm going to do this because I can't sit on my hands, and because they won't let me go where I most want to be: with Katerina and my girls.

So I'll find her, and kill him if I can. And if I can't, at least I'll know that for a fact. I will have tried.

I stand and turn, and as I do, I see that someone has slipped a note beneath the door. I walk across and pick it up, then fling the door open, but the corridor is empty. For all I know the note has lain there this last twenty minutes.

I unfold it and read.

'Meet me on the walkway above the labs at midnight.'

And that's it. It's not even signed. So it could be Kolya. Only I don't think it is.

Midnight is almost three hours off, and I'm of a mind to jump there straight away, to go in at a slight distance at five past midnight, and then – when I've seen who wants to meet me – to jump back here and then return naturally, by foot.

If it's safe. If it isn't Kolya.

304

So that's what I do. I slip out, moving unseen down darkened corridors, passing like a shadow across silent courtyards, down steps and out across moonlit lawns, until I find the place, located to the north of the main quadrant, between the massive rectangle of the labs and a long, windowless block. The walkway passes overhead, spanning the gap between the gym – which towers beyond the nearer buildings – and the fight school, concealed behind me, a long, straight length of softly lit *kunstlichestahl*, suspended eighty feet above the ground.

Looking about me, I quickly find the right spot, secluded on three sides, but giving a clear view of the walkway. Then, looking all about me, making certain that no one's watching, I jump: back first to Four-Oh, and then back again, to the same spot, only three hours further on.

And see myself, standing in the moonlight on the walkway overhead, waiting patiently for the author of the note, turning casually as a cloaked figure approaches from behind me to my right – from the direction of the fight school.

Coming closer, the figure stops, and for the next minute or two they exchange words. Then, suddenly, there's the faintest noise – a groaning, or maybe an animal lowing – and they both turn, looking down over the waist-high rail towards the labs.

I move forward a step, trying to see just what they're looking at, but as I do the wind blows up, rustling the leaves that surround me, and, unsettled, I turn to check there's no one there.

And when I look again they're gone.

I jump out, then jump back into the room above the kitchens, arriving the moment after I'd left, three hours back. And there I wait, until ten minutes to midnight.

305

I turn, watching the cloaked figure come towards me, just as I saw it from my hiding place below. They stop, giving the slightest bow, and I see that it's a young man.

'You came,' he says, and smiles. 'Good.'

Only he looks wrong. Too young, for a start, and too . . . open. Whoever he is, I'm pretty sure he doesn't work for Kolya.

'Who are you?'

'It doesn't matter. Let's just say I'm an intermediary. The thing is—'

'Did Kolya send you?'

'Kolya? Who's Kolya?'

'Then why are you here? Who sent you?'

He's about to answer, when a strange sound – a groaning – comes from below, from the direction of the labs. We both turn and go to the rail.

'What was that?'

'One of the prisoners.'

'Prisoners?'

There's a sudden gust of wind and he looks to me, his blue eyes flashing. 'There's a vent, above the room they're kept in. You hear them sometimes, especially at night, when it's silent. You want to see? I know the codes.'

'The codes?' I consider it, then nod.

I follow him, back along the walkway and down a long, twisting flight of metal steps. At the bottom a door.

He turns to me. 'Speak quietly. They'll be sedated, but . . . don't lean over the pens. That sets them off sometimes. They'll start braying, like dogs. And then the guards will come.'

He turns, facing the door squarely, and taps a code into the keypad. At once a beam of purple light flashes out, reading his 'indent'. A moment later the door irises open, and in we go, into a long, darkened room, the only light coming up from the 'strips' in the floor. I have a vague impression of work benches and of great, looming machines to the sides, against the windowless walls, but I've no time to stop and look.

My guide moves swiftly, unerringly across the floor, following one of the faintly lit strips, and I hurry to keep up with him.

On the far side there's another door. Again he taps in a code, again the light flashes out, scanning the indent. And in we go, into a brighter, much colder space, the ceiling lower than in the main laboratory. As the door hisses shut behind me, I take it all in at a glance. The room is about fifty yards square, the walls a glinting white, like porcelain. In the centre of the space, in neat rows, on small, island-like platforms, are the 'pens', though they look much more like giant baths, or sinks, with their chest-high porcelain sides. The light comes up from them in a soft, pale blue-white glow.

My guide touches my arm, then leads me out across the floor. I keep my voice low, like I'm in the presence of sleeping children.

'You said prisoners . . .'

'Political prisoners. Traitors, I'd guess you'd call them. The courts send them here. They used to execute them, but they've found a better use for them these days. The courts have ruled that they've no rights, you understand. Not even the right to breathe. So they end up here. The Doktor uses them for experiments. To teach the boys.'

'And you . . .?'

'Clean up after them. Wash out the pens.'

We stop beside the first of them and, careful not to lean over the thick, chest-high porcelain walls of the glowing pen, look in.

I don't know what I expected, but it isn't this. It's a young woman, shackled at both wrists and both ankles, chained there on her back on the cold white floor of the pen, naked and emaciated, her head shaved, dark flecks covering her almost translucently pale flesh.

'They've not started with this one yet,' he says, matter-of-factly. 'They don't normally. Not until they've assimilated.'

I look to him. 'What do you mean?'

'They starve them a while. And cut them. Little cuts, but painful. You see.' And he points to the flecks. 'The idea is to break them. Make them more compliant. That way it's easier.'

'Ah . . .' But I feel sick looking at her, imagining her as a child, cuddled up in her mother's arms; see her through a father's eyes – somebody's daughter – and weep inside at her fate. Whatever she did, it could not have deserved this.

'Are they all . . .?'

He looks to me, waiting for me to complete my sentence, but I can't. I've just seen what's in the pen beside hers. I walk across and, ignoring his warning, lean in, looking closer.

'*Doppelgehirn*,' he says, with what's almost an air of pride. 'They've almost perfected the technique.'

I swallow, then nod. I can see where they've joined the two skulls. The scars are fresh and raw, scabbed over, the stitches still in place. The skin is stretched tight across the bone, so that every vein is visible and raised, like a junkie's legs.

'I thought it would be more . . . sophisticated.'

He smiles. 'It is, generally. But the boys have to learn . . .'

I notice that there's the faintest trembling in the limbs. The creature's eyelids flicker in disturbed sleep, and then the body spasms and kicks, and then it groans: a long, low, animal lowing. The same sound we heard from up on the walkway.

'It takes a while to meld,' he says. 'The two brains. They fight at first. One has to be dominant, you see. You can't have both in charge. Hence the spasms, that faint trembling in the limbs. They all get that. Some never quite lose it. You see, that's where they fight it out – in the muscles. They both try and send signals to control the muscles. Each tries to colonise, if you like, different parts of the body. But only one can win.'

I look to him. 'Is this the only one?'

'No. There's seven of them in here right now. They've been trying to perfect the technique. The Doktor is very proud of what's been achieved these past few years.'

'Can I see the others?'

'Sure.'

None of them proves to be Reichenau, but it makes me feel that maybe this is where he came from. From this cold, underlit hall, and maybe even from this time.

Only how to find that out? Would there be records here?

'Have you seen enough?' he asks.

'Yes. Thank you.'

We go out, and as the door closes behind us, so I find myself shivering, part from the cold within, but also from the memory of the young woman.

It ought not to surprise me, yet it does. How often in the past, after all, has a civilising force depended on such barbarities?

I look to him again. 'Were you specifically asked to show me that?'

'Only if you wanted to.'

I take that in. So somebody *wanted* me to see, *wanted* me to make connections.

I'm about to ask him more, when he touches my arm again.

'Good,' he says. 'She's here. Come, quickly now, before we're seen.'

We cut across the grass, beneath the walkway, and as we come into the shadow of the facing building, so I see her, standing in the self-same spot I stood. A small, heavily pregnant woman with familiar eyes.

The *staritskii* is in my pocket. I could burn her before she said a word, before she had a chance to call out, and kill the living foetus. Only is it really Kolya there in her belly?

Just seeing her there makes me think this is a trick of some kind, or a trap. I look about me, expecting figures to materialise out of the air, only it's just us three, and as we stop before her, a little breathless from hurrying across the space, so my doubts grow.

Would Kolya have let me get this close?

I stare at her, searching her pale blue eyes, trying to see some sign of the madness that's in her son, but she seems just an ordinary woman, unaware of her significance to me.

'You came,' the young man says. 'I wasn't sure . . .' He looks to me. 'I was told only to bring you two together. I . . .'

'It's okay,' I say, slipping my hand into my pocket. 'I've only a few questions.'

She looks to the young man then looks back at me, clearly lost as to why she's there.

'The child, in your stomach, whose is it?'

She looks down sharply. 'I don't know . . .'

I don't believe her, but now she's here, I know I can find her any time I want. Go back to my room and jump back in. Waylay her and drug her and ask the question again, confident of an answer.

I reach out with my left hand and hold her chin, forcing her to look up at me. 'Do you have any other children?'

Her eyes resent my touch. 'One. A boy.'

I move my hand away. 'Can I meet him?'

She hesitates, then. 'Yes. But *he* comes. I don't trust you.'

'You don't . . .' I almost laugh.

But she's right not to trust me. After all, I could kill her in a second.

306

Her room is small and sparsely furnished, but I'm barely aware of it, because *he* is there. Kolya, I mean. Or if it isn't Kolya, it's his twin. Nine years old he is, and as he sits there on the bed, so his eyes watch me with a smouldering hatred that I can't explain nor understand. Has he always hated me? Or has he been taught to? *Schooled* to?

He looks past me at our guide. 'You can go now.'

And that, too, surprises me, for it's said with such authority that one might think that this ill-dressed child was a prince, born to rule.

The young man nods curtly and backs out, leaving us alone – the three of us. Me, Kolya, and Kolya's mother.

Then I was right not to shoot her . . .

He waits as she takes off her shawl and then settles in a chair in the corner. Then he focuses his attention once more on me.

'What do you want?'

'I want to know who you are.'

'I am Kolya.'

My hand rests on the *staritskii*, trembling slightly. A bead of sweat rolls slowly down my brow.

'Do you know who I am?'

He laughs coldly. 'You call yourself Scholl, but your real name is Behr. Otto Behr, and you are Meister of the Germans.'

I draw the gun, aim it at him.

'There,' he says, and smiles. 'What did I say? I *warned* me about you.'

And, even as the beam arcs across the room, he's gone, leaving only a searing after-image in the air, the sound of the woman screaming as I jump right out of there.

307

Back at Four-Oh I call a council of war.

The experience with the boy Kolya has shaken me. Once again he seemed to know precisely what I'd do and how I'd act. But it's not just that. It's the hatred in his eyes, the authority he exuded. As a father, I know just how angry – how dogmatic and petulant – a nine-year-old can be, but this wasn't that. What I saw in the boy was an arrogance born of certainty. An arrogance beyond *any* of the cadets at the Akademie.

What I saw was a boy who thinks himself almost god-like. Unafraid to face a laser. Smiling at death.

When we're gathered – and there are twelve of us this time, crowded into Hecht's room, the lights dimmed, the tree glowing in the semi-darkness – I put it to them bluntly.

'How exactly does he know? What is Kolya doing that allows him to anticipate our every move?'

One of the Elders, Meister Kempner, speaks first. 'He *knew* you were Meister? He *said* that?'

'Yes.'

'And who else knows that, apart from us?'

'Right now, nobody. But if he's looking back, from up the line . . .'

'Is that what you believe?' Zarah asks, from immediately to my left.

I turn and look at her. 'He must be. How else would you know what's yet to happen?'

Old Schnorr speaks up. 'Our friend, Schikaneder . . . you said to me that Kolya stole his journal.'

'Yes, but Schikaneder knows nothing about what's happening *now*.'

'True. Only think of the file we prepared. Kolya stole that. Maybe he's stolen other things. Memoirs written by one or other of us. Journals documenting these times in detail. Reports we've made.'

'It's a possibility,' I concede, 'if only because we know that's one of the ways he operates. But we still don't know why he's doing this, or what he's trying to achieve. I mean, why show himself to me, knowing that I'm armed, unless to taunt me in some way? To show me how powerless I am.'

Freisler speaks up. He sounds a little subdued. 'Is that what you think he's doing, Meister? Taunting you?'

I look across at him, thinking it strange to be addressed that way by him, even if it's my title now. 'I could have shot him, and he knew that.'

'Yes, but he would have changed it. He *knew* how you'd react.'

'Maybe.'

And maybe I've grown soft. Maybe those months at Cherdiechnost have taken off my edge. In the past I'd have shot the woman immediately she was in my sights, and thereby ended

Kolya. Far better that *she* should die than the *volk* be endangered by a madman.

'You should go back,' Zarah says. 'Go back and finish what you've started.'

'But it *is* finished.'

'Is it?' Freisler asks, leaning towards me, the Tree of Worlds reflected in his dark eyes.

'But Kolya's gone.'

'Has he? Meister Schnorr . . . tell us when the records say he was born.'

Old Schnorr smiles. 'April 2343.'

'You mean . . .?'

'What we mean,' Zarah says, 'is that we believe Kolya – the nine-year-old you met – was 'adopted' by his real mother.'

'Why?'

'So he could be there with her,' says Schnorr. 'Close to her. Protecting her and, by association, *himself*. As a grown man he couldn't have done that. The servants are kept segregated as to sex. But as her son . . .'

'Then he'll have to come back. To keep an eye on her. To make sure I don't harm her, and thereby *him*.'

'Precisely,' Freisler says.

'Then I have no choice. I *must* go back. In fact, I'll go now.'

'Not so fast, Otto,' Old Schnorr says, gesturing to me to sit down again. 'There are things here you must attend to first.'

Freisler, across from me, nods and takes up Meister Schnorr's comment. 'That's right. We've some reports we'd like you to study.'

'What, now?'

'You ought to,' Zarah says. 'As Meister you need to know the full range of what's happening.'

I know that, and it's one of the reasons why I don't feel I make a good Meister. I'm an agent – perhaps the best we have – but being Meister is a different thing altogether. It demands different skills. Skills I don't think I possess. But this is what they want. What Hecht – even knowing what he knew of me at the end – wanted.

'You want me to look at them now, is that it?'

Old Schnorr and Zarah and Freisler all nod, as do several others about the seated circle.

'Then you'd better let me see them.'

Meister Schnorr looks to Zarah. 'Send him back, then we'll resume here.'

'Send me . . .?'

It is as if they vanish. But I am still there, in the same room, on the same chair, only I know it is hours – days? – earlier, and beside me on the floor are a stack of files and a silvered data card.

Reports . . .

Several hours into the task, I look up from the screen, realising that Old Schnorr was right. I needed to know this stuff. Much of it is composed of brief resumes of what projects are green-lit and running – a page to each, giving the salient details – together with similarly brief CVs of the main agents involved. But there are a couple of files which are much more interesting because they deal specifically with matters that override the concerns of individual projects.

For a start there's a file on Reichenau and the platforms; another on Kolya and his abduction of his 'selves' through Time. Yet another deals with the quite recent phenomenon of agents coming back from up ahead. And the last, and perhaps most fascinating of all, is on me.

These latter files – the non-project files – are all Hecht's work, found among his 'papers' when they were clearing out his rooms. This, I learn from an appended note, is what they believe he was working on in those final thirty days of his life. Trying to make sense of things. Attempting to weave all of it into a coherent pattern. Much of it – and Hecht, true to his nature, takes great pains to say that this is so – is speculation, the filling of gaps with surmise. There's not much that's new, information-wise, but Hecht's thinking on certain matters is worth consideration.

For instance, he thought there was a connection – perhaps even an intimate, familial one – between Reichenau and Kolya. Why? Because wherever we find traces of one, we find similar traces of the other. Instances? Back in 1952, and again up in 2343. Hecht's belief – and my instinct is to agree with him – was that this was hardly likely to be coincidental.

On the subject of agents coming back from our future he was far less certain, perhaps because of lack of evidence. He had visited himself, certainly, but that was an isolated incident, and he had travelled only a relatively short distance into his own future. Overall, it was his feeling that, if it *were* happening, we would know for sure, because we would be flooded with agents coming back, and as that hadn't happened . . . Even so, the possibility of it happening remained large. It was now, he asserted, *theoretically* possible for it to happen, and so it would. Given time.

And I agree with him on that, and what he writes in his conclusion: '*We are all living this segment of our history first time round, but next time – and the countless times after that – they will be here, changing things, making alternations, and we may not even know it's happening.*'

Which brings me to the file I found most difficult to read, the file Hecht had compiled on me. I don't want to speak of it here, only to say that it was remarkably clear-eyed and open-minded considering Hecht's personal feelings on the matter, but I looked up from it finally with a mixed sense of shame and love, chastened by the experience of reading it.

No. One fact I will mention, something he said towards the

end of the report. That he had asked the Elders to appoint me Meister *despite* my aberrant behaviour, because he knew I would, eventually, make a fine Meister. A Meister suited for new times and new circumstances.

Such faith in me he had, even after his disillusionment.

And, sitting there, I find my eyes welling with tears at the thought of his loss, finally – *finally* – able to grieve him. Accepting him once more into my heart, as he, in his final days, had accepted what I was.

An hour later I am back, seated once more in the circle of my peers. Old Schnorr looks to me and smiles. 'Well, Otto? What have you to say?'

'One question. Why didn't Kolya try to kill *me*?'

308

I look up from the file and scowl at the boy sitting opposite me. He is by far the most unpleasant of them yet, a sneering, supercilious young man, not yet sixteen, who thinks himself not merely superior to me, but above being questioned by the Ministry.

His name is Paul Woolf and his father is the Chief Geneticist at the Institute in Vienna, and a very close friend of the Doktor – something young Woolf has dropped into the conversation on at least two occasions thus far.

'Just answer the question.'

'*Why?*' he says, leaning back a little, hoping to wind me up even further by an act of casualness. 'Both you and I know I'm not the student you're interested in, so why maintain this ridiculous charade?'

'You *know*, do you?'

'Of course I know. It can't possibly be me. I'm not a traitor. And besides, I object to the tenor of your questions. It seems to me like simple prying into what ought to be my own private concerns.'

'As far as the State is concerned, *nothing* is private.'

Woolf just laughs. An insolent sound.

I stand. 'Come round the desk. Stand before the viewer.'

He gets up slowly, sullenly and does what I've asked, and for a long while there is silence, while I make my observations and jot down my notes. Ironically, there's nothing particularly special about our young friend's chromosomes. They're the same mishmash of the good and the bad, dominant and recessive, the useful and the harmful. The Woolf clan are far from being supermen.

'It must be difficult,' he says, when I've finally done and he's seated again.

'Difficult?'

'Knowing what you are. What – *genetically* – you're capable of attaining. One day, you see, all of the subspecies will be identified. That's what my father says.'

I stare at him dumbfounded. '*And?*'

'What do you think? The lower kinds will serve *us*, of course. The Betas and the Deltas. Whatever we decide is necessary. Only they will be *glad* to serve us, because they'll understand the evolutionary distance – the vast, unbreachable gap – between us and them. Why, eventually they'll not even be able to breed with us any more. You see, that's what it's about, this society of ours. That's what's beginning here. We're taking the first steps even now. But in the future . . .'

In the future, I think, *you will all be dead. And your foul ideology with you.*

'It's the language of the blood,' he says, almost to himself. 'Not evolution so much as *destiny*.'

499

The language of the blood. I've heard that phrase before, two, maybe three times since I've been here, but in his mouth it sounds almost poetic, and I wonder where it comes from. Angossi? I'm about to question him further, when the door on the far side of the room bursts open and three uniformed men march straight in. I'm about to object, when I realise who they are. They're inspectors, like myself.

'Meister Scholl,' their leader says. 'Forgive the interruption, but we have business of some urgency and I must consult you.'

He looks to Woolf, who is surprised, and just a little intimidated, to see such reinforcements to my cause.

'Herr Woolf,' I say. 'You are dismissed.'

He stands and, with the most marginal of bows, hurries away, glad to be gone.

I turn and look to my superior. He's a big man, taller than me by a good six inches and broader at the shoulder. Facially, too, he is imposing, with large, almost sculpted features, jet black hair and eyes of an almost sapphire blue. *Aryan*, it makes me think. *A creature of the dark woods.*

All of this in an instant, and then I notice his insignia – Inspector, First Class – and bow my head. 'Meister . . .'

'Sit down, Scholl. And listen. I've not had time to contact Breslau and see what you've filed, so I'll need you to inform me what's going on here – what your brief is and which student is under suspicion. I'll also need to look through whatever ZA forms you've completed.'

'ZA forms?'

'Yes. You have them here?'

'No. In my room. I . . . I'll get them.'

'Good. But meet us back in the main building. At the Doktor's office. Oh, and bring the official report sheet along, too. I want to see who instigated this. It's too much of a coincidence that we're both here at the same time, don't you think?'

'Master . . .?'

'Yes?'

'You know my name, but . . .?'

'Schultz,' he says, and puts out a hand. 'I run the operation at Bremen.'

309

Zarah goes through it with me.

'ZA. That's zygote analysis. The indents . . . you took notes, I take it?'

'Yes.'

'Good. Then we'll use those to mock up some forms. Same with the official report sheet. It won't take long: an hour or two at most. Get some rest. I'll come to you when they're ready.'

'Thanks.'

I watch her go, then turn, looking about me at the room. I still feel an intruder here. This is still Hecht's room and always will be. I'll always see him in my mind's eye, sat in the depression in the centre of the floor, his long, pale fingers moving quickly across the keys, the Tree of Worlds glowing in the air above him.

Meister? I am not Meister. Meister means something else; requires a different mindset to my own, whatever Hecht believed. I am merely a stop-gap, a . . .

A fake, I think, and it makes me wonder about the life I've led and just how much of it was real, how much of it actually *meant* anything.

The parts with Katerina. Those last few months in Cherdiechnost . . .

And the rest? All those failed attempts to tinker with Time?

Standing there, I feel strangely depressed. Master of Time, I am, but can I change anything – can I *really* change any of it – for the good? Or am I, despite the potential power I wield, as much a victim as any time-bound man?

You see, that's it. The power I have seems illusory right now. Why? Because I can't wield it the way I want to. To rescue those I love and . . .

And put aside the Game.

But how can I do that? How can I ignore the call of duty? Would it be right to abandon my people to their fate? And besides, if I did – if I tried to, that is – then surely they'd prevent me. If I endangered them, they would be perfectly within their rights to stop me, even to kill me if necessary.

And then there's the Russians, and Reichenau, and Kolya . . .

No. The time's not ripe to put away the Game. The Game goes on, whatever my wishes. Meister I might be, but the world will not leave me in peace. It is not my destiny.

Ahead lies the loop, and death and birth and all the in-betweens of life.

The door hisses open. It is Zarah again.

'Forgive me, Meister, but we need to show you something urgently.'

Behind her, I realise, is one of our agents – Kessemeier, I think it is. He dips his head respectfully, but his eyes are ablaze, his whole body trembling with excitement.

He's holding a book in one hand, and as Zarah steps aside he almost thrusts it at me.

'There, Meister! That's it!'

I take it and study the beige cloth cover a moment. I recognise it. It's one of the books I had sent to the library. The language looks like German, only it isn't. Nor is it a sister-language. It's an altered version, the product of an alternate timeline.

'*Abwechseindrealitisch,*' Kessemeier says, giving it its proper, German term. 'I've done a transcript, if you want to read it for yourself.'

I notice now that Zarah too is excited, but I'm still confused as to why it should be so important. 'Just tell me what it is,' I say. 'If I need to, I'll—'

'It's *him*,' Kessemeier says, unable to contain himself. 'Kolya!'

That sends an electric jolt through me. '*What?* He's *mentioned* in it?'

'Mentioned? It's all about him, Meister! It's *his* history. How he rose, how he fell . . .'

'Wait. Slow down a second. His *history*?'

Kessemeier goes to speak again, but Zarah beats him to it. 'Our friend Kolya was a great leader. An emperor, you might say. Until we changed things. Until we took it all away from him.'

310

For the next six hours I am absorbed, reading about Kolya and his world and his struggle to reach the top and stay there. A world so similar and yet so different from our own, ruled by that proud, fierce eagle of a man. Until we came along and sucked his world into the Game, destroying it piece by piece, and then discarding it, like a broken, rusting machine shunted off on to a weed-strewn side-track of time.

Kolya. Undoubtedly Kolya from the portraits of the man. Ruler of an empire vaster than any other in human history, an empire that contained Europe and Asia, and most of Africa, and that was industrialised a good three centuries before its time.

And the agent who was in charge of all of this? Myself, of course. Not that I remember *any* of it. But who else could it have been? Why else would such hatred smoulder in his eyes?

Only how did he find out it was me? More to the point, how,

503

if he was born in 2343, did he come to rule this other world nine
centuries before that date?

And when did Kolya discover how to travel back in Time?

But that's the trouble with this. Exciting as it is, it begs more
questions than it answers. But at least we know *something* about
him now. At least we have a possible motive for why he's doing
what he's doing. All the more reason, then, to find him and
confront him.

Closing the book, I look up at Zarah. 'I'm going back,' I say.
'I need to find out how it's all connected.'

311

I jump back to the room above the kitchens, then hurry to meet
the others at the Doktor's office, the file of mocked-up forms in
one hand, my head full of questions.

If the answers aren't here, then where are they? Back in 1952?
At Krasnogorsk?

One thing's for certain: I can't go back to Kolya's world. That
timeline was snipped off long ago, and is now as inaccessible as
any fantasy. Whatever happened there – whatever he did and I
did – is veiled in mystery now. Unless . . .

And this is the thought that has been nagging me the last hour
or more. What if Hecht kept a record of it, back at the Haven?
After all, he kept copies of everything else back there. If I could
go there, then maybe I'd get my answers.

Only if that's so, then why didn't Hecht uncover it? Or is it
just that he didn't think to look?

After all, why should he? His memory – like all of ours –
changes from time to time to accommodate major alterations in
the timestream. So, while a record would have been kept – a

copy – there would have been nothing in Hecht's mind to set him off – even to suggest that somehow Kolya had already crossed our tracks.

No. I'm convinced of it. He wouldn't even have thought to look.

Yes, but what about his brother? Surely he'd have cross-referenced it somewhere?

Surely they had some kind of index, to make all that information more accessible?

But then again, why? If those timestreams were done with and left to rot . . .

Maybe that's why he evaded us. Why he was such a mystery all that while. Not that he's any less of a mystery now.

I arrive breathless at the Doktor's door, to find the other three waiting for me patiently. Schultz even smiles at me as I hand him the files.

'Thanks, Otto. Leave this to me from now on. It's time we taught these insolent bastards a lesson.'

I'm surprised, because it's almost certain that the Doktor, seated in his room the other side of the door and looking on via his camera, hears what Schultz says. But if so, he doesn't react to it, because when the door swings back and we enter, it's to find him crossing the room with his hands outstretched, as if to greet an old friend, a beaming smile on his face.

'Auguste, it's been a long time.'

And I realise with a start just what this means. Schultz was a student here. He is a product of the Akademie.

'Herr Doktor,' Schultz says, and bows low, even as we three, standing behind him, do the same.

'What do you want?' the Doktor asks as he straightens up, giving Schultz the respect he never showed me. 'Is it bad?'

'It isn't good,' Schultz answers him. 'It's never good. But I must have them all gathered. They must see this. Remember it.'

The Doktor nods, subdued. 'It shall be done. But come now, let's share a drink. To olden times . . .'

So it is, with the taste of brandy in my throat, I find myself standing up on the stage once more, only this time behind Schultz and his two assistants, as he looks out over a sea of shaven heads. There is an atmosphere of fear now in that massive space between the buildings, and as Schultz steps forward a chill silence falls.

When he speaks, his voice is strong and deep. It carries to the very back of that gathered crowd, echoing back from the walls of the buildings.

'I stand before you today not as a single man – not as an individual, acting as an individual – but as a representative of the State. A servant of the Fatherland. Indeed, we are all of us here servants of the State, and as such fulfil perhaps the highest purpose to which we might aspire. Today, however, we are here on a matter of the most serious nature; a matter that touches the very core of our social being.'

Schultz looks about him, his cold, clear gaze raking them like the brightest, most penetrating light.

'As a society we must always look to one another. Always recognise that while each has his task, his role within the greater fate of the nation, there is a common goal, a unity, to all our efforts. When that unity is broken – deliberately, *maliciously* – then it is our duty, one might almost say our sacred task, to root out the source of that breach, that *corruption,* and, by whatever means, *cleanse* the social being. Should we fail, should we even hesitate to act, then, like a disease in the very marrow of the bone, that disease will spread. The bone will rot and the body will fall.'

Schultz pauses, hovering on the edge now, close to revealing who is to be punished and why, and the mass of boys below him know that, and there's a kind of dark expectancy among them. They have heard this speech before and have seen what follows, and though some are fearful, many more are secretly excited at this moment, for the great, all-encompassing power of the State is about to be expressed, corruption rooted out and the unjust punished.

Schultz nods slowly. 'Have no illusions. We must have no mercy for those who transgress our laws. As a society, we cannot afford to be merciful. Mercy is only for the weak. For the feeble-minded who lack clarity of vision. Mercy is the tool of our enemies. And so we must not think of being merciful. We must think only of cleansing the race. Of how, through this act, the *volk* grows stronger and more certain of its ultimate victory.'

Schulz makes no sign or gesture, yet as he says those words, so his two assistants step out, away from him, heading for the steps that lead down into the massed ranks of the boys, one to the left, one to the right, moving with a determined gait.

Schultz's voice booms out. 'Francke, Roland Francke, where are you, boy?'

There's a moment's silence, and then a hand goes up near the front, over to the left, and a voice, frail, struggling to be brave, answers him.

'I am here, Meister!'

'And Baeck, Leo Baeck, speak up!'

Again a hand goes up, further back, somewhere in the middle. 'Here, Master!'

'Good. Make yourselves known to my men.'

I swallow, my mouth dry, knowing suddenly what's to come.

Their fathers are traitors – caught passing secrets to the Russians – and as the boys are led, their hands manacled behind their backs, up on to the stage, so Schultz speaks on, spelling out their wickedness, such that the two boys half stumble up the steps, their faces shocked and bewildered, and on to the stage, unable to believe that it is *their* fathers Schultz is speaking of.

Traitors. Enemies of the State. And therefore, by association, their sons are also traitors, for it is all genetic, after all. The rottenness is in the genes. *Ineradicable*. Best then to cauterise it, to *remove* the genes from the racial pool.

The boys – sixteen-, seventeen-year-olds – are half pulled, half pushed towards Schultz, his two assistants brutal now, forcing the young men down on to their knees before the Inspector. Necks are craning now, down there in the mass below us. There's a low buzz and boys are breaking their neat ranks, straining to get a better view.

'Roland Francke,' Schultz says, looking down at the bowed head of the first boy, even as he pulls the heavy gun from its holster. 'You have been sentenced by the court to die. Have you anything to say?'

But young Francke is too petrified to speak, and as Schultz presses the muzzle of the gun against his temple, he pisses himself.

The gunshot makes us all jump, it is so loud. There's a spray of blood and bone and the body slumps and topples to one side.

Schultz steps across, his cloak billowing out momentarily, his booted feet the last thing young Baeck will ever see.

'Leo Baeck. You too have been sentenced by the court to die. Have you anything to say?'

'No, Meister.'

His calmness surprises me and I take a step towards him, yet even as I do, the gun goes off again.

Schultz slips the gun back into the holster, then steps past the two bodies. Blood pools beneath his feet. He takes a deep breath and addresses the audience again.

'Good. We are almost done now. But we have one final piece of business to attend to. One last matter that must be resolved.'

He turns and looks to me, then turns back. 'Paul Woolf . . . come up here.'

I open my mouth, then shut it again. He *can't*, surely. The investigation's incomplete, and besides, nothing's been proved. Nothing *can* be proved. Yet I have a sudden gut certainty that Schultz means to settle it right here and now, whatever the state of the evidence. I know that he hasn't read the file, he hasn't had time, only time enough to memorise Woolf's name.

Woolf comes slowly, reluctantly up the steps and on to the stage, and whatever I felt about him, facing him earlier, I feel pity for him now, for Schultz is relentless. He might as well be the figure of death itself, standing there in his black cloak and shining black boots, his face stern like the face of an ancient statue.

Woolf approaches to within a couple of paces and then stops, bowing his head low. 'Meister Schultz.'

Schultz studies the boy, almost as if he can *see* guilt, and then he speaks in that booming, commanding voice of his. 'You have two choices, Herr Woolf. You can confess and save your family, or you can die anyway, and your family will die with you.'

'But—'

It is not Woolf, but I who says that 'but'. Schultz turns and glares at me, then turns back to young Woolf.

'*Well?*'

Woolf is trembling. He cannot speak, let alone make a decision. Schultz draws the gun.

'Stop it!' I yell. 'For Urd's sake!'

The gunshot startles me. I can't believe he's done it. I feel sick, because – foul as young Woolf was to me – he wasn't guilty. He hadn't done anything. Not anything to die for, anyway.

Everyone's looking at me now, staring at me, like *I've* done something wrong.

'Herr Scholl,' Schultz says, turning to me, the gun still in his hand. 'Have you something to say?'

But I've nothing to say, except, perhaps, how foul this age is, how perverse its values, and, turning away, I hurry from the stage.

312

I have packed my case and am ready to depart when the young servant comes to me again, the same who met me on the walkway the previous night.

'Come with me,' he says.

I'm not sure I want to, but I follow anyway, down the main stairwell and left, along a narrow corridor I've not been down before. At the end there's a short flight of steps, leading down to a small, metallic door set into a bare brick wall.

We go through, into a narrow, dimly lit corridor.

'What is this place?'

But he doesn't answer, just sets off down the passageway, as if it's my choice whether to follow him or not.

I follow.

We go left and then sharp right and come to a narrow wooden door, set into the hacked stone of the wall. Facing it, I find my heart is racing.

The young man stands aside. 'Go on,' he says. 'Go in. He's waiting for you.'

That's what I fear. My hand moves toward my chest. I look down at it, then lower it again. My palms are damp.

There's no handle, so I push it open, The room is poorly lit – a cell of a room – not that I can see anything at first. There's a kind of narrow hallway before it opens out, to my right. And there, sitting on a chair beside a bed, is one of them – one of Kolya's 'brothers', a big man in his mid-thirties, long-haired and with that prominent, balding brow they all seem to possess. He's like Kolya, only he lacks the intensity, lacks his *eyes*.

I stand before him, noticing only then that the boy is also there, curled up on the bed behind him, facing the wall.

I try to seem confident, but my nerves are on edge.

'What do you want?' I ask.

'To tell you—'

'Tell *me*?'

'That you can't touch us. Do you understand that, Otto? We're way ahead of you. We know everything you do. We know *when* you do it, and *why*. As for tracking us down . . .' He laughs. 'Kolya *let* you meet us. Me and the boy. He *wanted* you to. So that you'd understand.'

'Understand?'

'That he's not afraid of you. Despite what your people did to him.' He smiles. 'Oh, he knows that you know that now. The book . . . he knows about that. But that too will be reversed. *Everything* will be reversed, in the end.'

'Then why is he so angry?'

'Angry?'

'At Krasnogorsk.'

The man shrugs. He clearly knows nothing about Krasnogorsk. 'Tell him . . .' I begin. 'Tell him I'll see him in the loop.'

And with that I jump. Back to Four-Oh. Back to chaos.

313

There's the smell of cordite in that big, circular room, and over to the side, a group of the women have left their posts to huddle around another of them, who is down, clutching her arm. As I go across to them, Zarah looks up from among them, shock in her face.

'Otto! He was here! Kolya was here!'

If I hadn't come straight from where I'd come from, I might have laughed in disbelief, only right now I think he's capable of anything – even of jumping right in here, on to *our* platform, with *his* DNA.

By rights he should be dead, scattered into a billion little pieces, like the fake Burckel I brought back that time. Only he isn't.

'What happened?' I ask, crouching over the injured girl. It's Leni, I see. 'Why did he shoot her?'

Leni swallows, then. 'I tried to grab him. I leapt up on to the platform and—'

'There's a note,' Zarah said, and shakes her head in wonder. 'He jumped in just to leave you a note!'

She hands it to me.

It's just a single sheet of folded paper. I unfold it and read.

Otto.

Time isn't safe for you any more. What's more, I have that which is most precious to you. Your family. You will not see them again; not unless I choose to show them to you. To make you burn inside, the way you made me burn. Ah, but I forget. You don't remember that, do you? It isn't in the book. But ask Hecht's brother, sometime.

I'm sure he has it somewhere among his papers.

Yours in hatred,

Kolya.

To say that I am chilled by what I read is to understate it. My blood goes cold with fear. I look to Zarah and her eyes show that she has read it and knows what I am feeling at that moment. Or thinks she knows. Because this is awful; this feels like death itself. Forget the bigger questions that his note throw up – how Kolya knows and does these things – it is his blunt statement that he has them that destroys me.

'I have to go,' I say to Zarah quietly. 'I have to try to see them.'

And what's to stop me? If I jump in *before* I left . . . Only even as I make to ask Zarah to do just that, the platform activates behind us and I turn to see Ernst materialise in the air, his face as shocked as ours, his eyes bleak. He looks close to breaking down, and his voice, when he speaks, shakes, heavy with grief.

'Oh, my dear, dear friend. Oh, Otto, Urd save us, you've got to come and see. The things they've done. The *things* they've done . . .'

314

We jump in, into the trees behind the 'Hump', Cherdiechnost spread out below us. And what a scene of desolation it makes. Fires are burning everywhere. A great pall of thick black smoke drifts slowly in the wind. And the dead . . .

'What's happened?' I ask Ernst, the words the merest breath. 'How . . .?'

But Ernst doesn't answer. He seems as shocked as I am. And that's understandable, because only a day has passed here since I left, since I was taken back to Four-Oh.

And this . . .

'Kolya,' I say, but Ernst shakes his head.

'No, Otto. This was Nevsky. Come. You'll see.'

Only I don't want to see. My heart is breaking. Because, even from where we stand, I can see the bodies, strewn here and there, lifeless, across the burning fields, and running through my head is the thought that my girls – even Katerina – could be among them. That I could stumble on them . . .

The thought of it robs my legs of strength.

'I can't . . . I . . .'

But I know I must. This is no time to give in to weakness. If anything can be done . . .

Only I can see with my own eyes how complete the devastation is. Barely a single house is untouched, not a structure unmarked.

Slowly, side by side, guns drawn, we walk down the slope towards it. I feel sick. I feel, well, suffice to say that nothing in my long and oft-bloody career has prepared me for this. Because these are my friends, people I loved. And as we go, we pass first one and then another of those loving, happy people, and every last one of them is dead, bloodily disfigured, men, women and children: what did it matter to Nevsky who they were? All that mattered wás our defiance. And from seeing it, an anger begins to burn in me. An anger the like of which I have never felt before. An anger that threatens to consume me, just as the flames consume Cherdiechnost.

But the worst is to come. We cut across to the right, making for Razumovsky's half-completed house. I make to go inside, but Ernst pulls me back.

'No,' he says. 'You don't want to see.'

But I do. In those few moments since we descended from the Hump I have swung the other way. Now I *have* to see. For my revenge, I swear, will be terrible, and so I *must*. Even so, what I do see makes me groan; makes my heart break again, for there is my father-in-law, that big, larger-than-life man with his great black beard and his fierce ways, dead in his own bed, his young wife beside him, their throats cut, the sheets stained black with their blood.

Outside, I fall to my knees. I *must* see. Only I'm not sure I am strong enough to bear what I *might* see. Fear grips me now, and as I raise my eyes and look across to the big house and see the flames that still climb into the air from it, I wonder how I shall bear it, seeing the unseeable. How can I possibly go on living if life itself has been taken from me?

Crossing those few hundred yards is the most difficult thing I have ever done, because my head is filled with dark imaginings, with pictures beyond enduring, and so to find the house abandoned, empty, is a numbing surprise.

I turn to Ernst. 'Do you think ...' I swallow. 'Do you think he's taken them?'

'Nevsky?'

Ernst thinks a moment and then shrugs. His eyes meet mine. 'What shall we do, Otto? How shall we ...?'

But he doesn't finish. A shout has gone up, from over near the mill. We run down towards it and see, emerging from one of the grain stores, three villagers. Our people.

The miller, Terekhov, and his wife and daughter.

Seeing us, all three of them fall to their knees.

'Meister ...'

'What happened?' I ask. 'Was it Nevsky?'

'They came in the night, Meister,' Terekhov says. 'Hundreds of them, on horseback. They started putting houses to the torch and killing anyone who ventured outside.'

'And Katerina and my girls?'

Terekhov drops his head. 'I ... I didn't see, Meister. They were killing everyone. *Everyone*.'

So I've seen. But Nevsky. How did Nevsky get here so quickly? Unless ...

Unless he was here, in Novgorod, already. Unless that small troupe of his men who ventured out here were part of a much larger force.

And I know, as soon as I've thought it, that it's the truth. There can be no other explanation.

I turn to Ernst, meaning to speak, to tell him what, in that instant, I have decided, only I hear the hoof beats of horses, behind us and to our left and, turning, see a troupe of horsemen – five in all – heading towards us.

I look around and see, close by, a sword, lying there on the grass. I pick it up and, almost without thought, walk towards the approaching horsemen.

They slow and stop, laughing among themselves to see me, alone, walking towards them. They huddle together, then, some decision made, one of them straightens and, kicking his horse forward, begins to ride at me.

I meet him, taking him waist-high, almost disembowelling him. And walk on, towards them. Four of them now.

They don't mess about this time. All four of them kick forward. But that's the trouble with being on a horse. Manoeuvring. Only two of them at most can get close to me at a time, and I make that hard. As they flash past me, one more of them is lying on the ground, dead, his head severed.

They turn, focused on me now. Three of them. And as they do, so Ernst gives a bellow and throws himself at their back, taking one of them out with his bare hands – leaping on the fellow and bringing him down, his hands at his neck.

I yell, giving a blood-curdling cry, startling their horses who start to rear, plunging my sword pommel-deep into the chest of one of them. No pity in me. Dead to pity. Wanting these bastards dead for what they've done here.

Yet even as he falls from the horse's back, he takes my sword with him, leaving me facing the last of them, unarmed, defenceless.

Only he's lost his courage. He's seen me kill three of his fellows single-handed, and he doesn't want to die, and, turning his horse, he kicks its flanks, making ground between us. And I watch him go, my chest heaving, aching to kill him, but knowing he's beyond me. Yet not. For I still have the gun. Realising it, I draw it and, taking aim, fire at his back, burning him, making him shriek and topple from his mount.

And then I'm running, panting breathlessly across the space between us, until I'm stood above where he's writhing on the floor, and, kneeling down, I grasp his hair and pull his head back viciously and, making sure he sees me looking at him, end it.

And then I'm done. Not that it's purged. Not that I couldn't kill a thousand more of them for what they've done here. Only . . .

Only I'm trembling now, and afraid, oh, so afraid, that I have lost them for ever. That, whatever I do in time, this is it. This slaughter. This hideous awfulness.

And, putting my head back, I bay out my pain and my fear, making Ernst look up from where he's crouched over the dead man he has killed and look to me, fearful for my soul, afraid that he has lost me finally to the darkness that he knows so well.

315

Zarah, it seems, can't even look at me, nor can Old Schnorr. Freisler, however, is staring at me brazenly, like he's studying my every move as I pace up and down before them.

I have called another council of war, demanding that they give me the support I need to go back in there. I want forty experienced agents. To take Nevsky out. To save Cherdiechnost.

Only they don't want to. The vote is eleven to one against me. Even Ernst – even after what he's seen – has voted against me.

I stop, and, leaning against the table, look about me. 'So what am I supposed to do? Let them *die*?'

'Six agents,' Zarah says quietly, and Schnorr and Freisler nod.

'Six? Just *six?*'

'We can't afford to be sucked in,' Schnorr says. 'Besides. This is Nevsky. Kill him and we make a major change. The Russians . . .'

I know what he means. It would be like the Russians going in mob-handed after Frederick. We would have to respond. But I am determined. Even if this pulls the whole house down, I *shall* destroy him. 'Six then,' I say, and, turning from them, leave the room.

Only that isn't it. We have to plan this thing. Send agents in to find out where he is and when. How many men he has, and how disposed. And then I have to come up with a plan. Where do I take him? Do I ambush him on his way north from Novgorod, or at the estate itself? In the end we decide to do it in Novgorod. To raise a riot against his men and use that as cover for a bloody attack on Nevsky and his immediate retinue – his *druzhiny*.

And to my surprise, even as we finalise our plan, I have a seventh volunteer. Freisler. He even smiles at me: a sympathetic smile, unexpected from a cold fish like him.

'I'm sorry, Otto. I know how you must feel. But it's for the best. Besides, eight of us will be enough. *If* it works. If the Russians *let* it work.'

And the way he says that makes me look at him, because he seems to know more than he's letting on, but he just shrugs.

'Well?' he says. 'Are you ready?'

316

News comes back swiftly from our agents. Nevsky is indeed in the locality, in Gorodishche to be precise – in the old town, just south of Novgorod. He arrived that same afternoon I was taken back, his army – over five hundred strong – setting up camp outside the ancient walls.

And we learn that Nevsky has a 'meeting' that very evening, with the *veche* – the town council of Novgorod. I say meeting, but his scheme is a simple one – to threaten the boyars. To demand that they pay up or else. He does not come to bargain

No, Nevsky is unhappy, it seems, with how little *tamga* they have collected this time around. His masters, the Mongols, are planning new wars, and Novgorod is rich, and so he, and forty of his *druzhina*, will ride up to the *Sofiyskaya storona*, the 'cathedral side' of town, and beat upon the door of the council chambers with the pommels of their swords until they're opened to them.

It is there that they will learn news of what happened at Cherdiechnost.

That sobers me, for it means there was a spy in my camp. Someone willing to flee to Novgorod and betray his own people for a handful of gold.

Our agents don't know who it was, nor, in planning this, does it really matter. Only I swear to myself that I will kill them, whoever they are.

Some context here. It is late August 1256, and it is four years since Nevsky last returned from visiting the Horde, a Tartar army at his back, sent home to crush his rebellious brothers and enforce the dominion of the great Khan; a traitor not only to his people, but to his closest kin. Four years from now Novgorod will rise up against his impositions and throw out the Mongol tax-collectors, refusing to have anything to do with their census, but Prince Alexander, once more at the head of a Tartar force, will enforce the Mongol census, taking his army into the streets of Novgorod itself, brutally suppressing any opposition.

Our hero. The man the Russians made a saint. It makes me sick.

Prepared, the eight of us gather for a final briefing. And then we're in, jumping into an unlit side-alley on the *Torgovaya Storona*, just across the river from the cathedral. We pause a moment, gathering stones, filling our pockets with them, and then we hurry on, heading for the wooden bridge that spans the Volkhov.

The bridge is unguarded. We wait nearby, crouched behind a low wall, watching until Nevsky's retinue has passed across, then follow, swiftly, silently, like shadows.

Seeing Nevsky again I burn with hatred of the man. There's such a gap between what he seems and what he is. *So devils are*, I think, and swear – for the second time that evening – that I shall slit his throat before this night is out.

Such bloody thoughts I have as we run towards the council chamber, the log paths dry beneath our feet, a full moon shining down on us.

A crowd of several thousand has gathered in the streets surrounding the square in which the *veche* meet. At the centre of it all is the two-storey chamber itself, torches lighting the pale stone from which it's made, the thick wooden doors barred to Nevsky who, still on his horse, leans down to hammer at the door, demanding entry.

The crowd are angry, seeing Nevsky and his men. The common townspeople of Novgorod are no friends of his, and they shout and bay and hiss, knowing that his presence there can mean only one thing. Yet he seems undaunted by them, his men forming a ring about him, facing the crowd with their horses, pushing back at the mass of people surrounding them.

We slip among them silently, working our way through to the front. In the wavering torchlight I see one of our agents looking on from over to the right; see him look to me then flicker out of existence.

His disappearance is our signal. Taking a heavy stone from my pocket, I heft it in my palm, then launch it at the head of the nearest of Nevsky's men, and as I do, so a small rain of stones fly out of the crowd, connecting with men and horses, making the warriors cry out, their horses rear.

There's a moment's confusion and then all hell breaks loose, Nevsky's men lashing out with spear and sword while the crowd, pressed tight, unable to back off, find they have no option but to fight.

Out-numbered as they are, there should only be one conclusion, only among the common townspeople are eight trained killers, moving here and there, ducking in to severe an artery, cutting a tendon here, a throat there, moving with deadly intent until Nevsky, not quite knowing what has happened, makes a determined break-out, cutting and slashing his way to the edge of the crowd, six of his men about him.

The mob surges after him, but now they kick hard, and, running down anyone who dares oppose them, head for the bridge.

And as the crowd moves on, so it leaves us eight, standing among the dead and dying in the square.

I look to Freisler. 'Jurgen. Cut them off at the bridge. I'm going inside.'

Freisler nods, then jumps. An instant later all the others follow him, blinking out of existence, leaving me alone.

I turn and look across, even as the great doors to the council chamber swing back.

There's a little crowd of them in the doorway – boyars in their thick furs. There's even one or two I know, from Razumovsky's gatherings. But their faces in the torchlight are fearful, and as they slowly emerge into the square, I can almost read their thoughts. They are keen to be gone from there – to flee with their families and belongings, before Nevsky returns with his army.

Only Nevsky won't be returning.

I walk towards them slowly, and as I do, so one of them spots me and, pointing at me, cries out.

'It's the *Nemets*! From Cherdiechnost . . .'

My arms are slicked in blood. Blood spatters my face from where I've done my butchery.

'Where is he?' I demand, coming right up close to them. 'Come on, tell me! Where is the fucker hiding?'

Eyes look away, and I know I'm right. He's in there, whoever it is. Pushing through the little mob of them in the doorway, I go inside.

There's about a dozen of them, crowded about the far end of the table, and among them . . .

'Heaven help us all . . .'

For there, still in his priestly garb, with his over-stuffed belly and his long, bushy black beard is Father Iranov, my priest from Cherdiechnost. I stare at him, unable to believe my own eyes. And then, remembering what he's caused, I draw my knife.

'Stop him!' someone cries, only I won't be stopped. Jumping up on to the table, I run at Iranov across the table-top, even as he turns and scrambles towards the door. Hands grab at me, but I lash out, severing fingers with the diamond-sharp blade. I jump down, between two of the boyars, elbowing them aside. Iranov is at the door, but even as he makes to close it behind him, I hurl my knife, lodging it deep in his back, making him shriek and stumble, down on to his face.

I am on him in an instant. Tugging the knife from his back, I savagely lift his head and draw the blade across his throat, even as hands reach down to pull me from him.

Only they clutch air. For I am gone. Back to the bridge. Back to face Nevsky.

We form a line across the bridge, eight of us, shadow figures, dressed in black, our knives drawn, the fast-flowing Volkhov beneath us, visible between the close-packed logs, as Nevsky and his men come down the slope towards us.

They are flying along, like they're pursued by demons, and though there's no sign of the mob, we can hear the great roar of human voices coming towards us.

Church bells sound. Just two at first, and then others, taking up the alarm, waking the town with their discordant clanging.

And still Nevsky and his fellows come on.

I count the riders, then turn and look to Freisler. 'Two lines,' I say. 'The first four cut the horses' tendons and then the second line moves in, goes for the riders. But Nevsky's mine. You let him through.'

Freisler nods. Gesturing to three of the others, he jogs quickly forward, the four of them making a line about thirty paces in front of us, halfway across the bridge.

Nevsky is in front, his six companions just behind. As they come out on to the bridge and see us, they slow momentarily, but then Nevsky cries out something and they kick their mounts forward, meaning to run us down.

I see how our men crouch, flexing like wrestlers, and I feel a moment's pride. Then, knowing what I've got to do, I jump.

And jump back in, half a mile to the south, in the street where Nevsky will have to come if he is heading back to Gorodishche and his main force. Quickly I uncoil the rope about my waist and fasten it to the two spikes that our agents have already driven into the houses to either side, and then I crouch there in the shadows, hearing the cries and yells from the bridge, the more distant sound of the mob and of the church bells clanging tunelessly, and then – the noise I've been waiting for – the sound of his horse's hooves coming relentlessly towards me.

The horse hits the rope at speed and almost somersaults, the whipcrack snap as its back breaks, a sickening sound. As for Nevsky, he's thrown against the wall to my right, the impact almost bringing the wall down.

As I walk across, he groans and tries to sit up, then slumps back again, pain making him whimper like a child. Standing over him, I can see that he's badly hurt, maybe even dying, but it's not enough. I've seen what this bastard did. Seen how heartless this Mongol-loving cunt can be, and so I steel myself and, crouching, reach out and grasp his face, pinching his chin to make him open his eyes and look at me.

'You!' he says, surprised. 'I should have guessed.'

'Then you know why.'

And, drawing my knife, I push it deep into his throat and twist, then hold it there as he struggles, watching his face, watching the light leak slowly from his eyes.

Yes, I think, *but will it hold? Or will the Russians simply change it back?*

And I jump.

318

Beneath the moon Cherdiechnost sleeps. All is peaceful. No riders will disturb this night. I stand there a moment, before the *dacha*, breathing in the sweetness of the air, looking about me at that sweetest of all homes, then turn and, walking to the door, push through, making my way inside.

And stop, sniffing the air.

I don't know what it is, but something's different. Something about the smell of the place. Something . . . unfamiliar.

Even so, the house is quiet. Slowly I make my way upstairs, listening, craning to hear the soft, distinctive sounds of my sleeping darlings. Only there's nothing.

Maybe the doors are closed. Maybe . . .

But already my senses are prickling. Already I know that something's wrong. Because this stillness is too still. This silence *too* silent.

The landing is empty, flooded by the moonlight. The door to our room is just over to my right, my daughters' rooms beyond that, only as I look inside I see that the bed is empty, the sheets disturbed.

'Katerina?'

I call softly, as if not to wake the children, yet I am fearful now. The utter silence of the house is ominous. And now I smell it. The unfamiliarity I'd noticed earlier. A distinctly male smell.

I draw the *staritskii*, and even as I do I hear a sound – a stifled noise – from the guest room over to the left.

'Katerina?'

I say it loudly this time, and am answered with laughter. Deep, masculine laughter. And then a man's voice, mocking, high-pitched. '*Ot-to*? Is that you? *Ot-to*?'

I walk across, then stop, seeing him, knowing now why they weren't here the last time I came. Knowing now who'd taken them.

'Kolya?'

His eyes smile maliciously at me from where he stands. 'Meister Behr. How good to see you again.'

Only I'm not looking at him. I'm looking past him, to where six of his 'brothers' stand, each of them holding a bound captive. My daughters and my wife.

Seeing me, Katerina tries to struggle, but it's in vain. They are each of them bound tightly, at wrist and ankle, and gagged. Even my darling little Zarah.

It's an unbearable sight.

I look to Kolya. 'What do you want? What do I have to do?'

'Nothing. I have what I need. I've *taken* what I need.'

The gun is in my hand. I raise it, aiming it at him, but he only shakes his head.

'Try that and they're dead. I guarantee it. Now throw it down.'

'If there's nothing you wanted, then why did you wait here for me? Why didn't you just steal them away? To gloat?'

His lips form an ugly sneer. 'You misunderstand me, Otto. I did it because I could. Because I wanted to. Now throw the gun down or I'll kill them, one by one.'

I throw it down.

'Good.' He turns, looks to his helpers. 'Okay. We're finished here.'

I cry out. I can't help it, but I do. Because suddenly they're gone. Suddenly it's just Kolya and me and the moonlit emptiness of the room.

'Where . . .?'

'Have I taken them?' Kolya smiles and takes a step towards me, holding out his hand. 'Come and find out. Jump with me, Otto. Stay with them.'

His hand is an arm's length from my own. I stare at it, then shake my head.

'Very well. Then you will never see them again.'

Slowly, very slowly he retracts his hand, but all the while his eyes are on mine, smiling, like he knows what I'm going to do.

Oh, I know this is a trap, and that if I take his hand something terrible will happen, only what else can I do? If I don't go with him then they are lost for ever.

Jump back, you say. Get to them before he does? But Kolya is a step ahead of me, remember? He always has been, and I sense he always will. What other choice have I?

And so I grasp his hand and even as his fingers lock around my own, so I feel that sudden sideways lurch in time and know we've jumped.

Into a room, sun pouring in through a window to my right, even as Kolya frees his hand from mine and shoves me away.

I go to grab at him, to hang on for dear life, but he's anticipated that. His knee comes up, making me double up in pain, and then his elbow slams hard into the side of my face. I fall to my knees, and as I do he gives me a snarling smile.

'Goodbye, Otto. Have fun.'

And vanishes.

I straighten, gasping for air, trying not to be sick, then bring my hand up to my chest.

Nothing.

I try again. Nothing. Like there's nothing there.

Impossible, I think. *I'm in a loop. I'm . . .*

Trapped. The bastard has trapped me here. Jumped me in and snipped me off.

Using the side of the bed, I haul myself up, then lie back, wheezing, the side of my face pounding where he elbowed it. For a moment I close my eyes, my thoughts swirling, unable to believe I let him do that to me. Then, struggling up, I make my way over to the window, wanting to know just where he's dumped me.

I must be eight or ten floors up, the street below packed with cars and people. I'm in a city somewhere. Only where? And, more to the point, *when*?

I hold on to the sill a moment longer, then slowly turn, looking back into the room. Voices drift through the paper-thin walls. Spanish, or Portuguese, or something like that. Beside the bed, there's a chair, a desk, a chest of drawers and a small bookcase.

There's one door over on the left, another just past the door in the corner on the right.

Whoever it belongs to, it isn't mine, that's for sure. There's a case under the desk, and some papers on the desk. And there, on the floor beside the bed, is a newspaper.

I hobble across, feeling sick, and lower myself slowly on to my knees, staring down at the paper, amazed by what I see.

It is the *New York Times* for 8 November 1984, and beneath a banner headline is a picture of a man I last saw in West Berkeley, thirty-two years – or was it just two weeks? – ago. I read the headline: 'DICK, TAKING 49 STATES AND 59% OF VOTE, VOWS TO STRESS ARMS TALKS AND ECONOMY.'

White-haired, and in his fifties now, Phil stares up at me from the page, exuding confidence, like he's everyone's favourite uncle. Security men, in dark suits and wearing shades, surround him on all sides, while a snowy owl – his 'trademark' so the caption reads – perches on the shoulder of his charcoal-coloured suit. Phil Dick, my old science-fiction writer buddy, and now President of the United States of America.

Acknowledgements

This one, as you'll see from the dedication, is for Rob Carter – friend and fellow writer – who spent so many evenings sharing a beer with me and debating the notions that eventually became this strangest of tales. Thanks again. The next one's on me.

Thanks go once again to my agent, Diana Tyler, and to my dear friends and fellow writers, Mike Cobley, Ritchie Smith, John Kavanagh, Brian Griffin and Brian Aldiss, for their comments and suggestions. Thank you, guys.

Huge thanks, too, to my editorial team at Ebury, Michael Rowley and Emily Yau, for their close attention to detail. Long may we work together.

Love and thanks go to my darling wife, Susan Oudot, and my four darling daughters, Jessica, Amy, Georgia and Francesca, for keeping me sane throughout this weirdest of science fictional trips.

The two quotations from Hermann Hesse's *The Glass Bead Game* are from the translation by Richard and Clara Winston, published by Jonathan Cape in 1970, and are used here with their kind permission. The passage from Philip K. Dick's *The Man In The High Castle* is from the Penguin Books edition of 1969, and used here with their permission. If you've not read this book, do so now. Finally, the passage quoted from Friedrich Nietzsche's *Beyond Good And Evil* is from the R. J. Hollingdale translation, published by Penguin Books in 1973 and used here with their permission.

As before, I want to thank the great Al Stewart, whose

David Wingrove

wonderful song, 'Roads To Moscow' inspired me to take this
journey into the vast ocean of Time.

David Wingrove, February 2015

The story continues in

THE MASTER OF TIME

Read on for an exclusive extract . . .

DEL REY

Part Eleven

Exiles

319

For a time I just lie there on the bed, facing the wall, the tears trickling slowly down my face. The hurt is simply too much, the pain too fierce. I try to fight it, to be 'manful', only I keep seeing their faces, their eyes wide with fear, pleading with me – Katerina and my brave Natalya, young Irina and Anna, and Martha and my darling little Zarah – and an overwhelming sense of hopelessness, of sheer, soul-numbing impotence stops me dead.

How can I live without them?

But giving up will not save them. Only by living can I help them. Only by forgetting the hurt and setting it aside. But it's hard. Perhaps the hardest thing I've ever had to do.

I sit up and look about me, trying to think, trying to function like the time agent that I am. I used to be good at this – at living off my wits – but it seems I've grown soft.

I know two conflicting things for certain. First, I am trapped in some cul-de-sac of Time; trapped and unable to escape. Second, I can't possibly be trapped, because I'm still in the loop. How, for instance, can my children have been stolen from me when they do not yet exist? For surely, unless I escape from here and conceive them, they cannot come into being.

Or am I missing something? Has Kolya, perhaps, robbed me even of that?

I stand unsteadily, then begin my explorations. First I must know where I am and when. The newspaper on the floor – a *New York Times* – suggests I'm in that city in November 1984, but is that so, or is it a false clue left by Kolya?

Yes, and why here? Why now? Or was this hastily contrived?

I think not. I don't think Kolya does anything hastily or without a reason. At least, that's my experience so far. He's a control freak. Perhaps the ultimate control freak. A control freak with the ability to travel in Time.

I walk across and try the left-hand door. It's locked. I put my ear to it and listen, and sure enough I hear movement out there.

Turning, I walk over to the other door and try it. It opens. Beyond it is a short passageway with rooms off: a bathroom, a kitchen and a lounge. Four rooms, then. And not a hotel by the look of it. An apartment. But whose?

Not knowing when someone will return, I decide to search the lounge first. There's a TV, of course, and a big leather sofa – an old white thing, well-kept and relatively unscuffed – only what interests me most is the standing shelves.

Whoever this guy is – and I'm almost certain from the décor that it's a male – he's heavily into his military history, though there's a smattering of books about various media and sports personalities, as well as politicians. What novels there are are cheap thrillers of the kind you'd buy in airport lounges. Well-thumbed paperbacks.

What else? The carpet's wine red, the curtains the same. There are no pictures on the walls, and no photographs on display. Not anywhere. It's neat rather than fashionable and suggests our tenant is single. A very organised man.

I walk through to the kitchen. Again it's neat, everything in its place. But what stands out? A coffee grinder and, nearby, an expresso machine. One of those expensive Italian jobs. Three big mugs hang from hooks below one of the wall units. The bowl in the sink is empty and there's no washing up on the drainer. I turn, looking three sixty about me. No. There's nothing here that gives him away. Nothing except the coffee machine, which suggests expensive tastes.

The bathroom is a surprise. Marble. Real marble, not fake, and a top-of-the-range shower unit with one of those variable heads. This guy likes to shower. It's the nicest room in the apartment, and speaks volumes about his habits.

I look in the little wall unit over the sink. There's a shaving kit here, but it looks like a spare. I'd guess he has his best kit with him, wherever he is. And no sign of colognes or after-shave. Even the soap is unscented.

I nod to myself then move quickly on, returning to the bedroom.

It's hard to see this room without thinking of Kolya's presence. He jumped in here with me, so he knew this room. He'd been here before. So what's the connection? Does he know the tenant? Or is this one of *his* apartments?

Somehow what I've seen doesn't fit with Kolya's 'profile'. I can't see him being obsessed with showering, for a start.

I walk over to the bed and, crouching, drag the case out from underneath. It's locked, but that doesn't trouble me. As I click the locks open and push the lid back, I frown. It's full of old newspapers, some of them going back to the fifties. If they belong to our tenant, then that puts him, I'd say, somewhere in his forties.

Without studying them in depth, I can't see any obvious connection between them. They come from all over the USA, and the dates seem random, though I'm sure they're not.

Closing the case, I replace it, then go over to the desk, flicking through the papers there. And get myself a name.

DeSario. Joseph P.

It's there, on three of the bills, and on two of the letters.

Not only that, but there's an address – presumably the address of the apartment where I am right now.

Apartment 8D, 357, Seventy Fifth Street, New York.

The desk has three drawers on the right-hand side. I try the top drawer first, and find it full of the usual kind of stuff – paperclips, biros, scraps of writing paper and a packet of gum.

There's a stapler, too, and in the corner at the back a small glasses case.

I take the last item out and open it. The glasses look ordinary enough, only when I try them on, I realise that they're not spectacles at all. The glass is plain, the lenses perfectly flat.

I put them back, then try the middle drawer. Empty.

I slide it closed and, not expecting anything, pull the bottom drawer out.

And almost smile.

There's a handgun. A .357 magnum, if I'm not mistaken. And beside it a box of bullets. I open it and, sure enough, they're .357s. Live ammunition, not blanks. Careful not to touch the gun, I ease the drawer right out, peering into the back of it, and am rewarded with the sight of something else.

A small diary with a black leather cover.

I reach in and take it out. But if I'm expecting any kind of revelation, then it's not to be found within its pages. The diary is mainly blank. There are barely any entries at all, only hand-drawn lines linking blocks of three, four or five days, with the word 'OUT' at the start and 'BACK' at the end. Business journeys, presumably. But doing what? The bills give me no clues, nor do the letters. Only I know now when our friend DeSario will be back. Three days from now, if the newspaper is accurate, on November 11th.

And then I think about that. According to the diary he was 'OUT' on the eighth, so he probably left the newspaper on that day. Which would make it . . .

I go through to the lounge and switch the TV on, changing channels until I find a news programme, and there – beneath the headline – is the date. The Tenth of November, 1984.

Back tomorrow, then.

I'm about to switch it off and go back through, when I realise what I'm watching. It's a state funeral. There's a gun carriage, pulled by two black horses, and on it is a coffin draped with an American flag. There are lots of troops and important-looking men in sombre coats, and there, walking just behind the coffin, next to a small, slim woman in her late middle-age, his head bare, his whole demeanour immensely sad, is Phil.

I stare and stare, beginning to understand, beginning to remember what I know about this period. The guy in the coffin . . . Reagan . . . in our time-stream he went on to win a second term, his running mate – Bush, was it? – following him as President. But in this time-line Reagan has died somehow, and instead of Bush for a running mate, he had Phil.

The idea is so preposterous, that for a moment I entertain the idea that I've been drugged. Reagan, if I remember rightly, was a Republican. And remembering Phil . . . well, I don't know what his politics were, really, but they certainly weren't Republican. He hated all that authority shit.

I'm still watching as something flutters into camera view and lands on Phil's shoulder, perching there, preening itself even as he walks on, his step unchecked, behind the gun carriage.

An owl. A snowy owl.

I switch it off then hurry back to the bedroom. Picking up the New York Times, I flick through it until I come to a full-page article that fills me in with some of what's been going on.

The man in the coffin was indeed Reagan – Ronald Reagan, the thirty-ninth President of the United States of America – and the woman walking beside Phil, following the carriage, was his widow, Nancy.

Having survived one assassination attempt, just two months into his first spell as President, Reagan was shot a second time, while touring Wisconsin, only weeks before a poll which, most commentators agreed, would have seen him re-elected with a landslide victory over his Democrat opponent, Walter Mondale.

I read down the page, looking for details, then find what I'm looking for. According to this, Reagan was in a coma for the best part of six days before he died, while his running mate, the senator for California, Philip K. Dick, took over the campaign, choosing a relative unknown, the Governor of Texas, George Bush, as the new prospective Vice President.

The sympathy vote was huge. Dick, seen by many as a strange choice for running mate, representing, as he did, the softer side of Republicanism, had carried the day, not only riding the tide of Reagan's popularity, but coming into his own with his dignity of bearing and his clear, straight-spoken manner.

I close the paper and sit back, trying to think this through. If I'm to get out of here, I've got to find out just how far back the changes go, because that's where I'll find my way out of here. That'll be the point – the one and only point, in fact – where I can jump back to Four-Oh, back to the main trunk of the Tree.

Only there are two problems. One – I don't know enough about the specific history of this time and place to make that judgement and isolate that point where the changes began. And two – even if I did, how in Urd's name would I get back there?

I go over to the door again and rattle it, hoping maybe that the lock will prove weak enough to give, only it doesn't. It feels good and solid and secure.

And there's no way I can use the windows. There's a straight drop of eight floors to the sidewalk.

I walk back through to the kitchen and check the fridge. There are one or two bits of food, but barely enough to feed me for a day. Searching the wall units I come across a few cans and various packets, but again there's not much. If DeSario doesn't come back tomorrow, then I'm going to have to try to break out of here, if only to feed myself.

I go back into the lounge and stand in front of the bookshelves again, staring at them, as if the answer's there. Then, some kind of instinct driving me, I go over and start pulling books out and looking behind them. It's fairly random at first, but then I notice something. There's a small section on the bottom shelf where the book spines seem pushed back a little in one place.

I crouch and remove a couple of them, and there it is. A small wooden cigar box. And inside? I smile, knowing already that they're going to fit. For it's keys. A set of keys to this apartment.

320

I spend the next day and a half mainly on the sofa, the door open, giving me a clear view of the passageway and the front door, the TV on low, the .375 magnum resting on my chest. Loaded, of course. Just in case.

Because what's a man doing with a 'thirty eight' magnum if he doesn't intend to use it?

I've tried the keys and they work. Not that I intend to go anywhere just yet. Not until DeSario returns.

And if he doesn't?

Then I'll go out. See what's to be seen. Buy myself a steak dinner, maybe.

Because I've got cash now. Over eight thousand dollars. Money that was in the box where I found the key, in a sealed envelope marked 'expenses'.

I don't intend to steal it. Just borrow it a while.

For a while I channel surf, getting a feeling of this age through its images and idioms. It's very different from the fifties, and not just in its degree of sophistication. This is an age that has recently discovered sex, and in what I see and hear there's a constant battle raging between those who think things have gone too far and those who don't think things have gone far enough.

I stop at a music channel – a new one, so I believe: MTV, it's called – and watch for a while. The music's bland to my ear, the beat repetitive, the tunes insipid. Even jazz, I think, is better. But what do I know? Besides, at the volume I've got the TV, who can tell what the dynamics of the music are?

Only I've sat in the same room as Beethoven and seen him play piano, like a man possessed, and know this is not the best humanity can do.

I wait all of that day, and all of that evening, too, and still he doesn't come. DeSario is late. Either that, or he doesn't actually exist. Maybe this is all a construct, created by Kolya to keep me occupied. But why would he do that?

Is he watching me? Is that what this is? A controlled environment?

I decide to risk going outside, onto the streets. I've money and a key, and a gun. What harm can come to me? And if this *is* a construct, I'll find out quick enough. Kolya doesn't have the resources to people a whole city for my benefit.

I go to the window, to check out the weather, then return to the bedroom, to search through DeSario's wardrobe. Looking through his clothes, I note that he's no style guru, but that doesn't really matter. What does – and *is* it just coincidence? – is that he's my size, right down to our matching shoe size.

Slipping out of my old clothes I get dressed, then study myself in the bathroom mirror. It's far from perfect - denim jeans, a black T-shirt and a pair of casual slip-ons – but it'll do.

Last of all, I look for a coat to wear against the weather. There's one dark, woollen jacket that'll do me and I pull it on, noting how snugly it fits.

I pocket one of the hundred dollar bills, slip the gun into my jacket pocket, then pick up the key. I'm about to go out when I hear noises from outside, in the hallway.

There's a peep-hole in the door. I go to it, placing my eye against the glass.

There, in that shadowed space between the apartments, two men are gesturing violently and shouting at a woman. It's not a pretty sight. She has her arms up, as if to defend herself, and they keep leaning in to her threateningly; leaning in and shouting, until, finally, one of them shakes his fist at her and turns away, quickly followed by the other.

I watch her watching them go, real fear in her eyes, then see how she slumps, one hand gripping the half open door behind her, as if she's about to collapse. There's a part of me that wants to throw the door open and go out to console her, but I don't know whether this isn't yet another of Kolya's little games.

I step away, then turn, my back to the door, waiting, *listening*. And in a while I hear the door to her apartment slam shut.

I give it a minute, then slip out, locking the door behind me. Whatever it was, it'd be best not to get involved. For all I knew she might have been at fault. Only I don't think so.

I make my way down the stairs and out onto the grey streets of New York City. It's cold, a faint flurry of snow in the air. On the corner, just across from me, is a grocery store, its cluttered interior lit up against the encroaching darkness. I go across, buying myself groceries, a torch, a notepad and a packet of pens, the old guy on the till growling in his best New York fashion.

'You not got something smaller, buddy?'

I make an apologetic face. 'Sorry, friend. It's all I've got.'

The old guy makes a face, then rummages through his till, hiding the hundred dollar bill beneath the tray, before handing me my change.

I was going to head straight back, settle in and make myself supper, only I notice a bar, a few shops further on. A cosy-looking place. The kind you find scattered all over New York in this place and time.

Why not? I could have a steak and a beer, perhaps.

Yeah . . . but what if DeSario turns up while you're gone?

That's a risk I'm going to take. Besides, the mere thought of a steak is too much for me. After all I've been through . . .

Okay. Let me make this clear. There's not a moment I'm not thinking of them. Agonizing. Wondering how I can get out of there and rescue them. Only . . .

Only a man has to eat. Whatever age he's trapped in.

I walk across. There's a neon sign above the window. *Joe's Bar*, it reads, as if it could be called anything else.

I go inside.

It's small, one long room with a bar to the left and a row of tables and chairs to the right. It's also unexpectedly empty. Or almost so. There's a barman cleaning glasses, a small, stout, bald-headed man in his forties, and, sat on a stool at the far end of the bar, his one and only customer.

My instinct is to turn about and leave. Only that would seem strange, impolite. Not that the barman seems to notice that I'm there. He doesn't even look up, just continues to clean glasses, the clink of which is just about audible over the sound from the small TV screen that's just behind the bar.

Yes, and to add to my awkwardness, I've a heavy bag of shopping. I've only taken two steps towards the bar when I'm hailed.

'Hey . . . buddy! Let me buy you a drink!'

There's a small part of me that's deeply suspicious. I don't know the fellow, after all, and what better way for Kolya to keep tabs on me than to have his men scattered all about the area? In bars and shops and on the streets nearby. Watching me. Keeping tabs.

I go across. He's younger than the barman. Mid-thirties at the most. A tall, rather handsome young man, in a dark grey suit, the jacket of which is laid over the back of the bar stool, a packet of

Tareyton Long Lights – cigarettes, I'm guessing – on the counter next to his wallet.

'Hey,' I say, setting my shopping down and offering him my hand. 'Name's Otto . . .'

He smiles. A pleasant smile. 'Hey, Otto. I'm John. John Patrick Kavanagh.' And he takes my hand and shakes it firmly. 'What'll you have?'

I note that he's drinking a Coors Lite. A lager, by the look of it. I nod towards it.

'I'll have what you're having.'

He looks past me. 'Sure . . . Joe! Another Coors!'

And so our friendship begins. And within half an hour any doubts I had about the man are gone. He no more works with Kolya than I do. In fact he's a lawyer, and that accent in his voice that I couldn't place is from Illinois, from downtown Chicago, to be precise, where he's a corporate lawyer. When I ask what he's doing in New York, he laughs and, drawing from his cigarette, tells me.

'I'm attending subcommittee meetings of the NAIC. That's the National Association of Insurance Commissioners. But in my spare time I'm visiting the Museum of Modern Art. Oh . . .' And he leans towards me, lowering his voice confidentially, '. . . and cranking a woman named Patricia. She's from Chicago too. Moved out here after her divorce.'

By 'cranking' I assume he means having sex. And for some reason I think of the women in the apartment across from where I'm staying and a cloud falls over my face, which he sees.

'Hey, buddy. What's up?'

And I tell him what I saw, and he takes a long draw on his cigarette while he mulls it over, then, nodding slowly to himself, meets my eyes.

'You know what? I think you were right not to get involved. This is a hard town, Otto, and there're some hard people out there. You cross them and you'll end up dead.'

I can believe that. Only now that I've had a few beers, I feel like telling him more. Telling him *all* of it, in fact. Only then he'd think I was insane. That I'd escaped from some asylum. And then I'd be alone again. And I don't want to be alone. I realise that now.

'I'd better get back,' I say. But I sound only half convinced. There's part of me that wants to stay here and get drunk, and Kavanagh, realising that, buys me another drink. And another. And all the while he's telling me all about what's been going on – as he sees it – as if I've spent the last ten years on the dark side of the moon, which is near enough the truth – and I begin to get a picture of this time and place. And there's yet another part of me – the part that is *Reisende* through and through – that takes all of that raw information and makes a pattern from it. A *gestalt*.

And then – and who knows how it came about? – I'm saying goodbye to Kavanagh in the snow outside the bar, shaking his hand with my one free hand, the other clinging on to my groceries, then watching him as he disappears into the night, like a spectre. Or like some figure from a dream. And I return to the building where I'm staying and, unsteadily climb the stairs back up to the unlit apartment on the eighth floor where I have washed up, like a sea-sculpted spar from some shipwrecked vessel.

And DeSario?

Of DeSario there's no sign. Not that I expected anything. Because I know now. There *is* no DeSario. That's just a name. A peg for my imagination. And all of this is a construct, to keep me busy, guessing, running about like a hamster in a cage. Going nowhere fast. All for Kolya's sick amusement.

And, locking the door behind me, not bothering with the lights, I throw myself down on the big double bed and weep once more. For my girls. And Katerina. And because, despite all of Kavanagh's kindness, I am alone in this alien place.